Born again to kill . . .

Something new teased at the edge of my memory—the sensation of falling, the thrum of wings beating against the stale air, and a brilliant light that both warmed and blinded me. A soft voice had emerged from the light. A voice with a beautiful face and gossamer wings. An angel, and it offered to let me live. Offered to pull me back from the nipping flames of hell.

Offered me a future and a chance to atone for my multitude of sins. Lying. Stealing. Drugs. Larceny.

And, yes, attempting cold-blooded murder.

I didn't fully understand the bargain I'd made, but at the time, I made the only choice I could.

I chose life. But as I stood up and once again faced the reflection in the mirror, I had to admit that this wasn't exactly what I'd expected.

Titles by Julie Kenner

TAINTED

CARPE DEMON
CALIFORNIA DEMON
DEMONS ARE FOREVER
DEJA DEMON
DEMON EX MACHINA

THE GOOD GHOULS' GUIDE TO GETTING EVEN
GOOD GHOULS DO

FIRST LOVE

Anthologies

HELL WITH THE LADIES
(with Kathleen O'Reilly and Dee Davis)

HELL ON HEELS
(with Kathleen O'Reilly and Dee Davis)

FENDI, FERRAGAMO, & FANGS
(with Johanna Edwards and Serena Robar)

Book One in the
Blood Lily Chronicles

JULIE KENNER

THE BERKLEY PUBLISHING GROUP
Published by the Penguin Group
Penguin Group (USA) Inc.
375 Hudson Street, New York, New York 10014, USA
Penguin Group (Canada), 90 Eglinton Avenue East, Suite 700, Toronto, Ontario M4P 2Y3, Canada
(a division of Pearson Penguin Canada Inc.)
Penguin Books Ltd., 80 Strand, London WC2R 0RL, England
Penguin Group Ireland, 25 St. Stephen's Green, Dublin 2, Ireland (a division of Penguin Books Ltd.)
Penguin Group (Australia), 250 Camberwell Road, Camberwell, Victoria 3124, Australia
(a division of Pearson Australia Group Pty. Ltd.)
Penguin Books India Pvt. Ltd., 11 Community Centre, Panchsheel Park, New Delhi—110 017, India
Penguin Group (NZ), 67 Apollo Drive, Rosedale, North Shore 0632, New Zealand
(a division of Pearson New Zealand Ltd.)
Penguin Books (South Africa) (Pty.) Ltd., 24 Sturdee Avenue, Rosebank, Johannesburg 2196,
South Africa

Penguin Books Ltd., Registered Offices: 80 Strand, London WC2R 0RL, England

TAINTED

An Ace Book / published by arrangement with the author

PRINTING HISTORY
Ace mass-market edition / November 2009

Cover art by Craig White.
Cover design by Annette Fiore DeFex.
Interior text design by Laura K. Corless.

ISBN: 978-0-441-01784-3

ACE
Ace Books are published by The Berkley Publishing Group,
a division of Penguin Group (USA) Inc.,
375 Hudson Street, New York, New York 10014.
ACE and the "A" design are trademarks of Penguin Group (USA) Inc.

PRINTED IN THE UNITED STATES OF AMERICA

10 9 8 7 6 5 4 3 2 1

To Jess, thanks.
What more can I say?
Except, maybe, that you know I still owe you big-time.

PROLOGUE

. . . And by her hand that which would be open
may be closed . . .

—*The Prophecy of the Orb*

Can I just say that dying sucks?

All that bullshit about seeing the light and having this final moment of inner peace, blah, blah, blah. It's crap.

Dying is messy and terrifying and it hurts like hell.

I ought to know. After all, I was the one on that basement floor in a puddle of my own blood and bile. And there was no peace, no light, no *anything*. Nothing except the ice-cold knowledge that the sins I'd racked up in the last twelve or so hours were more than sufficient to push me through the gates of hell.

Forget everything else I'd done in my twenty-six years on this earth, good and bad. You go out planning to kill a man—even a man as vile as Lucas Johnson—and your fate is pretty much sealed.

From a practical standpoint, the moment of death is a little bit late to start getting all profound and reflective. As they say, what's done is done. But that doesn't matter, because even if you're the least introspective person on the planet, you still go through the whole Psych 101 rigmarole. You tell yourself that maybe you should have said your bedtime prayers once in a while. You wonder if all those torture-porn horror movies you watched while your boyfriend copped a feel weren't actually a sneak peek into what hell had to offer.

In other words, you get scared.

When you're living, you might tell God to take a flying leap for putting your mother six feet under when you were only fourteen. For leaving you with a stepfather who decided to cuddle up with Jack Daniel's because he no longer had a loving wife in his bed. For leaving you in charge of a pigtailed little half sister who thought you hung the moon.

And for making you arrogant enough to swear that you'd protect that precious kid no matter what, even though that wasn't a promise you could keep. Not when there are monsters like Lucas Johnson trolling the earth. Monsters who suck the life from little girls.

For all those reasons, you might turn your back on God, and think you're oh-so-righteous for doing it. But you'd be wrong.

Trust me. I know.

I know, because even as my life faded, the fires of hell nipped at my toes.

In the end, I got lucky. But then again, luck is all a matter of perspective, isn't it?

ONE

I woke up in total darkness, so out of sorts that I was convinced I'd pulled on the wrong skin along with my blue jeans. Couple that with the fact that anvils were about to split my head wide open, and I think it's fair to say that I wasn't having a good time. I tried to roll over and get my bearings, but even the tiniest movement kicked the hammers in my head to triple-time, and I abandoned the effort before I even got started.

"Fucking A," I said, and immediately wished I hadn't. I'm no *American Idol* contestant, but my voice doesn't usually inflict extreme pain. Today, it did.

Today? Like I even knew what day it was. Or where I was. Or, for that matter, *why* I was.

I'd died, after all.

Hadn't I?

Disoriented, I lurched up, only to be halted before I'd barely moved.

I tried again, and realized my wrists and ankles were firmly tied down. *What the—?*

My heart pounded against my rib cage, but I told myself I wasn't afraid. A big hairy lie, but it was worth a try. I mean, I lied to myself all the time, right? Sometimes I even believed my own shit.

Not this time. I might have dropped out of high school, but I know when to be scared, and tied up in the dark is definitely one of those times. There was no nice, cozy explanation for my current sitch. Instead, my mind filled with high-def NC-17 images of a long, thin blade and a twisted expression of cruel delight painted on a face I knew only too well. Lucas Johnson.

Because this had to be about revenge. Payback for what I'd tried to do. And now I was going to die at the hand of the man I'd gone out to kill.

No, no, no.

No way was I dying. Not now. Not when I'd survived this far.

I didn't have a clue why I was still alive—I remembered the knife; I remembered the blood. But here I was, living and breathing and, yeah, I was a little immobile at the moment, but I was *alive*. And I intended to stay that way.

No way was I leaving my little sister to the mercy of the son of a bitch who'd raped and brutalized her. Who'd sent her black roses and mailed erotic postcards. All anonymous. All scary as hell. She would see him in stores, lurking around corners, and by the time she screamed for help, he was gone.

The cops had nailed his sorry ass, but when the system had tossed him on a technicality, I watched Rose come close to losing it every single day. I couldn't stand the thought that the system had kicked the monster free when he should have been in a cage, locked away so he couldn't hurt any more little girls. So he couldn't hurt Rose.

So I'd stolen the gun. I'd tracked him down. And God help me, I'd fired.

At the time, I thought I'd hit him square in the chest. But I must have missed, because I could remember Johnson rushing me. After that, things were blurrier. I remembered the terror of knowing that I was dying, and I recalled a warm flood of hope. But I had no clue what had happened between warm, fuzzy hope and the cold, hard slab that made up my current reality.

I peered into the darkness again, and this time the velvet curtain seemed to be lifting. The room, I realized, wasn't completely black. Instead, there was a single candle against the far wall, its small flame gathering strength against the blackness.

I stared, puzzled. I was certain there'd been no flame earlier.

Slowly, the area around me shifted into a reddish gray with dark and light spots contrasting to reveal a line of angular symbols painted above the candlestick.

My eyes locked on the symbols, and the trembling started up again. Something was off, and I was overwhelmed by the frantic, urgent fear that the monster I knew was nowhere nearby, and that when I saw what I was *really* up against, I'd desperately wish it were Johnson's sorry ass that was after me.

A cold chill raced up my spine. I wanted the hell out of there.

I was about to start thrashing again—in the desperate hope that the ties would miraculously loosen—when I heard the metallic screech of a creaking hinge. I froze, my breathing shallow, my muscles tense.

The creak intensified and a shaft of anorexic light swept wide across the room as the door arced open. A huge shadow filled the gap. A dark, monstrous form was silhouetted in the doorway, emitting a scent that made me almost vomit.

A monster. And not of the Lucas Johnson variety.

No, Lucas Johnson was a Boy Scout compared to the putrid creature that lumbered forward, bending so that it could fit through the door frame. It lurched toward me, muscles rolling under an elephant-like hide. The creature wore no clothing, and even in the dark, I could see the parasites living in slime inside the folds of skin. Could hear them scurry for safety when the beast moved toward me.

The fetid smell that preceded it made me gag, and I struggled to sink into the stone slab as the beast peered down at me, a string of snot hanging precariously from the orifice that served as a nose.

The creature's mouth twisted, dry skin cracking as the muscles underneath moved, thin lines of blood and pus oozing out from the newly formed fissures. It swaggered to the candle, then leaned over and breathed on the flame. As if its breath were gas, fire leaped into the air, painting the wall with flame and making the symbols glow.

I cried out in alarm and pain, my body suddenly burning from within—the sensation passing as quickly as it had come.

The beast turned to sneer at me. "You," it croaked. Black piggy eyes lit with fury as it brandished a short, bloodied dagger. "Now we finish this business."

A piercing shriek split the dark, and I realized the sound was coming from me. Fire shot through my limbs, and I jerked upright with a fresh burst of determination. To my surprise and relief, I managed to rip my arms free, the ties flapping from my wrists like useless wings.

The creature paused, drawing itself up to its full height. It took a step backward, then dropped to its knees and held its clawed hands high. With the dagger, it sliced its palm, then let the thick, black liquid that flowed from the wound drip into its open mouth. "I serve the Dark Lord, my Master," it said, the words as rough as tires on gravel. "For my sacrifice, I will be rewarded."

The "sacrifice" thing totally freaked me out, but I took advantage of this quaint little monster ritual to reach down and tear at the ties that still bound my ankles. As I did, I noticed that I was wearing a silky white gown, most definitely not the jeans and T-shirt I'd left the house in.

Not that I had time to mull over such fascinating fashion tidbits. Instead, I focused on the business at hand: getting the hell out of there.

About the time I finished ripping, the creature finished

praying. It barreled toward me, dagger outstretched. I rolled over, hiking up the skirt as I kicked up and off the slab to land upright beside it. There's probably a name for a move like that, but I didn't know it. Hell, I didn't even know that my body would move like that.

I didn't waste time savoring my new acrobatic persona; instead, I raced for the door. Or, at least, I started to. The sight of the Hell Beast looming there sort of turned me off that plan. Which left me with no choice but to whip around and try to find another exit.

Naturally, there wasn't one.

No, no, no. So far, I had survived the most screwed-up, freaky day of my life, and I wasn't giving up now. And if that meant I fought the disgusting Hell Beast, then dammit, that was just what I was going to do.

The beast must have had the same idea, because as soon as I turned back toward the door, it lashed out, catching me across the face with the back of its massive, clawed hand. The blow sent me hurtling, and I crashed against the huge brass candlestick, causing it to tumble down hard on my rib cage.

Hot wax burned into my chest, but I had no time to reflect on the pain. The beast was on top of me. I did the only thing I could. I grabbed the stick and thrust it upward. The beast weighed a ton, but I must have had decent leverage, because I managed to catch him under the chin with the stick, knocking his head back and eliciting a howl that almost burst my eardrums.

Not being an idiot, I didn't wait around for him to recover. The candlestick was too heavy to carry as a weapon, so I dropped it and ran like hell toward the door, hoping the beast was alone.

I stumbled over the threshold, never so happy to be in a dark, dank hallway. The only light came from medieval-looking candleholders lining the walls every eight or so feet, but as I wasn't sightseeing, the lack of light didn't bother me much. All I wanted was out of there. So I raced on, down musty corridors and around tight corners until finally—*finally*—I slammed into the push bar of a fire door. An alarm screamed into the night as the thick metal door burst open, and I slid out, my nose crinkling as I caught the nasty smell of rotting food, carried on the cool autumn air. I was in an alley, and as my eyes adjusted, I turned to the right and raced toward the street and the safety of the world.

It wasn't until I reached the intersection of the alley and an unfamiliar street that I paused to turn back. The alley was silent. No monsters. No creatures. No boogeymen out to get me.

The street was silent as well. No people or traffic. The streetlights blinking. *Late,* I thought. And my next thought was to run some more. I would have, too, if I hadn't looked down and noticed my feet in the yellow glow of the streetlamps.

I blinked, confused. Because those didn't look like my feet. And now that I thought about it, my hands and legs seemed all wrong, too. And the bloom of red I now saw on the breast of the white gown completely freaked me out. Which, when you considered the overall circumstances, was saying a lot. Because on the whole, this experience was way, way, way trippy, and the only thing I could figure was that someone had drugged me and I was in the middle of one monster of a hallucination.

Then again, maybe the simplest explanation was the right one: I was losing my mind.

"You're not."

I spun around and found myself looking down on a squat little man in a green overcoat and a battered brown fedora. At least a head shorter than me, he was looking up at me with eyes that would have been serious were they not so amphibian.

"You're not losing it," the frog-man clarified, which suggested to me that I was. Losing it, I mean. After all, the strange little man had just read my mind.

He snorted. "That doesn't make you crazy. Just human."

"Who the devil are you?" I asked, surprised to find that my voice worked, though it sounded somewhat off. I glanced up and down the street, calculating my odds of getting away. Surely I could run faster than this—

"No need to run," he said. Then he stepped off the sidewalk and into the street. As if it had been waiting for his cue, a sleek black limousine pulled to the curb. Frog-man opened the rear door and nodded. "Hop in."

I took a step backward. "Get lost, dickwad."

"Come on, kid. We need to talk. And I know you must be tired. You've had a hell of a day." He nodded down the alley. "You did good in there. But next time remember that you're supposed to kill them. Not give 'em a headache. *Capisce?*"

I most definitely did *not capisce*. "*Next* time?" I pointed back down the alley. "You had something to do with that? No way," I said, taking another step backward. "No freaking way."

"It's a lot to take in, I know." He opened the door wider. "Why don't you get in, Lily? We really should talk."

My name echoed through the night. I looked around, wary, but there was no one else around. "I want answers, you son of a bitch."

He shook his head, and I could imagine him muttering, *tsk, tsk*. "Hard to believe you're the one all the fuss is about, but the big guy must know what he's doing, right?"

I blinked.

"But look at you, staring at me like I'm talking in Akkadian. To you I probably am. You're exhausted, right? I tell you, jumping right into the testing . . . it's just not the best method." He shook his head, and this time the *tsk, tsk* actually emerged. "But do they ask me? No. I mean, who am I? Just old Clarence, always around to help. It's enough to give a guy an inferiority complex." He patted my shoulder, making contact before I could pull away. "Don't you worry. This can all wait until tomorrow."

"What testing? What's tomorrow? And who *are* you?"

"All in good time. Right now," he said, "I'm taking you home."

And before I could ask how he planned to manage that, because I had no intention of getting into the limo with him, he reached over and tapped me on the forehead. "Go to sleep, pet. You need the rest."

I wanted to protest, but couldn't. My eyes closed, and the last thing I remember was his amphibian grin as my knees gave out and I fell to the sidewalk at the frog-man's feet.

TWO

I woke up on a bathroom floor, curled around the base of a porcelain throne. My stomach felt strangely empty, and the lingering taste of bile hung in my mouth.

Other than that, I had no general complaints, and the fact that I was alive—despite Lucas Johnson, despite the freakish monster, and despite the strange little frog-man—seemed something to celebrate.

At the same time, I had to wonder if it had all been a dream.

Surely, I thought, it had been a dream.

I sat up, then dragged my fingers though my hair, frowning to find the hair longer than I expected. I drew my hand back and looked at it, only to find that it wasn't my hand at all. Or my toenails, painted that dainty shade of pink. And the Hello Kitty pajamas I now wore were most definitely not my style.

Bile rose in my throat again as I remembered how out of it I'd felt when I'd been running for my life, and I reached up, grabbing the side of the sink, and hauled myself to my feet.

I pressed the heels of my palms against the countertop and stared at the face staring back at me.

Who the hell is that?

The girl I usually saw in the mirror carried ten extra pounds that refused to come off—probably because she refused to give up the Kit Kat bars she kept behind the counter at Movies & More. Her ears were double-pierced and she had a single, tasteful stud through the side of her nose. Her thick mousy hair was cut into a super-short, no-muss, no-fuss style.

That girl no longer stared back at me.

Instead, the face in the mirror had perfectly trimmed coal-black hair that hit midway down her shoulders and moved with all the grace and shine of a shampoo commercial. Her green eyes were shown off under plucked eyebrows that arched slightly in an expression of either interest or disdain. Her complexion was perfect, not the ruddy skin I was used to seeing. And tiny little diamond studs graced her single-pierced ears.

A strange wooziness came over me, and I realized that I was hyperventilating. Purposefully, I dropped onto the toilet seat, tucked my head between my knees, and breathed.

What the fuck?

What the fuck is going on?

I couldn't be someone else. It was impossible. That didn't happen. It wasn't real.

I am me.

Me, I thought, and I could prove it.

Frantically, I yanked the Hello Kitty top up, exposing my belly. My fingers probed taut, unblemished skin that had never once been stabbed in the gut. Confused, desperate, I shoved the waist of the loose pants down, searching for a wound but finding nothing. But I remembered it. The searing pain. The grin on Johnson's face as he plunged in the knife. And the pungent smell of blood and bile as it gushed out of my body.

I trembled—the kind of shaking that's deep in your

bones. This wasn't the kind of thing that happened to people. It wasn't the kind of thing that happened at all.

I'd turned into someone else.

Holy fucking shit.

My body might have bled out, but the essence of me went on, alive and kicking in this stranger who was becoming more familiar by the second.

I didn't understand how, but I couldn't escape the truth staring back at me from the mirror. That was *me*. No matter how unfamiliar she looked, that body with cutesy PJs, perfectly trimmed hair, and unblemished tummy really now housed me.

Dear Lord, how?

For that matter, *Why?*

I turned away from the mirror, my whole body shaking. Then I saw the crumpled white gown on the floor, and the shakes turned into near convulsions. A bloom of red spread out from the bodice, and my mouth went dry. *Oh, God. Oh, God. Oh, God.*

I turned back to the mirror and ripped the T-shirt off over my head. As with my belly, my chest—or, rather, *this* chest—was unblemished, the skin marked only by a small tattoo on her left breast. I looked closer and realized the tattoo was a small dagger. Not what I'd expect from a girl who wears Hello Kitty jammies and keeps bubble bath above the toilet, but hardly nefarious.

There was, in fact, nothing about this body that suggested foul play. Certainly nothing that suggested she'd recently been cut by a knife or stabbed with a dagger. But how could that be possible? She'd been covered in warm blood. *I'd* been covered. A sacrifice strapped to a cold slab. A feast for a monster.

There had to have been a cut. A stab. Something.

But there was nothing. Just my own memories, and those were faded and spotty.

I sank to my knees and bent forward, resting my forehead on the cool bathroom tile, the sacrificial gown clutched tight in my hands as I fought to remember. To organize my thoughts and bring some semblance of normalcy to a completely not normal situation.

My memories. *My* life. My own personal nightmare.

Lucas Johnson. Rose. The haunted terror in her eyes. My rage. My promise to keep her safe.

The taunting snarl on his tattooed face before I'd pulled the trigger, intending to blow him away. And the icy glint of steel before he shoved the knife deep into my flesh. The horror of knowing that I was dying and that, despite my best efforts, he would live on.

Something new teased at the edge of my memory—the sensation of falling, the thrum of wings beating against the stale air, and a brilliant light that both warmed and blinded me. A soft voice had emerged from the light. A voice with a beautiful face and gossamer wings. An angel, and it offered to let me live. Offered to pull me back from the nipping flames of hell.

Offered me a future and a chance to atone for my multitude of sins. Lying. Stealing. Drugs. Larceny.

And, yes, attempting cold-blooded murder.

I didn't fully understand the bargain I'd made, but at the time, I made the only choice I could.

I chose life. But as I stood up and once again faced the reflection in the mirror, I had to admit that this wasn't exactly what I'd expected.

THREE

My body's name was Alice Elaine Purdue. Appropriate, I thought, because I'd definitely entered Wonderland.

I'd learned this tantalizing tidbit of information the old-fashioned way: I'd snooped, poking around in the medicine cabinet until I found something with my body's name printed on it. A good plan, as it turned out, because Alice was the proud owner of both birth control pills and a prescription cream for athlete's foot.

I grimaced. Considering the firm state of Alice's ass and the fungal state of her feet, I assumed we'd been working out regularly, then showering in the public stalls without wearing flip-flops.

I scowled down at my toes, which thankfully didn't itch, then decided that it was time to leave the bathroom. It opened, conveniently enough, into a bedroom, and I stepped inside the darkened room, lit only by the single bedside lamp. The room was sparse, but still looked lived in. Two paperbacks were tossed carelessly onto the floor beside the bed, both Jane Austen novels. A variety of pastel necklaces hung from a hook glued near the top of the bureau mirror. A pink leather jacket lay balled up on the floor, half in and half out of the closet.

Beside the lamp was a small snapshot, snug in a cheap, plain frame. In the picture, a huge black cat sprawled on the back of a sofa, two adolescent girls snuggling against it from behind. I recognized the face that belonged to Alice. Or, rather, to me. The other girl seemed older, but so similar in appearance I assumed she must be a sibling. Serious brown eyes with long lashes above high cheekbones. Thick black hair pulled back in a high ponytail. A firm, strong mouth that seemed determined not to smile, though Alice was locked in an expression of perpetual amusement.

Who was she, this serious girl? I stared into her eyes, thinking of Rose and searching for answers. I found none until I took the more practical approach of sliding the picture out of the frame. On the back, in a delicate hand that I assumed belonged to a parent, someone had written *Alice and Rachel snuggle with Asphalt*. No year. No convenient notation—"sister" or "cousin." Tears pricked behind my eyes. Somewhere out there, Alice had a family that knew nothing of what had become of her.

Just like my stepfather. Just like Rose.

Agitated, I tossed the photo onto the bed, then stood up and moved to the window. I pushed aside the blinds and looked out at the gray buildings that lined the opposite side of the street. Cracked cement steps led up to front doors littered with mailboxes tacked to the siding, and gray paint peeled lazily under the crisp autumn sun.

Sun. Apparently Alice had blackout shades in her bedroom. What I'd thought was predawn was actually late afternoon.

I pressed my head against the cool glass, focusing on the gray façades that faced me. Something solid and permanent and real. Something on which I could ground my undulating emotions. Even that view, though, wasn't doing the trick. I didn't know this street, these houses, and a tremor of panic shot through me. I quashed it firmly, hating my cowardice.

Everything I'd been through so far, and *this* was what was getting to me? A freaking street address?

No. Chill. I drew in a breath, trying to get my head in order. The fungus cream had a pharmacy label, and the address was Boarhurst. Not the Flats—not home—but I knew Boarhurst. Once a small community in and of itself, it had been consumed by Boston like so many other villages, now clinging to their identity as distinct neighborhoods within the Boston sprawl. My various entrepreneurial activities had put me on the T to Boarhurst a couple of times. I didn't know the place like the back of my hand, but I knew enough to get around.

I let the blinds fall back into place, and darkness once again consumed the room.

I stood there, somewhat calmer now that I at least knew where I was, and I tried to fit the rest of the pieces together. I'd died. That much I knew. And I'd come back. That much had become obvious.

What I didn't understand, was why.

"'Cause you're our girl," a voice said. "You're the girl who can keep the demons from opening the gate. Keep that puppy locked up tight."

I spun around, my heart pounding, and found myself staring at the mysterious frog-man, a beer in his hand and his fedora slung low over his face.

"Get the hell out of here," I said, pressing my back against the wall, fear so intense I thought it would shoot out of my fingertips.

"Hey, hey, hey." He held up his hands in a peacekeeping gesture. "I know you're scared, but give me a break. I threw my back out lugging you from the limo to this apartment. And then I had to suffer through hours of boredom while you conked out on the bathroom floor. Now that you're back in the land of the living, I'm hardly going to vamoose now." He took a step toward me, and I tensed, ready to attack and run if need be. "Come on, kid. You're gonna hurt my feelings. I ain't here to hurt you. I'm here to help you."

"Bite me." I shot him my best tough-girl glare, slightly less effective considering the Hello Kitty pajamas. "Now, get out of here before I scream my head off."

The frog-man just grinned. "Call me Clarence, okay? The frog thing isn't too flattering."

"Dammit," I said. "Stay out of my head." He'd done that number on the street, and I hadn't liked it any better back then. "And I want answers. Right now. You can start with who you are."

"Think of me as a human resources professional. I'm here to guide you through your first day on the job." His forehead scrunched up. "All the days, actually, but first things first."

"Job? What job? What are you talking about?"

"It'll come back to you."

"Humor me, and tell me now."

"It's the chance of a lifetime, kid. An opportunity for redemption. A chance to do some real good. To make the world the kind of place it should be. A paradise instead of a cesspool."

I shivered, suddenly fearful I *did* understand; my mind simply refused to go there no matter how hard the frog-man pushed.

"Clarence," he said, creeping me out again by climbing into my head. "And yes. Battle of biblical proportions. The ultimate battle of good against evil. A war that's been raging for millennia, and still rages today. The kind of thing that would make reality-TV executives drool if only they could get their cameras in on it. But it's down to the zero hour now. Things are heating up. Bad things. Apocalypse things. And that, Lily, is where you come in.

"Me?" My voice rose with both fear and incredulity. "Are you nuts? What does the Apocalypse have to do with me? And what did you mean, I can make sure the gate stays locked? What gate?"

He moved his hands through the air as if reciting the title of a movie, its name up in lights. "Gate. To. Hell. Eh? Eh? Gets your juices flowing, doesn't it."

I blinked. "Gate to hell? Gate to *hell*?"

"Damn straight, kid. The Ninth Gate opens, and the underworld swarms in. And I'm not talking the trickle of these past millennia, but a full-blown onslaught. There's an army gathering on the other side, all set to come through when the dimensions line up."

My head was spinning. "*Dimensions?* What are you talking about?"

"You think demons can cross over any old time? They can't. That'd be some serious havoc, wouldn't it, girl? No, demons can only cross over when a portal is open."

I was almost afraid to ask. "So how do portals get open?"

"Got a few sorcerers in this world who know how to do the dark tricks, but even they can't hold a portal open for long. Get one, maybe two, demons at a time that way. But when there's a natural convergence like we got coming up . . ."

"Okay, slow down. What the devil are you talking about?"

"The next full moon, pet. We've got a full-fledged interdimensional convergence coming up. You know what that means?"

"I'm going to go out on a limb and guess the end of the world." I wished I could say I didn't believe any of this crap, but I'd just awakened in another body, so I was pretty much all about the bizarre right then.

"My star pupil. Only trust me when I say there are a hell of a lot more than four horsemen. Do you think that would be pretty? So do you think the world as we know it would survive?"

"Wait," I said, because even though my tolerance for all things freaky had increased, this still crossed the line into seriously fucked-up. "Back up. What?"

"A group of demons is preparing to open the last of the nine gates to hell," he said slowly and clearly. "Over the course of millennia, the other eight gates have been permanently sealed. But this one—" He cut himself off with a shake of the head. "Well, they just might manage to get this one open."

"But . . . But . . ." I was still about seven steps behind him. "Even if everything you're saying is true, what's that got to do with me?"

"The prophecy. That's where you come in. You're gonna protect it, Lily. You're gonna stop the demons and lock the gate up tight."

"Are you crazy?" I asked, thinking that he most likely was. "I'm not—I mean, how? How could I possibly manage that?"

He lifted the bottle of beer, his head cocked to one side as he examined me critically. "You really don't know? You remember so little?"

"Dammit, Clarence. Just tell me."

"You're an assassin, Lily. And if the prophecy is true, you're a damn important one, too. It's you who's going to kill the demons. It's you who's going to stop the ceremony."

"An assassin," I repeated, completely dumbfounded. "That's insane."

"Is it? You've already picked up a gun to hunt down a man. Now you'll use a blade."

"No. *No.*" An *assassin*? Not damn likely. "I did the hunting and killing thing once. *Once*," I repeated, my voice tight. "And I had good reason. That son of a bitch destroyed my sister. Fourteen years old, and she was in the hospital for a week, her face so swollen I could barely recognize her, her vagina so ripped she needed stitches. *Fourteen years old.*"

I could barely see him through the red haze of my memories. "He sent her postcards after. Called her. Stalked her." I caught a memory of Rose falling to her knees in terror, and me standing right there, promising to make it all better even as I burned with rage and the violent desire to rip Johnson to pieces.

"He wasn't going after her when you went out to kill him," Clarence said, his voice as flat as his eyes.

I lifted my chin. No way—no *way*—was I feeling guilty for that. "He *destroyed* her. He fucking destroyed her and they just kicked him back onto the street." I trembled, sucked in a hard breath, and faced Clarence dead-on. "I went after *him*. Only him. And I had damn good reasons. But I'm not a killer. That's not *me*. It's not who I am. It's not what I do."

"Don't think of it as killing. Think of it as saving the world."

"But—"

"Look," he said sharply, "what did you want to be when you grew up? Before your life made a left turn, I mean."

I clenched my teeth together and didn't say a word. I really wasn't interested in playing mind games. I needed to think. Needed to figure out what I was going to do about being stuck in a body in Boarhurst while Rose was unprotected and alone in the Flats.

"Humor me," he said. "Before. What did you want to be?"

"A doctor. I wanted to be a doctor." That dream had died with my mother. When my stepfather had sunk into uselessness and I'd become the one who had to put food on the table at the ripe old age of fourteen. I love my stepfather—or at least I know that my mom loved him. But sometimes I hate him for his weaknesses. And for not protecting me as I tried to protect Rose.

"Pretty self-sacrificing profession, medicine. Putting others first. Taking care to keep other people safe."

"It is," I agreed. "And in case you missed the memo, I'm not a doctor." The most I'd been able to manage was a few EMT courses picked up when I landed a job with shifts that lined up with the community college schedule, and when I could scrounge or steal money that didn't have to go toward food or the mortgage or the occasional hit. Most often, schedule and money didn't align.

I'd told no one, not even Rose. If I didn't finish, I didn't want the stink of failure on me any more than it already was.

And it was there all right, that rotten smell of decaying dreams. My failure had come complete with clichés—bad jobs, a few bags of pot or hits of X on the side, a wallet lifted here and there if I didn't think the owner would miss the cash too much, pirating DVDs and selling them under the table, and more shit, too, if I took the time to think about it. And, yeah, I even slept with a few guys I didn't like because I figured I could hit them up for a loan-turned-gift.

I'm not proud, but I did what I had to do, and I'd kept a roof over our head even when Joe did nothing but stare at the wall and scratch his ass.

I looked at Clarence defiantly through the haze of broken dreams. "I'm not a doctor. I'm not even close."

"Aren't you? Maybe you don't got a caduceus on your sleeve, but you went out to protect Rose." He leaned in close, his eyes so knowing it made me want to cry. "You did what you had to do so that she didn't have to feel the pinch. You did it, even knowing that in the end, it wasn't going to be good."

I licked my lips, remembering the feel of the gun in my hand as I'd made my way into the basement room Johnson had rented. I'd known I was going to die. I hoped I wouldn't, don't get me wrong, but the odds weren't great. I didn't care. I was willing to go into the blackness—the nothingness—that had terrified me so much as a kid. I was willing—so long as I could take him out with me.

I went out, in other words, intending to kill.

"Well, there you go."

But that didn't mean any of this made sense. I couldn't wrap my mind around why I was there. Why I was being given a second chance. I didn't get it. I really didn't.

Clarence sighed. "Come on, Lily. You ain't here 'cause you were a saint. A saint wouldn't need redemption, would she? No, girl, you're here because your *intentions* earned you another shot. What you did for your sister. Going out like that. Facing a monster like that. That was one hell of a sacrifice you were willing to make."

I blinked. Slowly . . . very slowly . . . maybe this was starting to make some sense.

"So here's the deal, kid. This is just like when you wanted to be a doctor—just like when you went all out to protect Rose. Only now you're protecting the whole big world. Keeping us all safe from demons and those that do their bidding. The enemy. The ones who are trying to bring a scourge upon the earth. To eradicate good. To destroy humanity. To bring hell to the surface and desolation to the land."

He pointed at me, his face animated. "And you, Lily—you're a barrier against their efforts. You're body armor protecting the whole human race. The secret weapon that's gonna fight to make the world right. And your first job's protecting the Ninth Gate."

I swallowed and tried to keep my face from betraying my emotions, which was ridiculous considering the little beast could get inside my head. But you know what? I didn't much care. Because I felt something inside me right then, something I hadn't felt in a long time. I felt hope.

More than that, I felt special. They wanted me. Lily Carlyle. They'd plucked me from death and told me I was special.

And how cool was that?

Except . . .

I gnawed on my lower lip.

"What?" Clarence said, eyes narrowed.

"You said something about a prophecy. Are you sure that's me?"

"You gotta have more faith in yourself, kid. And in us." He cocked his finger at me. "Trust me. The prophecy points to you. Only question now is, do you step up to the plate?"

I ran my fingers through my hair, getting them tangled in the unfamiliar length. I'm not sure why I was hesitating, because there was no way I was backing off from this. Like he said, I'd been *chosen*. I'd been plucked from obscurity to make the bad guys pay.

Men like Lucas Johnson.

I stood up and started pacing the room, the something I'd called hope growing in me. I hadn't felt it in a long time. Not since before my mother died. So fragile I wasn't even sure I should look at it. But it was there, peeking up out of the muck. A chance for a purpose. For a future.

And, yeah, a second chance at Johnson, too.

"It's yours if you take it," Clarence said, peering at me through narrowed eyes, his expression unreadable. I looked down, not wanting him to see the thoughts of revenge in my head. I had a feeling they were less than holy.

"What if I say no?" I asked, knowing there was no way I would. I was too pumped by the idea. Too keen on the prospect of doing whatever it took to wipe out the kind of evil that made men like Lucas Johnson tick.

"Is it something you're likely to say?"

I shook my head.

"Good. Because that would put you right back at square one, the sins of your acts staining your soul." He slipped his hand into a deep pocket of his trench coat and pulled out a lethal-looking blade, then shrugged ruefully. "And your blood staining this blade. Rules are rules."

"Holy crap! What kind of an angel are you?"

He slipped the knife back out of sight. "I never said I was an angel. I just work here. And now so do you."

FOUR

"All right," I said, starting to get used this über-girl idea. "Let's say I do this thing. What exactly does that mean? How am I supposed to protect this gate?"

"Good question, pet. Like to see you're on top of your game."

"Clarence . . ."

"First, you find them. The ones who seek to open the gate. Then you stop them. Turn their plans right around on them. Kill the demon priest and use the key to lock the gate instead of giving them a chance to perform the ceremony to open it. Oh, yeah. It's gonna be a beautiful thing."

"What ceremony?" I asked.

"A dark ritual, recently discovered, revealed in a scroll buried deep in a mountain in Turkey. Laid it all out. The ritual. The talismans. They get going on it, and poof. Too late's gonna come barreling down on us."

I swallowed. "When? When are they doing this thing?"

"Soon. We've learned that they still need one item. The

Box of Shankara. Open the Box during the ceremony, and it turns into a doorway, creating a portal to hell."

"Oh. Wow." Overwhelming much? "That sucks the big one."

"You could say that."

"And I'm supposed to jump in and muck up the ceremony?"

"We don't even want it to get that far. Our first line of defense is the Box. More specifically, the Caller."

"Oh. What's a Caller?"

"A demon possessed of the power to Call the Box back to him from another location. Even another dimension. Ancient stories say the Box was hidden away a couple thousand years ago. A Caller can bring it back."

"Oh. So not just any old demon can do that?"

"Different demons got different skills."

I pondered that. Demon subspecialization. Who knew?

"So how do I find the Caller?"

"Well, that's the problem, pet. We don't have a way to find the Caller. So instead, we're going to find what he's looking for."

"The Box," I said, because, hey, I'd been paying attention.

"A gold star for you." He grinned at me. "Give me your arm, and let's see if the bastard has summoned the Box yet."

"Excuse me?" I protested as he took my hand and pulled it toward him, stretching out my arm. "Hey!"

He'd pulled out a knife and was muttering over it in some language I didn't understand.

"Hello! What are you doing?" I tried to jerk my hand free, but he had me tight.

"Lily," he said sharply. "Be still."

And while I reeled from the verbal bitch slap, he sliced my arm horizontally, just below my elbow.

And the weird thing? It didn't hurt at all.

As I watched, a thin line of blood rose from the wound, and he pressed the edge of his knife against the blood, smearing it down my arm. Some stayed where the knife placed it, but some seemed to move of its own accord, forming a strange pattern on my skin.

I stared, confused, and then I gasped. Because *now* the pain was starting, and not from the wound but from the blood now burning into my skin. "Clarence! Shit! It's like acid! Get it off me!" I tried to shake my arm, but he was having none of it.

"One more moment, Lily. Just one more moment . . . There!"

Once again, he dragged the knife down, covering the burned area with a fresh smear of blood. All at once, the pain ceased, and he released my arm. I fell backward onto my ass, my arm clutched to my gut. "What the *hell* was that about?"

"Look at your arm, Lily."

"What? Look at my newly mutilated flesh? Screw you!"

"Look."

Damn me, I did. And what I saw was pretty amazing: a circle with strange symbols around the edge, like something Aztec. Or, I don't know, equally old. "What is it?"

"A locator," he said.

"But what's it doing on me?"

"The prophecy," he said, smiling up at me. "It's you, pet. And this is one more sign that proves it."

"Some freaky prophecy turned me into a map?"

"A locator," he repeated. "But it's pretty much the same thing."

"Fuck," I whispered, because this was not the kind of thing I could easily wrap my head around. "Fuck. Okay. Right. Fine. How does it work?"

He tapped the center of the circle, the one place not covered with images. "If the Caller had already retrieved the Box, then its symbol would be here."

"But it's not, so what does that mean?"

"The Box is still in a nether region," he said, then frowned. "They'll not retrieve it until the time for the ceremony is close. Reduce the risk that way."

"Of what?"

He looked at me hard. "Of you."

"Oh." I didn't feel particularly threatening at the moment.

"Right." I frowned at the design on my arm. "What about the rest of the symbols?"

"Some will become more prominent, and it is those that you'll use to find the Box's location."

"I will?" I was beginning to begrudgingly admit that this was pretty cool. Freaky, but cool.

"When the time is right, yes."

I decided to wait until the time was right to ask how exactly I'd do that. Right then, I was too overwhelmed by the fact that my arm was now the equivalent of a Shankara Box LoJack. "So what if it shows that the Box is in Tokyo?"

"The bridge would get you there," Clarence said.

"The bridge?"

He waved my question away. "Not to worry."

"But—"

"The odds of the Box appearing elsewhere are slim."

"Why?"

"Because the gate is here. At the convergence, the portal between worlds will open right here in Boston."

"No shit?" So much for all the hoopla in the Middle East. "Guess I'm glad I never bought real estate."

He shot me a hard look, and I shrugged. "Just keeping it light." I cleared my throat. "So, um, what now? I mean, since there's nothing in the center of my exciting new body art?"

"The circle will fade," he said, and in fact, it already was beginning to disappear. "But when the Caller utilizes his skill and brings forth the Box, the mark will burn, and we'll know where he has summoned it." He met my eyes. "So pay attention."

"Roger that. And in the meantime, what? I just sit around watching my arm?"

"In the meantime, you train."

"Right," I said, realizing that at the end of all this arm-watching was a big battle with demons. Yeah, training sounded like it definitely needed to be on the agenda. "So, I'm training with a team, right? And when my arm burns, we'll all go in together?"

"Sorry, kid. This is a solo act."

"Sorry?" I repeated. "Sorry? Are you insane? What is this, a suicide mission? I don't think so . . ."

He snorted. "As strong as you are? I don't think suicide's in the game plan."

"But . . . but . . . a team. Why can't I have backup?"

"That's just the way it's gotta be, kid."

"What? Why? This prophecy comes with an instruction manual?" Did prophecies work that way? My knowledge was limited to television and movies, probably not the most venerable of sources.

He chortled. "No, that's the big guy's mandate. Because what if we send you in with a team, and one of them is a mole? A plant for the forces of darkness? Pretty nasty result all the way around."

"A mole in heaven?"

"I know, kid. Hard to even stomach the possibility. But this is war. And we gotta be careful." He shrugged. "So that's the bottom line, pet. You find. You destroy. The Caller and the Box."

"Oh. How?"

"Your blood destroys the Box," he said.

"No shit?"

"That is the lore of the prophecy. As for the Caller . . ." He trailed off with a shrug. "The Caller you simply kill."

I drew in a breath, my I'm-a-cool-über-chick hubris fading in the cold light of reality. It was one thing to want to go out there, battle evil, and score big ticky points on the side of good. It was another matter altogether to realize just how much was riding on me not screwing up. Like, oh, the entire fate of the world.

"You got strength, Lily. Speed. All sorts of handy skills and tools. Comes with the prophecy. You're good, trust me. And with training, you'll be even better."

"Training," I repeated, taking a deep breath. Okay. Training was something tangible. Something I could latch onto.

I glanced at my arm—at the funky symbol now fading

from my flesh—and shivered. How much good was training against demons? Against the forces of darkness and the Apocalypse? That was big, scary shit, and I was only one girl. One girl not allowed to have backup. A fact I pointed out to Clarence, in an embarrassingly whiny voice.

"Don't underestimate yourself, Lily. You can do this." He looked at me seriously. "For that matter, you're the only one who can."

I started to pace, my thoughts bouncing from saving the world to what had gotten me here in the first place—trying to save Rose.

"I want to see her," I said. "I want to see Rose."

"Can't help you there, pet. You're dead, remember? Can't have you running around telling folks you're not really Alice, now can we? You can't tell anybody. Not your stepdad. Not Rose. Not anybody."

"But he's out there. He's going to start up again, Clarence. I know he will. And I'm not going to stand back while my sister's tormented." I met his eyes dead-on. "I won't do that. Not for anyone."

"Yeah, pet. I get that. But it ain't a problem, is it? The kid's safe now. You took care of that."

I blinked at him. "What?"

"Johnson," he said. "That plague on humanity is dead."

I plunked my ass back down on the sofa. "No. No, I shot him, but he kept on coming."

"Maybe it was a second wind," Clarence said. "But he blew through it. Trust me. The worm is dead."

"Really?" A sense of relief flooded me. Along with a disturbing hint of disappointment, and I realized I'd actually been looking forward to facing the bastard again. "You're not shitting me?"

He crossed his finger over his heart. "Would I lie?"

I licked my lips, trying to process the information. *Johnson is dead. Rose is safe.*

She'd lost her big sister—and that really did break my heart—but I hadn't been so naïve going into it to think that I might walk away unscathed. I'd always understood the risks. But if I took Johnson down with me, then I'd been prepared to call it a victory.

Which meant I'd won. Rose was safe.

I'd actually, really, truly *won*.

"You know what, Clarence," I said, smiling so broadly it hurt. "My crappy day is turning out to be not so bad after all."

He chuckled, then dropped down on the couch beside me. "Glad to hear it, kid. So we're clear?"

"Absolutely," I said. "Rose will never know her sister's alive."

"She's not, you know," he said, looking at me earnestly.

"Not?" I asked, assuming he was talking about Rose.

"Alive. Rose's sister isn't alive. You're not the same Lily that you were. You've been reborn." He patted my knee. "It may seem a minor thing, but trust me when I say it's the key to adjusting."

"I'm adjusting just fine," I said, then pushed up off the sofa. "I'm some prophesied superchick, right? So come on. Let's take me for a test-drive."

Clarence stared at me for a moment, and I found myself wishing I could read his mind like he could read mine.

"You know what? You're right. Time for you to get to work."

"Yeah?" I couldn't keep the eagerness out of my voice. "So, what does that mean exactly? I get a sword? A secret decoder ring? Fencing lessons?"

He eyed me sideways. "There's your work, and then there's Alice's. And for that, you're running late."

"Oh." I could feel the excitement levels spiraling downward, and I eyed him warily. "So what do I do?"

"You're a waitress," he said, and then he grinned. "Wear comfortable shoes."

FIVE

I have to admit that the ride to Alice's work in the limo was pretty cool. I'd ridden in it before, obviously, but the ride was much sweeter when I was conscious.

Tucked in near the cemetery and Torrent Park, the Bloody Tongue had been founded back in the 1600s and, according to local lore, had been owned by the same family ever since. It's remained in its original location and now was on the cusp, straddling a not-so-great neighborhood and an urban redevelopment area that was drawing in the young professionals. Haunted Boston tours ended there, which was how I knew about the place. Right after I'd started working at Movies & More, my manager had taken me out for drinks and screams. The tour had been more interesting than the guy, which made for some uncomfortable late shifts until he decided that the exciting world of video rental wasn't for him.

As the limo idled in a loading zone, I stared nervously out at the façade. I'd changed into the traditional waitress garb I'd found hanging on a hook inside Alice's closet. Black pants. A black tank top under a white sweatshirt with the

Bloody Tongue logo. Not a drop of pink to be found—thank goodness. But though I looked the part, I didn't feel it, and I was stalling.

"So tell me about Alice. I get the kudos and she gets the knife? What's up with that?"

What I didn't ask—what I wanted to ask, but couldn't—was whether Alice had died because I'd chosen life. The mere thought made me want to spew chunks. But what really got my stomach twisting was that even if I'd known that my words would have nailed Miss Pretty in Pink, with death and hell on the line, I would have made the same damn choice.

I closed my eyes, hating my cowardice even as I owned up to it.

Clarence eyed me from under his fedora. "Her death had nothing to do with you." I looked down pointedly at my new body.

"Ain't what I meant," he said. "She was murdered."

I hugged myself. "Who did it? And how did I end up . . . you know . . . *in* her?"

"I don't know who did it—honest Injun—and hers was the only available body when the opportunity arose."

"She's not like me, is she? Alive in another body, I mean." A horrifying thought struck me. "She's not in *my* body?"

Clarence chuckled. "Your body's tucked in at the morgue, and Alice's soul has moved on. Don't worry. You ain't gonna run into your own body on the street one day."

"Oh." Said that way, the scenario seemed rather silly. Still, I was glad for the reassurance. "Do they know? Rose? And Joe?" I asked, referring to my stepfather.

"Yeah. Neighbor found you in Johnson's basement. Cops came. Whole nine yards. Joe identified your body." The compassion I saw in his eyes almost brought me to tears. "Sorry, kid."

I nodded, afraid to try to speak right then. After a moment, I drew in a breath. "So why couldn't I just get my body back?"

He looked at me patiently, as if talking to a child. "You died, Lily. You did a dumb thing, and you died. Not like we're gonna just give you your old body back. It really doesn't work that way."

"Right. Forgive me for being a little hazy on the details of how resurrection or whatever it is does work."

"Eh. You'll figure it all out," he said magnanimously.

"And you really don't know who killed her? Isn't he going to be a little pissed to find out I'm still alive?"

"He? You didn't strike me as the sexist type."

I stared, wanting an answer.

"I really don't know, and I really couldn't say."

"I thought that God knew everything," I countered.

"He may, pet. But that doesn't mean he's going to tell me. Now, quit stalling." He nodded at the limo door. "Time to go."

As if on cue, the door opened, and I saw our tall, thin driver on the sidewalk.

I slid to the door and started to climb out. "But don't I need a cheat sheet or something? A primer on How to Be Alice?"

He tapped his head and grinned. "You'll figure it out."

And as he said it, the driver took my arm and gently tugged me the rest of the way out of the limo. Then he slammed the door. I stood there, gaping, a cry of "Hey!" hanging on my lips.

The driver, however, was uninterested, and though I knocked on the window and tried the door, Clarence didn't emerge.

I stood there seething as the limo pulled away from the curb, and then, as it disappeared around the corner, I turned to face the doors to the pub, remembering what he'd said only moments after I'd met him on the sidewalk near the alley. About being thrown into the testing. *This* was a test. Prove I was clever enough to play Alice, and I got a gold star. Screw up, and I'd be up close and personal with a blade. Again.

No pressure or anything.

I took three deep breaths, said a quick prayer for courage,

and pushed through the battered double doors, still accented by the original stained glass. On my first visit, the place had been bustling, filled with the late-night crowd. Now it was early Monday evening, with only a few patrons nursing beers or snacking on any number of fried delights. Most looked up as I entered. A few nudged each other and pointed, and a smattering paid no attention at all.

The knot in my stomach tightened a bit, and I wondered how I'd manage to pull this off. I'd waited enough tables over the last few years to know the general routine, so I figured I could muddle through the forest of pints, fish and chips, and Scotch eggs. It was the friends, coworkers, and regular customers that were worrisome.

I took a deep breath and forced myself to move before I got arrested for loitering. Two stairs led down to an uneven wooden floor, and I managed them without falling on my face. On the whole, the place looked as it had on my last visit. Tables dotted the dim interior, all the more dark from the oak-paneled walls and the red velvet booths that lined the south wall of the establishment.

There were no booths along the back wall, but the area bustled with the activities of serving drinks and food. To the right of center, metal doors swung open and shut, revealing glimpses of a hopping kitchen and giving the corner a feeling of hyped-up energy. A few yards over from the kitchen commotion, at dead center, a dark hall led into the back of the pub, the cavernous entrance marked by a neon sign announcing *Lavatories*.

A massive stone fireplace filled the space to the left of center—part of the original construction and highlighted by an ornately carved mantel now littered with framed photos of celebrities and politicians who'd stopped by the pub over the years. A couch on spindly legs with cloven feet dominated the area in front of the flames, and the two dark-haired women who sat there took a moment from their intense conversation to turn in unison, their curious eyes drinking me in.

I swallowed and looked away, now focusing on the U-shaped bar that commanded the center of the room. Dozens of bottles in varying degrees of emptiness cluttered the tiered center display area, and sparkles danced off the glass in a poor man's version of a chandelier.

The U itself was made up of polished oak, tall bar stools spaced every two feet or so. In the U, behind the bar, a white-haired man stared at me. His brows had lifted as if in surprise as I'd come through the door, but now he watched my approach with flat, expressionless eyes.

"You're late," he said mildly, when I was about ten feet away. "You okay, girl?"

"I—I'm sorry." I rushed forward. "I wasn't feeling well, and—"

"That why you disappeared on Saturday? I send you to the stockroom and you never come back?"

Saturday. That was the night I'd gone after Johnson. Which meant it must have been the night Alice died, too. And if she'd run out, then maybe she'd known she was in danger. More than that, maybe it meant that the danger was at the pub.

I glanced around the bar, checking out the faces, trying to discern whether anyone seemed surprised to see me alive. As far as I could tell, everyone was more interested in their beer than in my living, breathing presence.

"Yo. Whatsa matter? Your ears stuffed up?"

I snapped to attention. "Sorry. I was, um, sick Saturday. I shouldn't have run out like that."

"Damn straight. Shoulda called in on Sunday, too." His brow furrowed and his mouth pulled down into a frown. "Let me know you were okay."

"I'm really sorry. It won't happen again."

"Better not. You okay now?"

"I'm fine. Promise. Just a little fuzzy-headed." I managed a weak smile. "I didn't really eat much the last day or so."

"Hmmmph. Tell Caleb to make you up some fish 'n' chips."

"Thanks."

He made a gruff noise in his throat, then reached for a bar rag and began polishing the brass. "Can't have you passing out while we got customers needing food. And Gracie can't handle this place alone. I think we pretty much answered that question in the negative this weekend. Had to call Trish in, and she weren't none too happy."

"Oh." I hadn't a clue what he was talking about until I followed the direction of his gaze and landed on a ponytailed twentysomething in a white T-shirt with the Bloody Tongue logo silk-screened on the back. She was fumbling with the half apron she wore around her waist, trying unsuccessfully to count out change and make small talk at the same time. Gracie, I presumed. The unhappy Trish, however, was nowhere to be seen.

I conjured a smile. "So, I guess I should get to work."

"I'd say so. What's with your hair?"

"My hair?"

"You forget the rules? Get it back in a ponytail."

"Oh. Right. Wasn't thinking." A tall blonde with pencil-thin legs and severely highlighted hair came in from the back holding a prep tray of lemons and oranges. Trish, I presumed. And her hair was in a high ponytail, the same as Gracie.

"So what are you standing around for? Get it done and get to work."

"Right." I hooked my thumb toward the kitchen. "I'll just go find a rubber band."

I was passing Trish on my way to the kitchen when a female yelp underscored by the clatter of breaking glass stopped us both. The sound came from a far corner of the bar, and I turned in time to see Gracie on her rear, shattered pints littering the floor around her.

But compared to the spectacle playing out above her, Gracie sprawled on her ass was hardly even worth commenting on. Because even as she picked herself up off the floor, the limp body of a huge man was hurtling through the air.

He collided with the wood-paneled wall with such force it

shook the sconces, then slammed down, shattering a table beneath him.

"Goddammit!" shouted the bartender, rushing out from behind the bar.

I took a step forward, but Trish's hand on my shoulder stopped me. I started to protest, then saw who she was looking at: a man, tall and dark, rippling with uncontrolled rage and thrumming with raw energy. He stood a good ten feet from the injured man, but there was no doubt, no question in my mind, that this mysterious man had tossed his victim like so much garbage that entire distance.

Now I watched, unable to draw my eyes away, as he clenched and unclenched his hands. He took one step forward, then stopped, the effort clearly costing him. At any other time, I imagined that his face was uniquely handsome—a strong jawline, a once-broken nose, and eyes that took in the world beneath a strong brow. Now that face was contorted, still lost to whatever dark urge had powered his victim ten feet through the air.

"I gotta check him," I said, my EMT training kicking in. I hurried to my charge, purposefully avoiding eye contact with his attacker. I bent down, speaking softly as I gently probed his flesh, manipulating his limbs as I looked for breaks and fractures.

I heard movement behind me and turned long enough to see the mysterious attacker cross the pub in long, even strides. He met my gaze once, his eyes a brown so dark they looked black, with tiny flecks of gold that caught the light. Powerful eyes, and for a flash I saw recognition there, so intense it made my heart stutter. But it was stifled in an instant by the fury that boiled beneath the surface, so close to bursting I feared the explosion could well destroy the man.

Without warning, he lashed out, swiping two pints off a nearby table before stalking out the front door, leaving the pub so silent you could hear the beer seeping into the floorboards. The door slammed behind him, and we all breathed a sigh of relief.

I swallowed, my attention returning to the guy on the floor, my demand for a flashlight ringing out above the nervous titter of resumed conversation.

Trish appeared at my side, and I checked the battered man's eyes.

"What are you doing?" Trish asked.

"Making sure his pupils are dilating evenly," I said. "I, um, read about it in a first-aid book."

"Yeah? No wonder you're always acting like such a smart girl."

I cut her a look, but she smiled sweetly. Apparently Alice and Trish weren't exactly the best of buds.

We tried to help him up, but the man was clearly back to his old self, full of masculine self-sufficiency and gruff embarrassment. He pushed us away, then climbed to his feet, shooting a malevolent glance toward the front door, following the direction his attacker had taken.

"Go home, Leon," Trish said. "Cool down. You don't want to take him on when he's like that, and you know it."

The look Leon shot her was pure contempt, but he took the advice, stalking to the door and disappearing into the night.

I looked around for the bartender, then found him coming in from the back, pushing a mop and bucket.

"Shouldn't he have gone after that guy?" I asked Trish. "I mean, this is a lot of damage."

She lifted a brow. "What planet are you on today? Like Egan would go after Deacon when he's like that. Not damn likely." She shrugged, then pulled out a handful of tips and started counting them, as if this were any old conversation between waitresses. "You may think he's not too bad, but honestly, the guy scares the crap out of me."

She headed off, and I stared after her before cutting my gaze over to where Deacon had disappeared.

If I'd been smart, I'd be scared, too. But my brains must have taken a hiatus. Because right then, it wasn't fear I felt. It was curiosity. And more than a little attraction.

SIX

After Leon left and the crowd dispersed, I cleaned up the broken glass, then continued on to the kitchen where the cook, Caleb, made me a basket of the best fried cod I'd ever tasted. The only thing missing was a pint of Guinness, but I seriously doubted that drinking on the job was copacetic, even though I'd probably do a better job waiting tables with a hint of a buzz. While I was eating, Gracie came in and graciously gave me an extra ponytail holder.

"Table four," Egan the bartender said as I came in, full and ponytailed and ready to start my shift. While I'd been eating, he'd carted the splintered table off somewhere, and everyone in the pub had gone back to business as usual. Not me; I felt itchy and out of sorts, and my mind kept returning to that look in Deacon's eye. It was Alice he was looking at, of course, but I couldn't shake the sensation that he'd seen *me*—Lily.

"Get your head out of the clouds, girl," Egan said, pushing a tray holding two pints a few inches down the bar toward me. "Get to work."

I hurried to take the tray. A laminated sheet with a handwritten layout of the tables hung behind the bar, and I used it to get my bearings. Table four was in the back, opposite the corner where the now-smashed table had been earlier. I headed that way, walking carefully so I wouldn't spill the lager, my head full of questions, most of them about Deacon. Who was he? This man from whom rage had burst like a volcano? Trish had said that Alice didn't think he was "too bad," an assessment that made no sense whatsoever. Either Alice had a seriously screwed-up view of life—a theory I was willing to get behind, considering her apartment vomited pink—or I was missing the bigger picture.

Or, perhaps Alice had been wrong about Deacon. Maybe he *was* so bad after all. And maybe it was her calm complacency around such a dangerous man that had ultimately cost Alice her life.

"You picked a bad day to piss off your uncle," a biker dude at table four said, pulling me out of my thoughts.

"Apparently," I said, mentally connecting the dots and realizing that Egan the bartender was Alice's uncle.

"Where did you go, anyway?" his companion asked, this one in jeans and a flannel work shirt, his eyes hidden behind aviator glasses. "After you pulled your disappearing stunt on Saturday, it took forever to get my bangers and mash."

"Oh. Um. Sorry."

He held up his hands. "Hey, don't apologize. I'll just take it out in your tip."

"I—"

He barked out a laugh. "Gotcha."

"Lighten up, Alice," Biker Dude said to me. "You're walking on fucking eggshells."

"Headache," I said with a shrug. "More like a migraine."

I turned away, not sure I could take another round with those two, and returned my attention to more important things. Being Alice. Sliding into her life. And, hopefully, reaping some clue as to what had happened to her.

That hope was countered by the more mundane tasks of

my new life. Things like learning how to draw Guinness from a tap. Struggling to check the table-number chart without anyone catching me peeking. Even carrying on an innocent conversation with Gracie as we refilled saltshakers and balanced ketchup bottles precariously on top of one another.

All things that required my full concentration if I didn't want to give myself away.

"So how come you didn't call me back?" Gracie asked, after we'd finished with the saltshakers and had moved on to pepper. Previously, our chatter had centered on whether she should take Caleb up on his offer to make her an order of cheese fries. Now, apparently, we were getting to the meat of the issue, and I wasn't sure whether I was dreading the conversation or desperately curious.

"When?"

"Forget it," she said, standing and picking up a tray loaded with saltshakers.

"No, wait. I'm serious. My uncle told you I got sick, right? I've been a complete head case."

The tray went back down.

She turned slowly as she scoped out the tables, looking to see if anyone needed a refill or a check. Apparently we were safe, because she slid back into the seat and pulled out her tip money, then started organizing it by bill. "Really?"

"Totally. I haven't even checked my messages."

"Oh. Well, okay, then. But I was bummed you didn't call. We were supposed to go to the movies Sunday before work, remember?"

"Oh, man," I said, trying for sufficiently contrite. "No wonder you're pissed."

"I'm not all that pissed," she said, blue eyes looking up from under her bangs. "But I was worried. You've been so—you know—these last few days."

"Yeah? How so?"

"Well, distracted, for one. That's what you called it, right?"

"Yeah," I said, starting to load up another tray of

completed shakers. "That about sums it up. I told you why, though, right?" I said it with a smile—a confidence between friends.

"Very funny."

Apparently I hadn't told her. "Sorry. I'm just teasing. But I should have said something. I mean, if you can't share stuff with your friends—"

"Exactly." She leaned in closer. "Do you wanna talk about it now?"

I waved off the question. "Nah. It's no big deal. Guy trouble."

"Noah?"

"Excuse me?"

"Him just picking up and heading to Los Angeles. I mean, what a prick."

"Major prick," I said, making a mental note to search Alice's apartment for anything related to a Noah. Maybe he killed her and then fled the state.

"It's been over a month, Alice. It's kinda time to move on."

"Right. I know. You're right." Cross Noah off my suspect list.

"Brian's interested, you know. I can tell he wants to be more than just friends."

"Yeah, well, you know," I said, hoping I sounded non-committal instead of absolutely freaking clueless. I had no idea who Brian was.

Gracie laughed. "Try not to look that uninterested around him, okay? You might hurt his feelings."

"Sorry. It's just—"

"You've got someone else in mind," she said, sounding like a girl with a secret.

"I do?"

She rolled her eyes. "Come on, Lily. Do you really think Deacon Camphire's gonna be interested?"

I sat up straighter, my eyes wide and hopefully innocent. "What are you talking about?"

"Come on. I saw you talking to him last week."

"So?"

"So?" she repeated, incredulous. "Don't you think he's kinda scary?"

"Like tonight, you mean."

"Well, duh. I mean, Leon was being more of an A-hole than usual, but what Deacon did—I mean *whoa*."

Her *whoa* pretty much summed up my reaction to the mysterious Mr. Camphire on all fronts. Not that the people I hung with were all that straight-arrow, squeaky clean. You start scrambling to pay the bills at the ripe old age of fourteen, and you either stick to your principles and stay broke, or you cut a few corners and meet some unsavory individuals. My corners were so cut I only owned circles.

I had a feeling that Miss Hello Kitty didn't have to scrape the way I had, though. But before I had the chance to prod Gracie for any more info about Alice's recent conversations with the enigmatic man, Egan's booming voice interrupted. "You two gonna gossip all night? Or is someone gonna finish the side work and close out these checks?"

We both popped out of our seats like he'd sent an electric shock to our butts. Our eyes met, and we started laughing. Real laughs, as if the world were going to collapse around us, but we didn't care because something was just too damn funny.

I hugged myself, trying to get control despite the fact that I didn't want the moment to end. I felt alive right then. I felt as I had with Rose, before Lucas Johnson ruined everything. The way we'd bump hips in rhythm when she washed the dishes and I dried. The way we'd laughed. Rose was the reason I'd busted my tail—and stained my soul. To keep Rose safe and normal and protect her from the dark underworld I'd moved through while trying to keep us all alive. It had almost worked, too. *Almost*, however, isn't worth shit. It won't keep you alive, it won't pay the bills, and it damn sure won't get you into heaven.

"Alice?" Gracie asked, peering at my face.

Without thinking, I reached over and gave her a hug, needing human contact. She flung her arms around me exuberantly and hugged me back, and the intimacy—the connection—was so real it almost broke my heart. Because it wasn't real at all. I hardly knew her, but I'd latched onto the first light of humanity I'd found.

From behind the bar, Alice's uncle glowered at us, until we had to either calm down or risk psychiatric evaluation. Gracie grabbed a tray and moved away, then turned as a new thought occurred to her. She came back, then leaned in so she was speaking directly into my ear. "I got a callback on that receptionist job. I'm nervous as hell—but thanks for setting it up."

"Anytime," I said, wondering why Alice would be shooing her friend away. Better money? Better career track? Or something else altogether?

I grabbed my own tray, the questions circulating in my head, and went back to work. The rest of the shift whizzed by like a final exam, the night passing quicker than the traditional turning of a clock's hands. At one point, I grabbed one of the paper menus Egan kept by the door, then scribbled down the names of everybody I'd met that night. Later, I'd run through the list, making sure the names were burned in my brain. Alice homework.

The pub closed at nine on Mondays, and by the time Egan announced that I needed to cart the trash to the alley, my feet and calves ached, and I realized that I'd actually managed to learn quite a bit about Alice's life. On top of that, I also hadn't blown my cover. All in all, I considered the evening a success.

As I wrapped a twist tie around the top of a bag filled with greasy pub food remnants, Egan went to lock the front door. The pub had been expanded from the original tiny tavern, but the back section that snaked behind the public areas and ultimately opened to the alley was original construction. The kitchen, of course, had been thoroughly modernized, but as I passed through the door into the section the staff called the "Back," I left stainless steel and bright lights for damp wood, ancient brick, and low-wattage lightbulbs suspended from the ceiling by thick insulated cords.

The dim light barely permeated the darkness, and I imagined monsters hiding in the shadowy corners, their cackles barely disguised by the creak and gurgle of ancient plumbing coming from the lower level.

I knew the set of stone stairs led down to a stockroom and a second walk-in refrigerator supplementing the one in the kitchen, and I was curious about what else was down there. Now, though, exploring wasn't on my agenda. Instead, I followed the rough brick walls to where a steel fire door had replaced what must have once been a thick wooden entrance.

I pushed the exit bar with more force than necessary and escaped into the relative illumination provided by a few sputtering streetlights. The Dumpster was about twenty yards away, shared with all the tenants that opened onto this alley. I hefted my bag and moved toward it, holding my breath against the inevitable stench of garbage from a row of restaurants and bars.

The Dumpster lid was open, which I considered a blessing as I didn't want to touch the nasty thing. I lifted the sack and tossed it in, surprised at how light it seemed. It landed with a satisfying thud, and I congratulated myself on a job well done.

I'd pulled my hair from the ponytail, and now it fell in my eyes. I brushed it back behind my ears, not used to this new length. That was when I saw him. The creature from my awakening. The Hell Beast I'd coldcocked instead of killed.

And damned if he wasn't rushing right at me.

SEVEN

"I do *not* need another freaking test," I screamed, a complaint that had absolutely no effect on the beast rumbling toward me. Much more effective was the kick I landed. Straight up, so that my heel collided with what I assumed was his sternum, resulting in a satisfying smack that sent the creature spinning backward.

Because the idea of hanging around to tangle with a Hell Beast wasn't tops on my list, I made a dash for the back door to the pub, desperate to get out of there. Clarence might insist I was some hotshot assassin for evil, but at the moment, I really wasn't feeling the love.

Unfortunately for me, the creature cut for the door at the same time, tackling me even as I lunged for the handle. We tumbled backward, and I gagged on the putrid stench, my hands slipping on the thin layer of slime that seemed to cover its otherwise scaly body.

A clawed hand reached back, then lashed forward, razorlike fingernails catching my arm and slicing from shoulder to elbow, drawing a narrow line of blood. The sting came after that, an intense burning that could only be the result of something poisonous in the creature's touch. I yowled in pain, flinching back as if I could press myself into the concrete merely by trying hard enough.

Of course I couldn't, and that left me only one option. I had to fight.

With the beast straddling me, I couldn't get up, but that didn't stop me. My fingers were free, and as much as it disgusted me, I jammed my thumbs straight up into the creature's eyes. It roared in agony, shifting back and giving me the leverage to get it off me. I shoved with all my strength, and the thing went flying backward with way more velocity than I'd anticipated.

I jumped to my feet, awed by my own strength, and faced with the chance to test Super Me out again when the beast made a second rush forward. I kicked up and out, landing a solid thrust to its chest. The move wasn't artful, but it was effective, and the beast tottered backward. It rallied, coming back toward me with strength that matched my own, and skill that far exceeded mine. Apparently, Super Me needed some super training.

What I didn't have in skill, I made up for in hard and fast hitting, kicking, and pounding. Not a bad method, frankly. I hadn't yet won the battle, but at least I was still in the game.

And the game was getting pretty damn aggressive. Our fight sent us tumbling all over the back alley, slamming up against hard brick walls and rusty trash bins. Against drainage pipes and a rickety fire escape ladder.

We bounced off the ladder, breaking off a rusty metal bar in the process. It clattered on the ground, the sound the only thing other than my breathing that made it past the dull roar of ferocity inside my head.

We rolled along the wall until the monster pinned me, his hand encompassing my entire neck, and his grip tight enough that I began to wonder if I wasn't about to die again. I started to thrust my hands up in an attempt to break its hold when I saw a flash of something bright, then a dull thud as the something connected with the demon's head. The demon released me, and spun around, and when it did, I saw Deacon.

"What are you—"

But I didn't get to finish the question. The demon launched himself, and Deacon twisted, turning to get out of the beast's path, but it was no use. The creature tackled him, knocking him to the ground near the fire escape and kicking him soundly in the ribs before bringing one heavy foot down on Deacon's throat. A tiny bit more, and Deacon's neck would snap.

And I was *so* not letting that happen. At least not until I had some freaking answers.

I shoved off from the wall and leaped onto the creature's back, pulling him sideways off Deacon and sending us both tumbling to the ground. The beast landed on top of me, knocking my breath out, but even so, I was able to heave him off of me, throwing him down the alley a hell of a lot farther than your typical Boston waitress could probably manage.

I climbed to my feet as the creature did, and found Deacon up on his knees beside me. Slowly, he lifted his head, his dark eyes locked on the demonic target, his features skewed with rage, his eyes neither drifting nor blinking. I stood rooted to the spot, watching both of them, unsure who I feared more.

Deacon smiled then, and the malevolence seemed to drip like honey. The demon looked at both of us, then made a decision. It turned to run away.

No, no, no. Because this was one creature I had no interest in meeting for a third time, I scooped up the part of the fire escape that had fallen. Even as Deacon sprinted after the beast, I hauled back and heaved the beam like a javelin. Whether skill, blind luck, or divine intervention I didn't know, but it hit the mark, penetrating the thick skin and sending the demon crashing to the ground.

The body stuttered and shook, then went limp, life abandoning it. As I watched, Deacon reached into his jacket pocket and pulled out a switchblade. The earlier fury had vanished, replaced by a battle-worn acceptance, as if this were any other day, any other fight.

I watched, mortified, as he toed the corpse over onto its back, then bent over and plunged the blade into the beast's heart, releasing a thick black liquid that I had to assume was demon blood. Then he wiped the blade on the beast's haunches before retracting the blade and returning it to his pocket.

I stood there, dumbstruck, as the demon dissolved in front of me, the oil-like substance disappearing into the cracks and crevices of the alley's pavement, a faint greasy stain the only remaining evidence of this surreal encounter.

As I watched the demon, Deacon watched me. And this time, it wasn't rage or acceptance that filled his eyes—it was curiosity. But not about the bizarre creature he'd just slain in an alley. No, this man's curiosity lay with the pub waitress standing in front of him.

"What are you doing out here?" I demanded.

"Saving your ass, I thought," he said, without even a hint of the rage I'd witnessed, both inside the pub and as he'd battled the demon. No, this man stood calm and controlled, the wildness I'd seen now buried beneath the surface, burning deep, but locked in. "Then you turned around and saved mine. Guess we owe each other a debt."

I opened my mouth, then closed it again, not at all sure what I'd planned to say. Instead, I backtracked. "Are you here because of the test? I passed, right?" I indicated the greasy stain. "I mean, that has got to be a pass."

"The test," he repeated, his head slightly cocked as if he still couldn't figure me out.

"Never mind," I said, gingerly removing my foot from my mouth. Hopefully the ability to keep my mouth shut around civilians wasn't part of my final exam.

"Was this what you meant?" he asked, easing closer to me. "When you told me that you thought you were in danger?"

I blinked, wishing I knew the details of *that* conversation.

"And how'd a slip of a girl like you manage to piss off a demon like that?"

"I—I don't know," I said, but my head was spinning. *Alice had known she was in danger. But in danger from what? Or from whom?*

"No? Funny, because I think I do."

"You do?" The fear that rippled through me wasn't because of the man himself, but what I was afraid he saw inside me—Lily hiding within the shell of Alice.

"I think you've taken up killing demons," he said, his eyes locked on mine as I desperately tried to maintain an innocent countenance. He stepped closer still, then stood broad and foreboding in front of me, the tension within him so tight I feared I wouldn't escape the fallout if he exploded. And all of that intensity was aimed right at me, those dark eyes seeing everything. "Or have I misread the situation?"

I swallowed, my palms sweating and my entire body singing. I told myself I was too nervous to be turned on, and yet there was no mistaking my reaction. A physical reaction to a gorgeous man, yes, but also more than that. He was taking my measure, and I feared I wouldn't pass the assessment.

"Maybe I am," I said, boldly. "Everybody needs a hobby, right?" Clarence might not approve, but it wasn't like I was revealing that I was some anointed demon assassin girl. And if Deacon was right, maybe it was her new career choice that got Alice killed.

"Interesting," he said, a grin tugging at the corners of his mouth. He kept me locked under his gaze as he walked around me in a circle. "And curious."

"Nothing curious about it," I said, trying to keep my cool. "There's obviously a need."

"And you were coming to me why? Because you were afraid you'd pissed off the wrong target?"

"Something like that," I said. I cast a glance toward the spot where the demon had fallen, now just a stain on the pavement. "He and I have tussled before."

"Have you?" His eyebrows rose, and I regretted my big, fat mouth.

"Least I don't have to worry about him again." I frowned, remembering Clarence's instructions to kill it, not give it a headache. "Did I kill it? Or did you?"

"That would be you," he said. "All I did was make sure the thing didn't come back."

"Oh."

"Maybe you need a little more on-the-job training before you jump straight into this new career."

"I'll take it under advisement," I said wryly.

A hint of a smile touched the corner of his mouth. "I'm just messing with you. You did good work, Alice. Unexpected, but good."

"Rather unexpected for me, too," I said, then caught myself. "I mean, I never expected to get jumped."

He looked me up and down. "Are you okay?"

There was such concern in his voice that I had to remind myself that only hours before, this man had tossed another person across a room as if he were nothing more than a sack of laundry.

"I'll be fine." Possibly not the truth, but it was the best I could do.

His eyes raked over me, his assessment like a physical touch.

I forced myself to remain steady, my legs suddenly not working properly. "Okay, then." I nodded toward the pub's back door. "I should get back inside."

He moved closer, his hands closing around my upper arms, one hand warm and the other strangely cold. I took a step backward in a futile attempt to keep some distance between us, but he mirrored my movement. He was too close, and I was finding it harder and harder to think. As if he were radio interference keeping me from tuning in to my very own head.

"You haven't told me why you were here," I said, as much for something to say as because I was genuinely curious. His presence was a lucky break for me, but most men didn't hang out in dark alleys waiting for damsels in distress.

"You're the reason. I don't handle being stood up well. I wanted to get to the bottom of it."

"Oh." I figured that was my cue to skedaddle. I took a sideways step toward the door. "Now's not the time. I need to get back in before Egan—"

He stepped into my path, effectively blocking me.

"Hold up a second."

"No, I really—" I looked him firmly in the eyes, then pressed my hand against his chest to push him away.

And that was when it happened.

The world around me melted away, starting with his eyes. They shifted, turning from brown to black to a boiling red.

I tried to gasp—to scream—but it was like I wasn't there anymore. I was watching, but I wasn't controlling.

And what I saw scared the shit out of me.

A kaleidoscope of images. Dark. Dangerous. Heat and lust and power and fear.

I heard myself gasp, but the sound was muffled by the distance between my body and my reality. Instead, the beat of my pulse filled my ears, the dull, rhythmic rush of blood through vessels, of life humming along with each beat of my heart.

Blood.

Hot and demanding, pulsing and throbbing.

Red silk, crushed velvet. A sensual feast full of terrifying pleasures.

Blood.

I tried to pull out of this vision, this dream, this whatever-it-was that had grabbed hold of me, but it wasn't letting go. *He* wasn't letting go. He was holding tight, pulling me close, his pulse matching mine, the beat hypnotic and deep, drawing me in, threatening to drown me, to pull me under.

Hot fingers.

Bare flesh.

And desire as sharp as a blade.

Somehow, I'd gotten lost inside his mind. A vision I didn't want but couldn't stop. We were wrapped up in horrific images and sensual pleasures, and my instinct to run was countered by a desperate desire to stay.

Behind this strange curtain, my nipples peaked and the insides of my thighs ached. I moved closer, squirming against him, desperate to find satisfaction. But whether this was real or only in my mind, I didn't know. Right then, I didn't care. Right then, I knew nothing more than the touch of his hand and the desperate thrum of desire.

His fingers roamed my back, his body pressed so close to mine I could feel his heartbeat along with the steady tickle of his breath against my hair. Caution abandoned me as quickly as modesty had, and all I wanted was his touch, the feel of his skin against mine.

As if answering my prayers, his lips danced across my skin, finding my mouth, then claiming me in a wild, violent taking that left my body shuddering and my mouth begging for more.

He moved to break the kiss, but I pulled him back, frustrated when he resisted, as if he knew that some change was coming.

And then it was there—a flash—and suddenly my mind's eye turned gray, painting us in black and white, all lights and darks, highlights and shadows. The shadows sucked us in, and with another flash, my mind was seeped in gold.

We were horizontal now, our bodies naked and slick and joined, and his eyes—I could see only his eyes. Warm and soft, without any hint of the rage I knew lurked beneath the surface. Only desire and need and longing so intense it pulled me—compelled me—until I wanted nothing more but to melt into him, to merge into one.

It didn't last.

Those eyes, they changed in a flash. Snapping to a dangerous black, like a shark's eyes. The change so fast, so sharp, I flinched, as if I'd been chastised for trusting too easily despite the man I'd seen earlier in the bar—the man inside Deacon who terrified me.

I tried to pull back, but I was too far gone. The lens of my mind turned red, but those eyes stayed black. A deep, yawing black that sucked me in, consumed me.

I recoiled from the abyss I saw before me. *There is evil here.*

I wanted to look away—I didn't want to see. But I couldn't help it.

And what I saw broke my heart.

Pain and loss and fear. It pummeled through me.

His pain. *His* loss. *His* fear.

All held out in front, like a talisman to hold at bay a flood of dark rage, bloodred anger, and a vile malevolence the depth of which could burn a hole in a man's soul.

I struggled then, trying to pull away. Trying to get my head out of this dark place.

But I couldn't break free. His hold on me was too strong.

You're mine, his voice seemed to whisper in my head, the words so intense I would almost swear they were real. I looked down, my eyes finding a dozen white flowers, rivulets of blood running down the petals like rivers.

Lilies.

I gasped, dread shooting through me as the not-so-subtle symbolism broke the spell.

The images evaporated like so much mist, and I jerked suddenly, as if awakening from a trance, only to find my body pressed hard against him, my crotch rubbing against his thigh.

Mortified, I jumped back, my blood still pounding with desire and fear.

And when I looked up, I saw none of my confusion on his face. Instead, all I saw was anger.

"Goddammit, Alice," he growled, snatching my upper arm with a motion too quick to dodge. "You swore if I helped you that you'd stay the fuck out of my head."

EIGHT

I probably shouldn't have run.

Running made it seem like I was scared. Which I was. But that wasn't something I wanted Deacon to know.

No, I should have stayed. Should have pretended I didn't know what he was talking about. Should have pretended I'd never been inside his mind. Never felt that sensual burn, never seen the vile sheen of evil.

But so help me, I had. And so I'd broken free of his grip, and I'd run. And even though I heard him call my name, I didn't look back. Instead, I ripped the door open and stumbled inside. I slammed it shut behind me, then threw the heavy bolt into place.

I leaned back against the metal, my breathing shallow and my heart pounding in my chest.

The Hell Beast might be an over-the-top, freak-me-out, blow-me-away terrifying monster, but it was a pussycat compared to what I'd glimpsed inside Deacon's head and what I'd heard in his voice just now. Dark stuff. Scary stuff.

The kind of stuff that made Lucas Johnson seem like a stellar babysitting choice.

There *was* evil in Deacon—of that I was sure. But, dammit, I'd seen more than just the scary stuff. He was battling it back, fighting the good fight.

Whether he was winning, though . . . Well, that I couldn't say.

From what he'd said, I was guessing that Alice had seen the stain of evil on him, too. And that her peek inside the mind of the man had pissed him off. Probably terrified her. She'd gone back, though. And she'd asked him for help.

Then she'd never shown up to get it.

She'd been murdered instead.

But Alice had thought that Deacon could help her, and now I had to wonder if he could help me. Maybe she'd told Deacon something. Given him some tidbit of a clue that would lead to her killer. And that was something I wanted to know despite Clarence's warning. I *needed* to know it. Both to keep this new body of mine safe, and also to avenge the woman whose life I'd usurped. Clarence might think it was best left in the past, but I knew that wasn't possible. I *would* find Alice's killer. And right then, Deacon was the only lead I had.

Which meant that at some point I had to stop running and go face the man. A little tidbit that, frankly, should scare me to death. But it didn't.

Deacon compelled me. He excited me. This man who recognized demons for what they were—who held fury at bay behind the thinnest of barriers. This man who had set my body on fire with the slightest of touches.

A man who had promised aid to a frightened girl, and then worried for her when she hadn't shown up.

A dark man, yes, but with light around the edges.

And a damn sensual man, too.

I was no stranger to instant lust—to that internal thrum when a hot guy presses you close on a dark and sweaty dance floor. This, however, was different. This was deep and pounding and almost sinister.

I wanted to feel the heat of his touch and taste the saltiness of his skin. I wanted to consume him, and be consumed.

Even now, his voice echoed in my head. *You're mine,* he'd said. *You're mine.*

There was something there—something between Deacon and me. But whether it was between Deacon and Alice or Deacon and Lily, I didn't yet know.

Right then, I really didn't care.

No. I closed my eyes, mentally lecturing myself. *Don't fuck up.* This second chance was, literally, the answer to my prayers. I had a real chance to do some good here, to make up for a life that had taken a wrong turn toward crappy jobs and shady deals. And I wasn't about to screw this opportunity by screwing Deacon.

I *was* making this work, and I *was* going to ask all the questions I needed, and I *was* going to be über-save-the-world-chick.

I just wasn't quite sure how.

"Alice!" Egan's heavy voice boomed back from the front of the pub, saving me from my morass of thoughts. "What the hell, girl? You gone and get yourself lost again?"

I closed my eyes and drew in one deep breath as I tried to find myself in the mental mist. With some relief, I took stock, feeling like myself for the first time since I took down the demon.

I pushed away from the wall, mentally pushing Deacon away as well. Time to abandon the mysteries of that man and my reaction to him for the more immediate problem of sliding seamlessly into Alice's real life.

I pulled on the sweatshirt I'd earlier removed, needing to hide the long gash on my arm. Then I assured Egan that I had neither gotten lost nor abandoned my duties, and hurried to assist with the final closing chores. He'd sent everyone else home, and we went through the routine in companionable silence. If he noticed my hesitation as I considered the proper way to accomplish each task, he didn't say.

I stood awkwardly when we were done, unsure. Would he offer me some bit of affection? A peck on the cheek or a pat on the shoulder?

When I'd been waiting tables earlier that evening, things had gone smoothly. Or, at least, smoothly enough to let me believe I'd fallen convincingly into the role of Alice. Now there were no shouted orders, no spilled drinks. Only me and this man who was supposed to be my uncle. A man who'd known Alice since she was born. Couldn't he see? Couldn't he tell?

As if sensing my fear, he looked up from behind the bar where he was gathering his things. He rested one beefy arm on the polished oak, then caught me firmly in the net of his gaze. "You in some sort of trouble, girl?"

"I—no. Nothing."

He rubbed a callused hand over his beard stubble, his eyes never leaving my face as I forced myself not to squirm under his intense inspection. "Befuddled," he finally said.

"Excuse me?"

"All night. You been out of sorts. And what with the way you ran out of here on Saturday, I can't help but wonder if there's not something you're wanting to tell me. Like maybe you weren't sick? Like maybe something happened to you on Saturday."

I swallowed, then shook my head a fraction of an inch.

He exhaled loudly through his nose. "Have it your way. I ain't gonna let my sister's girls down. So if there's something on your mind . . ."

I hesitated, fighting an unexpected urge to find an ally in this man. He was Alice's uncle, after all. Who better to help me fit into her life? The words, however, eluded me as much as trust did. I wasn't Alice; he wasn't my uncle. And the job I now had was a solitary profession.

I managed a shrug, trying to look bored and unconcerned. "There's nothing. Honest. I was sick as a dog. So sick the weekend's a blur, you know? I hardly ate, did nothing but sleep, and now I'm dead on my feet. I'm tired, Uncle Egan. That's all."

"Lost weekend, huh?"

I pressed my lips together and nodded.

His eyes narrowed. "You got the sight back?"

"What?" I swallowed, hoping the shock didn't show on my face.

"You ain't had a vision since you were a kid, even before your mama died. If you start seeing again, you need to tell someone. Don't try to deal with it on your own."

"I wouldn't," I said. "I'm not." But my mind was whirling. Alice's visions must have come back, because Deacon had known. But she'd kept the return of the visions secret from her family. Why? And had Alice told Deacon? Or had he discovered the visions on his own? Maybe even when Alice was poking around inside his head.

None of these was a question I could answer, so I fell back on that old standard. Denial. "I haven't seen anything," I said, meeting Egan's eyes. "I swear. And if I did, I'd totally tell you."

For a moment, I thought he was going to argue. Then he gave me a curt nod. "Then what the hell you hanging around for? Go on. I'm ready to go upstairs and crash," he said, referring to the apartment he occupied above the pub. "Get home. And don't be late tomorrow."

"Right. I won't. Right." I hurried toward the door, more than ready to be out of there, even if that meant walking five blocks before I finally found a cab.

I started walking, warm in the red leather duster I'd found among the riot of pink in Alice's closet. I kept my eyes open, searching the shadows, because now I knew what hid in the dark.

The velvety blackness seemed to shimmer as I moved, and I imagined dozens of yellow eyes peeking out at me, watching and waiting. I stepped up my pace, the boots I'd shoved on my feet clomping on the pavement. In my mind's eye I saw the goblins gathering in mists, creeping up from sewers, soaring down on the backs of vultures. They were coming for me, and I wasn't ready. Lord help me, I wasn't ready.

In the distance, a taxi turned onto the street, and I stepped off the curb, my arm raised high. I stood there, willing the driver to see me, feeling naked and exposed as the devil's minions watched me from the shadows.

Thankfully, the cab pulled over, and I climbed inside, wrapping the illusion of safety tight around me.

Because the reality was, I was never truly going to be safe again.

NINE

The cab pulled to a stop in front of Alice's apartment, but I didn't get out. That was a new life in there. A new name, new friends, and new rules to follow.

The truth was, I'd never been much good at following rules.

"Miss?"

"I'm sorry," I said, sliding away from the door and back to the middle of the seat. "I need—I mean, can you take me to the Flats?"

He turned in his seat with a frown, an old man with skin the color of chamomile tea.

"I have the fare," I assured him, then rattled off the familiar address. "It's home," I added, though why I felt compelled to share that tidbit I didn't know.

His forehead creased before he turned back to the wheel and reengaged the meter. A town on its own before Boston annexed it, Boarhurst—called "the Boar" by the locals—sits at the south edge of the Boston metro area. The Flats was north and east, a low-rent area near shipping channels. Industrial, blue collar, and utterly lacking in charm. During the day, the monotony of dismal façades was broken by splashes of washed-out color—laundry hanging out to dry, children's toys broken and abandoned, potted flowers struggling toward the sun. At night, the entire area was monochromatic. I sat back in the cab and watched the black and white blur into gray.

The trip was pretty much a straight shot down the expressway, and at ten fifteen on a Monday night, traffic was light. I leaned back against the upholstery, trying to ignore the hell and damnation nipping at my toes. After all, it wasn't like I'd promised not to go to the Flats, right? All I'd said was that I wouldn't tell Rose what had happened to me.

I'd never once said I wouldn't watch her.

"Here," I said, leaning forward and pointing to the next exit off the expressway. "Then a left and a right at the light." I fed him directions, weaving the cab through the dark streets to the shabby neighborhood that had been my home for so many years. "Anywhere's good," I said, my eyes on the gray clapboards that covered our nondescript house.

Once upon a time, the gray had been trimmed with bright blue and the yard had been awash with flowers. But that had been a long time ago, when my mother was still alive. Now the yard behind the chain link was dust. Two recycling bins stood like sentries, one on either side of the porch steps, overflowing with whiskey bottles and crunched-up cans of beer. A single planter—now brown and crumbling—remained as the only evidence that the residents had ever tried to bring life into that grim yard.

I'd tended those plants myself—robust lilies and dusty pink roses. Not the typical fare for a container garden, but I hadn't been aiming for aesthetics. The plants were for me and my sister, something Rose could look at even when I wasn't home. Something that would remind us both that even if I was away, we would always be together.

I couldn't offer that reassurance any longer. At least I had the cold knowledge that I'd ended Lucas Johnson to comfort me, but Rose, my sister, had nothing.

I paid the driver and got out of the cab, then stood on the sidewalk until he drove away. The house was dark, and I wasn't sure what I intended to do. My hubris and determination had fizzled, leaving me feeling unsure, afraid, and just a little bit guilty.

"Get over yourself, Lil," I whispered. Then I took a deep breath, opened the gate, and marched to the front door. At almost eleven, the neighborhood was quiet. Late, but not late enough to send me walking away, especially because I could see the light and shadows from the television playing behind the frosted glass of the front door.

I lifted my hand, took a breath, then rapped four times on the door. No point ringing the bell—it had been broken for years.

At first, I heard nothing. Then someone crossed in front of the television, temporarily casting the interior of the house in darkness, as well as the porch. I shivered, my skin prickling as I twisted back toward the street, suddenly certain I was being watched. Nothing jumped out from the dark, however, and no creepy golden eyes peered from behind the bushes. If something was waiting out there to drag me down to hell, at least it was polite enough to let me finish my business.

Still unnerved, I turned back to the door, then gasped as it burst open and my stepfather's weathered face peered out at me.

"Wha?" Joe asked, bathing me in the scent of bourbon, the scent I'd always associated with his failure. Now it seemed like home.

I swallowed, and fisted my hands at my sides, determined not to reach out to him. "I—I—Is Rose home?"

His eyes narrowed, then he moved away, shouting down the hall for my sister as he lumbered back toward the den, never once turning to look at me again.

I fidgeted in the doorway, not sure what to do, but certain a piece of my heart had just shriveled up and died. I almost walked away, afraid I'd made a mistake by coming here, then stopped as my sister stepped into view. Fourteen years old, her skin so sallow she might as well be pushing fifty. Dark circles shadowed her eyes, and she moved with a heartbreaking wariness toward the door. The bruises Johnson had once put on her fragile skin might have faded, but my sister was still damaged goods, and that knowledge sat like lead in my gut. She wasn't healed and happy. Joe hadn't stepped up to the plate to be a good father.

My sacrifice hadn't worked any magic in her life.

I told myself it had been only forty-eight hours since I'd gone out to kill Johnson, and that nothing much would have changed in such a short time. I told myself that Rose needed time to get over my death and that Joe needed time to step up to the plate. In a month or two, things would be better around here.

I told myself that, but I didn't believe it.

"Who're you?"

"I'm . . . Alice," I said, shoving my hands into the pockets of my jeans so I wouldn't throw my arms around her. I waited until I was certain I could hold back the tears, then added, "I was a friend of your sister's."

She cocked her head, the way she did when she was thinking. "I hardly ever met Lily's friends."

I cringed, hearing the reproach, wishing I could go back and undo everything I did wrong—including the fact that most of my so-called friends had been shits. Shits who could get me cash, but shits nonetheless.

"She talked about you all the time," I said, truthfully. "And I wanted to come by now to make sure you're okay. She'd want to know that you're doing okay. Are you?"

Her large eyes blinked, and my heart skipped in my chest, so desperate was I for good news. For the assurance that my death had made this world a better place for her. That I'd somehow managed to keep my promise.

Instead, she only shrugged, her eyes as dead as I remembered. I'd wanted a fairy-tale ending, but no matter how much I wished for one, it just wasn't happening. Johnson had left his scars, and erasing his presence had not erased them from my sister's soul. If anything, my death piled on top had made them worse.

The bitter comfort I'd latched onto when I'd learned that he was dead shriveled in my stomach.

From the den, Joe hollered for Rose to shut the door. She started to, not bothering to say good-bye.

"Wait!" I yelped. She paused, and I rattled on. "I—I'll be at the funeral."

She stared at me, then nodded. Then the door clicked shut, leaving me standing like an idiot on my own front porch. "Right," I said, but this time only to myself. I pressed my fingers against the glass and whispered a quick "I love you." Then I squared my shoulders, lifted my chin, and walked across the beer-can-littered yard toward the street.

I knew I should head back to Alice's apartment, but before I could do that, I had one more errand. I turned right down the sidewalk, still haunted by the sensation of being watched. I stepped softly, listening for footfalls behind me. I heard none, but twice when I turned quickly, I saw shadows slipping over the sidewalk, disappearing into the trees and sliding down into the sewers. By the time I reached the video store, I was sweating, and my heart was tripping to an unfamiliar rhythm.

The overly bright fluorescent lighting seared my eyeballs as I stepped inside, the posters of a dozen movies staring back at me.

"Help ya?" Jeremy slouched behind the counter, an unlit cigarette dangling from his lips. I'd never been sure if that was his way of complying with the no-smoking rule, or if it was his way of saying *Screw you.* With Jeremy, sometimes it's best not to ask.

"I'm a friend of Lily's," I said, taking a Kit Kat bar from a candy display on the counter. "Was, I mean."

His eyes narrowed, and I could see the wheels in his greasy little head spinning. Jeremy did a nice business illegally copying DVDs, and I got a cut for any customers I shot his way.

I stood there, letting him size me up. More important, letting him wonder if this new chick was there to rat him out. Trust me when I say that it's a lot easier to get what you want if your mark thinks he's avoiding something worse by giving in to you.

"So?" he finally asked, shifting his weight from one foot to the other so that he teetered behind the counter.

I casually lifted a shoulder as I opened the candy. "No big. I was hoping you could do me a favor."

"Yeah? What kinda favor?"

"You got some cash on the books you owe Lil, right?"

"Who're you? Her accountant?"

"If it makes you happy."

"I don't owe her shit. I only work here. You gotta talk to Sean."

"I gotta talk to you, dickwad," I said. "'Cause I'm not talking her piddly-ass minimum-wage paycheck. I'm talking commissions. And she's got about three seventy-five coming her way."

He hesitated, and I could see denial on his face. Fortunately, he made the wise choice and didn't try to go that route. Instead, he tried diversion. "She's dead. Dead girls don't need cash."

"Her sister does," I said.

"So, like, what? Now you're social services, too?"

"If it makes you happy. But probably you should think of me as the problem that's going to be perpetually up your ass. Because I know where you get the vids to copy, and I'm thinking Sean doesn't have a clue." I took one long step toward him, so that I was right there, the thin plywood of the counter the only thing separating us. "And I know your customers, too."

"Bullshit," he said, but sweat was beading on his forehead.

"She told me, dude. She told me a lot." I put my hand on the counter, palm up. "So fork over the cash."

"Oh, come on," he said, but that was *all* he said, because I thrust forward and caught him around the scrawny little neck, pulling him toward me until my face was right there in his.

"You listen to me, you little shit. You open up your wallet. You give me what you've got. And if it's not three seventy-five, then you get the rest of the cash to me or to Rose by the end of the week. Otherwise, we'll have to have another chat. And honestly, I don't much like talking to you."

"Feeling's fucking mutual," he said, lurching back as I let him go, then smoothing his shirt as he glared at me.

"Now."

For a second, I thought he was going to hesitate again. And, honestly, I don't think I would have minded. Because I really was in the mood to kick some ass. But then he got wise and pulled out his wallet. He laid two C-notes on the counter, then followed that up with a fifty, a twenty, and six ones.

"And the rest?"

"I'll take it to Rose," he said. "I woulda, anyway. Kid needs a break."

"Right," I said. "You're all about spreading the good feelings and sharing the wealth."

"Damn straight," he said. "Not like I had a chance to say nothing with you going all Mojo Bitch on my ass."

"Rose," I stressed, deciding to ignore the *bitch* comment, especially since it seemed rather accurate. "Not her dad."

"I got it," he said. "Now, get the hell out of here."

"Pleasure talking to you, too." I slid a dollar back toward him. "For the candy."

I started to walk away, then stopped. "You touch her bike?"

He hesitated, and I knew he'd tried to. I'd locked it up good, though, before I'd caught the bus out to Lucas Johnson's shit-hole of a house.

"Never mind," I said.

"I'm gonna get someone to cut the chain off," he said. "Make a new key. Ain't no sense it sitting back in that alley with no one to ride it."

"You're right, Jeremy," I said. "That doesn't make any sense at all."

I took two bites of candy as I crossed the store, knowing he was watching me. Red stickers plastered the back door, warning that alarms would sound if I opened. I pushed. No alarms. So much for truth in advertising.

My decades-old Triumph Tiger was still parked there, a heavy chain around her. I didn't usually chain the bike up, but I also didn't usually keep it parked behind Jeremy's place. I'd locked it up tight Saturday night, though. Whether out of extra caution or premonition I didn't know. I was glad of my forethought now, though, and I reached under the fender for the magnetic metal box. It held two keys, and I had the chain off the bike in no time.

I straddled the machine, the bike warm and familiar between my legs. I'd just slipped the key in the ignition when Jeremy peered out the back door and into the alley. "Ain't your bike," he said.

"It is now. You got a problem with that?"

He considered it, probably weighing how much he could sell the bike for against the long-term income stream on his counterfeit DVD operation. I turn him in for that, and the door shuts on his little retirement fund.

Jeremy might be slow, but he's not stupid, and after a few moments of staring and pondering, he nodded, then disappeared back inside, the door slamming shut behind him.

I revved the throttle, relishing the sweet purr of the engine. "Come on, baby," I said, then kicked it into gear and peeled off down the alley, only to careen sideways to a halt as someone familiar stepped from the shadows in front of me.

Clarence.

Well, hell.

TEN

"Looks like we've got a few issues to work through," Clarence said as soon as I'd pulled off the road and killed the engine on the bike.

"I didn't break any rules."

"You were supposed to stay away from your sister."

I shook my head. "No way. I said I wouldn't tell her the truth. And what the hell are you doing spying on me, anyway?"

"I like to think of it as protecting our investment. Making sure the agreement we reached was solid."

I held up my hands. "I totally abided by the letter of the law. Didn't step off the path even a millimeter, and you know it."

His lips pressed together, and I watched as he pondered my words, irritation boiling below the surface. I was right—technically, I was absolutely right. But as for the spirit of the thing . . .

Well, maybe a *micro*millimeter.

"Nice of you to admit it," he said.

"I had to see her," I said simply. It was the truth, and I hoped it was good enough.

Clarence cupped his hand thoughtfully over his mouth and stared so long at me I began to feel antsy under the inspection. Finally, he shook his head. "You gotta be smarter than that, pet. You're our ace in the hole, remember?"

I nodded, wondering what that had to do with anything.

He released a long-suffering sigh. "What do you think's gonna happen to little Rosie there if some badass demon figures out who you are? You think he's gonna try to take you down?"

"Maybe," I said, but my voice had lost some of its edge. I had a feeling I knew where this was going.

"Yeah, maybe is right. But if he's a smart demon—and if he knows you got a kid sister out there, someone you're pining over, someone you love—whaddya think he's going to do then?"

I shook my head, not wanting to go where he was leading me.

He mimed a knife across his throat. "And not you, pet. Her. You hang with her. You talk with her. You let that girl into your life, and you are putting her life in danger." He spread his hands wide, then shrugged. "That's just the way of it, and unless you got some pieces missing up here, you know I'm right." He tapped his temple and looked at me solemnly.

After a moment, I nodded, because, dammit, I couldn't argue the point. Rose had been through hell once. I wouldn't be responsible for putting her through it again.

But this wasn't forever. I'd fight the demons. I'd make sure the gate stayed closed. And then, by God, I'd get my sister back.

In the meantime, though, I had a pissed-off frog staring me down. "Am I in huge trouble?"

He cracked a small smile. "No, kid. Guess I shoulda known you wouldn't stay away. That's who you are. Loaded with fluffle."

I lifted my brows. "Yeah. I'm fluffy."

He snorted, then shoved his hand deep inside his overcoat. "Got you a little something. Thought it might take off the edge."

"Yeah?"

He passed me a small, wrapped package. "Open it," he said, gruffly.

I peeled the paper back to reveal a plain white box, the kind in which necklaces come wrapped at Christmas. I looked curiously at him, then lifted the lid and made a little gasping sound when I saw the gold chain and heart-shaped locket.

"Took it off your body," he said. "Thought you might want it."

I nodded, unable to force words past my dry mouth and throat. I'd worn the necklace on Saturday, when I'd gone out to kill Lucas Johnson. It was a piece of my past, a part of my personal history, and something I'd never expected to see again.

I pried it open with one of my manicured nails and found the familiar, tiny picture of me and Rose, arm in arm, sitting on the swing on our front porch. "Thank you," I said, slipping the chain over my neck and tucking the locket under my shirt, close to my heart. "This means . . . everything."

"Yeah, well. You know."

"Won't the police miss it? I mean, I'm a murder victim, right?"

"They might," Clarence said. "But that's not our problem, is it?"

I couldn't help the grin. "Why, Clarence, you devil. You're a bit of a rule breaker, too."

He snorted, then shuffled his feet. "Let's keep that to ourselves, okay?" But whether he meant his bad-boy propensities or the locket itself, I didn't have time to ask, because he pulled himself up to his full—albeit short—height, then cleared his throat. "There are a few rules that are inflexible. But because we haven't covered them yet, I'm going to give you a pass. This time."

"And we're talking about what?" I asked, trying to sound innocent. Because I'd made an end run around two rules this night, and I had a feeling that telling Deacon that Alice was taking up killing demons was going to turn out to be an even bigger no-no than visiting my sister.

"The demon," he said. "I got sources, kid, and they tell me that you took out the Grykon nice and neat."

I blinked, completely thrown for a loop. "The 'Grykon'? You mean the Hell Beast in the alley? I broke a rule doing *that*? Are you schizo? You're the one who told me to! Kill it; don't give it a headache. That's what you said, right?"

"Killing the Grykon's a big ticky mark in the good column. Absolutely. It's the circumstances that we got some problems with."

"Oh." That thudding sound I heard was the other shoe dropping. Apparently, I hadn't dodged the Deacon bullet after all.

"You're supposed to be working alone, kid. So what am I doing hearing that someone was with you when you killed the critter?" He paused, and even though he was a full head shorter than me, right then it seemed like he was the one looking down on me. "Who was it? Who was with you?"

"You don't know?" The possibility was so startling that I completely glossed over the fact that my frog friend was royally pissed. "You don't keep some sort of constant watch? Like God looking down from heaven? A little handheld video device tuned to me? All Lily, all the time?"

He snorted. "Wouldn't that be handy? But no. You're pretty much on your own, unless I get a whim to follow you around town."

"But you just said—"

"Sources, kid. I said I got sources. And they told me the general drift; now I want the down and dirty. So let me ask again—who finally took the demon out?"

"Maybe I did."

He shook his head. "No."

Couldn't argue with that. "Someone else was in the alley," I said, trying to think softly. "But it's not like I revealed my secret identity. I still have my supersecret decoder ring, I promise." I kept my face bland and hummed "Row, Row, Row Your Boat" in my head, hoping to drown out any errant thoughts even more. Deacon had pushed my buttons but good.

The song was a trick I'd learned with my stepfather. Because Joe was an expert at reading faces. He used to always be able to tell when I'd been getting into stuff I had no business getting into. And inevitably, I'd ended up with a smack on my backside.

But once I'd learned to fill my head with mundane things—children's songs, stupid nursery rhymes, ditties from *Schoolhouse Rock*—the smacks were less and less frequent. I watched myself in the mirror once and realized why: even as my head blanked out with the mindless ditty, my face went blank as well.

With any luck, my little trick worked on heaven's messengers, too.

"Lily . . ."

"What was I supposed to do?" I snapped. "That thing was on me, and he pulled it off, and then we fought it together. I stabbed it, and I thought I'd killed it. Then he stabbed it again, and poof, a big puddle of demon."

"He, who?"

"Deacon Camphire."

His eyes narrowed, and I swear if my life were a movie, creepy music would have crescendoed. I swallowed and took an involuntary step backward, the dark images I'd seen in Deacon's mind stirring now within my own head. "He helped me, Clarence. What's wrong with that? Why is that bad?" I heard the high pitch of my voice and hated myself for it.

"Helped? Oh, no, pet. Deacon Camphire wasn't there to

help you. I don't know what he was really up to, but he damn sure isn't an ally."

"What do you mean?" I asked, afraid that I knew exactly what he meant. "What's wrong with Deacon?"

He looked at me, his expression curious.

"Dammit, Clarence," I pressed, when his lips stayed stubbornly closed. "Tell me. What's wrong with Deacon?"

"Everything," he announced, flatly. "He's a demon, Lily. A filthy, lying, stinking demon. He's bathed in the fires of hell, and the stench of the evil he's done clings to him, as pungent as rotting flesh. A demon," he repeated. "Exactly the kind of creature you were created to destroy."

ELEVEN

"*A demon,*" I repeated, something acidic roiling in my stomach. I stifled a shiver and forced myself to keep up the children's-song serenade, because these were the kinds of thoughts I was certain I'd be broadcasting loud and clear otherwise. *Deacon is a demon.* I didn't want to believe it—couldn't get my head around it—but at the same time I was utterly certain it was true. That flash of rage. The creeping, tingling sensation, like something dark and sinister had come to call. Something sensually compelling, but totally dangerous.

"What's the matter? Not expecting eye candy to be one of the bad ones?"

I kept my mouth shut; that one hit a little too close to home.

Clarence snorted. "Gotta get rid of those worn-out expectations, Lily. Things aren't always what they seem, pet."

"Like you?" I snapped, wanting to hurt him. Because as inexplicable as it might be, his news about Deacon had cut me deep. I'd been an idiot, pulled into an emotional trap, and I hated myself for my weakness.

"Me?" he asked, apparently oblivious to my inner turmoil, and thank God and *Schoolhouse Rock* for that. "With me, what you see is what you get."

"Yeah? Well, don't take this the wrong way, but you're hardly my idea of a heavenly messenger."

"What would be your idea?"

"I don't know. Good manners, for one. More paternal. Softer. And a hint of holiness wouldn't hurt, either."

His mouth twitched with amusement. "Straight out of central casting. Did it ever occur to you that I'm here *because* of you?"

"What do you mean?"

He snorted. "Come on, pet. You'd turn an angel's halo black inside ten minutes. And you really gonna listen to a priest? You gonna ask questions and hound 'em, and get your head properly around what's going on? Oh, no, kid. I'm here because I'm the only one the big guy figured you'd listen to."

I frowned, taken aback. Because the truth was, he was right. Clarence irritated me no end, but it was a familiar, comfortable irritation. Like dealing with Jeremy or one of his ilk.

"Like I was saying—you gotta make an effort to look beneath the surface."

I had to grudgingly agree. I let my mind wander back to the bar, to the way I'd slid so seamlessly into Alice's life even though it hadn't been seamless at all. I'd stumbled in my duties. I'd tended Leon with paramedical training that Alice most likely didn't possess. And no one had noticed.

"It's not just me, is it? I mean, no one really looks beneath the surface anymore, do they?"

He didn't answer, his silence an invitation to continue.

"I waltzed into her life. No one even knew she was gone. No one mourned her. Nobody said their last good-byes. They just ordered another round and watched her ass fill out a pair of black jeans. Only it wasn't her ass in those jeans, not really. And nobody had one fucking clue."

My jaw was tight, and I blinked back tears for this woman

I hardly knew. A woman hardly known by the people with whom she'd spent every day of her life.

"You get it, then."

I nodded. Sadly, I did.

I frowned, remembering the way Leon had lain crumpled on the floor, and remembering the man who'd put him there. Even with that temper, there'd been no hint that Deacon was anything more than a man. Certainly not a demon. Certainly not the incarnation of evil.

In the alley, he'd spoken to me with genuine concern in his voice, and he'd helped me fight the Grykon. Only the fact that I'd seen the inside of his mind let me believe what Clarence said. And, yeah. I believed it.

"Why?" I asked Clarence. "Why would he help me?"

"Come on, Lily. You're not stupid. Why do you think?"

"He played me," I said, clenching and unclenching my hands at my sides, not sure if I wanted to slide a knife deep into Deacon's heart or simply never see him again. "The son of a bitch played me—or, rather, he played Alice—and I had no fucking idea."

"That's the way they operate, kid. Don't beat yourself up."

"You're not mad? You're not going to—you know." I glanced toward his waist, where I knew that blade was sheathed inside his coat.

"Not if you're giving it to me straight. He doesn't know who you are? What you are?"

"He doesn't. I swear. But—" Deacon's last comment about staying out of his head popped into my mind before I could stop it, and I saw Clarence's face pinch, his expression shifting from anger to fear before smoothing out to basic, boring bland. A lot like my studied new expression, actually, and for one quick, quirky moment, I wondered what *he* was trying to hide.

"What exactly did he say?" Clarence asked, his frozen face shifting back to its usual animated self.

"Only that I needed to stay out of his head," I said, adding a mental song blast just to be on the safe side.

"What did he mean?"

"I don't know," I lied. "I was kinda guessing that maybe Alice was like you."

His head cocked slightly to one side. "Why would he think that? You been getting in anyone's head, pet?"

"He thought *Alice* was like you," I said. "I'm not really her, remember?" I spoke over a backdrop of "Conjunction Junction." And I said it firmly, the way I'd learned to lie.

I also said it over a backdrop of guilt because here I was, rolling off yet another lie, made all the worse because I was lying to God's right-hand dude. But I couldn't help myself. I was less than one day into this freakish new life, and I desperately wanted to keep it. I wanted to be Superchick. I wanted to fight demons. I wanted the chance to even my own karmic scorecard.

And something in Clarence's eyes made me think that if I told him the truth about what was happening in my head, all bets were off.

I forced the thoughts back deeper behind the veil of children's songs. Clarence was looking at me, his expression thoughtful, and I had to hope he hadn't been able to sneak in around the edges of my mind.

"You think he was bullshitting?"

I shrugged. "I don't know. Maybe. We know he was pulling my chain. But it doesn't matter because Alice is dead. And there's nothing funky going on in my head."

"Then you're golden, kid. But you'll tell me if anything pops up there, right? Can't believe we didn't know that about Alice, but if she really can poke around in a demon's head, that could come in pretty damn handy."

"Can't you?"

He shook his head. "One, I ain't on the front lines. And two, I only do human psyches. Limitations of my gift."

"Oh." Wasn't that interesting? The kind of nifty little tidbit of info I could file away for a rainy day.

I thought about the nature of my job and lined that up with the nature of Deacon. "So, um, am I supposed to kill him?"

"Deacon?" He shook his head. "No."

I tried hard to stifle my sigh of relief. "Why not? He's a demon. I kill demons."

"That he is, and that you do. But he's not one to trifle with. He's strong, Lily. Damn strong. And until you have a few more kills under your belt, I think it's safe to say he's a damn sight stronger than you. He's taken out too many on our side for me to blithely put you in his path. Our endgame is too important to risk our resources going after scum like Deacon Camphire. You understand?"

I nodded, assuring him that I did, and filling my head with children's songs so he couldn't see the relief that flooded through me.

The truth was, the revelation about Deacon had flummoxed me. That he was a demon, I believed. That there was evil inside him, I believed. And perhaps I was being naïve, but I didn't want to believe that was the end of the story. I'd seen the fight inside him—the struggle for good. More than that, I knew that Alice had gone to him. Had trusted him. Had believed that he could—and would—help her.

Maybe he'd been playing Alice, too. Hell, maybe he'd planted the images in his head so that I'd think he was fighting evil, when in fact he was the very epitome of it.

Maybe that was why Alice didn't show. Maybe she'd learned that he was playing her.

I didn't know.

But I couldn't dismiss him out of hand as easily as Clarence could.

I needed to poke and prod and learn and see.

I needed, I thought, to know what made Deacon Camphire tick.

TWELVE

You haven't lived until you've transported a nonangelic amphibian mentor on the back of your motorcycle. My life, thank God, is now complete.

Actually, I didn't mind the trip too much. Talking on a bike is strictly for emergencies only, so I enjoyed a bit of in-my-head time. Or, rather, I enjoyed it once I let my mind wander to complete nontopics. I didn't *think* Clarence could hold my waist that tight and mumble in fear while poking around in my mind, but I certainly wasn't sure.

So instead of thinking anything important, I thought about nothing. About the quiet Boston night, and the chill in the air, and the wind on my face. A world of possibility and purpose had opened to me, and I felt free and happy.

At least, I felt happy for a moment. Then the guilt set in. A new world was opening up to me, but Rose was stuck in the same shit-hole, only now her sister was dead. I'd tried to protect her like I'd promised, but I'd done a piss-poor job of it. The only thing better about her sitch was that Johnson couldn't hurt her anymore. But his death hadn't really saved her. It had only kept him from damaging her more. I had seen that much just by looking in her eyes.

My guilt was all the more pronounced because even though I cried for Rose, I couldn't shake the giddiness that came from this feeling that I belonged. That I'd finally found a calling and all my past fuckups were about to become ancient history.

The gig was dangerous, sure. But it was important. And despite the fact that it was scary as hell, it felt good to be me right then, even in someone else's body.

Good enough to bring on heaping shovelsful of guilt.

"Turn here," Clarence said, as I slowed at a blinking red light. I followed his directions around twists and turns, until we finally parked my bike in a dim alley. I looked around at the Dumpsters overflowing with bits of rotten food and other odoriferous things, and wondered why we were in such a grim place.

"Time to get you ready," Clarence said, turning away and then walking deeper into the alley. Fetid water pooled in potholes, the surface still and oily. The smell of mold and fecal waste hung between the brick walls, and I followed carefully, hoping to avoid the actual source of the stench.

My heart pounded as I picked my way carefully around the refuse. Not in trepidation, but in anticipation. I'd been in similar conditions mere hours before, and considering the odd circumstances of my new life, I fully expected another beast to leap at us from the shadows.

Clarence hurried down a darkened street, then turned down another alley that was, remarkably, even filthier than the last. I picked my way around the piles of trash, debris, and biological refuse, trying very hard not to breathe in the process.

He moved quickly, stepping around a pile of something slightly green and highly rancid as he moved closer to a steel door. He slid aside a metal plate to reveal an illuminated keypad. "And here we are."

"High tech," I said.

"You expected the door would open by virtue of a miracle? Our battle may be celestial, but our resources are state of the art."

He punched in a code, and the thick door swung silently inward, revealing a pitch-black hallway. "Shall we?"

Reluctantly, I followed him over the threshold. What little light accompanied us in from the alley was snuffed out with the *thunk* of the door shutting behind us. The air around us lay still and stale, the lack of even the slightest breeze accentuating the claustrophobic conditions. I swallowed, my skin suddenly clammy as the memory of the last time I'd awakened in pitch black settled over me.

Perhaps I wasn't as ready as I thought.

I heard Clarence in front of me, then heard the metallic *clang* of a breaker switch being thrown. Above us, a bay of fluorescent lights twinkled on and a fan at the far end of the hallway whirred to life, stirring the air and fanning away a few of my trepidations. Graffiti adorned the walls of the narrow hallway, but the filth and stench of the alley remained outside.

We moved down the long hall, our steps echoing off the concrete walls and floors. Soon, the glare of fluorescents gave way to the dim light of yellow bulbs mounted at intervals along the walls. We continued through puddles of jaundiced light, turning, then turning again as we thrust deeper and deeper into the labyrinth.

At last, we reached an ancient elevator door. I leaned close, my hands clutching the mesh of metal as I looked down the shaft that seemed to end in darkness. The cable hung in front of us, seeming quite inadequate for the job it was required to perform.

"You were saying about high tech?"

Clarence shrugged, a broad Gallic gesture. "Eh. Renovations. Who has the time?"

I was tempted to point out that God did. Now, however, hardly seemed the time for jokes.

"Good decision."

"You *really* have to stop doing that."

"Then you need to quit thinking so loud."

I frowned, but he only chuckled, then pointed to yet another access device hidden beneath a metal plate. "Your turn," he said.

I calmed my jangling nerves, then pressed my hand against the cool glass. A biometric scanner did its thing, and after a brief *whirr* and *click*, the tiny metal room began to rise from the pit, finally coming into view, then clanking to a stop in front of us. Clarence took the initiative and pulled open the gate. He stepped to one side and gestured broadly. "Ladies first."

I drew in a breath, looked upward toward the flimsy cable, and stepped inside.

God was on my side, right? At least, he was for now.

The elevator was controlled by an ancient dial mechanism, and Clarence took the helm, shifting the stick downward from 1 to B3. The car jerked, and immediately we started our descent, the world—or at least the building—moving vertically in front of us, like a dull filmstrip from second grade.

Despite the high-tech entry procedures, there was nothing spectacular about the building. The floors we passed were abandoned, but clean, the debris at the entrance little more than camouflage. But there was no stained glass, no statuary. Nothing to suggest there was anything holy about the place. Instead, it was like a bunker, and I hugged my arms tight around me, feeling more out of place with each foot we descended into the bowels of the building.

Though it seemed to take forever, the elevator finally creaked to a stop. I didn't have to ask Clarence if we'd reached our destination; I could see clearly enough that we had. A raised platform, like a boxing ring, stood dead center in the massive room. Around it, various training accoutrements—a punching bag, an exercise bike, a weight bench. Were it not for the mace, the broadsword, and other various medieval-style weapons mounted on the wall behind the ring, the place would have reminded me of the cheap gym Joe had gone to before my mother died.

The smell reminded me of my childhood, the tang of old sweat and leather. A hard wave of regret tugged at my heart, and I squeezed my eyes shut, fighting a longing so intense I thought my knees would buckle.

I took a breath, forcing myself to concentrate, to focus. My old life was gone. And if I wanted to keep whatever tenuous hold I had over this new existence, I needed to focus. I needed to fight—both myself and the demons that made the earth a living hell.

"No rest for the weary, huh?" I asked Clarence, with a brief nod to the setup.

He'd been watching me, his expression unreadable, and I wondered if he'd seen my memories, if he'd felt my loss. I didn't ask, and after a moment, his eyes crinkled at the corners. "Are you tired?"

I considered the question, and realized that I wasn't. Not at all.

"I didn't think so," he said. "You might crave a nap, but you don't actually need it. Not any longer. Not unless you get banged up pretty bad."

My brows lifted in surprise. "Really?"

"Sleep is comfort, a luxury. What your body needs and what it wants are two entirely different things," Clarence said. "Isn't that right, Zane?"

I turned, startled, and saw a man approaching from the shadows. I hadn't noticed him before, which suggested that he'd come in through a side door. Because this was not a man that I would have overlooked. Not in a million years.

His chest caught my attention first. Bare, with only a smattering of hair, his café au lait skin seemed to glisten in the minimal lighting. That perfect chest narrowed as his abs approached the gray fleece of sweatpants. They rode low on his hips, and I couldn't help but notice the thin line of hair pointing down like an arrow to what was hidden below.

I swallowed as he moved toward me, my eyes drawn to the

bulge at the apex of his thighs. I forced my gaze to continue on its merry way, dancing down one of those exceptional legs until I found a leather thigh holster that sheathed a knife capable of gutting an elephant.

I drew in a shaky breath, remembering why I was there, then mentally backtracked, examining not his body but the face and eyes that were focused on me. Rugged, I saw, with a strong jaw and penetrating green eyes. His head was shaven, and the single diamond stud he wore in his left ear twinkled as he moved silently on bare feet.

A cat, I thought, then immediately amended. Cats suggest feminism, and there was nothing female about this man. I could practically smell the testosterone, and every female part of me was reacting accordingly.

He carried himself tall, like a soldier, his muscles so tight I believed he could have tossed a pickup truck across the room.

He stopped his advance right in front of me, eyes skimming down from my head to my feet and then back up again with an intensity that sent my already primed female parts spinning. To say I liked the sensation would be the understatement of the year. But somewhere, from the depths of a swirling sensual haze, a touch of sanity poked through. *This isn't me.* I didn't get all gooey for every attractive man I met. Was this Alice? Was it something about him? Or had my new circumstances brought me unexpected delights as well as unwanted dangers?

"Isn't what right?" the man called Zane asked, his words directed over my head to Clarence. Reluctantly, I left lust behind, realizing that though I'd been basking in this man for what felt like an eternity, in reality he'd crossed the room in mere seconds. Now, of course, he was answering Clarence's question—a question about which I'd already forgotten.

"Our Lily," Clarence said helpfully. "I was explaining that there are some things her body craves, but only a few things it actually needs."

The man took a step closer to me, those cat eyes taking in every inch of me.

Cravings. Oh, yes. I understood all about cravings.

I clenched my muscles, forcing myself not to look away, to keep my breathing under control despite the way my blood burned in the wake of his gaze, as if he'd reached out and stroked me, his fingertips skipping red-hot over my skin.

"*Oui, ma chérie,*" he said, the Cajun cadence thick in his voice. "But do not pay too much heed to this old fool." He bent forward so that his face was near mine, his breath soft on my ear as he whispered, "You are alive, are you not? And sometimes, living is as much about the want as the need."

I swallowed, which represented about as much physical control as I had at the moment.

Zane caught Clarence's eye. "She is exceptional in many respects. You are certain she is the one?"

The lusty haze that had settled over me began to dissipate. It was one thing to be the intense object of Zane's attention. It was another thing entirely to be under such scrutiny for practical rather than prurient reasons.

"I am certain," Clarence said. "She wouldn't still be with us if I were wrong, would she?"

"I hope you are right," Zane said, his voice almost wistful.

"Who are you?"

"I will be teaching you many, many things," he assured me.

I turned stupidly toward Clarence. "But I thought—"

"I'm your main man, pet, but take a look at him. Who do you want honing your fighting skills? Him, or me?"

"Right." I wiped damp palms on my jeans. "Great."

"Where do you want to begin?" Clarence asked.

"She prevailed against the Grykon?"

"Eventually. In their first encounter she failed to terminate the creature. I'm happy to say that she rectified that mistake a few hours ago." He scowled a bit. "And then some."

"She must learn not to hesitate. There is no room for error, no room for pity. Hesitation is an invitation, and the enemy has already claimed too many victories."

"*She* is standing right here," I said.

"So you are, *ma fleur*," Zane said. "Standing proud and battle-scarred."

I winced, certain he knew about the slice on my arm, even though there was no way he could have seen it, hidden as it was under both a sweatshirt and my duster.

"Your coat," he said, nodding to a bench. "And the overshirt."

I grimaced, then peeled off the garments, leaving me clad in jeans and my tank top.

"I see," he murmured, his eyes trained on the wound that now marred Alice's arm, courtesy of the Grykon.

"You heal faster now, Lily, and most wounds will fade by morning. This, though," he said, brushing his finger down my arm. "This was rendered with poison."

I rolled my shoulders, determined not to reveal any regret. "I'm a warrior, right? Now I look like one."

"I think we would rather you blend in. And I know that I do not wish to see you either dead or injured."

"Too late for that," I countered. "On both counts."

His lips twitched in amusement, but that didn't catch my attention nearly as much as what he was doing with his knife. He sliced the tips of his fingers, and then he stepped in closer to me, his eyes dark and serious as he traced that finger down the length of the wound. There was no need for me to ask what he was doing—I could feel my skin knit in the wake of his touch.

"How—"

But he pressed a finger to his lips and shook his head. "It is a gift, *ma chère*. From me to you."

"Then I'll only say thank you."

He inclined his head. "This creature who wounded you," he began. "He had the chance only because you let him live when you first encountered him in the ceremonial chamber?"

"Well, *technically*," I said.

"And why did you not kill the creature when you awakened?"

"I had no idea what was going on then. I was trapped. I

was terrified." My skin prickled as I remembered the shock of waking up, of seeing that beast enter the room and bear down on me. "We fought, and I managed to lay it out with a candlestick. After that, I ran."

"Escape is not your mission."

"I didn't know I *had* a mission," I snapped back.

"Your mind must be firmly in the moment," he continued, as if I hadn't said a thing. "Firmly on the goal."

"And that goal is?"

"You must kill, Lily. You must complete each mission, without exception. This is a take-no-prisoners war, and the only way to prevail is to win. Kill," he said. "Or be killed." He fixed me with a hard look. "Do you understand?"

"I do."

"Good. Because right now, your mission is to kill that demon."

THIRTEEN

I turned sharply in the direction he pointed, and saw that a portion of the floor had opened up to allow the rise of a steel cage on a hydraulic platform. But where I expected to see a another Hell Beast with long teeth and cold, scaly skin, all I saw was a young girl. About sixteen, with a thick black collar around her neck. And when she lifted her eyes to mine, I swear it was Rose who stared out at me.

I drew in a breath. "That's not a— She can't be a demon—"

"She can," Zane assured me. "And she is."

"But—but— Where? How? You have a stash of demons tucked away for—"

I cut myself off. From the look on both their faces it was easy to see that was exactly what they had. A little demon collection, all hidden away, ready to be dragged out for training purposes.

I swallowed, not sure if I was disgusted by the reality or impressed that the training was so damn serious.

Zane was apparently oblivious to my mental meanderings. He held a small black device with a number of buttons. Now he pushed one, and the front panel of the cage descended into the floor, leaving three sides surrounding the wary teenager, looking ultra Goth in black with spiky silver jewelry.

Beside me, Clarence pulled a notepad and pen from his interior jacket pocket. "I'll be evaluating your performance, of course," he said. "Try not to be nervous."

"Nervous," I squeaked, gesturing toward the girl, who remained crouched on her haunches, unmoving, looking up at me. "This is insane."

"If that's the way you feel, *ma fleur*, you have failed already." He reached down and pulled a ten-inch blade from his sheath. He handed it to me, the blade landing cold and deadly in my palm, the blue stone on the hilt sparkling under the harsh light.

I wanted to argue, to give it back. But Zane's thick hands closed around my upper arms, and he lifted me up to the platform as easily as a child might lift a rag doll. I stood for a moment, unsure. Surely I wasn't actually expected to fight—to *kill*—this child!

"Maintenant!" Zane said, and although I know absolutely no French, I got the idea: *Get moving!*

But I *didn't* move. A mistake I would soon regret, as my opponent had no qualms. She sprang up and came at me, snarling like a feral animal. Her fingers splayed out like claws, and she was on my face before I could even react, her fingernails ripping my skin, barely missing my eyes.

"Holy shit," I cried out, as I smacked her hands away, instinctively turning my face from hers. Apparently instinct wasn't the primo option, though, because now I couldn't see her, and she took advantage of that mistake by hauling herself up and jumping on my back.

"Untrained," I heard Zane say, from what seemed like a thousand miles away. "I have much riding on this. I hope you are sure . . ."

Clarence's reply was muffled, but I heard Zane's grunt of acknowledgment clearly enough. What I *wanted* was to scream that they needed to get this little bitch off me.

What I did was fight.

And as soon as I made the decision—as soon as the very *thought* entered my head—a burst of power exploded through my body, even stronger than the surge I'd felt in the alley. The strength they'd put inside me was coming out in fits and starts, and I instinctively knew that I still wasn't fully primed. But it was going to be a sweet ride getting there.

I twisted at the waist, pressing my hands against the mat to get leverage even as I kicked over, my heel connecting to her head with a sickening *snap*. I finished my spin and arched to my feet, the knife held at the ready as she recovered and rushed me, snarling like a wild thing.

It was me, though, that gave in to the wild thing within. I don't know if it was frustration, anger, or just plain fight-or-flight, but I kicked into action with a vengeance. More, I wanted blood. *Her* blood. This sassy little bitch who wanted to take me down. *No freaking way.*

The girl lunged, and I thrust, forgetting that although I might have the strength, I definitely didn't have the skill. She used the back of her forearm to knock against my wrist, then reared back for another hard lash that had the knife flying out of my battered fingers before bouncing uselessly on the mat.

I allowed myself about half a second to mourn its loss, then realized it really didn't matter. I had all the weapon I needed inside me, and I set on her with a vengeance, ripping and clawing and beating and pummeling. More animal than woman, I was pounding the shit out of this demonic kid who would kill me if I didn't kill her first.

"Ah, *c'est vrai*. There is fight in her, after all," Zane said, his voice seeming to fill the hall.

"Told ya the girl had fire."

"Resourceful, too. Though there is still much work to do," Zane said, his voice matter-of-fact as I kicked out blindly, catching the girl under the chin and sending her stumbling back until she landed hard against the ropes that enclosed three sides of our ring.

"On so many levels," Clarence said, his tone suggesting I

was going to require quite a bit more work than he'd anticipated. I glanced over and saw him scribbling notes, and for some reason that innocent action fueled my fury. I turned to take it out on the girl, but she was already taking advantage of my distraction.

With a guttural howl, she leaped, landing hard and knocking me down. My lungs emptied with a *whoosh* as she deposited her full weight on my chest. My brain ordered me to struggle, but before I could put that innovative thought into action, the girl had her knees hard in my sides, as if I were a bucking bronco and she were hanging on for dear life. At the same time, she pressed her whole body forward, our faces intimately close, and her thumbs digging deep into my windpipe.

My body spasmed as my cells screamed for oxygen, and I struggled to get her off me. Apparently, though, demons are endowed with much the same strength I'd been blessed with. Which kind of sucked, when you thought about it.

Her face contorted, and I no longer saw Rose. Instead, I saw the true dark depths. I struggled beneath her, trying to get free, trying to breathe. And as I did, I saw hate and vileness and pure evil.

And, yes, I saw something familiar in those shadows. A cold darkness that had moved in, taking residence in the secret places of my mind. A longing to step up to the kill.

The thought that anything—*anything*—in that beast of a girl could be reflected back on me filled me with disgust. I pulled my knees up hard and fast, slamming them into her backside even as I rocked forward, my head smashing hard against hers. Starbursts screamed behind my eyes, but pain wasn't enough to stop me. Not anymore.

I heard her low grunt of surprise, then felt the lessening of pressure around my neck. That was all it took. I twisted at the waist, rolling left, then thrusting back to the right when I felt her center of gravity shift. I had the advantage then, and I took it, rolling her over and over until we were only inches from the knife.

I saw the realization spark in her eyes, felt the twitch in

her arm as she tried to reach for it—and I felt the lust of pure power as my fist smashed hard into her nose.

She howled, and I lunged sideways, my fingers closing around the knife even as she grappled at my face, her fingernails clawing at my cheeks, mere millimeters from my eyes.

I'd won, though. We both knew it, and I saw the flash of resignation as my blade hand arced back, the cold steel glinting in the air before I thrust it hard under her chin, a single line of blood rising under the edge as I pressed down, silently daring her to struggle.

She didn't.

Instead, I watched as fear flooded her face. Tears glinted in wide eyes, and she said the first recognizable word I'd heard her utter: *"Please."*

My will evaporated; I was being pulled back home, those eyes taking me to Rose. To everything I'd lost, and to everything I'd loved.

My hand shook, and I released the pressure ever so slightly. That was all it took—she was up and on me, slamming me backward as she clambered on top, her quick hands snatching the knife from my reluctant fingers even before I had time to register the victorious smirk distended across her mouth as the knife arced toward my chest.

Time seemed to slow as my mind grappled to find some scenario that didn't end with me dying right there. But no ideas sprang helpfully forward.

I had no place to go.

She'd gotten me smashed up against the corner of the ring, a steel pole pressed hard against my ribs, and her own body blocking any movement to the opposite side. Beneath me was a solid floor, and above me was the sharp steel of my blade.

I was screwed, and I knew it.

I struggled anyway, not inclined to die gracefully. Not really inclined to die at all.

I thrust out my hands, and she sliced my palm with my own knife, drawing a thin line of blood.

Fire shot through my hand, the sting of steel against flesh.

I screamed, my hand closing around the blade, my blood smearing over the angry metal.

No good. The pain burned through me, and when she lashed out with her other hand to pummel my face, I let go, failing, and dreading the inevitable. As I knew it would, the knife continued its treacherous arc toward my heart, and I knew without doubt that this time I was truly going to die. And damn it all, I was terrified.

The scream erupted from my throat, a living thing composed entirely of sound and fear, as the tip of the blade caught my shirt. I was dead, and I knew it and—

I was free.

The demon released me with a bitter howl, clutching the collar around her neck and straining as if her life depended on ripping that thing off. Then she fell to the mat, totally still except for the erratic rise and fall of her chest.

I scrambled sideways, my eyes on Zane. He held up the remote control. "To allow for training of our warriors."

I glanced sideways at Clarence. He didn't look back, still scribbling furiously in his notebook.

I drew in a trembling breath, desperately wanting his reassurance. Too bad for me, none was coming.

"*Now* you understand," Zane said, entering the ring with me and moving to the demon, who still lay motionless on the mat. "Kill or be killed."

He picked up my knife, holding it carefully. I nodded, not trusting my voice to speak.

"You did not kill," he said. "And you almost suffered that fate at the hand of your enemy. You failed us, *ma chérie*. I had such high hopes that Clarence was right. That you were the one. It is most disappointing," he said, his voice low and hypnotic.

I stood there, my palm throbbing in pain as I drank in those vibrant tones carried on his masculine scent, floating away on a sensory mist. The man was sex personified, so silky and sensual that I could concentrate on nothing else, even though a deeper part of my mind was screaming that this was off, that I needed to push through the mist. That whatever I felt in the presence of this man, it absolutely wasn't real.

I didn't care. I could stare at him forever, drinking in the sensual pleasure, relishing the tingle that his mere proximity sent coursing over my skin.

I sighed, my body humming even as through the haze, I saw his hand tighten around the hilt of my knife.

The steel glinted in the spackled light, the flashes an encoded warning only for me—*Wake up, wake up, wake up!*

The mist parted and I understood—I'd failed. And now it was my turn to die.

The blade slashed down, breaking the spell. I grabbed Zane's wrist with my sore hand and pulled, bringing the blade dangerously close to my chest, but also pulling him off balance.

He tumbled toward me, and as he did, I shifted, taking his arm with me as I rolled over. The haze evaporated, drowned out by the singular need to survive.

My hands locked on his wrist, and I pressed forward, ignoring the sting from the wound in my palm, wanting only to move the knife as far away from my flesh as possible.

And, yes, wanting to cut the son of a bitch who was trying to take me out.

I heard a sharp *snap* as his wrist broke, going limp as I forced the blade through the taut, caramel skin. Blood flowed, warm and sticky, and I opened my mouth, a wisp of an *oh* filling the otherwise silent room.

"Ma petite coeur," he whispered as a blood bubble formed on his lips. *"Je suis mort."*

FOURTEEN

Mortified, I fell to my knees, pulling the knife free as I tried to take back what I'd done—even as I watched the final spark of life fade from Zane's eyes.

"No," I whispered, letting the knife clatter to the floor. My gut clenched as something strange and otherworldly seemed to fill me—a surge of power followed by a burst of sweet, almost sexual pleasure that had me biting back a moan.

What the fuck?

I forced myself to open my eyes, as embarrassment, lust, and desire ricocheted through me, not to mention the abject terror that Clarence would slip a knife into the back of my neck and finish the job that Zane had started.

I flinched, my mind holding me steady while fear urged me to cut and run.

But Clarence wasn't moving toward me. Wasn't even looking at me.

Instead, he was watching Zane's body. And when I turned in that direction, I knew why. Beneath the rent in the material of Zane's shirt, his skin was knitting back together, as if I were watching an autopsy in reverse.

I swallowed, more fascinated than scared, my attention moving from his chest to his mending wrist and then to those dull, dead eyes. Dull, that is, until I caught a glint of something that seemed to come from behind the irises. A something too deep to be a reflection, but instead seemed to be a pulse of pure, internal energy.

I watched—astounded, flabbergasted, the whole range of shock-and-awe emotions—as Zane blinked, stretched, and sat up.

For confirmation's sake, my eyes dipped once again to his chest, but the man was healed.

More than that, the man had come back from the dead.

"So did you," Clarence said, his voice making me jump. I'd forgotten he was standing there, watching me even as I watched Zane.

"But I—but—" Honestly, what was there to say?

Zane rubbed the spot on his chest, then flashed me a smile so knowing it made my cheeks flush.

I took an involuntary step back. He would, I knew, finish what he'd started. And this time, the trainee wouldn't be victorious.

The expression that crossed his face as he looked at me, though, lacked any murderous intent. On the contrary, what I saw reflected back at me was . . . pride.

"Bravo, Lily," he said, taking my knife from the floor and then standing up, his shirt ripped, but the flesh underneath pure and perfect. "You understand now."

I stood there, my throbbing hand screaming for attention. But I wasn't interested in the pain right now. I shoved it away, compartmentalized it, and focused on the miracle of this man now standing before me. "How did you—"

"We all got gifts, Lily," Clarence said. "Zane trains. Makes sure we got the best warriors, and that they're gonna do whatever they got to live. To keep on fighting." He shrugged. "Wouldn't do much good if he permanently died each time a warrior passed the test."

I swallowed, his words enveloping me. *Passed the test.* "Then I really did kill him?"

"Oh, yeah. You nailed him. And you're stronger for it."

I frowned, at first assuming he meant metaphorically. But I soon realized he meant more than that. The blood seemed to pump through my veins with more purpose. My muscles primed. My senses acute.

I'd killed—and I *was* stronger for it.

I'd killed—and I'd enjoyed it.

"You got it, kid. Each kill with your blade makes you that much stronger. That much more of a fighter. That much more unbeatable."

I looked at Zane, who'd come back from the dead. "So what are you? An angel?" He certainly looked the role. Masculine beauty with eyes that seemed to go on forever, and a sensual allure that pulled you in, featherlight, but with a warrior's fire.

"Far from it," he assured me. He moved closer, making my skin tingle as if I'd stepped too close to a live wire. "Remember, *ma chère*. You can't let anything distract you. Not compassion, not curiosity, not eyes that look like your sister's," he added, looking back at the still-immobilized demon. "You have the skills. You lack only in commitment."

"I'm committed," I said. "I got you, didn't I?"

"She's not one to be trifled with, I see," he said to Clarence. "And *oui*, you did. But only after. And if I'd nailed your ass, *chérie*, where would you be now?"

Burning in hell.

His eyes suggested I was exactly right.

"Do you wish to survive, Lily? Do you want to fight our fight? Prevail in our cause?"

"Absolutely," I said, turning to stare at the little bitch who'd almost sent me to hell. "Absolutely, I do."

"Good. Then train," Zane said. "You complete your assignments. You don't hesitate. You go after the mission in the most single-minded of manners. Doubt will get you killed. Second-guessing is a doorway to death. You are not here to minister to them, to bind their wounds or cure their ills. Remember who we are fighting; their methods are tricky, their soldiers strong. But if you obey—if you *focus*—your gifts will see you through." He put his hands on my shoulders. "Can you do that, Lily?"

"Yes," I said, because no other answer was possible.

As I spoke, Zane moved with graceful intensity toward the girl, still on the ground, her face contorted with pain as she clutched the back of her neck.

He bent down and then, almost lovingly, stroked her hair before pulling down the neckline of her shirt, revealing an odd, raised tattoo. A serpent coiled around a sword, his mouth open, fangs bared, and poised to swallow the tip of the blade. "She is a vile demon, Lily. A Tri-Jal. You see this mark? That is the sign of the Tri-Jal, and they are the worst of the worst. So violent—so deadly—that even their sense of reality shifts. This girl only appears to be flesh, to be human. But there is no humanity in her, nor was there ever. She is a demon, Lily, through and through. Less than that, even. She is an attack dog, and evil is her master." He bent down toward the girl's face. "Woof."

She snarled in response even as she grimaced against the pain from the device in her neck.

"Some are able to be trained. They walk. They talk. They blend in. An elite force, if you will. A most dangerous breed. One day you will meet another one. And I'll tell you right now, that day won't be pretty."

I licked my lips, eyeing the girl warily.

"*This* is what you let live, Lily. This is what would have killed you."

He held out my knife. The one I had lost in the fight. The one that she had cut me with. The one I'd killed him with. "Come," he said. "Finish the job."

I hesitated only a moment, then took the knife from him. He took a step back. "Now," he said, pressing a button on the remote.

The demon girl howled, then stood tall. Her skin rippled, as if something were living beneath it, moving around, disfiguring her, but when she looked at me, her eyes still belonged to Rose.

"The hell you are," I said, and I lunged. She countered, but I was ready, and I tackled her, sending us both to the ground. I could feel the new strength in me, burning through me, filling me. And damned if I didn't put it to good use.

I had one hand on her neck, holding her down. Those eyes opened, but I looked away. "You're not her," I said, even as I slashed my blade straight across her neck.

An unearthly yowl split the air as the black goo oozed from the wound. I jumped back, then watched, fascinated, as the body shifted into a bottomless pit of slime that seemed to suck her out of this dimension and into some other unknown space, leaving nothing behind but a slight greasy mark on the mat, and me, suddenly broodish and dark.

I looked over the rest of the mat and noticed that it was stained in a number of places. The blood of demons and humans tainted the place, and there I was standing in the middle, the heir to it all. "I did it," I said.

"Indeed you did," Zane responded, with a small nod.

I frowned, thinking back to the Hell Beast. He'd also turned to goo, but his wound had been to the heart. "I sliced her throat," I said, only now recognizing the incongruity. "And she turned to goo. It doesn't have to be a heart wound?"

Zane looked between me and Clarence, clearly perplexed by my question.

"Earlier. When the Grykon—" I stopped myself, eyes on Clarence, unaware if I could share the fact that I'd actually encountered two demons—and that I'd let one walk away scot-free.

"Deacon Camphire has been up to his tricks," Clarence explained. "He took out the demon with his own blade in a rather obvious attempt to win Lily's trust."

I bit my cheek, forcing myself to stand there silently and accept the dressing-down.

"I see," Zane said. He lifted the short blade and showed it to me. "It is the blade, *ma chère*, not the nature of the killing blow. A demon taken out by a proper blade wielded by the blade's owner will not come back."

"Oh. So why didn't I have a proper blade before you guys sent me to the pub? I mean, I'm this kick-butt assassin chick and I had to grab something from the trash."

"Your test was fitting into Alice's life," Clarence said. "We didn't expect—"

"No," Zane said, interrupting. "She is right." He nodded to my hand, where I still held my knife. "A hunter makes a knife his own by spilling his own blood on the blade. She cut you across the palm with your own blade." I glanced at my hand, fascinated to see that the wound was already healing. "It is now yours, as you have seen. Use it well."

I licked my lips, unsure. "So this is all I need? A knife?"

"Do what you were made for and you cannot fail. Utilize your skill; take advantage of the element of surprise. Do that, and you will prevail."

I looked between him and Clarence, torn between going with the mystical assassin-chick flow, or diverting over to earthly practicality.

I chose the practical. "How about a gun, too? Just in case skill and surprise don't cut it."

"And what would you do with that?"

"Shooting between the eyes when the creature charges me leaps to mind."

"That would do you no good, *ma chère*. A bullet will not harm demon flesh. For that you need a blade."

I nodded to one of the many weapons cabinets. "Crossbows?"

"Slow them down, no doubt about that. And yes, perhaps a gun would do the same. But when it's time for the killing blow, that must come from your blade. *Your* blade, *ma chère*."

"Or else they come back," I said.

"Indeed."

I licked my lips. "So, they just stand up and come back to life?"

Zane shook his head. "It is not the body that returns, but the demonic essence. Use your own blade, and you kill that as well. It cannot find a new home. If you do not, the demon will find a way to return."

"Oh." I started to slide my new blade between my jeans and my belt, but Zane stepped forward. "Here," he said, removing the sheath from his thigh. He leaned over and strapped it to mine, his touch practical and economical, yet arousing nonetheless.

The transfer complete, he stepped back and nodded approval of my appearance. Then he returned to the ring and moved with a cat's grace to the place where I'd killed the girl demon. He rubbed the ball of his foot on the last bit of stain, then looked up at me, the import of what he was about to say telegraphed in his expression.

"You're here to eliminate demons," he said. "That is what you do now. If you don't do it, you're useless to us. And that," he added, returning to stand before me, "would be a shame." His eyes met mine, fierce, but with something buried deep that made me shiver, a reaction that only intensified as his eyes moved purposefully over me, taking measure of this tight new body I was coming to call home. "That really would be a damn shame," he added, as I instinctively reached for the knife sheathed on my thigh.

I closed my fingers tight around it, even as I fought the urge to move closer, to press my body against him and abandon all my responsibilities to the drunken frenzy of being lost in his arms. It wasn't real, though. That longing. I knew that, and I fought it. Like a virus, Zane had infected me, and instead of giving in to the fever, I backed off, crossing my arms over my chest and hugging myself. Whatever it took to feel less vulnerable. Less exposed.

Less goddamned horny.

If I wanted to survive, I needed to keep my focus. Most important, I needed to learn the rules of my new world.

And, I thought, glancing back at the barely discernible oily black stain, I needed to learn them fast.

FIFTEEN

I trained for another hour and killed three more demons that night—each one delivered to me in a cage and set loose in the ring. They came at me like feral beasts, some with blades, some fighting with only their hands. Some could toss me across the room with the power of their mind, and others leaped upon me, mouth open, trying to steal my soul. Zane taught me how to fight them all, how to protect myself. And most of all, how to handle myself with my knife. I can't say that my skill was elegant or refined. Mostly, I was scrapping, albeit with more skill and strength after each kill.

And the bottom line was that I survived.

Between sessions, I'd regroup on the sidelines, and Clarence would run me through Introduction to Demons. Showing me pictures of various types, telling me what type of mischief each was famous for, and relaying various bits of history. Tons of information, actually, and way more than my already overloaded brain could handle.

Honestly, it was easier to just fight, and that was what I did the most of, with Zane coaching me (or berating my skills, depending on your politeness factor) from the sidelines.

As for me, I thrust, parried, kicked, and lunged, all with an eye toward keeping myself alive and turning the demons into oily memories.

If that was the ultimate goal, I'd have to say I succeeded.

Which raised the question of why my mood was so black when Zane called for an end to the night's training. Truth was, I didn't want to stop. I wanted to pummel something. I wanted to rage against everything, to wail and beat and scream until the world shifted back to the way I wanted it to be. I wanted what *I* wanted and didn't much give a shit about anyone or anything else. I wanted to lash out against anyone who stood against me, and at the same time I wanted to curl up and let the darkness cover and console me.

I didn't like the mishmash of feelings, and I sure as hell didn't understand where they'd come from. I *wanted* this life. And dammit, I liked that I'd been handpicked. Liked even more that I'd survived the testing.

But it was there, this sinister, moldering mood. Like one of those dark cartoon clouds following just above my head. And try as I might, I couldn't shake it.

And that, of course, made me even pissier.

"Come on, pet," Clarence said as we walked toward my bike. "Lighten up. This too shall pass."

I squinted at him, trying to decide if he'd been poking around inside my dark mood. I'm certain I'd been broadcasting it loudly enough.

"Didn't have to poke," he said. "You're like that *Peanuts* character. What's his name? The one with the dust that follows him everywhere? That's you, only it's a funk that's surrounding you."

"Thanks," I said. "You're a big help. I feel so much better now."

He stopped walking, then turned and really looked at me, his expression managing to be both serious and compassionate. Quite a feat, really, when you factored in his overall amphibian-like countenance. "It's gonna pass, kid. Don't let it drag you down."

"And by *it* you mean the Pig Pen–like cloud that's making me want to curl up inside a blanket for the next millennium? Either that or go out and beat a perfect stranger to death."

"Yeah," he said. "That's the *it* I mean."

I made a noise. I didn't actually tell him to fuck off, but I think the sentiment was there in my tone.

He chuckled, apparently not put out by either my attitude or my actions. "It's the change, kid. I mean, what'sit? You've crammed a month's worth of living into less than a day's worth of hours. Got yourself a new bod, a new career, and one damn serious mission. So don't go blaming yourself if everything up here starts misfiring." He tapped his head and gave me a knowing look. "Go home. Get some sleep."

"I thought I didn't need sleep," I countered, feeling surly and not inclined to give an inch.

"I said you needed it to heal. You think you came through that transition unscathed?"

My frown deepened, because I was certain that he was right. My body ached like a bastard, though I wasn't particularly inclined to admit that little fact.

"Gonna take time, kid. So don't wig out on me just cause you're feeling a little premenstrual."

"Hello! Crude much?" Honestly, he was the freakiest little heavenly messenger. But he'd made his point. And, yeah, I was grateful.

"So give me an honest answer," I said as I settled on the Tiger. My hands tightened on the handlebars, and I realized my palm had completely healed. Nice. "What's the overall deal? The big picture, I mean. Are we gonna be making this trek to Zane's for training every day until that symbol on my arm does its thing?"

"I'd say that sums it up. You and Zane on a regular schedule. Side by side, getting all hot and sweaty and down with the kick-ass mojo."

I glanced sideways at him, my cheeks heating. He chuckled.

"Nice," I said, realizing Clarence had picked up on all my lust-filled thoughts. "And to think I thought you couldn't get any more crude."

"I'm just saying."

I sighed. "What's his story, anyway?"

"I guess the teenage girls would say he's got the pheromones from hell. Hard to resist, you know?"

"Yeah," I said. "I know."

He chuckled, clearly amused by my discomfiture. "This is where I leave you," he said, taking a step away from my bike. "I'll find my own way home."

"What? Wait! That's it? Don't I need an assignment? A document that will self-destruct? A password to a secret website?"

"I'll be in touch," he said, and then he tipped his hat, turned ninety degrees on his heel, and started burning up the pavement toward the end of the alley.

I grimaced, my anticipation for my upcoming assignment fading as I started the bike. I was going to be fighting some decidedly nasty demons in a battle that could decide the fate of the world. And I would wager that none of those demons was going to be particularly keen on rolling over for my blade when I came calling.

No pressure. No pressure at all.

The dark gloom still clung to me as I arrived back on Alice's street and squeezed the bike in between two parked cars. At after two A.M., the street was eerily silent, and the weight of the night pressed down on me. I could hardly believe all that had happened in less than twenty-four hours. I was literally a different person, and though I knew I should slow down and try to take it all in, I couldn't shake the buzz. I had a feeling sleep was going to elude me.

I climbed off, then mounted the steps toward the door, the key to the building in my hand. I'd just unlocked the door and was pushing it open when a piercing scream shredded the night, and I turned toward the sound, my heart pounding with a sick thrill at someone else's pain. Shame crashed over me, and I told myself to move. To go.

To save them.

I went. Running toward the noise and hoping desperately that my decision to get my ass in gear meant that the darkness bubbling inside me wasn't as vile as it felt. Maybe it truly had a purpose: Kill the demons. Save the world.

With a cacophony of thoughts swirling in my mind, I ran across the street, a welcome power surging through me as I urged my body to *move*.

I couldn't pinpoint the sound, but there weren't many options. Narrow passages separated the gray buildings on the far side of Alice's street. Once large homes, the houses had been converted to apartments, the grassy area between the homes paved, creating instant alleys leading to off-street parking, where children once played in grassy backyards.

I couldn't see anything as I rounded the corner of the closest alleyway, but I distinctly heard the muffled moans of a woman, most likely with a male hand clenched tight over her mouth. I edged closer, peering into shadows, ready for anything.

Hell, I welcomed it.

I didn't, however, expect what I saw: a dark creature—his eyes flooded bloodred—with one hand over a petite blonde's mouth, her neck gouged and pulsing blood directly into his gaping mouth.

I was on the move even before my mind finished processing. As I raced forward, he lifted his head, his lips curling up to reveal a bloody mouth feasting on living flesh.

His expression held no urgency, no fear. In fact, it was almost as if he were welcoming me to the party.

And it was that—even more than the freakish reality of meeting this creature in a dark alley—that made the tiny hairs on the back of my neck tingle with dread.

SIXTEEN

I saw all of that, analyzed it, and tucked away the oddity without slowing my approach. I saw the beast's eyes widen, surprise flashing behind blood-tinged irises as I hauled back and hit him—*blam*—in the nose with the heel of my hand. And damned if that didn't feel good. Like a release. All that dark stored up within me like a taut rubber band, bursting out with the full weight of my power behind it.

Man. Ya gotta love it. I know I did. Even when we got into it—when the demon snapped back to his feet and let me have it. We went at it down, dirty, and mean.

Our bodies collided, and I was knocked backward, landing on my ass before he leaped on me, bloody teeth bared. "You arrogant fool," he hissed, and then, remarkably, he stalled his attack, looking at me with something like kinship.

Revolted, I grabbed for the hilt of the knife, still strapped to my thigh. At the same time, I pushed my body up so as to free my arm for full movement. With all of my newfound power behind the motion, I brought the blade to the beast's neck, slicing through the skin, then the tendons and, yes, even bone. Not as easy as it sounds, but I was no longer your run-of-the-mill mortal, and I might as well have been slicing through butter. "Who's foolish now, you son of a bitch?"

The head lopped off, then rolled to one side, an astounded expression in those dead eyes. And then, in a blink, he melted into formless goo. *Yeah, well, don't underestimate a woman with a knife, buddy.* Next time, I'd have to try staking the thing—were bloodsuckers vampires even without fangs? I didn't know—but it was nice to know that beheading worked just fine.

Twisting around, I ran back to the woman. She was a mess—her throat ripped open and her skin gray and lifeless. For a moment—one brief, horrible moment—I reveled in her pain. Hell, I wanted to push it higher. Wanted to take it to the limit and see how much she could bear.

I gasped, the moment passing even before I could push it away, but not so fast that I couldn't escape the wave of self-loathing that crashed over me.

I wanted this new life. I really did. But at what price was I sliding into this role?

I shook myself, determination setting in. *Adjustments.* That was all this was. Just like Clarence said: stress and adjustments. I wasn't some blackhearted beast.

And to prove it to myself, I hurried to the woman, crouched by her side, and took her hand in mine.

"You're going to be okay," I lied, as life flowed from her. "I'm right here. I'm going to stay with you."

I pressed my hands over her throat, trying to stanch the flow of blood. No use. It pumped out of her, spraying through my fingers, covering my clothes, my skin, my face.

She gasped, a fish out of water, seeking a breath I couldn't give her. As for me, I breathed in deep, my senses primed and tingling. My thoughts seemed to separate from my actions, and I was aware of only one thing—an intense, undeniable hunger. But not for food. *For blood.*

Shaken, I stood, my gaze shifting between the woman and the stain on the concrete where the demon had been.

"What's happening to me?" I whispered, even as I gazed at my knife and fought the disgusting-but-oh-so-tempting urge to run my tongue along the still-bloody blade.

I closed my eyes as a wave of dizziness washed over me. I felt faint, desperate to satiate that most base of desires.

I knelt beside the woman, and even as I heard myself whispering, "No," I brushed a finger across her neck. Her body temperature was already falling, and the blood felt cool against my fingertip. I lifted my hand and pressed my finger to my lips, my tongue darting out to taste the sweet heaven of her blood.

No!

This time, the word echoed only in my head, but the force of it was strong enough to bring me to my feet. I slammed my hand down against my jeans, scrubbing the blood off and wishing I could scrub the sweet, sweet taste from my mouth, too.

First a sensual haze with Zane. Then that dark, violent brooding. Now a near-painful bloodlust?

It was all too freaking much. I needed answers, and I knew I couldn't go to Clarence. Somehow the idea of bloodlust in one of heaven's soldiers didn't sound like something I wanted to confess. Not when you considered that knife he had no qualms about using if I failed to prove myself.

I grabbed my head, trying to keep the throbbing at bay, a deep, rhythmic pulse that originated as much with confusion as it did from my battle to keep myself away from the blood that called to me like heroin to a junkie.

Run. It was the only thing to do. Run and get clear and find my head again.

I gave her one last look, guilty about leaving her, and knowing that if I stayed, I would surely debase us both.

Run.

It was the only answer.

Run, dammit, run!

I ran.

I ran as if the devil himself were behind me. Because you know what? I think he was.

SEVENTEEN

I ran, but I couldn't escape the scent, my own horrific desires, or the guilt that accompanied my overwhelming, sickening hunger.

The blood covered me, had soaked into my shirt, had stained my hands, and all I could do was run. Alice's apartment was right there, only meters away, but I didn't go in. Didn't want to surround myself in pastel pink and pretty images. Right then, nothing about me was pretty. Not the stains on my body. Not the anger in my heart.

And definitely not this sickening bloodlust that still burned through my veins.

Here I was, some big-shot, über-bad assassin chick, and the first time I stumbled upon a demon actually attacking a human I'd managed to do exactly nothing. *Nothing.*

Worse than nothing, I'd defiled her death by a perverse thirst that had come over me.

What was the point? What was the point if I couldn't save the innocent? I trembled, remembering the cold, gray death in the woman's eyes. Remembering as well that cold gray in the eyes of my sister.

Goddammit. I was supposed to be better now. Pulled out of the useless mess of a life where I couldn't even help my sister. I was supposed to have been chosen. A frickin' savior for humankind, but so far, all I'd done was fail. The woman in the alley, the demon in Zane's basement, my sister—raped and stalked and tormented. I'd killed, and yet I still couldn't help anyone. Couldn't keep my promises.

How the hell could I save the world if I couldn't save even one person?

I hugged myself, the reality of this world I'd slipped into pressing hard around me. Murderous demons in dark alleys. Girls with Rose's eyes and black souls.

Pretty freaking unreal.

Then again, I'd been plucked from the jaws of death. *Get thee to a new body, and go forth to slay the demon.* Yeah, perhaps astonishment at the revelation of horror movie–quality creatures in Boston was a misplaced emotion.

As my thoughts raged in my mind, my feet took me far away from Alice's apartment. The dark streets were mostly empty, but I caught a few stares, then remembered I was covered in blood. Nice.

At least, I realized, the bloodlust had faded. Which was good, because if I thought about it too much more, I would seriously wig out.

The red leather duster hid the blood, but the white Bloody Tongue sweatshirt was covered. I slipped out of the coat, then peeled off the shirt, leaving me clad in the thin tank top I'd put on at Alice's. Despite the chill in the October air, I didn't shiver, the heat coursing through my veins sufficient to keep me warm.

I dumped the shirt in a trash can, then slid back into the duster as I kept on walking, my strides eating up the pavement. At first, I heard nothing but the beating of my heart and my own footfalls. But after a mile or two, I heard the definite tread of someone behind me.

I wheeled around, hand on my knife, and came face-to-face with Clarence, looking as pissed off as a frog about to undergo dissection.

"I thought you didn't have a Lily-scope?"

"I went back to your apartment," he said. "Wanted to double-check. Make sure you're okay. Shoulda got there sooner, I guess," he added, his voice tight with control. "You're an assassin, Lily. You're not a vigilante."

"He *killed* her. And you're telling me I should have done *nothing*?"

With both hands, he raked his fingers through short, thick hair. "You did great. Awesome. You killed the big, bad, bloodsucking demon. Yay for you."

My mouth hung open, because I was absolutely certain I was now in Wonderland.

Clarence sighed. "I'm sorry to rag on you, kid. It really was a solid kill. Nasty demon, now gone from the world. Kudos to Lily."

"Then what is the problem?"

"You still don't get it," he said. "This isn't about eradicating every demon that's walking around out there—"

"I didn't kill *every* demon," I spat back in return, my mind flashing to Deacon before I quickly shoved the image away. "I killed *one*. One who was hanging around outside my apartment killing innocent women."

"You think you're invincible?" He poked me in the chest with one quick fingertip. "You ain't. But you *are* the one who's going to make sure the gate stays closed. And if you get whacked, you won't be around to do that, now will you?" He snorted. "We lose the war, you gonna be happy you took out a demon or three? A vamp who was getting his rocks off with some skank he picked up at—"

"Skank?"

"I'm making a point. You wanna let me make my point?"

I put my hands up in a gesture of surrender and stepped back.

"Point is, you might win the battle, but you sure ain't

gonna win the war. Not like that. Not if you go running off with your own agenda."

"He. Killed. Her."

"Everyone dies, pet," he said. "Like they say, 'That's life.' "

I crossed my arms, staring him down. "*I* didn't."

"My point," he said. "You got a job to do. You got a purpose. Don't screw it up for some tightly wound sense of justice."

"Tightly wound?"

"That woman was gonna die no matter what. Maybe not tonight. Maybe not next year. But she ain't living forever, and in the end, from her perspective, it's all the same. What *you're* fighting, though—that's eternal. More than that, you screw it up and maybe that little lady's soul don't have such a nice place to go. *Capisce?* You gotta be a big-picture gal, Lily. 'Cause if you're gonna go around sweating the small stuff, then we got loads of trouble ahead. Do you get that? Is any of this sinking in?"

"I get it," I said. And I did. I'd been trying to help. To use these newfangled powers to protect the weak and innocent. People like Rose. But I wasn't allowed to do that. Instead, I had to keep my eye on the mission and take my satisfaction where I was told.

Pretty lame for an über-chick.

"An über-chick who's going to save the world, pet. Trust me when I say that'll save a whole boatload of innocents."

I knew he was right, but it didn't feel that way.

He looked at me, eyes narrowed, searching my thoughts. "Come on, kid. Chin up. You can't afford to get distracted. We got too damn much to lose." He swung an arm around me and hugged me like a chum. "It's almost three, and you're due back at Zane's to train at ten, then you got a shift at the pub. You may not need sleep now, but I'm thinking downtime would be a good thing. Go take a little."

I nodded and ran my fingers through my hair. He was right, but that didn't mean I had to like it.

I told myself I had every intention of going home, of closing out the night in Alice's bed—*my* bed—and letting dreams carry me away from all this.

I told myself that, but then I kept on walking, twisting and turning down streets and alleys, not paying attention to where I was going, but letting the night lead me as I tried to empty my mind.

A steady bass thrum trembled through the air, the sidewalk beneath my feet throbbing with its syncopated beat. I stopped, turning as I tried to find the source of the music.

I realized then how far I'd wandered. I'd left the residential area far behind, and was now surrounded by warehouses and small businesses. The kind of off-the-beaten-path places that can repair your car or your antique typewriter and tend to be housed in metal buildings with garage-style doors.

The noise, I realized, was coming from a ramshackle warehouse on the corner, plastered with rain-stained posters advertising various bands I'd never heard of. I followed the music around the corner and found myself facing a guy in army fatigues smoking a cigarette as he lounged in a garden chair. He looked me up and down, his gaze barely even stalling as it hit the knife on my thigh.

"What's the cover?"

"Fifteen," he said. "We only got music, and we don't shut down until dawn." Which was doorman-speak for "We got whatever drugs and alcohol you want, but I'm not saying because you might be vice."

I still had my tip money, and I peeled a twenty from the wad of cash I intended to mail to Rose. "Keep the change," I said, then took a step for the door. His hand across my chest stopped me. I looked down at his palm over my breasts, then up at his face. The hand came off, flying up in a gesture of peace and goodwill.

"Gotta lose the piece," he said, nodding toward my knife.

"And to think I tipped you." I bent over and unstrapped the thigh holster. Then I pulled up the leg of my jeans, restrapped the contraption to my calf, and worked the denim back over the knife. A tight fit, and a very obvious bulge, but not so bad that it ruined the haute couture gestalt of my outfit. Whatever the hell that means.

"Not exactly what I had in mind."

"Well, I figure you have a choice," I said. "You let me in so I can dance and make merry. Or I go home, drown my sorrows in a beer from my refrigerator, and in my desolation at being rejected, drunk-dial the police and report the unsavory goings-on behind those doors. Because I'm pretty sure that *unsavory* is happening back there. Honestly, I wouldn't want in otherwise."

He stepped aside.

"Good boy," I said, bestowing him a quick pat on the cheek as I brushed past and into the deafening roar of the club's interior. *Club* being a loose term, of course, because these kinds of clubs changed geographical location almost nightly. But the place served my purpose—crowded, dark, boisterous, and too damn loud to even think.

I was tired of thinking.

The music pounded in my chest as I stepped through the inner door, though I suppose *music* is a loose term, too, considering the volume was too loud to hear anything but the bass beat. As far as I could tell, the song was meant to be enjoyed through vibrations in the air, as if those of us in the club were bats or something.

I considered the metaphor and decided it wasn't that far off the mark. I'd become nocturnal by default.

"Lily," I whispered, "you're a mess."

A bald man with a tattooed scalp shot me a curious glance. I ignored him and crossed to the makeshift bar of plywood and beer crates. I ordered a double shot of tequila and endured the bartender telling me they didn't have alcohol. "I'm not the cops," I said, then slammed back the drink he passed me. Easy enough, and because I figured good karma shouldn't be wasted, I ordered another, then took it with me as I wound my way through the crowd to the ladies' room, a haven of makeup, hair spray, and the most foulmouthed gossip you've ever heard.

Two overly coiffed sorority princesses stood next to a girl with a purple Mohawk and a pierced lip. All three turned and looked at me. I, in turn, looked at the sink, then aimed myself in that same direction. I plunked my drink down on the counter and proceeded to scrub the last remnants of blood off my hands, arms, and coat. Then I reached in front of Bitsy for a paper towel.

"Fight with the boyfriend," I said, conjuring a sweet smile, a not-too-difficult feat considering whose face I was wearing. In fact, anyone looking at the reflection in the mirror would probably assume I'd come in with Bitsy and Ditsy. Even after the night I'd had, Alice still looked cute and perky. Considering my old body used to develop bags under the eyes if I stayed up past nine thirty, I had to admit my new skin held some definite upsides.

The downsides, I discovered once I emerged from the ladies' room. Not fewer than seven men hit on me as I made my way back across the dance floor, and one of them actually reached out and grabbed my ass. I don't think I broke his nose, but he slid back into the crowd so fast after I belted him that I can't be sure.

I slid into the mass of people, arms high, my breasts pressed against the thin material of my tank top. Colored lights swept the floor, sweaty bodies moving in rhythm all around me, hips and fingers touching as we all moved in one delicious, sensual beat.

A lean man in a purple shirt slid in close to me, and I grabbed the waistband of his jeans and tugged him closer. A warm, sexy power was filling me, and I needed to explore it, to test it, to use it. I smiled at him and realized he was enthralled, which gave me a nice little rush.

His arm hooked around my waist and his hips pressed against mine as we gyrated in time to the music, a sensual bump-and-grind that only vaguely resembled dancing.

I closed my eyes as he slid his hands up from my waist, coming close to my breasts, teasing me, setting my body on fire, and taking my thoughts away from the specifics of my life to the pure, physical pleasure of touch.

And so help me, I wanted that. Wanted to be lost inside my head, even if only for a moment. I didn't want this man, didn't know him or care about him. Another face loomed in the back of my mind, but that was one of the images I pushed away, clinging instead to the safety of anonymity.

Whatever I wanted, this man would have to do; and if I could only quit thinking, maybe I could lose myself for a few minutes in his touch.

We moved in a mindless pattern of heat and desire, his touch fueling my need for release, but I wasn't desperate enough to go there with this man. It was enough to feel the power over him, a power I didn't understand, but that nonetheless consumed me.

I wanted it, though—wanted a touch so intimate it would truly shut my mind down, make all my thoughts and fears and doubts go away.

I wanted it, and it both terrified and fascinated me that the man who so dominated my thoughts—the man who tweaked my lust—was a man I couldn't have. A man I told myself I didn't want.

And, dammit, a man now striding toward me across the dance floor, the ocean of bodies parting in front of him as if he were Moses parting the Red Sea.

Deacon.

My heart stuttered in my chest. I told myself I should fear him, should at the very least be wary of him.

Instead, I simply wanted him.

"She's mine," he said, pushing my partner aside with little more than a glance. His arms slid around me, his hands on my lower back pulling me close as my body tingled from the electric storm surrounding this force of nature.

"I'm not yours," I protested, but I stayed in his arms nonetheless, tempting fate and testing the limits to my newfound sensual allure, not to mention my self-control.

He took his hand from my back long enough to hook a finger under my chin and tilt my head up. A smug grin tugged at the corner of his mouth. "Maybe not," he said with a cocky grin. "But you want to be."

EIGHTEEN

"The hell I do," I protested, pushing him away even as I wanted to sink deeper into his embrace. Because he was right. *I wanted him.* I wanted to see him squirm beneath me, and right at the moment I didn't care if he was squirming beneath my thighs or at the point of my blade.

I simply *wanted.* Low and visceral and desperate.

I gave him a shove, wanting to get my head together even more than I wanted to stoke my libido. "Go."

He pulled me closer, his embrace firm and demanding. "I like it here."

"Dammit, Deacon . . ." But he wasn't listening. The music was of the bump-and-grind variety, and even though the place practically vibrated with the beat, he held me by the hips and moved in a slow, sensual dance, and damn my ever-loving soul, right then I didn't care that he was a demon. Didn't care that he might have played me, set me up.

All I cared about was making that connection again—that

full-body, all-over tingling lust that had washed through me the first time he'd held me in his arms.

I sighed, remembering the longing and the sensual desperation.

And then I tensed, remembering the fear, the darkness, and the bloodred rage.

I gave him another hard shove.

"No." This time, I did break free. Gasping, I stepped back, eyeing him warily as the drunken ravers gyrated nearby. I had to keep my head on. I had to, because if I couldn't think, I couldn't figure him out.

The dim light cast the hard planes of his face in shadows. He watched me, his eyes hard and assessing. "Planning on running away again?"

"I'm not going anywhere," I said, the feel of my knife against my shin comforting me.

The corner of his mouth lifted ever so slightly, and his gaze raked over me. "Good. I'd hate to think I scared you off again."

I bristled. "Excuse me? You don't scare me."

"No?" Those harsh planes shifted into something resembling a smile, and damned if his eyes didn't twinkle. "I could have sworn that's why you ran so fast. Because of what you saw. What we both saw."

I flinched, realizing for the first time that he'd seen it, too. He hadn't merely felt me poking around in there. He'd seen what I'd seen, knew what I knew.

I didn't know much about weird psychic visions, but my impression was that they usually weren't shared. That this one had been didn't make me feel better. If anything, the knowledge made me even antsier.

And antsier still when he stepped closer to press his hand on my shoulders and bend his mouth to my ear. "Which part of the vision scared you more? The dark, bloody horror? Or the two of us, entwined and naked?"

"None of it scared me," I lied.

"No?" He leaned back enough so that I could see his face. His expression was harsh, unreadable, but anger seemed to roll off him in waves, and I had the feeling it was held in check only by the strength of his formidable will. "Then why did you run?"

"I didn't run," I lied.

"Of course you didn't."

"I was working," I said firmly, and a bit too loud. "I had to get back to work."

"Which raises the question of why you went into my head in the first place. You broke a promise to me, Alice, and an important one. Don't think I'll take that lightly."

I cocked my head, sensing more than just anger in his tone. This wasn't about a broken promise; it was about the revelation. And damned if I didn't understand why he was pissed. If I had that man's psyche, I'd want people to stay the hell out of it, too.

"I'm sorry," I said, and I meant it. "I didn't mean to. It just happened. I wasn't trying to turn it on. I swear."

He searched my face, and I let him, knowing with absolute certainty that he'd find nothing but the truth there.

"Anyone else gets in my head like that, and they'd be dead by now," he said, his voice matter-of-fact.

I lifted my chin defiantly. "Then why am I alive?"

He smiled in answer, then traced the line of my jaw with his fingertip. The simple promise in his touch shot straight through me, making my skin tingle and hum with both memory and anticipation. The need was ramping up again inside me, my body seeming to pulse with the lights of the club, desire so close to the surface I feared it would overcome me.

"It scared you," he said. "What you saw."

"I don't scare easy," I said, moving closer to him, proving to myself just how easy it was. How easily I could control this new power I'd found within myself.

"Is that a fact?"

I only smiled in answer, my fingertips tracing his shoulder, lightly stroking his arm. Closer still, the light burning inside me. That thrall. That trick. That sweet surrender I'd watched in the boy's face as he danced with me. I'd brought him in, caught him in a spell.

And I could do the same thing to Deacon.

And the power of that realization only fueled the fire inside me.

His head turned so that he could watch as my fingertip lightly grazed the soft skin of his forearm. "What does scare you?"

I lifted myself up on my toes, leaned in so that my breasts brushed his chest, nipples hard under the thin layer of my tank top. I placed my mouth close to his ear and breathed in the scent of bourbon mixed with mint. "You," I whispered, my voice little more than air.

"You should be scared," he answered, and the truth of that declaration shot all the way through me. Except it didn't scare me. It excited me. Made me want to push limits and test boundaries.

Apparently, all I'd needed in order to really feel alive was to die.

I pressed in closer and pitched my voice low. I was playing with fire, but until I got burned, I wasn't sure I could stop. "Does that mean you're dangerous?"

He stroked my hair, my head fitting into the palm of his hand. "You weren't scared of me last week. So you tell me, Alice. What's changed? And don't say the vision, because you stood me up long before that."

What's changed? Wasn't that the question—and I stepped back, the spell evaporating as reality circled around me. A reality in which Alice was dead, Deacon was a demon, and the mystery of Alice's death loomed over me.

"Alice?"

"Nothing's changed," I said, trying to figure out how to play this.

"Interesting."

I looked at his face, but he was giving nothing away. "What?"

"You told me twice you needed to talk—begged me to meet you, to be on time, to not forget—and then you stood me up."

"Last week I didn't—"

"What?"

I drew in a breath, quickly considering my options, and deciding to go with the big bomb. "Last week I didn't know you were a demon."

His eyes narrowed, but otherwise he showed no reaction. Almost imperceptibly, he moved closer, his body generating an electric reaction between us. "Didn't you?" he asked, the question confusing me. If Alice had known the truth about Deacon, then not only had I completely blown my cover, I'd also stumbled across the burning question of the century: What was pretty-in-pink Alice doing hanging around with demons? And had her less-than-savory acquaintances somehow gotten her killed?

"Does knowing what I am bother you?"

I looked into his eyes, the memory of everything I'd seen within him washing over me. The vile blackness. The raw fury.

I shivered. And then I caught myself, remembering what I was. "No," I said firmly. "Doesn't bother me at all."

The corner of his mouth twitched. "Should I be worried?"

I cocked my head, my brow furrowed.

"Because of your new career," he said. "You're going into the demon-hunting business, right?"

I tilted my head up. "That's right."

His head moved in, and he nuzzled my neck, my hair, his proximity sending little flutters and sparks ricocheting through me.

"Their scent is on you," he said.

Something hitched inside me, and I answered through a thick throat. "What?"

"You've killed tonight," he said. "Demon." He sniffed again, breathing in deep of the scent of me. "And there is blood on you as well."

He leaned back, looking at me with a question in his eyes that bordered on accusation.

"I didn't hurt her," I said. "I was trying to save her."

"Of course," he said. "It was, after all, the demon you were hunting. Not the girl."

"What do you want?" I said. Because right then, although I'd thought I wanted to lose myself in lust, I was more interested in him going away. Because with him that close to me, I really couldn't think.

"I want answers, Alice."

"I don't know the question."

"Then let me spell it out for you. You've changed. And trust me when I say I'm going to find out why."

"No, I—"

His finger moved to my lips, and I had to fight the urge to draw him in and suckle. "I didn't feel this way about the Alice who asked for my help, and I'll admit that bothered me. Made me think I'd been wrong about the whole thing."

I blinked. *What* whole thing?

"But the Alice in the alley?" he continued. "The Alice who let me watch while she slid into my head? The woman who got naked with me in a shared vision? She's the woman I've craved. She's the woman I want. And trust me when I say that I will have her."

I tried to say something, but the fact that my body was melting pretty much prevented speech. Instead, all I managed was a breathy little noise.

His lips brushed my ear, his breath hot against my skin. "So tell me, Alice. Tell me what happened to you."

A whisper of fear skittered down my spine. "I don't know what you're talking about."

"One way or another, I'm going to find out." He leaned back, his gaze riding hard over me before he turned to leave. He stopped once, then turned to look back. "And I take my promises very, very seriously."

NINETEEN

He knew.

Somehow, Deacon knew I wasn't really Alice.

I took a deep breath of the cool night air, far cleaner than the miasma of smoke and drugs and body odor I'd inhaled in the rave. The air not only cleaned out my sinuses, it cleared my thoughts. He didn't know. Not for certain. He was suspicious, yes, but that was entirely different from knowing. And even if he did have questions, I doubted that the possibility I'd hijacked Alice's body would pop to the front of his mind.

My long stride ate up the sidewalk as I turned it over and over and over in my mind, making myself dizzy with the permutations, making myself sick with speculation.

No question, Deacon was a threat. An unknown commodity I'd have to watch. A wildcard about whom I needed to learn as much as possible as quickly as possible.

Unfortunately, the thought of following him home and playing Nancy Drew had come too late. As a result, I was stuck with more mundane methods of research. I might not be a girl detective, but I did have the basic skills that come manifest with my age group: I could Google with the best of them. A skill that was thwarted as soon as I returned to Alice's apartment and saw absolutely no evidence of a computer.

Frustrating at first, but then I remembered the pink leather bag I'd seen in the back of her closet as I'd been digging for waitress attire. Sure enough, the bag was one of those fancy, girly laptop cases, and snug inside was a shiny white MacBook.

As I set the computer up on the kitchen table, I wondered vaguely if she'd been packing to go somewhere before she died. Surely most people kept their computers out and running, loath to be more than a minute away from e-mail or instant messages.

Feeling more than a little voyeuristic, I plugged it in and powered it up, reminding myself as I did so that I had a perfect right to poke around in there. Technically, the computer was mine now.

As the machine went through its startup routine, I pushed the button on Alice's nearby answering machine. She'd left a cheery outgoing message which, thankfully, included her phone number, and I made a point to memorize it. Then I listened as the digitized voice announced that she had three new messages.

One from Gracie—no surprise there. Another from someone named Brian wanting to know if she wanted to take in a movie. And the last from Sylvia, who had called to say goodbye before she left for a European vacation with her boyfriend.

Friends. Alice had friends and a life and people who cared about her. People who would have mourned her if they'd known that she died. I swallowed, realizing my throat felt thick, and wondered if anyone was mourning Lily Carlyle. Other than Rose and Joe, I rather doubted it.

I swallowed and forced the melancholy down, then eyed the machine again. Gracie was already in my new life and, honestly, that was about all the friendship I could handle. It was hard enough being the new me. I didn't think I could be the old Alice at the same time. Not yet. Not until I got better at the role.

I reached over and pressed the delete button, then listened as the machine whirred, erasing the friends. *Starting from scratch,* I thought. *Starting over.*

But a secret part of me wanted to meet Sylvia and Brian. Wanted to know them and have a beer and take in a movie. And a bigger part of me wondered if they would look at me and see Alice. Or if, like Deacon, they'd see that something had changed.

Frustrated with myself, I forced my thoughts aside. Alice's computer had finished its boot-up, and I was happy to see that not only had she not password-protected the system, but there were at least four wireless networks I could piggyback onto.

I had planned to type in Deacon's name, but instead my fingers insisted on my own, pulling up the rather morbid announcement that my funeral would be held on Thursday afternoon, at which time it was assumed the police would have released my body.

I shivered, the idea that I was walking around while my body was on an ME's gurney creeping me out. More than that, though, I thought of Rose and my stepfather. Of how they must feel, knowing I was gone. And of how it must have killed them to identify my body in the morgue.

An image of Rose, her face tear-streaked and battered, swam into my head. I still had the cash I planned to give her, and I found an envelope in Alice's kitchen and shoved it inside before scrawling out Rose's address for delivery. It wasn't much, but it was something. Just as the locket that now hung over my heart wasn't much, but to me it was also everything.

I wanted to give her more. Hell, I wanted to talk with her. Wanted more than the brief, shell-shocked girl I'd faced at the door. And even though I knew I shouldn't, I grabbed up the phone, then dialed our home number. Surely one quick phone call from Lily's supposed friend wouldn't result in all the demons of the world descending on her doorstep.

"Hello? Hello?" Her voice was soft, rushed, and I realized I'd probably caught her getting dressed for school.

I opened my mouth, but my words stuck in my throat.

"Dammit," she said, and slammed the phone down, cutting off my broken whisper of "Rose."

I held the handset out, staring at it until I felt the tears pool in my eyes. I'd scared her, and I hadn't meant to. I'd only wanted to hear her voice. To have that hint of connection.

And my selfishness had probably conjured up memories of Johnson's horrific phone calls.

He, at least, was dead.

The articles I'd found confirmed what Clarence had told me. Both our bodies had been found at the crime scene. So, yes, I'd accomplished what I'd set out to do—I'd killed Lucas Johnson.

I'd made a plan; I'd gone out; I'd killed.

And I didn't regret it for a moment.

I closed my eyes and drew in a deep breath, truly seeing for the first time what Clarence and Zane had already seen. What I'd experienced when I'd taken down that bloodsucker: I *could* kill. I could face evil down and thrust the blade in deep.

I liked that about me, I realized. I liked it a lot.

I shook myself, determined to focus. I had another mission here.

With grim determination, I typed in Deacon's name, but found nothing. The man was a mystery. Or, to be more accurate, the demon was.

Mostly to distract myself from blossoming thoughts of

Deacon, I switched my search to Alice Purdue, but the findings were also a toss-up between slim and none. A few measly hits about her high school graduation, a reference to her birth date and one photo showing her and Egan and a woman identified as Alice's sister, Rachel, standing in front of the Bloody Tongue at the ceremony to designate it a historic landmark.

I mentally filed the information about the sister, then gave up. For better or for worse, twenty-two-year-old waitresses don't tend to garner a lot of hits on Google.

A good deal of her life had been spent at the Bloody Tongue, and that was a place I wanted to know more about. I went first to the website and reviewed the standard PR material—the excellent restaurant reviews, the pub's long-standing history of ownership all within the same family, the authentic pub menu mixed up with a few new favorites. And, of course, the pub's reputation for being haunted and creepy. All of which I remembered from my Haunted Boston tour.

The truth was, the Bloody Tongue did good business playing up the rumors that it was dark and dangerous, that it had ties to witches and witch trials, and that witch hunter Cotton Mather himself had tried to force the pub's doors shut in the late 1600s but had been unable to pull off that feat. A fact that either supported the argument that the pub had no actual connection to the demonic . . . or suggested that the place was so firmly entrenched in real black magic that the false persecutors of the time couldn't touch it.

The website left the question open, the mystery adding to the allure of the pub. And though all the tourist websites that referenced the pub mentioned the tie to the dark arts as something amusing and a little kitschy, I had to wonder if there wasn't a great deal of truth tied up in the PR.

I poked around in her Internet browser, figuring I might get a clue as to what had been so important to Alice that she'd scheduled a clandestine meet with Deacon. But the history had been cleared, and so had the cookies. There was nothing, which meant I learned nothing. Nothing, that is, except the queer fact that little Alice obviously had some secrets. And she held them very, very close.

I drummed my fingers on the desk, considering where to poke next, and decided that I might as well learn more about my strange new world. Clarence had started teaching me about various demon species, but I'd never really been a lesson-oriented girl, and considering all that had happened to me in day number one of my new career, I think it's reasonable that the information pretty much poured out of my head as fast as he shoved it in.

Demons, I soon learned, are not a topic easily explored over the Internet. Rather than the scholarly information I'd hoped to find, I pulled up page after page of fan fiction, summaries of various television shows, and a few Apocalypse-related gloom-and-doom sites. There was some information I recognized—like Clarence's explanation about how some demons actually had a human form, whereas other demons dove in and possessed a real, sometimes willing human, which truly grossed me out. Goth girl had been an actual, human demon. I hadn't yet met a possessed human—willing or unwilling—but I figured in my new line of work, the odds were good that it was on my agenda.

Other than that, though, I couldn't tell where reality ended and fiction began. Apparently, I was going to have to pay more attention to Clarence's lectures and books. I wondered idly if I could just get the CliffsNotes.

At any rate, I gave up on learning about my newfound life's work pretty quickly, and decided to give Alice-exploration another attempt. This time, I poked around in Alice's file structure, hoping for some insight into the woman I'd become. It was a short-lived detour, though. Alice might not have password-protected the computer itself, but each individual file was locked to me.

I managed to open only one file, in fact. An odd stroke of curious, stupid luck, really. The folder on her desktop labeled "For Saturday" caught my eye, and I took a wild leap and input "Deacon" as the password. Lo and behold, the gates opened and I was in.

Not the most exciting of victories, though, because the folder contained exactly one file. A single photograph of a bear of a guy with pockmarked skin, sagging eyelids, and a don't-fuck-with-me demeanor. He was facing away from the camera, so I could see only about half of his face. The picture had been taken at night, and the image quality was poor, as if Alice had snapped it with her phone while walking. The file name was "T," and there was no other information. Nothing stood out as exceptional about the picture. It was just *there*. On the computer. Taking up space and, possibly, hiding some deeper meaning. But damned if I knew what that was. Certainly I couldn't guess why it had been password-protected any more than I could guess why Deacon's name was the password.

Was that merely a convenience because he was the one she'd been planning to meet on Saturday? Or did he know this man? If so, what could he tell me about T? I had no answer, but I'd be lying if I didn't admit to a low, tingling hum that coursed below my skin when I realized that I needed to see Deacon again. Yes, he was dangerous. Yes, he suspected me.

Yes, he was a goddamned demon.

And, yeah, that made it complicated.

But despite all that, I still wanted it. And damn me, I wanted *him*, too.

My thoughts were drifting toward the prurient pleasures that this forbidden lust could provide when a persistent—and puzzling—pounding at my door shut down my fantasies. Puzzling because it was barely dawn, and at least in my world, people do not come in the wee hours of the morning.

Frowning, I grabbed the knife off the table where I'd left it beside the computer, then stalked to the front door. I knew it wasn't Clarence—he wouldn't bother to knock—and I tried very hard to stifle the tingle of anticipation I felt at the possibility that Deacon stood beyond that door. After all, it could be anyone. Just because I and my demon-killing baggage now occupied the apartment, there'd been no announcement to that effect in the local paper. Which meant that this visitor was most likely calling for Alice. The original Alice.

I gripped my knife even tighter, realizing that Alice's killer might be a little perturbed to see her up and walking around. And the crack of dawn seemed like a good time to remedy that little problem.

Then again, a potential killer probably wouldn't be polite enough to knock.

I pressed my face to the peephole, then grimaced when I saw a tall woman with raven-black hair, familiar eyes, and an impatient expression. I'd seen that face before, but it wasn't until she pounded on the door again, calling out, "Alice! Dammit, open up," that I recognized her from Alice's picture and the newspaper article I'd seen.

This was Rachel. Her—or, rather, *my*—sister.

"You are *not* going to avoid me," she yelled through the door, loud enough for the neighbors to get an earful. "Ignore me all you want, but I've got a key and I'm not afraid to use it."

I considered the possible advantage of slipping onto the fire escape, but ruled it out. This was Alice's sister, and sooner or later, I'd have to deal with her. Might as well do it now.

One more solid *bang* and then the rattle of keys. "Okay. I'm coming in."

I snapped the lock, turned the doorknob, and pulled the door open, sending Rachel tumbling into the entrance hall, led by her key, now stuck in the lock.

She glared at me, righted herself, and then yanked the key free. "Could you move *any* slower?"

"It's early, Rach," I said. "You woke me up."

"Rach?" she repeated. "What's the matter, *Al*?"

I managed a weak smile. Apparently this was not a family that was big on nicknames. "It just slipped out."

"Slip it back in." She dropped her purse on the little inlaid-tile table by the door, then moved without preamble toward the kitchen. I lagged behind, taking stock. I recognized the Prada purse right away, and I could tell by the incredibly put-together look that Rachel didn't have an item of clothing on her that didn't come complete with a famous name. Alice, I'd noticed, was well put together, but the pieces were mostly discount cute. With Rachel, though, I caught the distinct whiff of money.

"Are you sleeping in your clothes now?" she asked from the kitchen.

"Huh?"

Her brows lifted and she nodded pointedly toward me. I looked down, then realized I was still in jeans and my tank top, the stench of blood on me, if not the stains. It had been one hell of a day. Literally.

"Nice jammies."

"Oh, right. I fell asleep watching television, and, well, you know."

"I think I do," she said, but before I could ask her what she meant by that, she disappeared from view behind the counter, then popped up again with a blender. She plugged it in, gave me an eagle-eyed stare over the breakfast bar, then turned to inspect the contents of my freezer.

"What are you—"

"I know you, Alice. And you're not eating right. I'm making you a smoothie."

I was quite ready to argue that I had a pathetically balanced diet when I realized I'd eaten nothing except a few bites of fish and chips in the last twenty-four hours. My stomach chose that moment to growl, Rachel looked at me triumphantly, and I realized two things. One, a smoothie sounded pretty good. And two, I had absolutely no experience in the younger sister role. So far, I had to admit, it wasn't too bad. Invasive, but tolerable.

"What?" Rachel squinted at me. "What's wrong?"

I rubbed my eyes, scrubbing away the tears that had threatened as I thought of Rose. "Nothing. I told you. You woke me up."

She didn't look entirely convinced, but she was too busy scooping out globs of yogurt to call me on it.

"So what are you doing here at this hour?" A risky question for one so clueless, but I figured I'd take the chance.

"Can't a big sister want to pay her baby sister a visit?"

I cocked my head, hoping I looked either irritated or resigned.

It worked. "Oh, stop it. I promised I wouldn't go there again, and I meant it. But that doesn't mean I don't think it's a piss-poor idea to start working at that place again."

"I know," I said, then shrugged in a manner that I hoped invited a longer diatribe.

The deafening *whirr* of the blender put a kibosh on that hope, and by the time she was pouring smoothies, I could tell she'd worked her way off the subject. With any luck, I could work her back on. Clearly, she hadn't wanted Alice working at the pub. Did that have something to do with it being a demon magnet? Or was there some other reason?

My thoughts circled back to Deacon. Had something she'd seen at the pub prompted her to go to Deacon for help?

I didn't know, but I needed to find out. Because when you added it all up, Alice had ended up dead. And I needed to figure out why. Not only because I felt like I owed her, but also because I wanted to protect my own new hide.

"So why *are* you here?" I repeated when she handed me my smoothie.

"I was worried, okay? And don't get all huffy and tell me you're grown-up and can watch out for yourself because I know how you can be."

"How's that?"

She shot me the kind of irritated-sister look I well recognized. "And since I have to fly out again this morning for London, I wanted to swing by and check on you. Remind you not to do anything stupid. Or anything *more* stupid, I guess I should say, since you've already gone back to work with Uncle E."

"It's a good job," I said, hoping to goad her into telling me why it wasn't. "I make great tips."

"A good job? The pub's always this close to shutting down, and you know as well as I do how Egan manages to get that extra little influx of cash every time."

"Yeah," I said, pretending I did know, and wishing there were an easy way for me to figure it out. This had to have something to do with the hints and whisperings that the pub had connections to the dark arts. But how? More important, how could I ask while at the same time sounding like I knew?

"Dammit! You promised me you'd stay away from all that dark stuff."

I took a sip of smoothie to cover my reaction. Alice wasn't as pure as she appeared, and I was beginning to think the little dagger tattoo on her breast was more telling than the pink wardrobe. But what exactly had Alice done that had landed her dead and me in her body?

I shook it off, cleared my face, and forced a smile. "I'm not dark," I assured her. "Only light here."

"Alice . . ."

"Sorry. But I'm fine. You're worrying too much. Or is there something in particular you're worried about?" *Great, Lily.* That *was subtle.*

"Why do I always get drawn back into this same conversation?" She started to scrub out the blender with a soapy sponge. "You got accepted to Harvard, Alice. You don't have to work at the pub. You don't have to slide into the family business. It's a one-quarter ownership in something you've told me over and over that you don't want. That you were perfectly content to walk away from."

"Like you did?"

Her eyes narrowed, her glare pure fire. I stepped back, surprised by the reaction to what I'd thought was a good question for digging a bit further. Hadn't realized I was using a pickax. "Don't be glib," she said coldly. "It doesn't suit you."

"Sorry," I muttered, genuinely contrite.

Her shoulders slumped and she exhaled loudly through her nose, then slammed the blender in the dish drainer. She dried her hands on a towel, then stood there, flailing a bit, as if she were at loose ends without a prop. Finally, she shoved her hands into the pockets of her formfitting jacket.

"Just promise me you're being careful rather than stupid."

"I promise," I said, vowing to figure out what exactly Alice had been stupid about.

"Okay, then." She moved around the breakfast bar, then pulled me into a hug. I stood there awkwardly for a second, then put my arms around her and sank into the comfort of being loved. By proxy, maybe, but right then I needed it however I could get it.

When we pulled away, she smoothed my hair back from my face. "I kept my taxi waiting downstairs, so I've really got to run. If I miss this flight, I'm completely screwed on the London end of things."

I nodded sagely, as if I understood completely why she'd be going to London in the first place.

"Can you do me a favor? Rick's popping down to D.C. on Wednesday, which means he can't watch Lucy and Ethel. I know it's a pain, but it's just the one evening. Do you mind? Rick's not leaving until lunchtime, so you can come late."

"Um, sure. No problem."

"Really?" I assured her that Lucy and Ethel would be in the best of hands, and was immediately pulled into another hug. "You're the best."

She clicked back to the door in high heels, gave me yet another kiss and hug, checked her hair in the mirror over the table, then disappeared into the hallway.

I stood in the doorway, watching her go and wondering what I'd gotten myself into. A great big mess, I figured, especially now that I belatedly realized I had no idea where her apartment was. Or, for that matter, where she kept her key.

Come to think of it, I wasn't even certain about the genus of Lucy and Ethel. I'd assumed dogs, but for all I knew, I'd be babysitting two hungry Venus flytraps.

I stepped into the hall, planning to chase after Rachel and ask her . . . What? I stumbled, realizing I couldn't actually go with that plan. Not and keep my cover story, anyway.

I was, I thought, going to have to wing it.

TWENTY

Here is an unexpected truth: shoving a knife deep into a demon is one hell of a lot easier than tapping a keg. Or maybe it was just me. After all, I'd spent the morning slaying demon after demon, tossing off the ones Zane threw at me like so much rubbish, my confidence growing with each ounce of praise he let leak out. I'd pored for hours over ancient texts, learning about various types of demons, studying more than I had in high school, and doing a pretty good job keeping the basics in my head.

But now here I was, befuddled by a beer contraption. Honestly, it all made my head spin.

This was only my second day on the job, but so much had happened to me, I felt like I'd been living this life for weeks. Months.

Which only underscored my frustration. Considering the time I felt like I'd logged, you'd think I would know how to tap one stupid keg. But no. So there I stood, befuddled in the pub's basement, in front of a long row of kegs tapped by long hoses that led upstairs to terminate behind the bar, where Egan happened to be waiting to dispense pints of Guinness to the riot-ready men upstairs. Separate an Irishman from his stout and trouble inevitably follows. That was one of those facts I was fast learning.

"Problem?"

I jumped, managing to knock my head on the overhead shelving through which the tubes ran. "Uncle Egan. Hey. I'm—"

"Dicking around and pissing off the customers?"

"I just can't quite get this thing to . . ." I trailed off, gesturing helplessly at the contraption that reminded me of a sci-fi movie prop, the tubes sending goo out to anesthetize the victims.

"First time I ever seen you fumble down here. Ain't like it's brain surgery." He squinted at me, barely paying attention to the hoses and clips as he handily retapped the keg. "Something on your mind?"

"No. No, nothing." I shook my head and managed a wan smile. "Just distracted, I guess."

He nodded vaguely, his eyes on me the whole time, as if he were sizing me up. "You got second thoughts about coming back to work here?"

"Of course not," I said, wondering if that had, in fact, been part of Alice's problem.

"Good, kid. Glad to hear it. You know I love you like a daughter. Rachel, too, even though she's got too big for her britches. Your mom, though . . ."

"What about her?"

"No way. Uh-uh. We ain't going there again tonight. You understand?"

"Yes, sir."

"Now, get your ass upstairs and take care of the customers."

I nodded and started scurrying toward the stairs, but stopped when he called my name. "Something else?"

"Just a sentimental old fool," he said.

I stood there, not sure what I was supposed to say to that.

"When you were little, you used to crawl into my lap. You'd tell me stories—things that had happened to someone else or someone you made up—but I always knew you were talking about you. You needed to get stuff out, and I was the one you shared your secrets with.

"You told me about the sight," he continued. "You told me even though it scared you to death. But you knew you could trust me to stay quiet. To help."

I licked my lips, not sure what I should say to that, finally deciding that the only thing I could do was take a chance. "I told you when it stopped, too," I said, then drew in a breath. "And good riddance."

But Alice hadn't told him when the visions had started up again, and I had to wonder why. Why had she run to a demon instead of her uncle, this man who loved her? And why was Rachel worried about what she was getting mixed up in?

The only answer that made sense was that Alice was getting mixed up in dark stuff, and she was turning away from her family. Not an unfamiliar story, really. But instead of drugs, Alice was dabbling with demons.

I had to believe that her dabbling had gotten her killed.

She'd chosen the wrong path, trusted the wrong people.

And one of the people she'd trusted had been Deacon. Or, at least, she'd trusted him until she'd stood him up. So what had changed? What had she learned that had kept her away? That he was a demon? Or something even more sinister?

I shuddered, not liking the direction of my thoughts, but unable to dismiss them.

"Alice," Egan said gently, his eyes searching mine. "I know things were rough there between us for a while, and it about broke my heart when you run off last year. But, Alice, you came back. And we were talking, and last week, I thought . . ."

"What did you think?" I whispered.

"I thought you were finally treatin' me like a dad again. Now, though . . . Well, you barely said two words to me since you ran outta here the other night. I don't know if you got yourself in trouble, or what's going on. I worry, Alice. That's all. I worry about you."

I'd never known my real father, and even though Joe had been around since I was little, that absence had left a hole in my heart. And now I found myself enveloped in Egan's arms, my face against his shoulder, breathing in the scent of hops and grease as he patted my back, his touch filled with concern.

He deserved to know the truth, and I wanted to tell him, but so help me there was a silent, shamed part of me that was glad I had to hold the secret close to my heart. Because it was that secret that let me slide into this life—this family and these friends—and at least have a taste of the world that I'd lost.

And it was that secret that pressed a new wave of guilt down on me. Because I'd been given a second chance and a new world. But Rose, whom I'd promised to protect, was still lost in the old.

TWENTY-ONE

"You fly all the way to Ireland to get that, little girl?" the bear in black asked as I slid the pint of Guinness onto his table.

I conjured a sweet smile, the kind that ensures a decent tip. "Sorry it took so long."

"Sit on my lap, sugar pie, and I'll forgive you."

"The thing is, *sugar pie*, I sit on your lap and I don't think I'll ever forgive myself. Besides, I don't fancy a shot of penicillin today." I turned on my heel as the bear's companion guffawed and revealed to everyone within earshot exactly where he'd like to see that sassy little mouth of mine.

God.

I kissed my tip good-bye and headed back to the bar, checking on a few tables as I did. Egan was back there again, and I looked at him fondly, happy to have found someone to ground me in this new life. If you wanted to get down to the rough-and-tumble details, I had no more information than I'd had a few moments before. Still clueless, still no idea who killed Alice or why. I'd asked a few questions but had been unable to get any helpful information from Egan. There's simply no elegant way to ask someone to reveal to you things that you've already confessed to them. *Gee, Uncle Egan, I've lost my memory—what exactly* was *I worried about last week?* wasn't the approach I wanted to take.

And so I'd drawn no information from our encounter. Even so, I'd walked away with something valuable, and as he smiled at me now, I felt warm and safe. But I remembered the way Rose's eyes had looked when she'd peered out the door at me, at Alice. She wasn't warm and safe, and the nice feeling that had been growing in my stomach shifted toward dark guilt and regret.

I was working the front section of the pub, Trish taking the tables in the back. Gracie was off today, having called in sick, although Egan had roughly commented that she sounded damn perky on the phone. I'd forced my features to remain bland even as I wondered if today was her interview for the job Alice had lined up for her.

With only two of us on the floor, we were running ragged. The Bloody Tongue draws the five o'clock blue-collar crowd, and that crowd comes in hungry and thirsty. Someone from the back section called out to me, insisting they needed their cheese fries right then, and I glanced around wildly for Trish.

She wasn't on the floor, but after a moment, I saw the kitchen door swing open. She rushed in, looking frazzled, a shaft of light arcing over a two-top tucked into the corner. I gasped as the light hit the face of the man sitting there. *Deacon.* For a moment, our eyes met, my stomach doing one of those butterfly numbers I remembered from junior high. And, like junior high, I turned and started straightening the salt and vinegar on a nearby table.

Half a minute later, I realized I was being a complete idiot and turned back around. He was gone.

"Where'd he go?" I asked, brushing Trish's sleeve as she hurried toward the bar to pick up a tray of pints.

She blinked owlishly, and I watched her face as she slowly processed my words. Trish was a decent waitress, but her bulb was definitely dim. "Who?"

"Table nine." I pointed unnecessarily. "Deacon Camphire."

She glanced over her shoulder, then looked back at me. "There's no one there."

"I know that," I began. "But—"

"If you know it, why are you asking me? I mean, come on, Alice. It's not like I don't have anything better to do than stand around talking to you."

And you know what? I felt the same way about her.

She hurried off to feed the masses, and I shuffled over to table nine to avoid my duties. Still no Deacon, but the chair was warm, and as I sat there with my hands pressed to the tabletop, I imagined he was right beside me.

I saw Egan watching me from behind the bar, eyes full of curiosity and concern. I didn't raise a hand, though, to reassure him. How could I, when I wasn't reassured myself?

In the kitchen, I lost myself to the bustle of activity and the thick scent of grease. I could feel it seeping into my pores. Odors defined a place, I thought, and now they defined me, too. The scent of the pub. The stench of a kill.

"Order up," Caleb called, and I took the three baskets of fish from the burly cook, then moved back into the seating area, handily depositing the baskets in front of a group of twentysomethings with law texts open in front of them. They barely noticed me, their discussion about Blackacre and adverse possession enticing only to the extent that I felt a bit adversely possessed myself.

I headed back to the bar, planning on bumming a drink from Egan, but he wasn't there. Instead, Trish was pulling pints with the expertise of a pro. I leaned over and grabbed the soda dispenser and an empty glass, then tried to fill it with Sprite. Nothing. Just a fizzle of carbonated water, and even that came out mostly air.

"Dammit. Where's Egan?" I asked, positively parched.

She hooked a finger toward the kitchen. "Stockroom, I think. All I know is he ditched, and now I'm stuck."

"Sorry 'bout that."

"Heh. It's your party, too." She shoved a tray of pints toward me. "Table seventeen."

"But I gotta—"

"You gotta help me. That's all you gotta do right now."

Okay, it was a fair point, but I was determined. Not being stupid, though, I took the tray and delivered the beers. What I didn't do was go back to the bar, and when Trish saw me heading toward the kitchen, her irritated cry was enough to turn heads in the pub. I snapped off a wave and promised to be right back. Probably not the way to win friends, but a girl's gotta do what a girl's gotta do.

I got to the stockroom on autopilot, heading down the stairs and past the walk-in and then the alcove with the taps where I'd met Egan earlier.

The pub's basement consisted of a series of twisting and turning wood- and stone-lined hallways, so much like a minotaur's maze that I wished I'd brought bread crumbs. The door to the stockroom was on the left, and as I walked, my right hand trailed along the walls made of river rock and concrete. As I passed the walk-in, though, I stopped short, realizing I was no longer touching stone but cold metal.

I hadn't noticed it before, but now I saw a narrow, bronze door etched with odd symbols that seemed familiar, but when I tried to latch onto the source of that memory, it slipped away like trying to grab a handful of water.

Experimentally, I pressed my hand against the metal, which seemed to thrum beneath my palm. I leaned closer, searching for a knob, compelled to go inside, to see what was behind the wizard's curtain. I found nothing, though, and I slammed my fist against the door in futile frustration.

Frustration morphed to obsession, and I think I would have stayed there forever, trying to will myself through that barrier, had I not heard Egan's voice echo down the hallway.

With no small bit of reluctance, I moved away from the

door, pushing through the mist until the pull of the voice was stronger than the call of that door.

"I need to know, dammit," he said, his words drifting back from the stockroom. "You can't fuckin' leave me in the dark like this."

I paused, partially curious but also not wanting to interrupt. I expected to hear a second voice, but when I heard only Egan again I recalled the phone mounted on the wall by the door.

"Yeah? Well, then you tell me what's up. You tell me what happened to turn this whole effing thing back on my ass." I heard the shuffle of his feet, then saw his shadow fill the doorway.

I shrank back, the stone wall pulling me close as I held my breath, willing him to back away. I didn't know whom he was on the telephone with or what he was mad about, but I did know that I didn't want to interrupt.

As if my will had power, the shadow receded, Egan's voice fading as he moved away from the door. "No way. No fuckin' way. I got a right to know. I've put my blood and soul into this pub, offered it up for you to come in and do your thing for how long? And this is the thanks I get? You got to be shitting me."

I took a step backward; whatever was going on, Egan was pissed. And because this seemed like a private moment, I wanted the hell out of there. I stopped short, though, when I heard the deferential slant of his voice in the words that came next. A fearful deflating, as if someone had taken a pin and stuck it hard in his puffed-up chest.

"No, no. Course I would never— Right. Right, yeah, I know." A pause, then, "I don't think that. No way. I was just blowing steam. She just got me worried. That's all." An even longer pause and then another moment of supreme ass-kissage. "Absolutely. Yes, of course. Anything you need. No problem at all."

After that, I didn't hang around to hear the ending. He'd be in a rage when he came out of that room—who wouldn't after being royally called on the carpet—and I wanted no part of it.

What I did want was answers.

To whom had he offered the pub up, and how had they screwed him over? And the "she" who had him worried. Was that me? Or, rather, was it Alice? Had she learned something about the people on the other end of the line? The folks who were scary enough to put fear into a bull of a man like Egan?

Had she been involved with whoever was threatening Egan? Or, if not threatening him, at least pissing him off. And definitely pulling his chain.

Like an Escher drawing, my thoughts kept circling back on themselves, the rapidity of each new idea acting as the engine that carried my feet forward and back through the maze to the kitchen and finally back into the seating area of the pub.

Trish yowled at me the moment I walked in, but I didn't answer. I was too lost in my own questions and in the utter sense of helplessness that came from knowing that the answers I sought would be a long time coming.

TWENTY-TWO

I'd parked the bike in the alley behind the pub without giving a lot of thought to what would happen if someone asked me about it. Or, rather, I'd given it some thought, but because I'd still discovered no evidence that Alice owned a car, my need to remain understated and in line with Alice's overall personality had given way to my need not to have to walk to work.

I was heading for the bike when someone touched me on the shoulder, and I whipped around, knife in hand, only to discover it was Gracie.

She yelped, and I did, too, then leaped back and shoved my knife behind my back.

Too late—she'd already seen it. "Whoa," she said. "My mom keeps telling me to carry a stun gun, especially with all those girls that disappeared over the summer," she added, referring to a series of disappearances a few months prior, mostly of young college dropouts. Girls with few resources and no family nearby. The case had made the news, and I don't think any of the girls were ever found. Maybe now, being super über-chick, I was fighting back at evil for them.

Gracie eyed the knife. "That's even freakier than that switchblade you used to carry." I blinked, surprised that Alice had gone anywhere armed. "And I still say that it's a stupid weapon. I mean, I took a self-defense class once, and we had to stick a knife in the dummy. And I couldn't do it. I mean, *really* couldn't do it. That skin was tough! And on top of that, the dummy just looked so real . . ." She trailed off with a shrug. "Stun gun. Moms always know best."

"It's silly," I said, tucking the knife back into my coat. "There were some guys on the street last night, and I thought about it as I was leaving this morning, and just grabbed the knife."

"So you figured that since you're enough of an idiot to walk home in the dark, you ought to be idiot enough to carry a knife, too? Don't you know those guys'll just take it from you? If they're looking to attack you, one blade isn't going to do anything, 'cept maybe help them."

"Is that your mom talking?"

She shook her head. "My uncle Tito. He's a cop. You know what he'd say to you?"

"What?"

"Pepper spray."

"Gosh," I said. "I never even thought of that."

She gave me a queer look, but I just smiled. I'd already realized that Alice had the most innocent smile on the planet, and I was putting it to great use. Then I grabbed the handlebars and swung myself up and onto the bike. "So what are you doing here?" I asked.

But she didn't answer. Just stood there gaping.

"Who are you and what have you done with my friend?" she finally asked.

My entire body turned to ice. *Holy shit.* I stared, my mouth hanging open like a fish, then finally managed a mousy, "What?"

"The bike, dude," she said. "I totally take back what I said about walking home. But come on. Did aliens reroute your personality? I thought you hated those things."

"Oh! Right! I do. Or, I did. I got over it."

"So were you just pulling Noah's chain?"

I flipped back through the information I'd processed over the last two days, finding *Noah* filed in the ex-boyfriend category. Apparently he'd had a bike. And apparently I hadn't been happy about that. "I guess I was a little touchy with him," I said, trying to sound like I was admitting a huge character flaw. "And he was too reckless. I'm safe," I said, my lack of a helmet underscoring that big fat lie.

Gracie, however, didn't notice. "He was, wasn't he? And that Harley he had was so loud!"

My ex-boyfriend had a Harley? Alice might just turn out to have been cooler than I thought. At the same time we were now treading in dangerous waters, considering my utter lack of information about Alice's boyfriend. Time to head home. But when I made noises about leaving, Gracie rushed to protest.

"I was thinking we could do something," she confessed.

"Do what?"

"Celebrate." She grinned. "Come on. Leave the bike and ride with me. I'll tell you about it on the way."

I had no idea what *it* was, and my gut was telling me to go home before I made a major faux pas and gave myself away. My gut, however, was easily ignored. Because the truth was, I liked Gracie. And even though I'd told myself that getting involved with Alice's friends was setting myself up for trouble, I wanted to go. After all, I saw Gracie every day at the pub. Like it or not, she was in my new life to stay. I might as well enjoy it.

"Okay," I said. I slid off the bike, then followed her to the end of the alley where her ancient, decrepit Chevy Nova took up two spots in front of a meter.

I climbed in, catching a quick glimpse of someone dark

lurking in the shadows by the pub. I watched long enough to see that someone climb into a car, and then Gracie turned off the street and my view was lost.

I pulled down the visor to watch our rear traffic for a tail. At a quarter past eleven, there were only a few cars on the road, and thankfully none stayed with us for more than a block or two. We made good time as she got onto the expressway, and I breathed a little easier, assuming either I'd been paranoid or my shadow had assumed I wouldn't be hunting any demons with Gracie at my side.

"So what are we celebrating?" I asked brightly, trying to get into the spirit of the thing.

"They didn't offer on the spot," she said, "but I really think I got the job. Thank you *so* much for hooking me up with them."

"Hey, no problem," I said, then shifted the subject, because I didn't want to be caught in the awkward position of having to admit that I didn't know who *them* was.

We ended up talking mostly about the customers and Egan, with Gracie doing most of the talking, and me feigning a headache that Gracie swore would be remedied by food. "I bet you didn't even eat dinner," she said, sounding so much like someone's mom, I couldn't help but smile. But all in all, the conversation was easy and friendly and I don't think I even came close to blowing my cover.

By the time she pulled off the expressway, I realized I had no idea where we were. I was about to ask when she made a U-turn, then slid to a stop in front of the valet stand for a restaurant that announced brightly in green neon that it was Thirsty. Fortuitous, I thought, because I was rather thirsty myself.

The raucous atmosphere felt familiar, and I followed Gracie to a booth in the far corner, not noticing until we were halfway there that we weren't following a hostess. "I told Aaron I'd meet him, okay?"

"Aaron?"

She stopped and turned to look at me. "I told you about him. The guy I met at the gym."

"Right. Sure."

"And I mentioned it to Brian, too."

I recognized the name from Alice's answering machine, and kept my feet planted. "Whoa. Hold on. What is this?"

She managed a guileless shrug. "You two would be great together, Alice. I know it."

A setup. This was a double-date setup, and I'd walked straight into it. "I don't know," I said, taking a step backward. It was one thing to be Alice at the bar, or even casually around Gracie. But to be Alice with a guy who was crushing on her? That really wasn't the best of plans.

Gracie's eyes turned all puppy-dog on me. "Please? I'll be totally awkward with Aaron if you're not around, and it's really not a date with Brian. He knows you just broke it off with Noah. And you guys are friends already. Come on, Alice. Don't bail on me."

I looked over her shoulder and saw the two guys at the corner booth. They looked nice enough, like the kind of guys you'd meet at school or a Red Sox game or something. The kind of guys who didn't know the street value of Ecstasy and had no idea how to pick a lock. The kind of guys I had absolutely no experience with.

They were talking animatedly about something—sports probably—and hadn't noticed us. While we stood there, though, one glanced over. I saw the recognition in his eyes followed by a smile and a wave. Because we were caught out, I smiled back and dropped my shoulders in surrender. Looked like we were going to go join the guys.

I told myself it wouldn't be too bad. After all, if I started feeling like I was totally missing the Alice rhythm, I could always bail.

Gracie led the way and we did the hug-and-greet routine. She slid in next to the boy-next-door type with short red hair. Aaron, I presumed. Brian, dark-haired with enough smattering of beard stubble to look edgily sexy, scooted over to make room for me. I sat down and managed what I hoped was a casual smile.

I was saved from jumping straight into conversation by the arrival of our waiter, who looked to be no more than fourteen. I ordered a beer and a basket of fries, then sat back to soak in the atmosphere while the others got in their orders.

All around us, couples and groups laughed and drank, the mood of the place convivial. People came here to be with friends. To hang with people they liked. To just spend time.

Had I ever had friends like that? Sure, I had people I'd gone out with. We'd hung out. Drank. Maybe took a hit of something on the not-so-legal side of the line. Definitely maybe went back to someone's flop to make the most of the high by getting naked. But I couldn't say they'd been friends. Not really. I'd never once told any of them about Lucas Johnson. Not about what he'd done to Rose. Not about the system setting him free. And not about my plan for revenge.

But I'd pulled away. I'd closed off, quit returning phone calls. Gotten utterly lost inside myself. And the more I slid into my own little revenge-filled world, the more my so-called friends drifted away. Not one had asked me what was wrong; not one had come by the house to see how I was doing.

I looked sideways at Gracie and tried to picture her exhibiting that level of disinterest. I couldn't, because Gracie was real, not someone casual who did shots in the back room and occasionally hit you up for money. Solid. A friend. And for the first time I was struck by the real difference between me and Alice: Alice might be dead now, but once upon a time she was a hell of a lot more alive than I'd ever been. She was also, I thought, a whole lot more mysterious. A pink and pampered girl who made friends, attracted cute men, and apparently dabbled in the dark arts. And kept some serious secrets.

I frowned, and if Gracie or the guys noticed my pensive

demeanor, none of them showed it. Instead, they were glued to Gracie as she bubbled about how she was certain she would get the job. "And I owe it all to Alice." She flashed me a smile. "You're the best."

"If you are," Brian said, "you'll set me up with a job, too. My boss is driving me crazy."

"Sorry," I said, deadpan. "I can only help those with actual talent."

He pressed his hands over his heart. "Zing! And she fells me with the first shot out of the quiver."

I grinned and took a sip of my water, thinking that maybe this was going to be easier than I imagined. And, actually, it was. I circumvented Brian's questions about why I didn't call him back about the movie, and dodged Aaron's general queries about my friendship with Gracie by turning the interrogation back on him. I was nursing my beer and trying to look interested while he talked about inventory at the auto parts store where he worked when I saw a flash of someone familiar near the entrance of the restaurant.

"Alice?"

"Nothing," I said, but not fast enough. Gracie turned in the direction I was looking. And when I heard her intake of breath, I knew she'd seen Deacon, too.

"Do *not* go over there," she said as I scooted toward the edge of my seat.

"I have to." I thought of how I'd seen him in the pub, and how he'd disappeared. And now here he was again. Watching me. Following me. And I intended to put a stop to that.

I stood up and smiled at the guys. "I just have to go clear something up with someone I know," I said, then turned away before they could ask questions or protest.

By the time I got to the front of the restaurant, Deacon was gone again.

"No, no, no," I muttered. "Not happening." I checked the bar area and didn't see him there, either. At least not until I noticed the double doors that led to an outdoor seating area. I headed that direction and pushed through the doors, then found myself standing amid candle-topped tables. Despite the October chill, the air was warm, courtesy of carefully placed propane heaters.

I glanced around and found Deacon standing at the outdoor bar, a bottle of beer in his hand. He watched, expressionless, as I approached.

"You keep disappearing on me," I said, my tone accusing.

"And yet here I am. Perhaps your perception of reality is faulty."

"Why are you following me?" I demanded. Behind the bar, the waiter cocked his head, then glanced at Deacon, eyes going narrow.

"This guy giving you trouble?"

"I can take care of myself," I said with a hard look at the bartender that had him backing off. Probably not the most polite way to handle the situation, but I could feel the slow boil inside me. A warm and soupy swamp of emotion just itching for a fight.

"You felled him with a mere glance," Deacon said, his eyes on my face. "You've been practicing your power stare in the mirror, haven't you?"

"I've been practicing a lot more than that," I said. "And answer my question. Why are you following me?"

"I'm pretty sure I've already answered that, or did you forget the promise I made?"

I hadn't. How could I? For that matter, how could I forget anything about this man? Every touch, every scent, every slight change in his expression was burned into my memory. And along with all of that, his promise to find out what had happened to me.

That wasn't a promise I could let him keep.

"It's dangerous for a man to have obsessions," I said. "Maybe this is one you should give up."

"I don't think so," he said. He took a step toward me. I held my ground, determined not to let him rattle me. "Not all obsessions are bad," he said. "Sometimes, they can be fascinating." He reached out and brushed a strand of hair behind my ear, his fingertips grazing my cheek as he did so. The touch, so simple, so casual, and yet it set off a chain reaction inside me that had my entire body warm and primed and ready.

"But sometimes," he added, "they can be dangerous." Before I could think, much less react, his mouth closed over mine. I heard myself gasp, and then felt my thighs warm and my nipples peak as I stayed with him, letting myself fall down, down, down into the kiss with him. A heated kiss, so hot he might have been pulling me down to hell with him. And so decadent and deep that right at that moment I would have willingly gone there with him.

The thought brought me back to myself, and I remembered who and what I was. Not to mention who *he* was. Or, rather, what he was.

My hand went automatically to my thigh, but the knife wasn't in its sheath. I'd been in waitress mode last, and I'd shoved my blade inside a pocket when Gracie had come along.

"You wouldn't kill me," he said. "Not here. Not now."

"Why the hell not?"

"Two reasons," he said, leaning casually against the bar. "First, you don't stand a chance against me, Alice. Trust me on that." I remembered what Clarence had said, and decided not to argue. There was a time for false bravado, and this was not it.

"And second?" I asked.

"Because you liked the way I kissed you," he said. His words flowed over me like warm whiskey, making me light-headed. "You liked it, and you want more."

I managed a small shake of my head. "You're wrong."

His smile was slow and full of promise, and he stared at me for a moment, then another, until I began to get antsy under his gaze. His eyes dipped down. My breasts, my crotch. Then lifted back to meet my eyes. "No," he said. "I'm not."

And then he slapped a twenty-dollar bill onto the bar and edged past me, quickly closing the distance between us and the door. He pulled it open and disappeared. And all that time I tried to find a snappy comeback, but never quite managed. Quite possibly because everything he'd said was true. A fact that left me itchy and needy and more than a little confused.

There was no doubt he'd won that round. Demon hunter reduced to sensual mush is not the way to fight the forces of evil.

Deacon pushed my buttons, and I needed to learn to steady myself around him. I had a job to do, after all. And to do it, I needed a clear head.

Because splashing water on my face might help, I headed back inside. Despite telling myself I didn't care where Deacon was, I skimmed the room looking for him, a knot of disappointment settling in my stomach when I didn't find him. *Good.* Because I was going to calm down and go hang with my friends. No Deacon was a good, good thing.

I intended to swing by the table and tell Gracie I'd only be another minute, but she and Aaron were in deep conversation, and Brian was no longer at the booth. Not being inclined to stifle Gracie's brewing vibe, I skipped the table and headed straight to the ladies' room.

The restrooms were tucked in the back next to a fire exit, and apparently the owners of the restaurant hadn't planned for the popularity of the place, as the line was eight women deep. Not being desperate, I decided to forgo the wait and step outside. Despite a red sign warning that *Alarm Will Sound If Opened*, someone had propped open the door, and no alarm was blaring.

I squeezed through the opening and found myself in an alley. I didn't know if it was Alice's vibe or the *Hi, I'm an assassin* label now plastered to my forehead, but I seemed to be spending a lot of time in alleys lately. Tomorrow, I thought, I'd make it a point to go someplace green.

I drew in a breath, almost wishing I smoked. At least it would be a way to pass the time while I gave Gracie a few more minutes with her male specimen.

Behind me, I heard the door slam shut. I turned, hoping it hadn't locked, as I really didn't want to circle the block. Inconvenience, however, was the least of my worries. Not that I realized that immediately. Instead, I stood stupidly, my supposedly hyperalert senses utterly failing to warn me about the wiry creature that launched itself at me from behind one of the trash cans.

It was small and round and apparently springy; its head landed in my gut, knocking me down and forcing me to exhale with a *whoof*.

"And now," it croaked, "I think it's time for you to die."

TWENTY-THREE

From my prone position, I scrambled to get my knife from the interior pocket of my coat—only to have the beast knock it out of my hand. I twisted to the side, watching it slide under a nearby pile of delivery crates, my fingers stretched out to retrieve it.

That was the wrong move. While I was reaching, the little beast leaned over and bit me, sinking its teeth deep into my wrist. I howled, jerking my arm up and slamming it down so hard that it crunched against the pavement with a bone-sickening *splat*. The teeth stayed in my arm, with the demon body firmly attached as well.

While the demon gnawed and chewed and growled and shook on my arm like a dog with a bone, I slammed my arm over and over on the pavement, trying to smash its ugly little head in. Demon heads are remarkably resilient, however, and I wasn't having much luck. Not having any other weapon, I smashed my arm—and its body—against the wall, then thrust my leg out, my heel smacking against the beast's neck.

Its mouth opened, leaving bloody toothprints on my wrist.

I jerked my arm away before it could bite down again, then pulled my leg back, too. With no support, the thing tumbled to the pavement, gasping for air through its smashed windpipe. Its tongue, black and oily, protruded as it growled and hissed and locked its clawed hands around my ankles.

I fell backward, trying to kick myself free, but couldn't manage it. The pressure of those hands tightened, cutting off my circulation. Any second now and that intense demonic grip would break bone.

I winced, not immune to pain no matter how much strength the Lord had given me, and searched for something I could use as a weapon. I saw two things immediately: a broken beer bottle that I intended to put to good use, and three dark figures racing toward me from the street. They weren't wearing their handy-dandy *I'm an Evil Demon* T-shirts; nevertheless, I could tell they were coming for me.

I didn't waste any time dispatching the demon that had me in a clutch. I'd seen plenty of injuries caused by broken glass, but I'd never caused one, and I was surprised at how easily the sharp glass slit the leathery skin of the creature's throat. That wasn't enough, though; the hand stayed tight around my ankle, and I had to forcibly pry the elongated, bony fingers up, wasting precious time.

Finally free, I kicked the lifeless carcass out of the way and dove for my blade, determined to take the dead demon out of the game permanently.

I didn't make it. With my fingers only inches from the blade, one of the newly arrived demons grabbed my feet and flipped me over, its sword descending at the same time, cutting a gash through my Bloody Tongue T-shirt as well as the skin above my ribs.

I lashed out in frustration and pain, managing to knock its blade back before the demon could try for a better shot, but I still suffered a quick kick in the chest, right at my fresh wound. I sucked in air and scooted backward even as I grabbed the foot and held on tight, flipping the beast up and back as I used the creature to leverage myself up off the ground.

I was standing now, but I can't say I was in a significantly better position. My three attackers looked pretty damned determined, and pretty damned scary, too. Two towered above me, with hide like an armadillo's skin, a snout where a human nose would be, and eyes as flat and dull as a shark's. Both walked on muscular legs with cloven feet, had tails dragging the ground as if for balance, and were armed to the teeth with so much metal I would have expected to see them in a video game.

The third appeared human in form, but I knew that meant nothing. Like the Goth girl, this demon's blood would run black.

The front-runner demon flashed the sword again, but I leaped over it in a perverse version of jump rope. The failure of its sword to make contact as expected knocked the demon backward. I, however, couldn't take advantage of its misstep, because I needed to focus on the mace that Demon Boy Number Two had whipped into a frenzy and sent flailing my way, the chain stretching out behind it.

In what was either an absolutely brilliant maneuver or a shining example of pure, blind luck, I reached up, grabbed the chain, and thrust downward, pulling Demon Boy Two to the ground with me. I grabbed the handle from its clawed hands, then thrust sideways, jabbing it in its soft underbelly even while I straightened up and whipped the mace around on its flail.

I held my breath, then let it fly, landing a solid blow on the third demon even as it was rushing me. It collapsed to the ground, pushing over the first demon—my friend with the broadsword—as it was getting back into the game.

"I don't think so," I said, then dove on it, landing a solid punch to its snout with one hand while I snagged the broadsword with the other. I whipped around, slicing Demon Boy Two down the midline as it lunged for me in a futile attempt to attack me or rescue its companion. I hesitated a second, waiting for the strength that should have fueled me, and when it didn't come, I realized that I hadn't killed the beast with my own blade. I didn't own the kill, and I wouldn't gain the strength.

No matter. I was strong enough as it was, and I whipped around, making the full arc with the sword. I ended by stabbing down, impaling the demon at my feet with its very own sword.

Bilious fluid from the two demons pooled around me, but I didn't have time to enjoy the rush of victory because the third demon—the human-looking one—climbed back to its feet and got medieval on me, the mace I'd tossed now in its hand. It held the handle, eyes burning with hate as it twisted at the wrist, spinning the spiked ball faster and faster. That, however, wasn't the scary part.

The scary part was the five additional demons racing up the alley.

"Bring it on," I whispered, feeling foolishly, desperately confident.

"Bitch," the human-looking demon shot back, releasing the mace. It arced toward me with pinpoint precision. I dove forward and down, the ball so close I felt the spikes comb my hair. I landed in a forward roll, then jumped up, the sword still in my hand. With absolutely no wasted movement, I jammed the sword into the human-looking demon's throat, then lifted my arm, raising it above my head.

Impaled on the blade, the demon's body twitched and shook. Blood dripped from the wound down my arm as life left the creature's body. I breathed in its coppery scent, letting the lust for more fill me and make me stronger.

With one hand on the hilt of the sword and the other on the demon's hip, I shook the body as a warning to the other demons who'd come to give me shit.

Then I tossed it to the ground. As I did, a gray cloud rose from it. A cloud that seemed to have eyes and teeth and a mouth that screamed in silent rage, opening onto a dark, black maw that looked like it could swallow the world. On the ground, the body twitched, and dim blue eyes stared at me. The mouth opened, a bubble of blood clinging to the lips. He uttered a single word, "Help," and then collapsed, lifeless, on the ground.

I shook myself, confused and overwhelmed, unsure what had just happened. All I knew was that the body was dead and the cloud was gone, and I considered all of that good. But the five demons in the alley were still there, and that was very, very bad. I widened my stance and stared down my five new foes. "Do it," I said. "I am *so* in the mood for more." I could feel the blood in my head—making me rage. Making me hungry for a fight.

The demon in front locked eyes with me, and for a moment, I really thought we were going to rumble. Then he stuck two fingers in his mouth and let out a whistle. That was all it took. The others ripped for the street.

I stepped over my trophy demon and started to give chase, then decided not to. I was tired. I was freaked.

And I wasn't keen on chasing demons down the streets of Boston.

I shouldn't have relaxed. I should have stayed on guard.

Because right then—right there—the leader of the five demons thrust his arm out, revealing a crossbow that had been hidden in his jacket. I saw it a half second too late—his other hand was already there, supporting the weapon—and as I dove toward the ground, he let the arrow fly.

It struck me in the chest, and the world turned red, my ears filled with the thrum of my own blood, my heart exploding under the point of the arrow.

My useless limbs collapsed beneath me as I fell to the ground, my eyes wide open and staring at the demon I'd tossed down only moments before. He was already dead, that one.

Soon, I'd be joining him.

I struggled to breathe, but only gasped, finding not oxygen but bloody spittle.

The demon's eyes stared out as the last bit of life slipped from me, his message clear: *See you in hell,* he was saying. *And see you soon.*

TWENTY-FOUR

"One, two, three. Breathe. One, two, three. Breathe. One, two, three. Breathe."

Blackness.

"Dammit! I need the defibrillator. Where's the—"

Serpents. Twisting around me. My legs. My arms.

"Charge!"

Pulling me under. Ripping me up.

"Clear!"

Their eyes glowing red.

Ker-thwap.

Forked tongues darting out.

"I got nothing. Again."

Tasting me.

"Charge!"

Wanting me.

"Clear!"

No!

Ker-thwap!

No!

"Hold on. I think—yeah. I got a pulse. It's faint, but it's there."

No!

"Alice. Alice, can you hear me? Squeeze my hand. Open your eyes."

I squeezed. Then opened my eyes to meet concerned compassion in the form of pale blue eyes. Eyes I knew. "Thom?" I whispered, the word barely coming out past the cotton in my mouth. I knew him from my EMT training ride-alongs, but Thom had known Lily, not Alice, and confusion crossed his face.

"Oh, God, Alice!" Gracie's voice, her whole body emphasizing her relief as she pulled my head into her lap and hugged me close. Brian and Aaron stood behind her, their expressions blank with shock. "Oh, God. Oh, God." Tears streamed down her face, and she clung to me. I sat there, not so much in shock as baffled. Something had *stabbed* me in the heart, and that wasn't the kind of thing a defibrillator fixed. So what the hell had happened?

"Thom!" someone called. "We're bringing in the gurney."

"I don't need it." I shifted, trying to sit up, hoping to prove my point.

"Stay still, Alice," Brian said urgently, but I shook my head.

"No. Can't. I'm okay." I remembered nothing except the demon's eyes and then blackness. And then the sound of the world coming back.

I shivered.

I seemed to be making a habit of dying.

I took the blanket Thom offered me and wrapped it around my shoulders. Then I looked around, taking stock. An easy task, because other than me, the paramedics, Gracie, Brian, Aaron, and the onlookers gathered in the fire door, the alley was empty.

"What happened to you?" Thom asked.

"There was a guy." Actually, there were several, and they were demons, but I figured I shouldn't mention that.

"What happened?" Gracie asked.

Don't I wish I knew . . .

"There was this guy, and he jumped me," I said, fabricating as I went. "And then he stabbed me—"

"Stabbed you!" Gracie said as Thom and his shadow shifted closer, faces both concerned and a little freaked.

"We didn't find any—"

"I meant *hit*," I said, brushing away Thom's hands as they came close to my blanket. The material of my shirt had been ripped by the arrow; I was certain of that. But I was equally certain of what he'd see if he pushed the blanket aside. Perfectly healed flesh, right over my heart.

I'd died, yeah. But once again, it hadn't stuck.

Dear God, dear God. What have you done to me?

"Alice? Alice!"

"He hit me," I said, shaking my head, forcing myself to focus. "We, um, fought. He ripped my shirt. Hit me. And I guess I hit my head. He . . . I guess he got away."

Or, rather, his buddies had carted him away. I grimaced, realizing too late that I could have used the dagger on which I'd impaled him to cut myself. I could have made it my own.

I could have used it and watched his body dissolve into demon goo.

"Blood," the other paramedic said, crouched down over where I'd dropped the human-looking demon. He dabbed at it with a latex-coated finger. "Definitely blood."

I shivered, suddenly light-headed and edgy as he stirred up the scent. A scent I'd keyed off earlier, the lust for blood fueling my lust to kill. Now, again, it filled my senses, primed me. But it was the blood I wanted now, not the kill. To imbibe it. To devour it.

The desire—the *need*—seemed to consume me, and I wanted away from these people, away from everything, because I couldn't stand it, and the craving disgusted me as much as it compelled me.

Dear God, what have I become?

"Cops are on their way," Thom said, forcing my mind out of its surreal haze. "And you're on your way to the hospital."

"No," I said, closing my eyes and trying to ignore the scent. "I'm fine. Honest."

"You had no heartbeat for over two minutes. You're going to the hospital."

"But—"

"Don't you dare argue," Gracie said. "You died!"

"Holy shit," I said, climbing to my feet. I *had* died. And I'd come back.

I'd come back just like Zane. I'd killed him, and then I'd watched him come back.

And he would have the answers I needed.

"I'm so sorry," I said, before taking off running. "But I have to go."

TWENTY-FIVE

"What have you done to me?" I asked, slamming Zane against the closed side of the equipment cabinet, making the knives and swords on the other side clatter. "What the hell have you people done to me?"

He looked me straight in the eyes, completely unperturbed by my fury. "You seem upset, *ma petite*."

"Do *not* fuck with me. I *died*," I said, and saw the slightest flicker in his eyes. "I died," I repeated. "And yet here I am. Again."

"Ma chérie," he said, his voice soft and almost hesitant. "I do not understand."

Because my knife was still lodged under the debris in an alley, I grabbed one from the cabinet and thrust it forward, slamming the blade through the thin metal beside his ear and burying it up to the hilt. "Bullshit! That's bullshit!"

Even as I ranted, some part of me very logically announced that coming back from the dead was a good thing. That whatever cool new gift came with my fancy demon-assassin package, it was a handy trick to have in my repertoire.

Because if the über-assassin-chick can't be killed, that makes her even better at her job. Right?

Right.

But calm, cold logic didn't quell the hot rush of anger and betrayal.

I didn't want immortality sprung upon me like a Cracker Jack surprise, and I sure as hell didn't want to be a mere tool, with everyone else knowing more about my life than I did.

I didn't like it, but I was afraid I was going to have to live with it.

"Tell me," I repeated, trying to force the answers I so desperately needed. "Tell me now."

"Explain exactly what happened."

"No," I spat. "*You* explain. You said I get strength when I kill with my blade? Maybe so. But I get a whole hell of a lot more that that, don't I? That sexual tingle. The bloodlust. The goddamned immortality. I take something inside me. *Don't I? Don't I!*" My eyes stung, and I could feel the tears hot and heavy behind my eyes. I knew I needed to rein it in, but something dark and bitter was inside me. Something raging and silent, pushing me along.

Demons.

With each kill, I was somehow sucking in their vileness. Their blackness. Their rage and desolation.

I soaked in what they felt, what they wanted, what they craved. Be it pain, or fury, or blood.

And I drew in their anger—an anger I was currently quite happy to inflict on Zane.

"You will release me now," he said, "and we will speak calmly. If not, I assure you it will not go well for you."

With a humorless laugh, I pushed myself back. "Go well for me? There's the understatement. Especially since there isn't even a *me* anymore. And there's less and less each day."

I ran my fingers through my hair and stalked to the sparring ring, my gaze on those oily stains, the evidence of slain demons. "Please," I said, my voice small. "I don't know if I can handle this."

I turned to him and was mortified to realize that not only had tears spilled down my cheeks, but he was close enough to brush them away.

The touch of his thumb across my cheek sent shivers through me, and when he pulled me close and stroked my hair, I lost it. "I can't do this, Zane. I can't fight for good if it's going to make me evil. If it's going to make me *wrong*."

"Hush, *ma fleur*. We will figure this out together, you and I."

I leaned back and examined his face. "You didn't know?"

"I swear to you that I did not."

I took in his face, tried to find the truth in there, and found more than I was looking for. I'd let down my guard, and before I could stop it, I was tugged in, dark images filling my mind, along with a desperate, deep sadness.

I jerked away, terrified he'd realize what I'd done, that I'd been inside his head.

But as my heart pounded fearfully in my chest, he merely held my hand. "*Chérie*," he said, "it will be okay."

I licked my lips, realizing he hadn't noticed. I'd slipped in quick and fast, and if he'd felt me in there, he must not have known what it was. "How?"

He stroked my hair, and the sadness I'd seen in his eyes filled his voice. "I do not know," he said. "There are times when I fear it will never be all right again."

I pressed my lips tight together, certain I'd just seen more of Zane than he wanted to reveal. I rested my head against his shoulder, wanting to ask him what was wrong. Wanting to know his past, and about the demons that troubled him, too. I didn't, though. Instead, I asked a simple question. "So what do I do now?"

He sighed. "You wait," he said. And then he left me there, alone with the dark thoughts oozing through my mind. I shivered, not much liking my own company anymore, and desperate to try to find the real Lily behind the black veil that was shrouding my head.

I don't know how long I stood there, sort of floating in a

sea of angst, but the next thing I knew, Clarence was in front of me, his fedora pulled low, his eyes bugging out in their usual froggy way. In other words, he looked like his normal, ugly, irritating self.

And I couldn't have been happier to see him.

"It's the essence, pet," he said without preamble. "You take a bit of the essence of each creature you kill."

"Thanks," I said, my voice dripping with sarcasm. "I actually figured that one out on my own. You want to tell me why you didn't mention it before?"

"Couldn't tell you what I wasn't sure about."

"What do you mean?"

"You passed a test, pet," he said, then spread his hands wide. "Congratulations."

"A test?" I'd done little more than get myself killed. I mean, yes, the resurrection thing was rather cool, but I hadn't exactly been in control.

"That's the point," he said.

"Stay out of my brain. And what's the point?"

"This is one of the signs. The signs that prove you were the girl of the prophecy."

"That I'd come back from the dead?"

"That you would absorb the essence of those you killed. You're our girl, Lily. No doubt about it."

I eyed him suspiciously. "I thought we already knew that."

He pulled off a Gallic shrug. "Eh. Hard to ever be completely sure. But I'd say we are now."

I raked my fingers through my hair. "So let's make sure I've got the full picture here, okay?" I didn't wait for either him or Zane to nod me on. "My job is to kill demons." I spoke carefully, as if talking to particularly slow first-graders. "And demons are evil. And when I kill them, I suck that evil inside me."

"That's pretty much the sum of things."

"But I thought I was getting a chance at redemption. A chance to make up for the things that I've done. A chance to kick evil's butt in the name of all things warm and fuzzy.

And now I find out I'm a huge storage bin for evil karma? What the *hell* have you people done to me?"

"Do you truly think you would have been chosen if we did not believe that you could handle this?"

"Handle? Handle what? Handle knowing that if I die, I'll rot in hell? Or, oh, wait. Dying is the least of my problems now. You people have tainted my soul."

Clarence moved toward me, getting right in my face. "You think the big guy woulda picked you if you couldn't handle it?"

"I don't know. I don't know anymore."

"There's a lot of things out there to be scared of, *ma fleur*," Zane said. "Don't include yourself in that group."

"Easy for you to say. With each kill, I become what I beheld. How am I supposed to live with that?"

"Because it ain't really you." Clarence took off his fedora and ran the rim through his fingers. "Compartmentalize, pet. Use what you need—the fury, the bloodlust—and lock the rest away."

"Blood." I looked at him, the import of the blood from the demon in the alley suddenly striking me. "He *bled*."

I watched as confusion crossed Clarence's face. "Eh? What are you—"

"He was *human*. Don't you see? The demon I killed—right before the other one killed me. He was *freaking human*! He was possessed," I said, remembering Clarence's lesson in Demonic Basics. I looked from Zane to Clarence, feeling slightly sick. "Oh, dear God, he was possessed, and I saw the demon leave. I killed him. I killed an innocent human. Killed," I repeated. "Not only am I a walking vacuum for demonic essence, but I'm also now a murderer." Twice over, actually, when you counted Lucas Johnson. And considering that killing him was what started this whole thing, I definitely added him into the mix.

Clarence looked at me calmly, his very coolness irritating. I wanted him to rage, to fly about. To exercise the same fury that burned in me. "Yeah, you killed. I get that. But check it out, pet. You killed something evil. Vile. And that, kid, is pretty much why you were made."

"Vile?" I repeated. "He was *possessed.* This big demon cloud thing came out of him."

"Not all possession's by force. Most welcome it. Want the power inside them."

I thought of the human's eyes and knew that he hadn't welcomed the demon in. "Not this one," I said.

Clarence sighed. "What do you want me to tell you, pet? That you fucked up? You didn't. Whether the human wanted it or not, the fact was he'd been possessed. Probably woulda stayed that way until his body wore out and the demon moved on. That wouldn't have taken long. Humans are frail, and this human was a tool—the body was a tool—and you destroyed that tool."

I shook my head, understanding what he was saying, but hating it nonetheless. I wanted to protect the innocent. Not slaughter them when danger got too close.

"In every war, there are casualties. You did exactly what you were made to do."

"I thought I was made to stop the demon priest from opening the Ninth Gate. I thought I wasn't supposed to run around killing demons without your say-so," I said, feeling more than a little surly.

"Don't whine, pet, and don't play stupid. You are what you are, and what you are is a weapon against evil. They know it. They know you're going after them; evil's gonna fight back. When it does, you defend yourself. You damn well better do that, or we really are lost."

I drew in a breath, deflating now because he was right. "Fuck." I slid to my knees, suddenly exhausted, the weight of emotion and horror pressing me down. "He wanted to kill me. They all did. Demon and human. This wasn't some random attack on a girl in an alley. This was about *me.*"

I shifted my gaze from Clarence to Zane, needing both of them. "How did they know where I was?" I shook my head, remembering the shadowy figure outside the pub. And remembering Deacon inside the restaurant. I hugged myself and filled my head with children's songs, hoping Clarence hadn't already taken a peek inside my mind.

"Someone set you up, pet," Clarence said. "Let's think on who coulda done such a thing. Who knows you're here? Who knows what and who you are?"

"The Grykon knew, but he's dead."

"I believe we've already addressed the fact that you failed to kill the Grykon in the ceremonial chamber," Zane reminded me.

"Oh, God," I said, finally understanding the import of that mistake. "There was plenty of time for it to have a beer with its little demonic buddies and spread the word."

"True enough," Clarence said. "But we've still got another suspect waiting in the wings. Someone else who saw you in action." He looked at me hard, his eyes knowing.

"Deacon Camphire," I said, the name coming reluctantly to my lips. "But he doesn't know what I am." Even as I spoke the words, I wasn't sure. What if he'd been playing me all along?

I closed my eyes and shook my head. "I don't know that I can do this. Constantly on alert. Danger in every shadow. I'm not that canny. I'm not the girl you people think I am."

"Trust me," he said. "You are."

"I killed. I killed just like you guys told me to." I thought of the pungent scent of the human's blood. "But now I have to live with myself—with what I've done and what I'm becoming—and I'm not sure I know how."

Zane stepped forward, then lowered himself, balancing on his heels, thighs straining against denim. "You live with yourself because you must. You sleep at night because you know that you are fighting the good fight. That, because of you, there is one less stain of evil upon the world."

"And if I become the stain?"

"Do not do this to yourself, *chérie*. Evil is a virus. You have eradicated an infection upon the world."

"Eradicated?" I asked bitterly. "It's not eradicated. It's inside me." I took a deep breath, tried to quell the sense of horror growing within me. "What if I can't handle it?"

"You will," he said. "Because, *ma petite fleur*, you have no other option."

No other option . . .

His words stayed with me, hanging on my shoulders like a cloak as I moved silently toward the elevator, not stopping, not looking back, even though they both called my name.

I went first to the restaurant. To that alley where I'd died the second time. It was quiet now. Safe. The stains on the concrete were the only signs of the violence that had come before. That, and the faint scent of blood on the air. Just enough to rile me. To get that hum going in my belly.

I licked my lips and rolled my shoulders, determined not to fall prey to my own damned nature. Instead, I did the one thing I'd come to do—I dropped to my knees and felt around in the grime by the door until I found my knife. Standing, I sheathed it, feeling suddenly more like myself simply because I knew it was there, its minuscule weight somehow grounding me.

I'm not sure where I walked, or for how long, but my steps ate up the streets as the night deepened. The streets cleared, workers going home to families, until only a few cars dotted the roads, and the only pedestrians were those who called the street home.

When I finally glanced around, trying to get my bearings, I realized that I'd walked through the night. Though the sun hadn't yet broken the horizon, already commuters were loading up and pouring off a nearby train platform. I hesitated, then made my decision, paying the fare and stepping on the train, letting the rumble of the train hypnotize me, my mind as empty as the car and kicking back to life only when we pulled into the station. I pushed through the living wall trying to enter the car as I was trying to leave, then stumbled to the exit, not entirely sure why I'd come.

No. That's a lie. I'd come for Rose. Or, more accurately, I'd come for me.

I caught up with her at the high school, standing off to the side as the number twenty-eight bus pulled up. I thought of Clarence's warning that I could be putting her in danger. But I wouldn't speak to her. Wouldn't single her out. I'd simply stand there and see and maybe, just maybe, feel a connection to myself again.

I swallowed hard, seeing her descend from the yellow beast like a sleepwalker, dark circles under her eyes, looking even more harrowed than she had when she'd answered the door only yesterday. The girls she used to hang with—the ones who'd claimed to be her friends—circled past as if she weren't even there. In a way, they were right. My sister was no longer in that shell. Johnson may have let her body live, but she was dead nonetheless.

Just like her big sister.

I wanted to help her, but I didn't know how. Not if sliding into her life would put her in danger. And the knowledge that I could do nothing but watch left me feeling sad and impotent.

As I stood there, she glided toward the door, then paused, almost as if she could feel my eyes on her. She turned in my direction. I saw her forehead crinkle in recognition, and my heart skipped a beat before I remembered that it was Alice she now recognized as the woman who'd come boldly to her door. To Rose, Lily was gone forever.

I managed to hold it together as she pulled the door open and disappeared inside. Then the tears started. Hot tears that poured down my cheeks and racked my body with sobs.

A few stragglers from the bus looked my way, curious. But I wasn't inclined to be inspected like a bug in a glass. Not now. Not with my heart breaking into tiny pieces. Rose existed as nothing more than a hollow shell.

For that matter, so did Lily Carlyle.

I wandered aimlessly, lost in a funk, letting my feet take me where they would.

They stopped six blocks from my old house near the small

Catholic church we used to attend on Christmas Eve. My mom had never pushed us toward a particular faith, but I had believed in God. I'd had faith in the world, in the knowledge that good would win over evil, and in the certainty that God was looking out for us.

I'd lost that faith when I'd lost my mother, and I realized now what a void that had left in my life.

Standing here now, by the little church, I thought of my mom and the way she brought us here on Christmas. Joe never came, but my mother brought Rose and me, and we sat in the balcony. I could remember the weight of boredom as we sat there, waiting for the service to begin. And then the choir would sing, and it felt like their voices were lifting me up toward heaven.

I needed that lift now. That spark of humanity reaching for something divine. So far, the heavenly creatures I'd met had a baser quality. A burning practicality I never would have expected, but that I had to admit I understood. Having looked into Rose's eyes, I think I understood the spartan nature of the mission more than ever: Eradicate evil. In all facets, in all forms. Take it out, no matter what the consequences, no matter whose soul was tainted in the process.

Cut out the evil, and clear the way for good to ride back in, tall and proud and victorious.

Without thinking, I crossed the street to the white stone church, my head tilted back as I looked at the spire that rose like an arrow pointing the way to heaven. Before I even realized I'd stepped into the street, I reached the door, my hand closing on the solid brass handle. I pulled it open and breathed deep of the scent of oil and wax, with just a hint of spice underneath.

I stepped inside and found myself in a foyer with another door facing me. I hesitated only a moment, then closed the distance, passing through another set of double doors and into the sanctuary.

A few people knelt in prayer, rosary beads held tight. No one turned to question me, and so I stood for a moment hugging myself, trying to get straight, to figure out what I needed and how I could find it here.

Along one wall, I saw an altar with dozens of white candles in red votive containers. Intrigued, I walked there, then let my hand drift over the flickering flames, letting the heat dance on my palm and the warmth seep through me.

"Are you okay?"

I jumped, then turned to find myself facing a young man in a priest's robes.

"Would you like to light a candle?"

I yanked my hand back as if the flame had burned, then shook my head, an inexplicable sense of guilt wafting over me.

"I shouldn't be here. I shouldn't have come."

"You're very welcome here."

"No. I mean, I know. I—" I couldn't get the words out, because they'd been blocked by an epiphany: I'd become the job. A killer. A tool. But it wasn't a job Lily could do, and hanging on to her would get me killed. It was what Clarence had said: I had to let her go. She was dead already, after all. I had to let the old Lily go and find the new woman underneath. A fighter. A killer. Someone who could stand up against evil and not even flinch. Who could take it in and smother it, burying it deep inside her soul.

A woman who understood the cost that had to be paid for the ultimate gain.

The one, Clarence had said. She was in me somewhere.

And now it was time for me to coax her out. To sacrifice the last remnants of Lily and welcome home the killer within. Welcome her, use her, and finish this.

Defeat the demons, seal the gate to hell, and protect the innocent.

Do that, and Rose really would be safe.

Do that, and I would have finally kept my promise.

TWENTY-SIX

I continued to walk the streets, lost in my own head, but my senses sharp. So far, I'd felt no one watching me. Perhaps the demons thought I was dead.

Or maybe they were regrouping, planning the attack that would finally take me out for good. I cringed, having grown rather fond of Alice's head, not to mention the steady beat of her heart. An unpleasant direction for my thoughts, but this was my life now. I was a fighter. A shadow. And, yeah, maybe I was someone who could make a difference to the whole big-picture part of the equation. I was a weapon, Clarence had said, and the responsibility accompanying that pronouncement terrified me, especially now that I knew that the better I did the job, the more humanity I lost.

Not an ideal situation, but what was? Not Lucas Johnson and Rose. Not my mom dying. Not getting stabbed in the gut by a sociopathic asshole. And not even being brought back to life to go chase down demons.

Like my grandma used to say, nobody ever said life was

fair. And if coping meant compartmentalizing, well, I could do that. I could shove away all the shit that washed into me after every kill. I could hide it. I could lock it up. I could ignore it. I'd focus on *Lily*. Not who she'd been, but who she was now. I'd focus on her, and I'd fight the rest of it.

And I knew I could because hadn't I been doing it my whole damn life? Living in shadows and loss. Scraping for a nickel. But I'd never lost sight of *me*. And I'd always had Rose out there, a bright light pointing the way.

I still had her. This was about saving the world, right? The world, and everyone in it.

The streets were bright again, the sun a violent counterpoint to the gray shadows of my thoughts. I'd left the commercial district, moving down side streets until I'd reached a section of town where even the bright rays of sun couldn't erase the shadows. Here, the disenfranchised loitered, the humans who were ripe to be recruited by evil, just like the human I'd killed in the alley. The human who'd asked for help too late. The homeless, the lost. Men and women on whom society had given up. They loitered in liquor store doorways, skulked into porn shops, and cut business deals through half-open car windows.

I wanted to tell them to keep themselves centered. To not take the easy route, and to trust no one who said they could help them. I didn't, though. I didn't say a word. Who was I, after all, to give advice to the damned?

Storefront signage flashed by in a haze, the colored signs sending a message that I was too stupid to get right away. When I did, though, I stopped and turned around, looking for the business that had finally registered in my hazy brain.

I found what I was looking for about twenty yards down the block. I'd passed it without noticing, and now I backtracked until I was in front of the window. Red neon announced *Tattoos*, and a smaller handwritten sign below informed the discriminating customer that the artist was onsite. And, as an added bonus, *Madame Parrish, Psychic* shared the space, presumably offering her services to anyone who wanted to know how their mother, father, lover, friend was going to react to the artistic creation our intrepid customer was bringing home.

I spent half a minute considering the door, reminding myself about infections caused by dirty needles, the possibly poor quality of the ink, and the painful process that accompanied the removal of tattoos. I ought to know. I'd had "Jimmy" and a heart removed at the ripe old age of nineteen.

Ignoring my own prior experience, I pulled open the door and stepped inside.

The dim interior was a shock, and it took a moment for my eyes to adjust to the light. When they did, I realized that the back section was brighter, and immediately beyond a curtain of beads, I saw a guy hunched over a woman's half-bare breast, his long hair swept back in a ponytail. His attention stayed focused on his customer until he shut off the needle, and then he looked in my direction.

"Yo. I've got about five more minutes. You looking to get a tat?"

"Yeah," I said without hesitation. "I am."

"Cool. Got a design in mind?"

"I want a name," I said. "Maybe some sort of picture, too. I don't know what."

"Look around. Anything in those books by the window I can do for you. Price is on the sheet."

He turned back to the girl without waiting for my reply, which left me no place to go except to the books. I was looking at intricate angelic designs when I heard someone move behind me.

I turned, expecting the guy or his customer. Instead, I found myself face-to-face with a woman who had to be on the bad side of eighty.

"Forty-nine," she said. "But don't apologize," she added, before I even had time to realize that I hadn't actually spoken my remark.

"Another one," I muttered, considering taking my business to the next tat house down the road.

"He'd never forgive me if I scared you off," the woman said. She moved to a darkened corner and eased herself into a stained velvet chair. "Please. Sit."

I eyed the hard folding chair opposite her, then listened as she laughed.

"I'm the one pushing ninety," she said. "My bones need the cushions."

"I'm so sorry about that," I said, her casual demeanor drawing me in, if not making me downright comfortable. "I never would have said that out loud."

"Of course you wouldn't. You're a good girl." She leaned over to pat my hand, and when she smiled, I saw that her teeth were stained brown, her gums red and swollen. I wanted to ask why—what medical anomaly had made her this way? But despite her graciousness and my own raw edges, I couldn't bring myself to be quite that rude.

"A disease would be the easy answer," she said, her smile easing my embarrassment. "No, it is my gift. It preys on me."

"You're Madame Parrish."

"I am."

"So what can you do?" I asked. "Your gifts, I mean. Read minds, I guess. Do you also see the future?"

Her brows rose slowly as she peered at me. "You sound dubious. You, who have surely seen things much more curious." She cocked her head, examining me. "You will learn to control it, you know."

"What?"

"What you see," she said matter-of-factly. "It was an unexpected gift. Unknown even to the giver. A legacy from the one who came before. But you will learn, my dear. It will take practice and focus and great strength, but it can be done. I promise that you will learn."

I licked my lips, suddenly not certain I should be there. Not certain I should be talking with this woman who could pick facts from my mind as easily as Clarence did, and who knew of my visions, and seemed to understand them better than I did.

"Not better. But I do have a different perspective. And, perhaps, I can help."

"I don't know how."

Her smile was soft, grandmotherly. "You want to learn how to close the door on your thoughts. Even now, you wish you could."

"I could if I wanted to," I said, obstinately. "Children's songs. Works like a charm."

"On some. Perhaps. But there is a better way."

I tilted my head, not sure whether I trusted her, but definitely wanting to hear what she had to say.

"A Secret Keeper. To do what you must to block your mind, you will have to find a Secret Keeper."

"A what?"

But she only smiled. "It is difficult, what you do. Being two people." I gasped, but she didn't slow. "That will change with time, too, and you will be only one."

I pushed up out of my chair. "I'm sorry. I should go." I brushed past her. "I'm not even sure why I came here."

"Ah, but I am. You wish to know if you are doing the right thing. The right thing, for the right reasons."

I stopped, my hand on the door, then turned back to face her. "Am I?"

She shrugged. "These questions of what is right and what is wrong. Of what is good and what is evil. They are not black and white. And sometimes we make the wrong choice for the right reason."

"And my choices? Are they wrong?"

The lines in her face deepened with her smile. "My dear. Only time can tell you that."

TWENTY-SEVEN

I can't say I was thrilled by the discovery of Clarence sitting on a portable stool in front of my door. I'd spent the last two hours lying facedown on a tattoo table, an experience that was both painful and surprisingly relaxing. I'd de-stressed, pondered my problems, and now all I wanted to do was veg with mindless television.

Alas, that wasn't to be.

"You over it? Centered? Got your chakras all lined up nice and neat?"

I stared down at him. "If you mean am I feeling better, then yes. Thanks so much for asking." I considered sharing the meandering path my mind had taken me on that night, but I wasn't really in the mood. If he wanted to know, he could tug it out of my head himself.

He shrugged, then stood up, folded the stool, and hoisted it under his arm. Then he barged past me, leaving the stool propped up against the hall table. I cringed, certain the aluminum would scratch the finish. Just in case, I moved it aside and rubbed my finger over the wood. Still pristine.

By the time I draped my coat on the rack and made it into the living room, Clarence was already rummaging in the fridge. "Getting pretty thin in here. You can't find time to schlep down to a grocery store?"

"You been sitting outside my door for how long? You can't walk to the laundry room and buy yourself a Diet Coke?"

"They don't got what I want in the laundry room," he said, rummaging around until he came up with a beer. "Ha! Always check the vegetable crisper." He popped the lid and chugged. Then he belched and sighed. Nice.

I shoved past him to open the refrigerator door myself. Because I wasn't inclined to have beer for breakfast, I grabbed a bottle of water. He was right about one thing—somewhere between training, waitressing, and visiting my past, I needed to add a trip to the grocery store to the agenda.

"So what were you doing waiting in the hall?" I asked, once we were both comfortably settled in the living room, me on the sofa with my feet on the coffee table and him in an overstuffed armchair that gripped him like an enthusiastic lover.

"Working up a thirst," he said, then raised the bottle to his lips to prove the point.

My reaction might well be considered gloating, but I couldn't help it. I finally got it—he wasn't allowed to come into the apartment uninvited anymore. I'd passed the test. I'd proved I really was Prophecy Girl, and that meant that my place was mine.

"You can't come in anymore," I sang, holding off on going so far as to hum the "Hallelujah Chorus." "It's *my* place now. Not a loaner. *Mine*."

"Don't get too cocky. I'm still your boss." But I swear I saw a smile when he said it.

"Mine, mine, mine." I knew I'd crossed the line into irritating, but I couldn't help it. I'd actually accomplished something in this freakish new life. I'd passed a test, made headway. And that, my friends, was sweet.

"Does this mean my head is off-limits, too?"

"Heh. You gonna give me grief about that? Not like you haven't figured out ways to keep me out," he said, then started humming a bar from "Conjunction Junction."

I blushed, which pissed me off. "It's *my* head. You shouldn't be allowed in without permission." I cranked up a rousing chorus from *Schoolhouse Rock* and reminded myself of what Madame Parrish had told me: a Secret Keeper. Whatever that was, I needed to find one.

Clarence swallowed a mouthful of beer, then shrugged. "Yeah, well, I'm getting into your head less and less. The song thing and . . ." He trailed off with a shrug, then took a long pull on his beer.

I narrowed my eyes, my antennae going up. "What? You can't get into my head as easily anymore? Why?"

He didn't answer, but he didn't have to, because right then I knew. I knew, and it sickened me.

Clarence couldn't get inside a demon's head.

And I was absorbing demonic essence. Every time I killed with a blade, I was becoming more and more demonic. Less me. Less human.

Dear God.

I sank onto the couch, then pressed my fingertips to my temples.

"Eh, don't get your panties in a wad. You're safe. I still got a line into your head."

I looked up at him. "But I'm right. It's exactly what I was saying at Zane's. The demons I kill—they're changing me."

"Kid, you changed the minute you ended up in Alice's body. Don't split hairs. You're here doing a job."

"But—"

"Dammit, girl. Didn't we already tell you? You can handle this; otherwise you wouldn't be who you are. You tuck it away. You don't let it turn you. You use it. Use the demon inside for good and you've got yourself some damn sweet poetic justice. *Capisce?*"

I considered what he was saying and had to admit that

despite his typically irritating way of saying it, my froggy friend had a point. Take the demon in. Twist it around. Use the strength and essence to take out more demons. In with the bad air, out with the good. Sort of like money laundering for demonic essence.

It wasn't perfect, but at least the image gave me something to hold on to. A way to do this without feeling like I was sinking deeper into the pit even while I was struggling to climb out.

"So can we move on?" he asked, sounding particularly pissy.

"Sure. So, uh, why are you here?"

"The way you walked out, pet. I was worried. Wanted to check on you. Make sure you were okay."

"Make sure I hadn't decided to back off? Decided not to do this thing anymore?"

"Did you?"

I shook my head, my thoughts from the night swirling inside me. "I'm good," I said. "Or I'm as good as I can get, I guess." I looked at him straight on. "At any rate, I'm down with the job. Warts and all."

"Glad to hear it, kid. Let's get you back to Zane. Get you training."

I thought with longing of a nice, warm bed and knew that wasn't going to happen. And, actually, I was okay with that. Because the thought of smashing down some demons was equally appealing, and it got more so as I thought of it. Thought of the strength that would fill me and the darkness that would ooze through me. I told myself I didn't want it, but in the deep, secret part of myself, I liked that it was there. That darkness gave me the strength to kill and the wherewithal to win. And, dammit, I wanted to win.

I got my chance soon enough. Zane was waiting for us when we arrived at his basement, and he put me in the ring without preamble. Before I knew it, I was jabbing the heel of my hand up toward a demon's nasal orifice. It growled and snarled, greenish snotlike stuff dripping from its eye sockets as it lunged for me, apparently pissed off that I'd gotten in more than my fair share of whacks and still remained relatively unscathed. *Relatively* being the operative word.

I was alive. I was well. And I wanted to stay that way.

My blade was tight in my hand just where it was supposed to be, and I pounced, dodging around the demon's outstretched limbs to grasp it around the torso with one arm even as I sliced its throat with the other.

I drew in a deep breath and leaped back as it shook with death throes, a surge of power filling me even as life spilled out of it. A surge so rich and liquid it was almost sexual, the rush of blood through my body almost orgasmic. I let it ripple through me, soaking it in, letting it fill me. Letting it *please* me.

But whatever pleasure I'd drawn from the kill evaporated when I looked down at my body and saw that I was completely covered in a thin layer of green slime.

Nice.

I bit back a gag. Nasty price to pay for a rush of power and strength.

I got a rag and started cleaning myself up, my body still humming from the kill. "Next," I demanded with an easy grin, but before Zane had time to lure my next victim into the cage, I doubled over, clutching my arm in pain.

"Lily?"

"My arm," I managed, as Clarence jogged over from where he'd been watching on the sideline. "Oh, shit, my arm."

I thrust it out in front of me, certain a million fire-tipped needles were embedded in my flesh. Instead, I saw that the Aztec-like symbol had come to life, the strange pattern now seeming to dance upon my flesh. "Holy shit."

"About time," Clarence said, his voice full of eager anticipation.

"You didn't tell me it was going to hurt so much," I raged.

"Blood," Clarence said, moving toward me with his knife. "It eases the pain."

The pain was so great that I barely noticed when he sliced my arm, then smeared the blood over the symbol. He was right; the pain lessened almost immediately, and I sighed with relief, and with trepidation. How many times was I going to have to experience that before this adventure was over?

Clarence turned to Zane, his expression serious. "Make her ready. Quickly."

Zane nodded, then cocked his head. "This way," he said, moving like a panther across the training room, his native sensuality clinging to him like early-morning dew. A sensuality I'd absorbed but had not yet learned to control.

He stopped in front of a gray, industrial-style cabinet, then turned to me, his gaze both warm and demanding. "It is unfortunate that you are undertaking this mission before dark, *ma fleur*. In the middle of the night, you can get away with carrying much more than mere blades."

He glanced at my thigh and the blade that was holstered there. The blade that had killed him, actually. A state of affairs about which he held no grudge.

"I thought I had to kill with the blade."

He grinned. "And I thought you wanted weapons that would slow the beasts down."

He reached for the two steel handles that protruded from the cabinet, turned them, then pulled the doors open with a flourish. The inside gleamed like a Gothic slasher movie gone bad. Crossbows, mace, daggers, and halberds, along with your standard switchblades, swords, and scary-looking hunting knives.

I whistled through my teeth, then pulled my hand back when I realized I was reaching out to snag a weapon without invitation.

Zane noticed, too. "You are eager, *n'est-ce pas*? *Bien.* The more primed you are, the more focused you will be."

"This stuff's for me?"

"Eventually." He grabbed a simple switchblade from the middle shelf. "As I said, these weapons are for the night."

"So whether or not I'm sliced down because I'm underarmed depends on the time of day I go hunting? Gates of hell, remember? Nasty, evil demons, right? So forgive me for being dense, but I'm thinking that going out with a broadsword in broad daylight is a much better plan. Trust me," I said, thinking of the demons in the alley. "The other guys aren't going to hold back on weaponry."

"I assure you, this blade is serious enough."

He pressed the switch and the blade zinged out, the steel glinting in the harsh light provided by the single, bare bulb that burned above the cabinet.

He held it out for me, and I took it. My fingers brushed his palm as I did, and with that minimal touch, my body burst into an electric overload of sensual awareness.

I snatched my hand away, afraid to let it grow.

I looked up, not on purpose, but as if my eyes were drawn to his face. His eyes, dark and knowing, watched me impassively. But his mouth curved, ever so slightly, in the faintest hit of a smile.

"It is good, I think, *ma fleur*."

"What is?"

"The connection." His thumb absently brushed his chest, the movement seemingly unthinking, but I knew better. He moved a step closer, and I caught the musky scent even as the beads of sweat on his smooth scalp and forearms glistened. "Who knows what will happen if we let it grow, eh, *ma chérie*?"

I stepped backward with a regretful shake of my head. Zane cocked his, examining me with thoughtful eyes. "Interesting."

"That I would say no to a man of your great charms?"

"*Mais oui*. And also, that there is another. I am correct, am I not? Who is he? This man who stays your hand? A remnant of your life before? Or a new fascination?"

I forced myself not to look guiltily in Clarence's direction. If either of them learned that Deacon was the object of my interest . . .

I forced my thoughts back to the moment. "The only thing I'm fascinated with right now is that blade." I nodded at the knife. "And I don't think that my libido is relevant to this mission. Do you?"

"Touché." He held out his hand. "Give me your palm."

I hesitated, realizing what he intended to do. The knife at my thigh belonged to me. This switchblade, however, had yet to be marked.

"You hesitate now?" he asked, amusement in his voice. "I can see the demons already quivering with fear."

I sneered at him and stuck out my hand. "Shut up and cut me, already."

The blade sliced through my palm, and I bit back a wince, not wanting to show pain. Not wanting to react at all.

He wiped off the blade, then retracted it and slapped the weapon into my hand. I flinched against the sting of it on my cut palm. But the truth of it was that the wound was already starting to mend. By the time I approached my quarry, I would be fully healed.

"All right," I said, after taking a deep breath for courage. "Where do I go now?"

"Now, *chérie*, you go change."

"Huh?" I asked, but Clarence stepped up in response, pressing a bundle of black cloth into my arms.

I eyed them both curiously, then unwrapped the bundle. A black jumpsuit and a matching black hood, with slits for eyes, nose, and mouth. "It's what all the fashionable demonic assassins are wearing this year."

"Indeed," Zane said.

"And if I'm running around like this, why can't I carry more weapons? This is hardly going to be inconspicuous."

"You can peel the hood off after the attack," he said reasonably. "And then you will look like nothing more than a beautiful woman in a skintight suit."

"Oh."

He pointed to the shower area. "Go."

I went, and when I came back, I felt like I should perform

a series of complicated martial arts movements. Or at the very least, creep silently around the room, ninja-style.

Zane, however, wasn't amused. Just the opposite, and I could see the desire that my rather formfitting outfit sparked in his eyes.

"You were right about skintight," I said.

"Now," Clarence said, "there is no more time to be wasted."

"Where am I going?" I asked. "My arm tells where the Box is, right? So where do I go now? The symbols are a map? Can you read them?"

"Pull back your sleeve," he said, as Zane stepped back, his gaze fixed on the two of us.

I did and found myself looking once again at that strange, pulsating symbol now burned into my arm. If there was a location carved in there, I sure as hell didn't see it.

Clarence took my left hand in his. "Cover it," he said. "Cover it with your other hand."

I almost asked why, then decided that I'd find out soon enough. I pressed my palm over the symbol and felt an immediate, uncomfortable tug at my navel, so hard and so quick that I couldn't even scream. Instead, I was being yanked through space, Zane's basement melting away to be replaced by blackness. Terrifying, swirling blackness, filled with low moans and winds and a million creepy electrical sensations that crawled over my body, making me writhe and squirm and open my mouth in a soundless scream.

And then there was nothing. Just blackness that seemed to curl around me like a blanket. I couldn't see anything, so I had no perspective, but even so, I somehow knew that I was moving fast, faster than was possible in the real world. I was hurtling through space, through dimensions, through time itself, and the thought both scared and fascinated me, and I felt myself tightening my hand, remarkably relieved to find that I was still clutching Clarence's fingers.

This was the bridge, I realized. And he was my way back.

Before I had time to think about where I might be going, I

saw my destination. A street, and a row of houses, and it was like I was a bird, high above the world. Only then the bird started falling, falling, falling, and the ground was rushing up toward me. I was going to crash. I knew it. I could practically feel the impact even before it happened, and I braced, fear clutching me, as the ground came closer, closer, closer, and then—

Nothing.

It was over.

I was on a patch of dirt in a trashy yard, and I was breathing hard, and Clarence wasn't holding my hand anymore, and when I looked up at the sky, I saw a strange, swirling mist, like a whirlpool consuming itself. And then it was gone.

The portal, through which I'd traveled. A portal, I thought, that had opened in my own body.

I stood up slowly and brushed myself off, and as I did, I realized I was smiling.

Now, this, I thought, *is cool.*

TWENTY-EIGHT

The yard belonged to a run-down shack of a town house with chain link surrounding a front yard that consisted of dirt, aluminum beer cans, and cinder blocks. *Charming.*

I stood still for a moment, trying to get my bearings, then realized I was standing in a pool of light coming from a strategically aimed porch light on the house I was targeting. Nothing like killing the element of surprise five seconds into the game.

I knew enough to move out of the light, but despite repeated *Law & Order* viewings, I had a less-than-honed sense of how to infiltrate a building that housed the target of an assassination. I doubted that a frontal assault in full view of street traffic made sense, though, and so I crept around to the back. I kept a knife in each hand, ready to flail and stab like my life depended on it. Which, of course, it did.

I entered low, proud of myself for remembering that little tidbit, and was almost disappointed to realize there was no one there trying to halt my progress, no one pressed in beside the refrigerator holding a gun aimed at my chest. I had a clear path through the moldering kitchen, and with the scent of rotting milk filling my nostrils, I eased through a dusty dining room, finally emerging at a wide-open foyer dominated by a staircase that must have once been a stunning focal point, but now stood forlorn and sagging.

I edged toward it, taking the first step carefully in case the wood beneath my feet crumbled. It seemed solid enough, and thus encouraged, I continued to climb. The balustrade shook under my hand, and I inched to the side, letting go of the rail as I climbed steadily upward, the tip of my knife scraping the plaster on the wall with a sound that resembled mouse claws on concrete.

I tugged the blade back, holding it close to my waist, afraid the mouse claws had given me away. I stopped, frozen on the stairs, listening for any sound, any hint of motion from above. I was met only with silence. Reassured, I recommenced my climb, this time with only the soft pad of my shoes against the stair tread to telegraph my presence.

The floorboards creaked as I hit the landing, and I tensed, certain that this time, I would be found out. But no light illuminated the darkness of the upper level, no face emerged from the shadow, no footfalls echoed in the stillness. It was so quiet that I was beginning to wonder if the magic map on my arm had delivered me to the wrong house.

I took the rooms one at a time, a knife in each hand, the penlight I'd tucked in my back pocket now wedged under my watchband so that both hands were free to cling like grim death to my weapons. The floor was empty, and from all evidence, no one had visited these rooms in months, possibly years.

I jammed the point of one of the knives into the balcony rail, then peered over it into the living room below. Barren, except for a few pieces of furniture covered with drop cloths. A shaft of light cut across the room, streaming in from the window overlooking the front porch and revealing a warped wooden floor covered with a perfectly smooth layer of dust marred only by a set of footprints leading from the back of the house toward the stairs I'd just ascended.

Curious and encouraged, I inched back toward the stairs, then shined the light down into the abyss. Sure enough, another set of footprints mirrored my own, continuing forward upon reaching the landing instead of turning as I had. With the beam narrowed, I followed the feet, then frowned as they walked up to a wall. Dead end.

What the . . . ?

I splayed the light on the papered wall, focusing on the seams, then trailed the beam down to the floor. Years of wear had smushed the central strip of the carpet that covered the landing. The edges, however, remained in good condition. Everywhere, that is, except for the spot where the footprints ended. There, the fibers were well-worn, as if a constant flood of visitors had pressed their bodies flat against the wall and stood there. Just stood there doing nothing.

Not damn likely.

I leaned forward, pressing my fingertips to the wallpaper seams, searching for a latch to operate the door. Another room back there, or perhaps another staircase. But whatever it was, it led to my mark. And I knew I couldn't leave without finding the Caller. Finding him, killing him, and destroying the Box.

I can't say that I've ever searched for a hidden room before, but after some delicate probing, I found the telltale indentation. I pressed the soft spot, and damned if the latch didn't click and the entire panel swing inward on greased hinges.

The small room that was revealed lacked the abandoned-junk miasma of the public areas. Both sparsely furnished and spotlessly clean, this section of the house screamed out with utilitarian function. What it didn't have—at least not that I could see—was an occupant.

Having already been through the drill once, I found the next hidden door with significantly less trouble. This one led to a winding staircase that circled up to the attic before opening onto yet another landing. This time—finally—I saw signs of life. A shadow moving within, but without any urgency. *Good.* With any luck, that meant my demon hadn't heard me coming.

The stairs were metal, and I moved at a snail's pace, fearful of causing a creak that would shatter the silence.

Somehow, I made it up without announcing myself to the world. I slowed as I approached the landing, then eased my eyes over the edge, peering up at the room while holding my breath.

Considering my lack of skill with regard to stealth approaches, I was pleasantly surprised to see that my tack worked, and I was even more pleased to see that I wasn't facing multiple occupants. The single demon stood at an angle to me, facing something in the corner of the room at about my nine o'clock. I could see the side of his face, angular and deceptively human. A familiar knot tightened in my gut, and I reminded myself that the beast was vile. More than that, he was working to end the world.

As I watched, the creature turned his focus to the fireplace behind him and to the left. It was the mantel that attracted him—glowing with inlaid gold and gemstones, and marked with etchings that seemed like some sort of bastardization of Egyptian hieroglyphics. The thing clearly had some intense ceremonial value, but though it might be ancient and powerful, it held no sway with me.

Or, it didn't until he pressed his palm flat against the ornamental center and a door to the left slid open, revealing an ornate golden box.

The Box of Shankara.

Perfect.

I'd arrived in time. Destroy the Box, kill the demon, get home in time for a few prime-time television programs on my glorious night off waitressing.

I sliced my palm with my knife, letting the blood flow. If my blood destroyed the Box, I wanted to be prepared. Then

I tightened my grip on my knives and considered my approach. Maybe ten yards between us, with a clear path over a carpeted floor. His back was to me, and if I moved slowly and stealthily, I might be able to continue my clandestine approach. I couldn't bank on it, though. For all I knew, the gems in the mantel reflected the room into his eyes.

I didn't want to be the assassin who blew her first mission because she trusted that her ambush would succeed. Instead, I was going to abandon caution and rush the bastard. I'd have to run like the fires of hell were nipping at my ass, but since they were, I figured I could manage that.

I took a deep breath and barreled forward at a breakneck pace, planning to launch myself over the Box and take care of that little detail first. The launching part went okay, but the rest was a complete nightmare. The kind where you realize after it's too late that the stealthy approach probably would have been better. Always go with your first instincts, after all.

As I leaped, the Caller turned, a set of broad wings bursting through the thin material of his shirt as they unfolded, then catching me across the middle as he spun around. The effect was a lesson in physics—two objects in motion collide with unequal force. And one guess which object absorbed the blow and went flying.

I landed on the far side of the room, knocked into a bookcase that teetered recklessly but didn't fall and brain me. The beast took a menacing step toward me, fangs suddenly visible on that advertising-exec smile. His fingers no longer looked like a man's—they had somehow elongated into thin, bony structures with sharp talons, each of which was now pointed right at me. "You."

The word was an accusation, and I fought the automatic response to edge backward, to deny. Instead, I burst forward, knives flying, and the words Zane had said when he'd first put my knife in my hand echoing in my mind: *Do what you were made for and you cannot fail.*

Apparently not words to live by, because one broad thrust of that wing sent the knife in my right hand flying. I clutched the left one tighter as the demon ripped upward, slicing my ninja suit to ribbons and bringing thin lines of blood up on my abdomen before sliding back and peering hard at me. "It is true, then. The prophecy." He blinked, lids closing side to side over marble-black eyes. "And on which side do you stand as you straddle the line?"

I thrust my left hand out, the tip of my blade pointed right at the demon. "Do not even try to play games with me. I'm on the side that will see you dead."

Those alien eyes narrowed only briefly before he was on me, so fast that I had no time to think, much less react. His wings spread wide so that I could see nothing but his face and torso and the thin, gray membrane of wings spread wide on spindly bones, fragile in appearance, but containing deadly strength.

The long, taloned fingers of his hand grasped my neck and squeezed, the grip like a vise. With the wing itself, he pressed my arm back. I struggled—so help me, I did—but I couldn't move the hand with the knife.

I was trapped. And that pretty much sucked. Because despite all my training, all my gifts, all the prophesied bullshit, I was no match for this creature, and as a reddish gray swirled around me, I couldn't help but wonder if this had all been a big cosmic joke. Kill Lily in a big way. Make her pay for trying to protect her sister. Crush her illusions that there was any justice in the world. Make her pay for doing what needed to be done.

The Caller's eyes burned into mine, the wings still holding my arms out to the side, useless. His hands were more deadly. One remained on my neck; with the other he pressed against my forehead, and so firmly I feared my bones would snap.

I wasn't going down like this, though, and I looked him in the eye, staring a defiant *screw you* deep into those black orbs even as I struggled.

All bravado, I knew. He would snap my neck. Any second, he'd snap, and I'd be dead. Again.

The snap didn't come.

Instead, as I looked into his eyes, my body convulsed, and my head filled with a pain not my own.

Touch and eyes.

Mist-encased images of the beast accosted me—images of him locked in combat with someone I couldn't see, but somehow knew was not me. *Who?* Even as my air supply dwindled and my body fought pain and terror, I searched my mind for a better angle. For some hint of what I was seeing and why.

I don't know how, but I knew this was not the past. This was a Thing Yet to Be, and though I didn't understand how that could be any more than I understood how I'd come about because of a prophecy, at the same time I knew that it was absolutely real. What I was seeing would happen.

Or, at least, it would if the path didn't alter.

The thoughts whipped through my mind, forming, but not cohesive. Instead, I was inundated with information. Thoughts. Images. Impressions. Conclusions. A nightmarish mishmash that centered around this vision of the beast locked in battle.

In the vision, the beast released his battle partner long enough to reach behind him and pull a broadsword from a scabbard I hadn't seen. Perhaps it hadn't been there, and like a dream, it had materialized only when needed. He brought it up and over, his strength awe-inspiring, and as he moved to the side to follow through with the swing, I saw the face of the person with whom he was doing battle: *Clarence.*

Like the bursting of a dam, the vision popped and my strength flooded back.

"Fiend!" the Caller cried, momentarily loosening his grip. "You play tricks in my mind!"

I didn't bother to retort. I simply lashed out, fueled by fury, and that coupled with the fear of losing Clarence. Yes, he got on my nerves, but I'd grown fond of the little amphibian. More important, he was the one link between my old and new lives. And no one—no one—was messing with him while I was around.

I twisted violently to the side, managing to loosen his grip on my neck. As I did, I shot upward, forcing our skulls together and setting off a July Fourth–style fireworks display in my head. I ignored the fact that it felt like my cranium had shattered and my brains were spilling out on the Oriental carpet. Instead, I did the only thing I knew how to do—I whaled on the guy. Arms weaving, knife flashing, I caught him across the arms, sliced the wings, and took off an ear with one fateful blow.

The kill shot, however, eluded me, and we dodged and parried, me bouncing and weaving and pretending I knew what the hell I was doing; him lunging with talons and claws and a strength borne straight from hell. "You are flawed," he taunted. "Incomplete. Failure is your destiny," he added with a black-eyed smirk. "For even if you win this battle, the war will not go your way."

"I'll take the battle," I said, then thrust my knife, managing to slide it into the narrow space left open between his flailing arms and wings. The shot went home, and as I watched, the demon sagged on my knife.

It wasn't a kill shot, though, and he stumbled across the room to the Box, with me right there with him.

He lashed out with his wing, knocking me back, and his talons fumbled at the Box even as I scrambled forward, trying desperately to touch the Box with my bloody hand, hoping that alone would be enough.

I didn't make it.

I was only inches away when he held the Box high. I heard the demon's whisper of *"Disparea!"* and in the blink of an eye, the Box disappeared.

"Noooooo!" I screamed, then rushed forward and thrust my blade through the beast's heart.

And with its last, dying breath, the demon smiled at me.

The Caller was dead.

But the Box was gone. And I'd failed to even take the battle.

TWENTY-NINE

I raced out of the demon's house, my head filled with failure and my emotions crowing a victory.

I needed to get away, to stuff these feelings inside. *Compartmentalize.* But I couldn't. The essence was too fresh, the emotions too raw. A swell of pride. Of victory. Of intense martyrdom for having the cunning to stop the beast.

I'd done things. Horrible things. Violent, awful, perverted things.

And they would be forgiven. Erased. Because in the end, I'd won. I'd served the master well, and I would be rewarded.

No.

I fell to the sidewalk, my hands pressed to the concrete as I forced myself to slowly and methodically think the truth.

That isn't me. I haven't won. I've lost.

I've lost, and the Box is still out there. Ready to be Called. Ready to open the gate.

The emotions racing through me weren't mine. I was experiencing the last visceral reaction of the lousy bastard demon who'd managed to defeat me.

The gates of hell were going to come flying open, and it was all my fault, and I did *not* want the smug son of a bitch doing a victory dance inside my head.

But he was, and as far as I could tell, I couldn't do a damn thing to stop him. Not yet, anyway.

Damn, damn, damn, damn!

So instead of trying, I pressed my forehead to the concrete, willing it to pass. Willing myself to absorb the essence. To metabolize it. Take it in. Fucking *process* it so that I could get on with the business of my life—and not the business of living the life of every Hell Beast I killed.

Gravel crunched in the distance, and my head snapped up, the adrenaline rush compartmentalizing my emotions in a way that blunt mental force could never have managed. The sun had dropped below the rooftops, and now shadows consumed the alley. A figure stood in the dim light, his identity enshrouded by the gloom.

I squinted, fighting the urge to run as I tried to get a look at his face. I couldn't make out anything. At least not until he took a step forward. Then I saw the glint of his knife, cold and malicious as it shimmered in the light from nearby streetlights.

I screamed, then yanked my sleeve up and slapped my hand over the symbol on my arm, desperate to rebuild the bridge and escape. I felt the tug, I saw the blackness, and then—*blam*—the handle of a flying knife knocked my hand away from my arm. Instantly, the portal fizzled and popped, and then disappeared.

It was gone. *The bridge was gone*. And though I pressed my hand again over the mark, the symbol had faded. It no longer worked.

It was done, and I was under attack.

The arm drew back then, and the blade went flying. I yelped, thrown completely off guard, then twisted my body down and to the side.

The knife missed my chest, but caught me in the shoulder,

slicing neatly through my svelte black bodysuit. At first I felt nothing, and then the pain registered—a deep burning sensation as my body processed the nature of this assault.

I bent to retrieve my attacker's knife, my shoulder aching with the movement even as I moved my other hand to the hilt of my own still-sheathed knife. Considering how fast my body now healed, I expected to be back at full capacity in no time.

Bring it on, baby.

At the end of the alley, he stepped out of shadows—a tall, thin figure dressed all in black, even his face covered. Just like me. Two anonymous warriors, ready to do battle. And since I had the whole immortality thing going, I was feeling decidedly superior. At least until I tried to grab my knife and discovered that I couldn't do it. The sensation in my arm was gone, replaced by a million red-hot pins jabbing into my nerve endings.

A burst of fear scurried up behind the hubris I'd just been spouting.

Holy shit, what is wrong with me?

The sensation spread. My chest tight with cold. My belly trembling as icy fingers moved through my body.

Poison.

He lifted a crossbow . . . Aimed . . .

And as he let the arrow fly, I forced my legs into action, my muscles screaming as I fought the subglacial temperatures that had settled into my bones.

I ran, and I kept on running, the world spinning around me, turning all sorts of interesting colors. I could no longer feel my arm or my chest. I was breathing, which I thought was a very good thing, but I had no visceral connection with that process. My lungs might be expanding, my heart might be beating, but from my perspective I was as stiff and unmoving as a mannequin.

I wasted a few precious seconds to turn and look behind me. He was there, that man in black, walking slowly toward me, his weapon at his side, ready to fire when he was in range. He wasn't hurrying, though, and I knew why. He'd infected me with a paralytic. And once my arms and legs quit pumping—once I lay helpless on the pavement—he'd pull off my mask and slide a blade into my heart.

I'd come back. That much I knew. But suddenly I was faced with a new fear—like, what would happen to me if he cut off my head? If he buried me in a pine box? If he trapped me in wet cement?

I couldn't die, but I could suffer, and right then I think I was more scared of living trapped or headless throughout eternity than I'd ever been of dying.

Move, Lily. Move your goddamned feet!

I stumbled into the street, dodging the few cars that zipped by. Horns blared, but I heard nothing, too obsessed with the picture that ran through my head over and over: the blade, dark boxes, my head. Mentally, I shuddered, though my upper body was no longer capable of such a reaction.

I thrust myself blindly in front of an oncoming car, holding my hands out in a desperate plea for it to stop.

I saw the female driver's eyes go wide, and she swerved, missing me even as she slammed on the brakes. The tips of my fingers in my right hand still moved, and I used that motion to pull open the car door, brandishing my knife.

The woman screamed, and though I couldn't speak, she figured out exactly what I wanted, stepping on the gas and thrusting us forward, her hands tight on the wheel as she shot terrified sideways glances in my direction.

As for me, I kept my eyes on the shadows, finally finding my tormentor standing in a pool of light from a single porch lamp. He turned, defeated, as the car went by.

I'd won this round, but it was a Pyrrhic victory. My body was giving out, I was in a car with a woman I'd kidnapped, and soon, I knew, I'd be meeting my foe again.

"What . . . what should I do?" the woman asked after we'd traveled a few miles down the road.

I stayed silent, my lips nonresponsive to my commands. I

craved a cell phone, but what good would it do me? I had no number for Clarence or Zane, and there was no one else I could count on.

Besides, I wouldn't be able to dial the damn thing.

The driver glanced at me, glanced at the knife, and made a hard right into a vacant lot. She opened the door with the turn and jumped out before the car had even stopped. It rolled forward, smashing into another vehicle, and slamming me forward so that I hit my head on the dash.

Immediately, a car alarm started blaring.

I tried to use my fingers to open my door, but they'd stopped functioning. There was still some life left in my legs, though, and I pushed and scooted and shoved until I fell like a lump of dead meat out of the car and onto the rough gravel and broken glass that covered the lot and now dug into my cheek and hairline.

I couldn't turn my neck, but managed with a few shoves and kicks to get my body oriented so that I could scope out the area. No one. My hijack victim had disappeared, though if I was any judge of human nature, I had a feeling she'd be back, and with the police.

I needed to get out of there, and with the last bit of strength in my legs, I scooted across the lot, ripping my oh-so-fashionable assassin costume as I aimed myself toward the edge of the lot.

This was where that extra oomph of strength really came in handy, because there was no way I could have managed this in my old life. At the same time, in my old life, there was no way I would have found myself paralyzed in a vacant lot after carjacking an innocent woman.

The lot ended at a grassy easement that sloped down to a second street. I rolled down the hill, pleased to find a smattering of tractors and bulldozers, all shut down for the night. I settled underneath a tractor, not because it seemed like an amazing hiding spot, but because my legs had finally given out.

I closed my eyes and prayed, hoping that God was keeping an eye on his nascent warrior . . . and hoping that the police would assume that a carjacker would leave the scene and not be stupid enough to camp under the nearby construction equipment.

Moments passed without a sound except for the gentle whiz of passing traffic. I closed my eyes.

Whether I died or merely slept, I didn't know. Certainly with the paralytic, my heart could have stopped. And with Zane's essence, it would have started up again.

Or, maybe I simply passed out.

I didn't know. Which, frankly, was a little freaky.

Not that I intended to dwell on the freaky. Instead, I needed to get the hell out of there.

I rolled out from under the tractor, my muscles stiff but once again fully functional. I saw no one nearby and breathed a sigh of relief. If the cops had come, they were gone now. And whoever my attacker had been, he hadn't found me.

My shoulder still ached, but a quick glance showed that the wound had healed. My clothing was ripped to shreds. I wanted a shower, but even more than that, I wanted answers.

And I knew of only one place to go to start asking questions.

THIRTY

It was past midnight by the time I reached Zane's door. I used my palm to gain entrance, then took the elevator down to the training center floor, my eyes searching for Zane even before the cage-style elevator came to a stop.

Empty.

But I knew he was there. He had to be there.

I scanned the room, finally noticing a small, unmarked door on the far side, beside a metal shelf that held white, fluffy towels. I marched to it and pushed the door open, then slid silently inside.

I was in a spare room, and Zane was there, on a metal cot, his body covered by a thin blue blanket.

I moved forward with stealth, then sat on the edge of his bed, my hand pressed flat on his naked chest, right over his heart.

His eyes flashed open, the warrior in them fading to relief when he saw me. "We've been concerned. The portal closed, but you hadn't come through. Then hours passed and you didn't check in."

"How do you stand it?" I whispered. "How do you stand knowing that you can't die but that you could suffer endlessly? That you could be hacked into bits and left for dead? But you wouldn't be. Or buried in a cement vault for hundreds or thousands of years? How do you live with that?"

I felt the sting of tears in my eyes, then the gentle press of his hand over mine.

"I live with it, *ma fleur*, because I have no choice." He sat up, revealing the rest of his bare chest and firm abdomen. The sheet fell around his hips, and I had a feeling that the rest of him was bare, too. "What has happened tonight, *chérie*?" he asked, his voice infinitely gentle.

I pointed to where the knife had sliced through my now-battered skinsuit. "I was attacked. After the assignment. Poison on the knife. Something. I'm not really sure."

At the word *poison*, he'd tensed, leaning forward to look at the now-healed wound. "Tell me," he said. "Tell exactly what happened."

I told, and watched as his eyes went hard and flat.

"They did not know the truth about you, *chérie*," he said. "But the greater truth—who you are and why you are here—*that*, they must know."

"That's what I figure, too. End me, and evil takes a holiday." I glanced sideways at him. "Then again, maybe they did know that I've sucked in your essence. Maybe they paralyzed me so that they could chop me into little immortal pieces." I shivered at the thought. That *really* creeped me out. "But I got away."

"Possible," he said, looking thoughtful. "Though it would not, I think, have been that difficult to locate you. It is after midnight now, and you left here before dark. Plenty of time to locate an unconscious warrior."

"Which is why I didn't come here to slice off *your* head," I said, giving voice to a suspicion that had been gnawing at me. His brows lifted, but I pressed on. "You would have known what to do. How to stop me for good. You would have found me, and you would have done that. But here I am. Which means you didn't sell me out."

His eyes narrowed. "Although I am pleased to be off your suspect list, I had no knowledge of where you were. The portal reveals its destination only to you."

I frowned. I hadn't realized they wouldn't know where I was.

"Beyond that," he continued, "I would like to know why you would think of me as a traitor for even a moment."

I tilted my head, but never took my eyes off his. "You're a demon. An incubus."

The hard edge to his eyes glimmered with amusement. "Am I?"

I swallowed, certain I was right, but at the same time knowing it was one hell of an accusation, especially considering whom we both worked for. But it made sense. His immortality. His intense sensuality. The way he was able to melt me with only a look.

And the way the heady power of that sensual fire now burned within me.

He was an incubus. He had to be.

He rose, the sheet dropping away to reveal his perfect, naked body. I stood firm, my knife held out, forcing myself to keep calm as he drew near. He might not have been the one who attacked me, but I couldn't fully trust him. Not knowing the truth about him.

He moved toward me, stopping his advance when his flesh touched my blade, a single drop of blood beading on that perfect caramel skin. "And what do you intend to do with that knife?"

"Isn't this what I'm supposed to do? Kill demons? Don't I at least have to try? Even against the immortal ones?"

He turned, ignoring my knife as he pulled on a pair of thin gray sweats. "You assume that is what I am," he said, moving back toward me with slow purpose. "That this sensual buzzing and humming between us comes from a dank, dark place." He'd pitched his voice low, and the thrum of my body deepened, all of my senses coming to life as he spoke.

I forced myself not to touch him, though I desperately wanted to. "Turn it off," I demanded, even though I knew that part of it now came from me. Our two natures—hot and quick and designed for pleasure—seeking each other out. Craving release.

I swallowed, my mouth gone suddenly dry. "Turn it off now."

He ignored me, coming closer still. "So quick to condemn what you do not even understand. Tell me, Lily, what is it you think an incubus is?"

"I already told you," I said. "A demon. One who draws strength and power through sex and drains the victim in the process." I glanced across the room to the cabinet that held the books I studied during breaks in physical training. "I've been doing my reading, remember?"

"You forgot the best part," he stated calmly, circling me as he spoke, his body mere inches from mine, his proximity working like static electricity and making my skin tingle. "An incubus makes love like no other. The pleasure he brings his partner is unrivaled, and his skills as a lover are unmatched."

"Back off," I demanded, my skin heating and my senses tingling.

"Ah, *chérie*. Sexuality is not about being ungodly. It depends entirely on how it is used. Pleasure?" he asked, running his fingertip lightly from my chin down my neck, and then brushing over my breasts ever so lightly. To my abject horror, I felt my nipples tighten and knew without a doubt that my panties were wet.

"Or control," he said, and before I could react, he'd cupped my ass and pulled me close, his rock-hard erection pressed against my Lycra-covered thigh. "There is a difference, no?" He released me and stepped back. I stood there, gasping for breath, the heat of this man starting a fire inside me.

"Sit," he said, nodding at the bed.

"I prefer to stand."

He shrugged. "Suit yourself." He moved and sat, and I had to wonder if I'd made a mistake. He was half naked and on a bed, and I was in a libidinal fog. Possibly not the best move on my part.

"You are right, of course. I am an incubus—or what human culture would call an incubus. But that does not make me evil, Lily. It does not make me a traitor. And it certainly does not mean that I am a demon."

"But I thought—"

"You thought that the bedtime stories were true. They are not." He reached for me, and without thinking I moved to sit beside him. "There is nothing inherently bad about those of us with sensual allure. It is only those who would control—who would use that allure for power and persuasion—who kneel at the altar of evil."

"And you?" I whispered.

His hand stroked my cheek. "Sexuality can also be a form of worship, *ma chère*. The connection, both physical and spiritual."

He sat back and drew in a deep breath. "Do not condemn me, Lily. I am not evil. Far from it. I am, in fact, much like you. Caught in the middle. We are alike, you and I, in more ways than the essence we share."

I pressed my lips together, feeling lost and foolish. As if I didn't know where good ended and evil began. Something that should be the simplest question in the world, and now it seemed unduly complicated.

"Poor Lily," Zane said, looking at me with gentle eyes. "The world is not like the stories of your youth, *n'est-ce pas*?"

"No, it's not."

"At least for you, it is simple. You hunt demons. Do not make it more complicated than it must be."

"But I'd always thought that an incubus *was* a demon—"

"Forget what you know," he said sharply. "You must let go of the old ways of thinking."

"I know! I understand. But—" I cut myself off, trying to form the thought that filled my head, demanding and yet amorphous. "Can a demon be good? You say kill them all. But are they all evil?"

The amorphous cloud in my head took form, and I concentrated on the floor, afraid Zane would see the reflection of my thoughts on my face: *Deacon.*

"A most interesting question," he said, his voice low and scholarly. If he had any clue as to the motivation behind my question, he kept it to himself. "Like all things, there is a hierarchy in the heavens, and the demons who thrived when the universe was a formless void drew back into the dark when God breathed light upon this world. The darkness shrank, shut out by the light. And the dark-dwellers—the demons—did not seek this new dimension. Not at first. Not until something new and wonderful appeared and walked there."

"Humankind," I said. "Evil came into the world along with humankind."

"For whatever reason, humans are uniquely subject to the temptations of the dark, without in fact being dark by nature. And those that dwell in the dark are uniquely tempted by humanity. And so evil crossed over. The first evil. The serpent of mythology. And once the crossing was made, the path was forged."

"Is this real or mythology?"

"If you are living it, it must be real."

I couldn't get my head around the idea of a cognizant darkness or a powerful snake that was the embodiment of evil, but I tried to go with it, because underneath the parable was the story of what I was fighting. "Go on."

"Once evil began to tempt humankind, it realized that evil could also exist *within* humans. Could merge. Could possess and influence. And with every human who took the dark inside, the dimension of evil grew larger."

"As evil spreads in the world, hell expands."

"Exactly."

"So that Goth girl. The Tri-Jal. She really was human. Just a really, really, really dark human?"

He shook his head. "The flesh became so key to the dark-dwellers that some species of demon learned to create a shell. But it is only packaging used to cross to this dimension, because a demon's true form does not blend in here, as you have seen." I nodded, thinking of the Grykon. "Evil is best able to get a grip when it is subtle. When it looks and feels like that we know best."

"So it looked like a girl, but there was no humanity inside. Not like that human who was possessed. There was still humanity in him. Just trapped inside with the demon."

"Trapped," Zane said, "and subjugated."

I stood up and wandered over toward the cabinet with the books as I considered everything he'd said. "If humans can suck in the dark, can demons suck in the light?"

He smiled. "Ah, *ma chérie*, that is the question. If a single man can expand the dimensions of hell by aligning himself with evil, can God himself not be enriched by a child of the darkness turning to face the light?"

"Can he?"

"All in nature can be good. And all can be evil. Free will, *chérie*. But each of us, human and demon, has a true nature. And very few among us are brave enough to fight it."

I took that as a qualified yes, then licked my lips, wondering what my nature was. Wondering more if it had changed when I became Alice, and if it was changing still as I absorbed the demons day after day.

"Do not question your nature, *chérie*," he said kindly. "Your heart is good."

"And you? What's your nature?"

His smile was tight. "I fight on the side of righteousness. That much, I will swear to you. Though I do pay daily for my hubris."

"Hubris?"

"In my youth, I wanted to live forever, a trait that is awarded only to the true angels and incorporeal demons. I acted rashly, trying to manifest a desire I did not truly understand and would not have wanted fulfilled had I considered the ramifications. I was punished for my foolishness." He closed his eyes, sighed deeply. "And now you share my torment."

"But that means you got what you wanted." I said, my voice a whisper. "Immortality."

"It would seem so," he said. His smile when he looked up at me was wan. "There are times when I believe that hell is the place where all your dreams come true."

"I don't understand."

"Do you know why I am down here, Lily? Down in this prison of concrete and metal?" he asked, and I realized that his voice was no longer accented. "Do you have any idea how old I am? How many lives I've had? How many places I've lived, wives I've had, years I've seen pass by as minutes?"

"I don't."

A sad smile touched his lips. "Neither do I," he said. "But it has been far too many."

"Zane—"

He lifted a hand. "No. Hear me. I have lived thousands of lifetimes, Lily, and I am tired. So tired, and I crave death. I crave the end of this life and the beginning of a new, in whatever form it may come. And yet I cannot have that which I desire. I cannot, because of my own foolish ambition. And so I have trapped myself in a nightmare of my own making."

"But what does that have to do with why you're here in the basement?"

"I made a deal. Long ago, I made a deal to train warriors. And in exchange, when the time is right, I will be granted freedom. I will be granted death." He met my eyes. "And all I have to do is stay and teach and train."

"Stay?" I repeated. "You mean you can't leave? You're not allowed to go upstairs?"

"I can," he said. "And if I do, the bargain is over." He stood, waiting for me to say something, but I didn't know what to say. "Do you know what the real hell of it is, Lily?"

I shook my head.

"I have, time and again, been tempted to ride that elevator to the street."

"But then you'd break the bargain and you'd stay immortal."

He exhaled loudly. "After so long, I fear death as much as I crave it. It is," he said with a smile, "a hideous conundrum."

I thought of him trapped down here in the basement, and realized that Zane was living my nightmare, albeit in a bigger box.

"How much longer do you have to train?"

"That depends on you, Lily. The fate of the world will be determined soon, and with it, my fate as well. The convergence," he said, a hint of dread flashing in his eyes, "it comes closer every day whether we want it to or not."

"Zane. I'm—"

"No. You of all people should not pity me. We are bound now, Lily. We share the same fate."

I frowned, disturbed.

"But enough about theology and eternity. You came tonight because you feared I acted against you. But trust me, *ma fleur*, I wish you no harm." His gaze grazed my face as I avoided looking into his eyes, afraid of what I might see there if I let Alice's sight take over. Afraid also to let him know I had the sight at all. "No, *chérie*. I would never wish you harm."

His lips closed roughly over mine, taking without asking and leaving me breathless and needy.

Needy, yes, but unwilling. Gently, I pushed him away, ignoring the desperate ache inside me begging to be sated. "No."

His eyes examined me, and I looked away, afraid my will would fail. He'd turned me on, yes. He'd fired my senses.

But at the end of the day, there was another man who filled my thoughts. A dangerous man whom I wanted in my bed, despite my better judgment.

He stepped back, increasing the distance between us. "You break my heart, *chérie*."

"Some other time, perhaps," I said. "If things are different."

"Is that a promise, *chérie*?"

I thought of the way I'd promised to always be there to protect Rose, and I had to shake my head. "I don't do promises anymore," I said, then turned away. Finally, it was time to go home.

THIRTY-ONE

I wasn't the least bit surprised to find Clarence sitting on his little stool outside my door when I arrived back a few minutes before one in the morning. What did surprise me was the present he shoved into my hand, a small box wrapped in purple paper. I took it, confused.

"Ain't no big thing," he said.

I frowned, but peeled the paper off, then tugged the lid off the box. A cell phone was inside, nestled in crumpled-up tissue paper. The phone itself was pink. With sparkles. I looked up at Clarence. "This would have come in handy earlier. Or not. Considering I couldn't move my freaking muscles."

"Company plan," he said. "Unlimited in-network calls, unlimited text messaging, unlimited e-mails. Gotta love technology."

I almost managed a smile as I shoved my key in the lock and let us inside. "Nice thought. Appreciate it. Not sure how I could have used it today—probably would have lost it in the battle—but here's the thing: I failed."

I glanced at him, expecting a pep talk. Instead, I got nothing.

"Right," I said, suddenly uncomfortable. "Anyway."

"Don't worry," he said, patting the pocket with the knife. "I ain't here for this."

"Glad to hear it."

"But don't expect platitudes, either, pet. Your failure may not have lost the war, but there's only one battle left. The big one. And everything's riding on you."

"Not that there's pressure," I muttered.

"Hey," he said, suddenly effusive. "You can do it, right? Wouldn't be here if you couldn't. You just gotta be confident."

"I am," I said automatically. Then I thought about it, and realized that I'd spoken the truth. Despite my failure with the Caller, I'd survived. More than that, I'd learned.

And I wasn't going to let evil win. I thought of Rose, and my resolve solidified even more. This time, I wasn't going to lose.

Already in the kitchen, Clarence tugged open the refrigerator, then snorted with disgust. "So how's the arm? Anything new popped?"

I shook my head, realizing that my arm would spark to life again when the Box was brought back into this dimension by a new Caller. I cringed, already anticipating the pain. Gee, it was fun being a map. Not.

"I just got home," I said. "You don't really think it'll pop again so fast, do you?"

"Time's running out before the convergence," he said. "They're gonna act fast. Probably already have another Caller on the job."

He opened the pantry and shoved things aside, peering at all the shelves. "So?"

"Huh?" It was the best I could manage.

"Keep up, Lily. Now we're moving on to the official debriefing. The poison. The guy who shot you. You wanna give me the lowdown or not?"

"I—yeah. Sure." I frowned. "Didn't Zane already tell you?"

"The basics. Now you tell me."

I did. Running him through the entire mission. "So how did they know I was there?"

"That's the question, ain't it? And we may not ever learn the answer. Coulda been a guard. Coulda been someone lying in wait to take you out. Someone who doesn't want you around."

"Who?"

"Dunno," he said, but I had a feeling he had a suspect in mind. "And we don't need to know. Right now, we just need to do the job. Time's running out. Gotta focus. Next time they won't Call the Box until the last minute. Right before the ceremony, maybe even during it. Whole thing'll be one hell of a lot harder."

"Great."

He slammed the refrigerator door shut in disgust, then started rummaging through the cabinets, finally coming away with a battered box of Hostess Twinkies. I snagged one, then ripped it open and took a bite of the preservative-heavy confection. "Why would anyone eat this?" I asked.

"If it ain't your taste, you don't have to," Clarence said, looking a bit bemused. "You only got her body, not her personality. Not her taste in food. And you don't even really got her life."

"Yeah," I said. "That's been eating at me."

"Come again?"

I rubbed my temples. "I still want to know about Alice. I need to know."

He blinked amphibian eyes. "Alice? Why?"

"What do you mean, why? Because I'm living inside her, and I don't know enough about her. She's the vessel, right? The vessel I'm stuck inside?"

"Come on, kid. We got bigger things to worry about."

"I can worry about both. Whoever killed Alice is a risk to me. To this body. They try to take Alice out again, they could fuck up the mission."

He stared me down, clearly not believing that my motive was purely mission-oriented.

"Or maybe I just need to know."

"Drop it, pet. Trust me. On that path lies madness."

I lifted my brows, and he shrugged.

"Maybe not madness, but frustration. What does it matter what the girl was like?"

"I'm trying to fake a life, here. Do you really want me wasting time trying to figure this out on my own? Time I could spend training or whacking demons?"

"Whacking?"

"Dammit, Clarence! Just tell me."

"Okay, okay." He moved the sofa and settled in. "Alice 101, here we go. Dad died of cancer. Mom fell down some stairs about five years ago. She was Egan's sister, by the way. Left her share of the bar to Alice and Rachel."

"Yeah?"

"Yup. You're a proud owner of one-quarter of the place. Apparently you come into it when you're thirty. Until then, Egan runs the bar, and your cut goes into trust." He shrugged. "Ain't no story there, pet. Not one worth telling anyway."

"It's a start," I said. "But I want more than just the surface stuff. Like what do you know about the Bloody Tongue? About how it fits in?"

He turned curious eyes on me. "Fits in to what?"

"Rachel's annoyed with me. With Alice. Said I shouldn't have gone back to the bar. That I shouldn't have gotten in with all that dark stuff again."

"Dark stuff?"

"The pub, I presume. It's got a rep. All the way back to witch trial days. And before, probably."

"Yeah, it's got a rep, all right," he said. "I don't know much more than what you get on that Haunted Boston tour, but I do know that Alice's parents dabbled in the dark arts. Her mother, primarily."

"Egan mentioned not getting along with his sister."

"There you go."

"Where?"

"Rachel musta thought Alice was gonna follow in Mom's footsteps. And if Alice was hanging with Deacon Camphire, that was a damn good bet."

"Deacon?" I was so surprised, I forgot to sing in my head, a little faux pas I immediately rectified.

"You said he was there your first night, right? Maybe he was trying to make Alice embrace her mother's beliefs. Persuade her to follow in Mommy's footsteps with him. Explore that dark world."

I shook my head, emphatic. "No, I don't think so."

"Why not?"

"I don't know," I said, looking away, afraid he'd read the truth in my eyes even before he plucked it from my head. "I—"

"And when she refused, that's when he did it."

My head snapped up. "Did what?"

"Killed her, of course."

All the blood drained from my body, and I stood there, frozen and desperate. "What?" I asked, barely managing to force the word out.

"My sources tell me that Deacon Camphire killed Alice. I told you, Lily. He's a bad one."

THIRTY-TWO

"No," I said firmly. "No. That can't be right."

Clarence cocked his head, examining me, his expression wary. "You got some special insight into the beast?"

"I—no. But he saved me. That first night at the pub. He swooped in and saved me—saved *Alice*—from the Grykon. If he wanted me dead, why would he do that?"

"Maybe because he knows that you're more than meets the eye now. Maybe because he saw an opportunity to get close to you and learn what you're up to. What you want. Who you're working for."

"No." I latched hard onto denial, clinging to it like a life raft and shouting out children's songs in my head. I wanted to process this tidbit on my own, without amphibian interference. "It doesn't make sense," I said. "How do you know this? Who's your source?"

"I got ears all over this town, kid. All over the world. Trust me when I say that I put stock in this tipster's info."

"Oh."

He examined my face. "Something you want to share, kid?"

"No. I'm just surprised. It doesn't feel like it fits." I turned away from him and walked to the window, wanting a smidgeon of privacy for my thoughts. Because I *was* surprised. Deacon killing Alice didn't fit the puzzle pieces I had in my head. If he'd killed her, wouldn't he have been surprised to see her alive and kicking? Would he have tried to save me?

Then again, maybe he had not only killed Alice, but had known that someone would be coming along to slip inside the body.

But that made sense only if he was in line with Clarence and company, and he *so* definitely wasn't.

I turned up the volume on my inner *Schoolhouse Rock* serenade as I turned the problem over. Maybe the bad guys knew that a warrior was coming, and Deacon was supposed to stop it. But if that were the case, then wouldn't he be trying to kill me rather than save me?

I frowned, wondering about the times I'd almost died. Outside the Caller's house. In the alley behind the bar, only moments after Deacon left me.

I released a shaky breath. Maybe he *had* tried to take me out.

Except that didn't feel right. Trouble was, where Deacon was concerned, I wasn't certain I could trust my own objectivity.

"Quit singing 'Conjunction Junction' and give it up," Clarence said, making me jump. "He's a demon. What do you expect? Demons lie. It comes with the job description." He dropped to the sofa and kicked his feet up on the coffee table. "Rest, meditate. Don't have a beer, since you haven't bothered with a grocery run. But relax. You got work at the pub today, and you need to go. Stay normal; stay busy. But when your shift ends, you go straight to Zane and train. From now on, that's what you do in your spare time. You got that?"

I assured him I did, and after he left, I wandered aimlessly through the apartment, trying to get my head around Clarence's revelation that Deacon had killed Alice. Could it be true? Was he really playing me for a fool?

I didn't want to believe it, but I couldn't deny the timing of the attack in the alley. Deacon had essentially told me he was dangerous, and only moments later, I'd died.

That was one hell of a coincidence.

But he'd picked the wrong woman to play games with. He'd gotten past my defenses and under my skin, and damned if I didn't want to make him pay.

How convenient that fate had given me the tools to make that dream come true. I could end the son of a bitch, and I could do it for revenge and in the name of God.

How sweet was that?

Trouble was, it didn't feel sweet at all. It felt bitter. Bitter and cold and wrong.

Not for the first time, I had to wonder if I wasn't all wrong for this job. What kind of prophecy hung the fate of the world on the shoulders of a girl like me? A fucked-up one, that was for damn sure.

My mishmash of thoughts irritated me, reminding me of just how much I didn't want Clarence to continue seeing inside my head. That meant I had two choices. I could quit trying to compartmentalize the demonic essence I took in, or I could look for this Secret Keeper that Madame Parrish had told me about. Because option number one was unacceptable, I went for door number two.

As far as I knew, a Secret Keeper was something you bought at Target, so I tried the Internet first, punching in a broad search request. When that yielded a million entirely irrelevant results, I went hog wild and added "demon" to the request.

Amazingly enough, I got a decent hit. A character in one of those role-playing games. A creature known as a Secret Keeper. I poked around and found out that in the game, the demon took in secrets from other players, shielding the secrets from the giving player's enemies. *Interesting.*

I did a few more searches, but found nothing else. Figuring that fiction often imitated life, I moved from the computer to an ancient, battered text that Clarence had given me. There was no convenient index, but I flipped pages, skimming the calligraphy-style text and getting more and more discouraged until, finally, my eyes caught the word *secret* as I was about to flip a page. I stopped, read the text carefully, then smiled broadly.

I'd found my man. Or, rather, my creature. An Alashtijard. Not a demon itself, but a demon's servant.

And to be fair, I hadn't found him; I'd only identified him.

But it was the first step. Because once I located one, I could kill it. And once I'd done that, I'd be a Secret Keeper, too.

And there was no way Clarence would get into my head then.

The thought made my smile even broader. Clarence might be my handler, and he might be one of the good guys, but I definitely didn't like him in my head. And the knowledge that there was a way to keep him out that didn't involve me losing my humanity went a long way to improving my mood.

I decided to celebrate with another preservative-laden Twinkie, and as I headed back to the kitchen, I noticed that the message light on the phone was blinking. I punched the button to play, more for the distraction than because I cared. There were eleven messages, the first making my stomach twist with guilt. *Gracie.* Her frantic voice sounded choked with tears, and I wanted to kick myself for not thinking about her. Of course she'd be worried. Even though it seemed like a hundred years ago, it had been only a day, and because Wednesday had been my day off at the pub, I hadn't seen her to reassure her. All she knew was that I'd been in a fight Tuesday night, I'd been freaked about my missing attackers, and then I'd raced the hell out of there.

I glanced at the clock, wanting to call and let her know I

was okay, but not willing to do that at almost two in the morning. I told myself she'd be just as relieved to learn I was okay at a reasonable hour, and that there was no point in waking her up. And the truth was that although I hated that I'd worried her, the fact that there was someone in this new life who did worry about me made me all warm and fuzzy.

The next message was from Brian, also worried, but not as tearful as Gracie's call. I smiled a little, sorry I'd worried them, but enjoying the warm feeling of having people who cared.

After Brian came a hang-up, and the two after were from Clarence, looking for me after the mission. Obviously, he had both talked to Zane and found me, so I deleted them.

After that, one more hang-up.

I frowned, wondering if Alice was plagued by telemarketers, or if the hang-ups were something more nefarious. In a sudden burst of technical savvy, it occurred to me to check the phone log, and as soon as I did, my stomach clenched. I knew that number.

My number.

Rose's number.

With a shaking hand, I put the phone down, remembering how I'd called just to hear her voice. She must have checked caller ID, too. And she'd decided to call back, curious. And, possibly, a little scared. Why wouldn't she be? She'd been stalked by Lucas Johnson, hadn't she? And now I'd put that fear back into her. Me, the girl who'd gone to the mat to try to protect her.

It was fucked up. All the more so because I couldn't tell her who I really was, and I couldn't really befriend her. Not if I wanted to keep her safe. But I could call her back. I could at least call as Alice and fess up to the earlier call. I could explain that I'd been looking out for her. That Lily would have wanted me to.

The plan made me feel somewhat better, and I headed toward the bedroom, figuring that snuggling under the covers with a magazine was just the ticket. I never got the chance, though, because it struck me anew that it was early Thursday morning. Otherwise known as late Wednesday night for those of us not yet in bed (or who no longer needed to bother with going to bed).

And I had a commitment for late Wednesday.

I had an appointment with Lucy and Ethel.

Damn.

I changed clothes—the ones I'd been wearing were in tatters, anyway—then rummaged in Alice's drawers until I finally found an address book with Rachel's phone number and address. No key taped conveniently in place, but on my way out the door, I thought to open the tiny drawer in that little tiled table. Five keys, each with neatly labeled tags: *Spare*, *Pub Bk Dr*, *Laundry Room*, *Noah*, and *Rachel*.

Thank you, Alice.

Fortunately for my mood, Lucy and Ethel were indeed dogs and not plants or fish. They were so excited to see me that I felt a twinge of guilt for the irritation I'd felt during the ride over, being much more inclined to sleep and brood than to play babysitter to the pets. Still, after the day I'd had, I needed some TLC, and who better to provide some anonymous comfort than a couple of fuzzy, squirmy muttlings.

The muttness of the dogs actually surprised me. Rachel struck me as the blue-blood type. The kind who would enter her dog in a show and then down a martini or three if she didn't get a ribbon. Or if she did, for that matter.

Apparently my assessment skills weren't up to par, because her apartment didn't reflect nearly the level of snobbery that her clothing suggested. Or, perhaps I was a reverse snob, making assumptions based on wardrobe and little hard evidence.

In fact, the apartment was warm and eclectic. She had a variety of candles in various shapes and sizes, but they were all black. An interesting palette, especially considering that her striking red furniture screamed color.

Above her mantel was a series of photographs showing

her selling jewelry as a child at street fairs, then smiling at the camera as she strung beads on a necklace. The middle part of her journey to fame and fortune was missing, and the time line skipped straight to Rachel holding her first corporate sales check, enlarged about a hundred times, her smile thin as the flash of the camera caught her eyes.

After that, the photos switched to pictures of family and the pub. There was even one showing the Haunted Boston tour guide with Egan, Alice, and Rachel. They were all decked out in Halloween attire, and Alice was grinning like a fiend under a gaudy witch's hat while Rachel, in similar garb, shot her little sister an exasperated look.

I couldn't help but smile. I'd aimed a similar look in Rose's direction many a time, and I had to wonder what these two had been quibbling about.

With the dogs following at my heels, I gave up my snoopiness and put out food for them, then poured myself a glass of wine while they indulged. When we'd all finished our snacks, I found their leashes hanging by the front door. "Come on, girls. Let's go do your business."

I'd noticed that Rachel or her boyfriend had spread the bathroom with newspaper, but it was clean and dry. Presumably, the little girls needed out. And I definitely needed to walk.

At that hour the park across from Rachel's apartment stood empty, and that was where I headed with the dogs, letting them lead me with their churning legs and snuffling noses to all the good smells that littered the ground. They whined and tugged on their leashes, wanting to be set free, but because I didn't know if they'd come back, I kept a firm hold. I still craved my long, hot bath—I really needed some thinking time—but standing there in the dark sufficed. And as the dogs snuffled and romped and did their doggy things, I let my mind wander. My curious fate. The darkness inside me. The mystery that was Alice.

And most of all, Deacon.

As if the whisper of his name in my mind were an incantation, he appeared, little more than shadow on the far side of the park. But it was him, there was no doubt in my mind, and when he stepped into the light, what I already knew was confirmed. I could feel his eyes on me. Watching me.

And I could feel the desire in him, too, and I hated myself for returning it.

More than that, though, I felt a deep malevolence. An anger. No, a *fury*. That seemed to roll off him in waves. A rage, I realized, that matched my own.

I needed to go after him. To end this.

I needed to race to him. To draw my blade. And to sink it deep into his heart.

He'd killed Alice. He'd betrayed me.

Worse than that, he'd played me.

He must have; everything I'd learned pointed toward him.

Everything except the way I felt in my gut.

I shook it off. Told myself that I wanted him dead.

But I didn't go; I didn't run.

I had the dogs, after all.

But as I stood there, my stomach in knots and my hands sweaty, I couldn't be sure whether I was staying put because of the dogs, or because of me.

THIRTY-THREE

Rose had already left for school when I called the next morning, but Gracie snatched up her phone on the second ring and gushed with such relief that I agreed to meet her for a late breakfast at Dino's before our lunchtime shift at the pub.

I found her in a back booth, already sucking down coffee. Her blue eyes brightened when she saw me, and she raised a hand, waving me over. She was up and in my arms before I could fend her off, her hug so tight I felt smothered. And loved.

"Hey," I said. "I'm alive. I'm fine. And I'm really, really sorry."

"What the hell happened to you? I mean, you were *dead*. They had to use those shocker things! You should have gone to a hospital, Alice. What the *hell* were you thinking?"

"I wasn't. I just ran."

She flopped back in her seat, then squinted as she looked at me. "From what?"

The waitress wandered over, saving me from answering.

Instead, I ordered a short stack of chocolate chip pancakes and lots of coffee. Comfort food. Gracie did the same, and as soon as the waitress left, she jumped back on me. "What were you running from?"

"To," I said, because there was no escape from the interrogation. "I was running to something."

"All right. To what?"

"Gracie . . ."

"No." She sat up straighter, looking remarkably firm for such a little blond thing. "Something's up with you. You've been weird for days. Don't you dare deny it."

"I'm not denying," I said, remarkably relieved to share something—anything—with someone outside the weirdness parameter of my life.

"Then what is it? What's going on?"

"I can't say. Really," I added, when she opened her mouth to object. "But it helps just knowing you care."

"I do." Her teeth scraped over her lower lip. "I won't pry. I swear. But tell me one thing. Are you in trouble?"

I shook my head. "No. I promise. But I guess you could say I'm trying to stop trouble."

She cocked her head, obviously trying to figure something out. "And Deacon? Is he part of the trouble?"

I tensed, and tried hard not to show it. "I'd really rather not talk about him."

"Alice—"

"No. We're done. Moving on to you. Anything happen yesterday with the job?"

At my question, her mood completely changed, going from pensive and suspicious to open and excited. "I got it," she said with a wild, exuberant laugh. "I got the job!" She grabbed my hands and looked me straight in the eyes. And, because I wasn't thinking about it, I found myself looking back.

That was a big mistake. A fact I realized when the world around us seemed to drop away. I heard Gracie gasp, felt her hands tighten on mine, and though I wanted to look away or let go, I couldn't. I was stuck. Right there inside the vision. Right there, with Gracie.

We were falling. Screaming. Thrust into a dark pit. A candlestick stood tall under a row of familiar symbols. And in the center, a single female figure, wearing a white silk nightgown and tied spread-eagled to a stone table.

"Alice!"

I blinked, jerking my hands free of hers.

"Oh my God," she said, her eyes wide. "What the hell was that?"

But I could only stare at her, trembling with the memory of how I'd awakened, trapped in a room just like that. Strapped down, just like that.

"Alice! Alice!" Gracie's voice shook with fear. "What the hell? That girl. That was—" She broke off, shivering. "What was that? What's going on? You saw it, too, right?" Her eyes were wide, freaked, and I knew just how she felt.

I couldn't afford to be freaked now, though, and so I drew in a breath and tried to quash the memories. *Calm,* I thought. *Control.* Those were my buzzwords now.

"I get these visions," I said, forcing my voice to remain steady. "Not often, but sometimes." I shrugged, pretending nonchalance. "It's weird, but I've gotten used to them."

"You told me before, remember?" Another shiver rippled through her. "But I never had any idea they were like that."

"Yeah. They can be unnerving." I managed a smile, absurdly grateful that Alice had shared the visions with Gracie. I had a feeling her advance preparation was the only reason Gracie hadn't run screaming from the restaurant. Even with warning, I could tell she was freaked, though she was trying to put on a good show. Probably she'd told Alice that the visions were no big deal, and she didn't think Alice was weird for having them. Now poor Gracie was getting the chance to put her money where her mouth was.

She gnawed on her lower lip and eyed me warily, slightly calmer now. "Are they, like, what? Predictions?"

"Sometimes," I admitted, and saw the fear flicker in her eyes. "And sometimes they're more like dreams. You know, you have to interpret what it means."

"And this one?"

"Dunno. Not really." I still didn't know how the visions worked, but maybe touching Gracie had triggered a memory in the body I now occupied. A memory of the sacrificial ceremony. A memory that, if I was lucky, could help me find Alice's killer.

"You're not telling me everything," she accused.

I started to deny it, but didn't see the point. "You're right," I said. "I'm not. And you were right about the other day, too. When you said I was distracted."

"Can I help?" she asked, though she looked like she'd much rather walk across hot coals.

"No way," I said, probably faster than I should have.

"You're gonna get yourself hurt," she said. "Killed, or worse. Aren't you?" Tears welled in her eyes. "If there's something freaky going on, Alice, you need to call the cops."

"Don't worry. I've got help."

"Deacon?"

"No," I said, probably too sharply. "Stay away from him, Gracie." I still didn't know why he killed Alice—and I still hoped that Clarence's source was wrong—but I wasn't taking any chances with my friend's life. "For that matter, stay away from the pub. When's your new job start?"

"Um, tomorrow. I know it's horrible of me not to give Egan a full two weeks, but it's okay, don't you think? Especially since the pub's gonna be closed tomorrow anyway."

"It is?"

"Yeah, remember? Oh, that's right. You have Wednesdays off."

"Why's he shutting down on a Friday?"

"Plumbing. They have to rip out some plumbing in the bathrooms. Egan's really pissed, but I guess it's all about health codes and stuff." She wrinkled her nose. "At any rate, it sounds nasty. But that should make it okay, right? I mean, that's almost like giving an extra day's notice, isn't it?"

"Totally. And I'll work an extra shift if Egan needs the help. Don't worry about it."

She rubbed her arms. "Hard not to," she said, and I knew we weren't talking about the job.

I shrugged, but had to agree. And the way I figured it, Gracie couldn't have picked a better time to have found a new job and gotten the hell away from a pub whose owners throughout history had made a point to advertise their dark allegiances.

In fact, maybe this was the reason Alice had pushed Gracie toward this new job. For that matter, I saw absolutely no reason for Gracie to go back to the demon-overrun pub. Gracie, however, insisted on following etiquette and giving Egan her notice in person. I didn't like it—I had no proof, but I did have a sick feeling that one of the bar patrons was behind both Alice's death and Egan's troubled telephone call. And if scary, creepy things were going down at the pub, I wanted the only friend I now had someplace far, far away.

Because I couldn't explain any of that to her, we walked to the pub together.

Egan looked up as we entered, then went back to polishing the brass on the bar. The place was mostly empty, just a few diehards nursing pints. A little closer to lunch, and the crowds would start to trickle in. I almost welcomed it. Juggling beers and food would at least clear my mind. Maybe if I could stop thinking about it for a second, an answer would manage to take root in the muck that was my brain.

I watched Gracie push through the doors to the kitchen, and as I hurried to catch up, Egan waved me over. "For Tank and Leon," he said, drawing two pints of Guinness.

"I'm not on yet."

"Alice."

"Fine. Whatever." I took the tray, searching the bar until I found Leon, the guy Deacon had thrown across the room. I assumed his companion, a big fellow with an acne-scarred face, was Tank. He looked somewhat familiar, but try as I might, I couldn't place the face.

I slid the pints onto the table, shifting my weight toward the door and trying to signal with body language that even though I was standing there holding beer, I wasn't really on duty yet.

"You back," Tank said in a voice like acid on nails. "Missed you, we did." His smile displayed of a row of rotten teeth.

"I was sick," I said, feeling my breakfast curdle in my stomach.

"Egan said." He looked me up and down. "Better now?"

"Great." I managed a watery smile, then hooked my thumb toward the back. "I should probably—"

"Alice not so friendly today. Got you something on your mind?"

I shook my head. "Not really."

His eyes narrowed. "Thought we were buds."

Well, shit. "You're right. I've got stuff on my mind."

He cocked his head, his expression all but asking, *Well?*

"Lucy," I said, hoping Alice had shared personal details. "She barfed all over the carpet."

"Heh," he said. "Bet Rachel not happy."

"Not at all." I tried the thumb trick again. "Sorry I'm such a spaz. But I'm late, and—"

I took a step away.

"Hey!"

I stopped, turned back.

He tapped his cheek with his index finger, decayed teeth flashing a bone-chilling grin.

I swallowed, then kissed my fingertips and pressed them to his cheek. "Time for me to go on duty," I said, then winked.

And then I walked away, holding my breath and looking straight ahead until the kitchen doors swung shut behind me.

Fortunately, the afternoon was busy enough that I didn't have any time to think about Tank and his scary teeth.

I'd pulled a short shift, filling in for Trish, who'd taken the day off to spend time with a relative who was in town from Nevada or Arizona or some other state with heat and horses. I was grateful for the reduced hours today. After all, I had a busy evening planned.

At fifteen minutes to the end of my shift, I started doing my side work, irritated to see that not only did I need to cut up some lemons, but there was only one lonely lemon in the fridge behind the bar. I looked around for Gracie, finding her near the table where Tank had been earlier. I didn't remember him clearing out his tab, but he was gone now, and good riddance, too.

Gracie caught my eye, and I held up the last lemon, then signaled toward the kitchen. She nodded, and I headed back, leaving the front to Gracie because Egan had disappeared to the stockroom fifteen minutes ago and still hadn't returned.

"Lemons," I said, as I entered the kitchen.

Caleb shook his head. "Downstairs. I used the last of 'em this morning and haven't had time to refill."

"Dammit, Caleb . . ."

The bear of a man only grunted and tossed me the key to the walk-in. "Grab me another gallon of coleslaw while you're down there."

"Only if you're nice."

My black sneakers made next to no noise on the stone stairs leading down to the basement. Not that I was trying to be Stealth Girl, but I have to admit that even only a few days into the job, the idea of arriving in a room unannounced had become second nature. A trait for which I was grateful when I heard the voices down below.

I edged to the side of the stairs, then folded myself into an alcove, drawing in a breath as if that would make me blend in with the stone and shadows. One hesitant step back up, but then I stopped. My conscience poked at me, but not much. Not when the form of the words started to settle in my head and I recognized the voice. Tank. And he was talking with Egan.

"—haven't got choice, Egan. The game, you know."

"I already played that game."

"Goods didn't work. You got paid. How that fair?"

I frowned, trying to follow the conversation. What goods? Drugs, perhaps? I'd done enough deals on my own to know that purity in drugs on the street was dodgy at best. And hadn't Rachel mentioned the bar's financial troubles? If Egan had gotten into dealing in order to up the cash flow of the bar . . .

"I gave you exactly what you asked for. How is it my fault if it didn't work? I did what you—"

"You question me?"

"Of course not. But—"

"You gonna return money?"

"I don't have—"

"But you can get?"

"Yeah, yeah. I know just where to get."

"Friday. Sunrise. You deliver, or you pay."

Tank stormed out, and though I knew I was well hidden, my heart pounded wildly in my chest.

Friday.

Tomorrow.

I didn't know what was going to go down, but I damn well intended to be there to find out.

THIRTY-FOUR

I vacillated between action and inaction, then finally decided to act like the badass I was supposed to be, suck up my courage, and ask Egan if anything was wrong. He looked up at me over the shot of tequila he was pouring at the bar, his doughy face forming into suspicious lines. "What? What could be wrong? Other than Gracie up and giving her notice. Or not giving it. Last day's today, and now she tells me. You know about this?"

I shook my head and hoped I looked perplexed. "So that's all that's bothering you?"

"What? That ain't enough?"

I debated a second, and then bit the bullet. Hard. "I overheard you and Tank. He sounded really pissed. And . . . well, it sounded like he was dragging you into something illegal." Egan hadn't seemed the type to run a drug shop under the table, but the truth was, nothing surprised me anymore. Not that I intended to accuse Alice's uncle. Better to play the *Are you getting sucked into something?* card and see if I couldn't get him to spill at least part of the truth. "I thought maybe you needed help."

For a moment he looked scared, then confused. Then, to my surprise, he burst out laughing. "Well, holy shit, girl, I guess that would sound like we were slipping a little heroin to the local populace. And Tank's sure as hell got the look about him, doesn't he?"

I blinked, taken aback by his forthrightness.

"For all I know, the bastard does deal," Egan went on, as if the thought just occurred to him. "But not here," he said, turning a gimlet eye on me. "I don't hold with that, and you darn well know it."

"Well, sure," I said, as if I did know it. "So it wasn't drugs. Was it, you know, dark stuff?"

Egan gave me a tight little shake of the head. "You know better than that, girl."

I nodded. Clarence had specifically told me that Egan had fought with Alice's mom over her involvement with the dark arts. A scary reputation for the bar was apparently okay with him. True scariness crossed the line.

"Well, then, what is it? What's going on?"

The amused expression was back, and he chuckled as he passed the tray of drinks off to Gracie, pointedly not looking at her. "Bastard's complaining the car I sold him doesn't work. That ancient Buick? The puke-green one? Worked fine when he picked it up, but he's saying I either return the money or get him another car, and . . ." He trailed off with a shrug.

"That's it? A car? That's what's bugging you?"

"You're the one said I looked like something was wrong. Me, I'm just annoyed I got to deal with a prick like that."

It made sense, and because I saw the truth in his eyes, I felt foolish. At least I did until he smiled at me. "I'm glad you came back to work here, Alice. It's nice to have family who cares."

"Yeah," I said, meaning it. "It is."

I leaned over the bar and gave him a quick kiss on the cheek. "I'm late. Gotta run."

I was late, too. I was supposed to be at Zane's, training hard and killing demons in the ring. Zane said it was to build both my confidence and my skill, but I knew there was another reason. They wanted me primed on demon essence. He and Clarence might give lip service to the whole "compartmentalize" thing, but I knew they wanted to keep me in a killing frame of mind. And how better to get there than to take a little hit of demon?

Cynical? Perhaps.

Maybe that was the result of an overload of demon kills, too.

I didn't know.

All I knew was that I didn't need the dark essence. Not today.

Today I could get to that dark place all on my own. Because today, I was going to my own burial.

I didn't go to the service itself. Didn't want to hear them eulogize me. Didn't want to see how sparse the turnout within the church was.

And I didn't want to feel like a hypocrite because my family had brought my body into a place of worship.

I'd lost my faith a long time ago, burying it with my mother. There was no heaven, I'd thought. No hell. And there was certainly no God looking out for us.

There was nothing but emptiness.

Now I knew better. But it wasn't faith that had brought me around; it was hard, cold reality. I knew there were monsters in the dark. And, yeah, I was scared. Not for me with my badass skills, but for people like Rose who'd had their faith snuffed by monsters like Johnson and needed to find their way back into the light before the dark pulled them down.

The small cluster of mourners at the grave site was already breaking up when I arrived. I hung back, out of place despite being the one person who truly belonged there. At first, I could only see Rose's back. But then she turned, and I saw the way the skin clung to her bones like a wraith, and I knew she wasn't eating. My death and her memories were sucking the life from her. Her hair hung limp, and even at this distance, I could see that her once-beautiful eyes were flat and dull.

I told myself that it had been less than a week since I'd died, and that time would surely heal her. But I knew that was a lie. I wanted to help. Wanted to do something more tangible than saving the whole world.

I wanted to go to my sister, but at the same time I knew that I shouldn't. And right then, responsibility was warring with desire. I held back, waiting to see which aspect of me won the battle.

From across the manicured lawn, I watched as Rose looked blankly at the few people who came up to offer condolences. Jeremy from the video store was there, too, and that tiny connection almost made me smile. Or it did until my stepfather stumbled next to Rose, useless with grief and alcohol.

My stomach clenched, my blood cold. I'd promised I'd take care of her, but now, standing in a cemetery in the Flats, that promise seemed cold and hollow. How could I have been so egotistical to swear to deliver something that could never be? I couldn't take care of her. I'd tried. I'd done my damnedest.

And in the end, that was what it had made us both: damned. Me with the stain of sin, and Rose with the fears that kept her locked inside after dark, a prisoner in her own home, tormented by her memories, her fears, and her sister's unkept promises.

"Rose." The word came out a whisper, forced past my lips by the tears that filled my throat. There was no way she could have heard me, but still she turned, and I saw her eyes widen. I froze, staying right there as she leaned over and whispered something to Joe, then marched to me.

I stayed put, despite Clarence's warning echoing in my ear.

"Why have you been following me?"

The question, so unexpected, brought me up short. "I haven't. I mean, I waited for you that one time at school. But—"

"But nothing. You stood there. And you watched. I saw you. And just because I haven't seen you the rest of the times doesn't mean I don't know you're there. I can feel your eyes. I can see you in the shadows. You think I don't know. You think I'm stupid, but I'm not."

"I'm not following you," I said, fear wriggling up my spine. "I swear it." Someone was, though. Someone was stalking my sister, and the thought of that made me go weak in the knees. I needed to be here, protecting my sister, not off fighting amorphous evil with a capital E.

She was still eyeing me warily, and I sighed, the sudden burst of exasperation with my little sister so familiar it warmed me. "If I were sneaking around following you, would I be standing out in the open at your sister's funeral?"

She thought about that, pouted a little, then shook her head. "Guess not," she said, rubbing the toe of her polished black shoe into the damp grass. "So why are you here?"

"To tell you that I meant it. What I said before. Lily was my friend, and I know she'd never have left you on purpose."

She nodded, eyes brimming with tears as she looked at me. Then her gaze dipped down and she frowned, her eyes narrowing as she reached toward me. I lifted my hand, unconsciously feeling for the locket I'd tucked inside my shirt. But it wasn't inside. It was hanging out. Right where Rose could see it.

I forced myself not to jump when her fingers touched it. And when she opened it, I heard a little gasp.

"She gave it to me," I said. "The night she—well, she gave it to me for safekeeping."

Rose simply stood there, and I couldn't tell if she'd bought my line of bullshit.

I reached up for the clasp. "Do you want it?"

She shook her head. "No. She wanted you to have it." Her

head tilted to the side, as if she were trying to figure me out. "You really are her friend."

"Yeah. I told you so. And I meant what I said. If you need something—anything—you can call me. Here. I've got a cell phone now." I still wore black jeans and a black T-shirt under the red leather coat. Probably not the most respectful of outfits, but I hadn't had time to change. Plus, I didn't figure a skirt would ride well on the bike.

I rummaged through all my pockets, but couldn't come up with paper or a pen. Rose hesitated a moment, then opened a small black purse that I recognized as once belonging to our mother. She passed me a pad of paper and a ballpoint, and I jotted down the name of the pub along with my number and my name, remembering to write "Alice" rather than "Lily." It was, I realized, getting easier and easier to think of myself as Alice.

"I mean it," I said, passing the paper back. "You need anything at all, you call." Clarence wouldn't be happy about that, but I didn't give a flip. If someone was following Rose, I figured she might already be in danger. No way was I staying away knowing someone was watching her.

She hesitated, then managed the briefest of smiles, the first one I'd seen touch her face in a long, long time. "All right," she said, tucking my number back into her purse. "Thanks." She looked back over her shoulder at Joe. "I gotta go."

She turned without another word and left me standing there, alone at my own funeral.

Honestly, now that I thought about it, the whole thing was more than a little creepy.

I shook the thought out of my head as I started to head in the opposite direction, my mind mulling over the question of who was following her. Clarence? To make sure I wasn't sneaking over to the Flats to visit? But that possibility didn't ring true, a fact that disappointed me. If it were him, at least I would have an answer. And an answer was better than this cold, vague fear that Rose was still in danger.

"Sad day for that girl."

I spun around and found myself looking into Deacon's black eyes.

My hand went to the inside pocket of my coat, where I'd stashed my knife. "Stay the fuck away from her."

His head tilted to the side. "She's important to you."

"Yes," I said. I couldn't bear to deny it out loud. And the truth was, he already knew it. I thought about what Rose had said, then remembered how I'd seen Deacon in the distance when I'd been walking the dogs. "You've been following me."

"Yes," he said simply. No excuses. Just confidence. And a hint of danger. Yeah, well, I could be dangerous, too.

"And the girl? You following her, too?"

"Why would I do that?"

"You tell me."

He came another step closer, and I felt that catch in my gut. A keening, visceral need that unnerved me. *She's mine,* he'd told the boy on the dance floor. And damned if right then I didn't think it was true.

Was that why I was so hesitant to believe the worst of him? I told myself it wasn't; I wasn't so shallow as to be controlled by lust. At least, I didn't want to think of myself that way.

No, I was hesitant because I feared that Clarence was being fed bad information and that either intentionally or foolishly someone was trying to set Deacon up to take the fall for Alice.

I couldn't be sure, though. Not about that.

But I did know that he was dangerous.

About *that*, I had no doubts.

"Why are you here?" I asked, walking away from the grave toward the far parking lot where I'd left my bike.

"Apparently I'm following you," he said easily. "So perhaps the real question is, why are you here?"

"I don't owe you an explanation."

"And I don't need one. It's clear enough, *Lily*, why you came."

He never raised his voice. Never let victory flash in his

eyes. But he'd won, and I staggered back before I caught myself. Only an instant. One small misstep. But he would have noticed. I had a feeling Deacon noticed pretty much everything.

"I don't know what you're talking about," I said, trying to salvage something.

"Don't play games," he said, his voice taking on a harsh edge. "At least do us both that favor."

I weighed my options and ruled out killing him. I could run. I could lie. But in the end, he knew who I was. Body and soul. And there was no point holding on to my secret. Not if I could use disclosure as a bargaining chip.

We were near a marble mausoleum, now burnished in the orange light of the setting sun. I stopped, then turned to face him. "How did you learn my name?"

Something dark burned in his eyes, like faith dying. "You're mine, remember?" His words were bitter. "We both saw it. Saw the lilies in the blood. Entwined there, you and I."

I shook my head. "Tidy story, but it's not true. Nobody would pull a name from that."

"Maybe not. But add in the tattoo on your back—the artist was happy to discuss it that afternoon, especially when I slipped him a fifty, by the way. Can I see it? By his description it must be quite a treasure."

"Bite me."

"I'd be happy to."

God, he was smooth. So smooth I wasn't sure if I wanted to jump him or kick him.

What I did know was that I wasn't afraid of him. And that in and of itself scared me a little. Because he was dangerous, right? And that's how dangerous things get close to you. They put you at ease. They sneak in.

I knew all that, and Deacon was creeping closer and closer.

"A tattoo's hardly proof of anything," I whispered, desperate to keep control.

He pressed his hand to my waist, and though I flinched, I

didn't push it away. Neither, however, did I look in his eyes. I didn't want a reminder of the evil inside him. Not now. Not when the danger already arcing between us was sending up enough sparks to light Boston for a week.

He drew closer, the hand easing under my coat to the small of my back. He pressed against it, but the tattoo had healed, and I felt no pain, nothing except the warmth of his hand. "A white lily," he said, "with droplets of blood. And underneath, in a delicate hand, a name written out—*Lily*."

We were hip to hip now, and my body sang with arousal. He was hard against me, and though I knew I shouldn't, I wanted him desperately.

"Not hard to figure out the rest. To search death records. To find a young woman dead, her body being buried today."

I felt the tears sting my eyes, foolish because I wasn't really dead. Or maybe I was.

"Lily." The whisper of his breath against my ear sent sparks ricocheting through me, and I had to force myself to keep my hand tight around my knife. I could play dangerous games, but I couldn't lose control.

"Big jump from a tattoo to a funeral," I whispered, glancing up at his face. My gaze skimmed over his eyes, and I felt the jolt of the vision. I forced myself to look away, to break that connection. I didn't want to go there. Not now. Not with him.

"Not really," he said, and if he had felt the vision coming on, he didn't show it. "I knew something had changed, after all. You're not the Alice I used to know. Alice didn't heat my blood the way you do. I didn't want to slam Alice against a wall and thrust myself deep inside her." His voice was rough with need as he slid his hand between my thighs. I trembled, as much from his words as his touch. "And I didn't want to toss her down on a bed and pleasure every inch of her until she came for me."

"Don't," I said, as his finger teased the skin above the waistband of my jeans. "Don't play me like this. It won't work."

"What won't work?" He took my hand, brought one finger to his lips, and suckled the tip.

"You're not going to distract me," I said, ignoring all the evidence to the contrary.

"Is that so? It seems to be working so far."

It was the confidence in his voice that jerked me out of the haze of lust. I pulled away, feeling the hard wall of the mausoleum behind me. "Word on the street is you killed Alice," I said, then watched his face for the shock of accusation or the acceptance of truth.

I saw neither. Instead, he looked pensive. He took a step back, increasing the distance between us. "I suppose that's fair," he said. "After all, her blood is on my hands."

A lick of fear flicked through me. "What do you mean? You killed her?"

"Did I take her life?" I saw the restrained anger at the accusation, held back by the tightest control. "Of course not. But you should know that better than anyone, shouldn't you?"

I blinked, confused. "What do you mean?"

"You tell me, Lily," he said. "You're the one in her body."

THIRTY-FIVE

"You think *I* killed her? Are you crazy?"

"Not at the moment, no."

"I didn't want this," I said, smacking him back with the palms of my hands so that I could get by. I spun around, fueled by fury. "I *died*, you son of a bitch, and then I wake up in some other girl's body and I learn that she was murdered. She's gone and I'm here, and there's not a minute goes by that I don't feel pretty goddamned guilty about that. But it wasn't my fault. It wasn't my idea. And when I find out who killed her, I swear to you I will rip their heart out and shove it down their throat."

I drew in a breath, staggered by my own wrath. And, yes, I knew it was fueled in part by the demons within me surfacing, their inherent rage egging me on. I could feel the beasts within crying to get out. To take their rage out on Deacon, and damn the truth to hell.

But it wasn't his fault. He hadn't killed Alice—I was certain of that now.

"I wouldn't have hurt her," I said. "I don't care whether you believe me or not. But I wouldn't have hurt that girl."

"I do believe you," he said, and I could hear the relief in his voice. "I thought I was wrong. That they were tricking me again. That somehow I'd lost my grip and sunk back into—" He cut himself off with a shake of his head. His eyes had hardened with the memory, but when they looked at me again, they were soft. "My Lily."

He took my hand, pulling me close, bringing my insides alive with need. I clung to him, the sharp edge of my earlier rage replaced by a knife-edge of lust. I needed him. Craved him.

"What is this?" I whispered. "What is this between us?"

"I don't know," he murmured, stroking my hair, my face. As if he couldn't get enough of me. As if breaking the connection between us would break him, too. "I only know that I saw you, Lily. I saw you, and I knew that you were the key to my redemption."

I eased back, searching his face, not certain that was a responsibility I wanted to shoulder. "Saw?"

"A vision," he said. "Months ago. I thought it was Alice I saw, but I understand now that it was you. We were fighting, side by side, and I knew that we would win, because we had to. *I* had to. If we failed, we would both be damned, and the world as well."

"I don't understand."

He turned away, not looking at me. "There are things I've done. Things I'm not proud of. Unforgivable things." The pain in his voice raked over me like sandpaper, and I wanted to cry. He drew in a breath and turned back. "But this—if I can do this—then I will have my redemption."

"But do what?"

"Seal shut the Ninth Gate to Hell."

I gasped, and as I did, he searched my face.

"That's why you're here, too, isn't it? Why you're in her body. You're here to seal that gate."

I nodded. "I don't know why it's her body I got thrown into. I swear I don't. But, yeah. That's what I'm trying to do."

"Let me help you, Lily. It's what I'm supposed to do."

I took his hand, the idea of fighting with someone at my side exciting me, especially after being told I was destined to fight alone. And yet how could he help? Clarence would never trust him. And like it or not, there was that whole prophecy thing. I was a solo act.

Even so, I couldn't deny that it was nice to have someone who knew my secret. Nice to have a bit of the loneliness lift.

I licked my lips, trying to get my head around this new development. Finally, I cupped my palm against his cheek and met his eyes. "Let me see," I said. "Let me see what you saw."

But before I could slide into the vision, he jerked free. "No."

"Deacon."

"No." Rage colored his voice, cold and dark. "I told you I seek redemption," he growled. "I have done things—horrible things. Things I won't share." He stepped back so that there was no contact between us and met my eyes. "You've seen part, but you've hardly seen the worst. I won't take you there now. And I sure as hell won't go there with you."

I wanted to cry for the pain I saw in his eyes. I understood the desire to escape your past, and I knew more than I wanted about doing things you regretted. But I still needed to know. "I have to know you're telling me the truth."

"You're going to have to take me on faith, Lily," he said. He moved toward me again and pressed his hand over my heart. "You're mine," he said. "And you know it."

"Deacon." He befuddled me, and that was not a good place to be. But underneath the confusion and the questions, I knew that he was right. We were linked, he and I. And right then, with him standing so close, I wanted that link to be more than metaphorical.

"I can feel the quickening of your pulse," he said. "And I can see the flush on your skin." He moved closer, his lips grazing my hair as he spoke. "You want me," he said. "And if that's the first step toward trust, then so be it. I'll take what I can now, but in the end I will have all of you."

I swallowed, my mouth suddenly dry and my mind searching for a response. The sharp ring of my cell phone saved me from replying. Thinking of Rose, I grabbed for it, disappointed when I heard Clarence's voice. "Zane's. Now." And then he was gone.

I frowned at the phone, then frowned at Deacon beside me. I wanted to take him with me—wanted him to fight at my side—and the fact that that was forbidden frustrated me.

"I don't like to see you frown," Deacon said, then kissed me so hard and so unexpectedly that my phone tumbled from my fingers in surprise. When he broke the kiss, his dark eyes smoldering, he gave me a small, knowing smile. Then he bent down to retrieve my phone, his dark hair shifting as it grazed the back of his neck.

I blinked, certain I couldn't have seen what I'd thought. I dropped down onto my knees and pressed my hands over his, stopping him from standing again. He looked at my face, and the soft expression faded to hard lines and angles. "What?"

"Your neck," I said. "What do you have on the back of your neck?"

I saw the truth in his eyes, even before I leaned sideways to look.

"No," he said.

But fear and fury were on my side, as well as my newly acquired preternatural strength. I flipped him over and straddled him just long enough to push his hair aside. Then I leaped up, certain the fear and loathing would consume me.

"A *Tri-Jal*? You're a fucking *Tri-Jal*?"

"Lily, calm down."

But there was no calming down. Not from that. He had the mark. The serpent tattoo. Zane had warned me that I'd meet one again one day. The feral demons. The worst of the worst. Attack dogs for their master, only some of which managed to assimilate in our world.

Deacon, I'd say, had done a damn fine job assimilating.

"Let me explain," he said as I lunged back down on him, the tip of my knife pressed to his heart.

"Just tell me the truth. Am I right. Are you a *Tri-Jal*?"

"Yes."

My hand tightened on the blade, and I told myself I needed to thrust it home. I couldn't, though. I hesitated, my mind filled with doubts and questions.

He saw it and used it, tossing me over and pulling his own blade, pressing it hard against my neck. "I've told you only the truth, Lily. I haven't betrayed you."

The next thing I knew I was flying across the yard, tossed aside like he'd tossed Leon the first day I'd seen him.

I landed hard on my ass and scrambled to my feet, prepared to take off after him.

I didn't, though, because my arm began to scream in agony. I doubled over, clutching it, and watched as Deacon disappeared in the red haze of my pain.

THIRTY-SIX

The portal dumped me out at a little church a few miles from downtown Boston. The place was ancient, battered, and abandoned, with plywood across the stained glass and scaffolding barring the door. I drew in a breath, then looked up, catching a final glimpse of the portal closing above me, the way back to Clarence and Zane now blocked.

This time, at least, I was allowed to bring toys. A crossbow. A sword. And a shitload of knives. Color me a happy warrior.

I stood, then looked around to get my bearings. Yellow caution tape encircled the building, and I had to wonder if the place had been condemned, or if the demons were trying to discourage unwanted visitors.

I'm certain I qualified as the latter, but the plan hadn't worked. I wasn't discouraged at all. If anything, my toes were itching to kick demon butt.

As stealthily as possible, I eased toward the church. I found my first guard at the front doors. A bored-looking doughboy dressed in black. I lifted the crossbow, aimed, and fired, taking him out before he even knew what had happened.

The ease of it gave me a buzz, and I began to think that maybe this was possible after all.

I considered entering through those doors, but I decided to walk the perimeter and take out any other guards. I found four more, and dispatched them easily as well. So much for security. I had to presume that they believed the attack on me had succeeded. That the poison had killed me, and that heaven had no warrior who would fight to keep the gate closed.

I was feeling better and better about the mission as I edged along the side of the building next to one of the guards I'd dropped. The plywood barrier over one of the windows had come loose, and I raised myself up on my toes and peered in. A demon in the form of an ancient, weathered man stood in the center of a golden circle that had been drawn with chalk on the floor. He was dressed as a priest, and his blatant nose-thumbing of heaven and tradition hit me like a slap in the face.

Around him knelt five demons, each in black robes with hoods covering their faces.

I ran my fingers through my hair, considering my options. Six to one did not spectacular odds make. Even with me sporting some damn cool weapons and a shitload of attitude.

Fuck.

I took two deep breaths, reminding myself of why it was me standing there out outside that window. Because according to the heavenly forces watching over us, I was the anointed super soldier who could take these bastards out. Whose blood could destroy the Box that would otherwise open the gate to hell. Clearly, I had a little holy sumpin' sumpin' going on. A fact that should have bolstered my confidence to an insane degree, but instead had me waiting for the other shoe to drop. The shoe that would squash me like a tiny little bug.

How's that for confidence?

Not great, I'll admit, and I forced myself to shake off the

fear and the hesitation and to own up to the fact that I could do this. I'd proven it over and over again already, and with each assignment, my strength grew. I might not be the most elegant fighter in town, but I'd already earned my street-fighting chops, I'd taken out their security team, and I'd been busting serious demon ass in Zane's ring.

One on one, I wasn't doubting myself.

Six to one, though . . .

That was going to take more than strength and cool weapons. If I was going to survive, I was going to have to get creative. I turned a circle in the courtyard, searching for things I could use to increase my arsenal.

An iron fence surrounded the property, and though I couldn't pry the arrowlike fence toppers off, I did manage to loosen one entire post—an iron bar with a deadly pointed end that fit perfectly in my hand, its weight remarkably well-balanced for throwing.

With my makeshift javelin in my hand, I scoured the area, gathering stones from a small garden and shoving them in the pocket of my jeans. That would have to do. I dropped my coat at the foot of an angel statue, hefted the crossbow in one hand and the javelin in the other, and edged around the building toward the back entrance.

The doors were unlocked, and I pulled them open and eased inside, armed and very, very dangerous.

I found myself in an unoccupied reception hall filled with tables and chairs. At the far end of the room, I could see the doorway, through which the gate-opening ceremony was in full swing.

No time for planning—I needed to get moving.

Keeping to the walls, I circumnavigated the room until I was right by the doorway. I lifted my knife, using its polished surface as a mirror to see into the room without revealing myself.

The demon in priest garb moved within a circle, touching each of the five kneeling demons on the head with a silver stick as he mumbled some sort of incantation. I waited, knowing I needed to destroy the Box. I didn't see it yet, and I held my breath, waiting for that key piece of the ceremony to be revealed.

I didn't have long to wait.

The high priest held his hand over the middle of the circle and a finger of blue flame shot up from the ground, the golden Box suspended in the middle of it. And as the flame disappeared, the Box sank slowly to the ground.

Showtime. I sliced my palm to ready my blood, then rounded the corner. I let the iron post fly and then took my stance with the crossbow even as my makeshift javelin hit its mark, sliding through the back of one of the kneeling demons. He splayed forward as his brothers rose, and I took aim and fired, the crossbow shooting true and nailing a second son of a bitch right in the eye. He staggered, screamed, and fell to the ground as the three remaining vassals moved to cover the high priest, who now held the Box in his hand.

I could still hear him chanting behind them, and knew that not only was this not over, but I had to move faster. I reloaded the crossbow, only to have it snatched out of my hands and tossed aside by the quick *snap* of a leather whip.

I gasped, my hand stinging, and looked out to face the hardened face of one of the vassals. "You will not succeed," he said. "Our quest is righteous."

"The hell it is," I countered, reaching into my pocket for a handful of rocks. I let them fly, scattering the vassals, and drew my sword from the scabbard. With it in my right hand and my blade in my bloody left, I rushed forward. I caught one across the middle, slicing him hard across the chest, my body immediately thrumming as the scent of his blood washed over me. It spurred me on, and I stabbed another through the heart with my blade. I owned that kill, and the strength of the act flooded through me like strong wine.

The one still standing remained in front of his master, a ceremonial knife held out as a weapon. But I was ready for him, willing to cut him across at the torso if that was what it took to get to the master. To destroy him and the Box.

I drew the sword back and put all my power into it. I lunged—and then my body spasmed with pain. The sword and blade tumbled from my hand, and I looked down to see the neat hole in the front of my shirt, the blood almost invisible against the black fabric.

I looked up to see the priest I'd sliced through the chest drop his arm as if weighted. And I had time for only one coherent thought before I dropped to the ground: *Gun.*

THIRTY-SEVEN

Blackness.

Silence.

And then something.

Pinpricks of light.

Hints of speech.

A babble. Voices. Nonsense.

An incantation.

Reality rushed back at me—everything. The demons. The ceremony. The gun.

And, of course, the gates of hell.

I kept my eyes closed and took stock of my situation. I was lying on something cold and hard. The floor, I presumed, as I could hear the shuffle of what sounded like feet near my head. I felt something heavy on my belly, and though I desperately wanted to open my eyes and look, I didn't. I needed to think before I acted because I was certain—damn certain—that I had only one shot at winning this for the home team.

My biggest advantage, obviously, was that they thought I

was dead. Soon enough, though, someone would notice that my wound had healed and my heart was beating.

I listened, certain I still heard only three. The injured vassal was at my feet, his breathing shallow. The strong one stood near my right hand, the priest near my left, muttering in a language I didn't understand.

My blade was on the floor somewhere, but I still had a blade in an ankle holster. I had something heavy on my belly. And I had the element of surprise.

What I didn't have was time. And because I could afford to waste no more of it, I opened my eyes, at the same time lashing out with my right arm and knocking the vassal down as I arced my hand down and toward my ankle. I didn't make it, instead grabbing the ceremonial knife he'd dropped and smashing it into his throat. Blood spurted, coating my hand and teasing my senses.

I tossed the athame aside and reached for my own knife, wiping the vassal's blood on the leg of my jeans. I needed my blood to destroy the Box, not the blood of a demon's servant.

To my left, the priest had rushed forward instead of back, and I realized that he was going for the Box of Shankara—which, I realized with a start, was the heavy thing on my belly.

I snatched it up, rolled to the side and over the bloody and fallen vassal, and sprang to my feet as the high priest and the injured vassal both rushed me.

My hand, however, had healed, and the Box remained intact as I carried it. I stopped everyone cold by dropping it and then slamming my blade through both my palm and the middle of the Box, even as the high priest screamed in protest.

"You must not!" the vassal yelled, rushing me, his eyes focused on the Box. I jerked my knife free of my hand, ignoring the pain, then used the Box to bash his head in. Even as I did, the Box was disintegrating, falling away like bits of golden dust in my hands. An ancient relic whose time had passed.

I felt a tug of satisfaction as I turned to the high priest.

"It's over," I said. "You lose."

He stared back, his eyes clouded with cataracts and his skin wrinkled and leathery. He spoke only one word, his head going side to side even as he repeated it over and over: *No.*

I moved to him, my knife at the ready. This wasn't over yet. I wanted more. I wanted *him.*

"Please," he whispered.

"Please?" I repeated. "You think I'll let you live for *please*? You're trying to open the gates of hell."

"No!" The sound seemed not to come from the priest at all, but to echo all around me, as if the demons I'd slaughtered were screaming out in protest.

The priest gaped at me with wild, wide eyes. "No, no. You don't understand. I'm not—"

"—ever going to finish what you started," I said as one final, evocative *no* echoed through the room. I ignored it, my blade sliding into the demon priest's heart like butter. His body collapsed, his expression one of disbelief.

Yeah, well, believe it, brother.

I drew in a harsh breath as my body spasmed, the deep regret of an unfinished job filling me, along with the pure, clean certainty that no matter what, in the end, the light would prevail. The feeling warmed me, calmed me, and, frankly, confused me. Not the powerful rage that usually consumed me when I killed a demon. This time I was filled with a sense of peace. Remorse, yes. But also something else. A sensation that in the end, good would prevail.

A sensation I could only categorize as faith.

It was, I was certain, my reward. The proof that I had secured the gate. The angels, I thought, were singing.

I wanted to revel in it. To drink it in. To bathe in it like someone discovering light after hiding, lost, in a cave.

I didn't have the chance. Instead, I saw the glint of a blade coming right at my head. And then I saw the man who wielded it—*Deacon.*

And that was when I realized the source of that final *No.*

Not the demonic priest, but Deacon. Now here to seek revenge.

He caught me before I had time to react, and the tip of his blade pressed into my jugular, his arm tight around my chest. He held me intimately, almost sexually, and a hundred regrets whisked through my mind, the most tangible that I'd been a fool. That I'd trusted a demon, and a Tri-Jal at that.

"At least now I know that you don't die the ordinary way," he whispered. "It was you at the Caller's, and leaving you for dead clearly wasn't good enough. I should have cut off your head. That's not a mistake I'll make twice. I don't like being used, Lily. And I damn sure don't like being lied to."

I closed my eyes and tried to be brave. "Do it," I hissed as the blade pressed in against my neck. "At least I'll know the gates of hell will remain safely locked."

He held me tight, the blade at my throat, his forearm clutching me firmly under my breasts. Then his arm relaxed and the blade fell away.

I sucked in air, realizing I'd been holding my breath, then stumbled as he shoved me to the ground. I looked up and found my own crossbow aimed at my head.

"Move," he said, "and you die. I'll cut off your head and bury your body if I don't like what you have to say."

I stayed perfectly still, watching him. The tenseness of his body. The tendons in his hands, his arms. He was rage personified, and I swear I would not have been surprised to see him turn into a swirling tower of flame, capable of destroying anything in its path. More than that, *wanting* to destroy.

He breathed. That was all he did for at least three solid minutes—the longest minutes of my life. He breathed. And slowly—oh, so slowly—the muscles began to relax. I watched as he brought the fury under control, reining it in like one might tame a wild horse. He even shuddered, as if shaking off something horrible.

"Talk," he said, but this time control edged the anger in

his voice. "What did you mean about keeping the gates locked?"

"What did I mean?" I repeated, my voice rising with disbelief. "You lying son of a bitch, you know what I mean. We talked about it. Hell, you said you saw me in a vision. Nice touch, by the way. Cozy up to the girl and get her to share her secrets."

"Tell me," he said, his voice low and deadly. "Spell it out for me exactly why you're here."

It was ridiculous, but because he was the one holding the crossbow, I complied. "I came here to do exactly what I did. To kill your little demon buddy there who was trying to unlock the Ninth Gate to Hell. You can kill me now, but I'll die knowing that because of me he's dead, and the gate to hell is still locked tight, just like it should be. And there's not a damn thing you can do about it."

"Locked," he repeated, the crossbow dropping slightly. "*Locked?* Do you have any idea what you've done? You killed the one man who knew how to *close* the Ninth Gate to Hell. To seal it up tight. The demons are still coming, Lily. And they're coming because of you."

THIRTY-EIGHT

"No," I said, shaking my head. "No fucking way."

He held the crossbow at his side, but his grip was firm, ready to draw the weapon if need be. "He's a priest, Lily."

"A priest in hell, maybe," I said, but some of the force had left my words.

"Dammit, Lily. Are you blind? The man was human. He was a priest. A very old priest who devoted his entire life to figuring out a way to close and lock the Ninth Gate."

I fought a wave of nausea. "To close it?" This couldn't be happening. It couldn't. I'd seen the angel. I killed demons. I worked for God, dammit.

"Yes," he said, his voice both angry and exasperated. "To close it. The gate's already opened. I told you. It's been open for thousands of years, and now it looks like it'll be open a thousand more. Worse, it'll be open at the convergence. Just a few more weeks, and they're coming through. The horde is already gathering on the other side. Waiting. And now they're praising you." He stopped, and I saw fury play over his features. "You're being played, Lily. You're being played for a fool."

I licked my lips, suddenly very parched. "That can't be. I was sent. They sent me to keep the gate from opening. To prevent the fucking Apocalypse." Even as I spoke, though, I knew there was nothing behind my words. They were as hollow as the lies Clarence had fed me. Lies. All of it lies. I knew it. Could feel it flowing inside me, the truth of Deacon's words, hidden there in the essence of the dead priest.

Without Deacon, I never would have felt it. Would have assumed the warm glow of faith was merely the glow of a job well done. But now, knowing, I could dig deeper. And I could see it, could feel it.

"They played me," I whispered. "Said I was doing God's work. Saving the world." I didn't look up at Deacon. I couldn't face him.

"You're not working for heaven, Lily," Deacon said. "You're a hit man for hell."

He bent down, touched me, and I whipped my arms back, flailing wildly to get away, beating and pounding on him to no effect, even as tears streamed down my face. "Oh God, oh God, oh God." I clung to him, silently begging for comfort.

He answered the call, pulling me close and holding me tight. And right there, with the priest dead on the floor beside us, I broke down and sobbed in Deacon's arms.

He let me go on for a moment, his strong hands stroking my hair, caressing my back. But all too soon, he pulled away, taking the illusion of safety with him. "We need to leave. There's no guarantee they won't come looking for you. Leave now, they'll see the result, they'll be happy. Job well done, and Lily's probably celebrating in a bar somewhere. Stay, and—"

"I'll fucking kill them."

"Or they'll kill you," he said, his dark eyes intense.

He stepped back and held out his hand for me. I didn't take it, though I desperately wanted to lose myself in his arms again. I couldn't, though. I had to be smart now. I had to be careful. "You're a Tri-Jal demon," I said. "Why the hell should I trust you?"

I could see the fight for control in the way his eyes flashed and his jaw tightened. "Right now, I'm the only one you've got."

"That's not good enough," I said. I stood up, ignoring his hand. "You're a demon, Deacon. Just like the ones who've pulled a hell of a con on me. They gotta know I'll be pissed if I find out. And now that they're done with me, I figure my days are numbered. Kill me off when I'm done, and keep their secret safe. And, hey, isn't it convenient that a Tri-Jal demon, the baddest of the bad, shows up to take me for a little stroll?" I shook my head. "Don't think so."

I started to walk away, and he grabbed my elbow, tugged me back.

"Take your hands off me," I said. "Or else I'm looking inside. You want me to stay? Let me see what you've got locked up in there."

He let go of me. "No."

"Bye-bye." I took another step.

"Lily."

It was the pain in his voice that made me stop.

"That's not for you to see," he said. "What's inside me. What I've done. What I'm still capable of doing. That's off-limits. Always."

"So you say."

"But I am not here to harm you. I swear to you. And you've already been inside my head once. You know the path I'm on."

"Redemption," I whispered, before I could help myself.

"We need to get out of here," he said.

I hesitated, certain the smart thing to do was run from him. But I couldn't. Right or wrong, in the end, I trusted him. More or less, anyway.

"I saw some apartments a few blocks east," he said. "We can go there. Find a vacant one. Hole up. Talk."

I saw the relief in his face when I nodded agreement, and

I gathered up my blades and followed him out. I retrieved my coat by the angel, and we left the abandoned church, leaving the carnage behind. "Turn off your cell phone," he said, after we'd traveled a block. "If it's on, they can find you."

I nodded, then clicked it off. "You said you tried to kill me. After I killed the Caller. Who, by the way, was a demon. Explain that one to me. If I've been working for demons, why did they have me killing them?"

"We can talk inside."

"We can talk now," I countered. I was still iffy on the trust thing, and I wanted more before I went into a closed room with this man.

He glanced sideways at me once, then nodded. "You're right that he was a demon," he said, "but Maecruth sought redemption."

"Maecruth?"

"The Caller."

"Oh." I wasn't sure I liked knowing that he had a name. "He wanted heaven?"

Deacon shrugged and kept walking. "The concept of heaven and hell is a mortal one. Let's just say that he was drawn to the light. He wanted the chance to take it in. To fill the shadows within himself. But the dark in him was too thick. Like oil. Like what you see when a demon is slain. And the task for redemption was great."

"He had to get the Box of Shankara to the priest," I guessed.

"Right. The Box has been missing for centuries. But Father Carlton needed it for the ceremony. Maecruth managed to steal it from a demonic vault."

"Father Carlton," I repeated. "That was his name?"

"Yes."

I said a silent apology to Father Carlton. "So what I've done . . . I can make it better by finding a way to close the gate again. Or even by finding a way to destroy all the keys? Changing the locks on the door?"

"The Box of Shankara was the only key that would lock the Ninth Gate."

"Oh, God."

He looked at me sideways. "There are legends, though. Stories of a key that will lock all nine gates."

A bit of hope fluttered within me. "Where is this key?"

"No one knows."

I nodded, determined now. "Well, I'm damn sure going to find out."

I watched his face, saw his approval, and smiled.

"Here?" he asked, nodding at an apartment complex that looked to be in imminent danger of condemnation.

"Luxury living. Let's go." I led the way, but stopped on a set of cement stairs. "We'll go in, but you need to finish telling me your story. I don't like it, I leave. And I get any hint that you're scamming me, I will take you down so fast you'll be a puddle of black goo before you have time to form a cohesive thought. Got me?"

He pushed past me up the stairs. "I mean you no harm, Lily. I know it, and you know it. So don't threaten me. It isn't becoming."

I could hear the knife in his voice and swallowed. He was right. I did know it. And right then, I was glad that Deacon was on my side.

We found an empty apartment on the third floor and settled in on the floor of the empty living room. The place smelled like cigarettes and urine, and the gray carpet was probably supposed to be beige. It wasn't the Ritz, but it would do.

"Maecruth," I pressed. "How did you come to be there?"

"I believe it's my turn to ask questions."

I shook my head. "Sorry. No. I want to hear about the night you killed me. Trust me when I say I'm really interested in that. And yesterday you told me that Alice's blood was on your hands. I'm a little curious about that, too. So tell."

"I think not," he said. "I seem to be doing all the talking, which I find ironic under the circumstances. I think it's time to hear your story."

"Circumstances?" I countered. "I'm not a demon. And I'm sure as hell not a demon from the darkest depths of hell."

"But you are the one who ensured that the gate stays open, for which all the demons say a hearty thank-you."

I scowled, because he had me there, but my mind was still on what I'd said, and my eyes were on the man. This normal-looking, albeit gorgeous, man. I'd seen the temper in him, the tight control. And in his mind, I'd seen darker things still. And yet I'd seen nothing feral. Nothing wild. Nothing that had been broken down by evil and left to rot. Zane had said most Tri-Jals lost their minds and never got them back. Deacon, I realized, was even stronger than he looked.

It made him more dangerous. And it made him one hell of a strong ally.

"I died," I said, making a decision even without realizing I'd made one. "I went out to kill a son of a bitch named Lucas Johnson, and I died."

"Lucas Johnson?" he repeated, and I saw the shadow of recognition in his eyes.

"Yes." I spoke warily, afraid of what Deacon would say. Afraid I knew it even before he said it. "Oh, God. He's a demon, isn't he?"

"Yes." A muscle twitched in Deacon's jaw as he held back temper. I empathized, as I was holding back a bit of temper, too. Because I understood the truth now: I hadn't killed Johnson with an owned blade. Which meant he hadn't stayed dead.

His essence had come back. It had found a new body. And Johnson was the one stalking Rose. The one she'd told me she'd seen. Eyes on her, watching her. Following her.

Fuck. I started to climb to my feet, but Deacon took my hand and tugged me back down. "No. Tell me the rest."

"I have to go."

"Tell me," he said.

I wanted to scream and kick and punch him in the face. I wanted to run to Rose and steal her back to safety. I wanted to find Lucas Johnson and slide my blade into his heart. And

I couldn't do any of it. Not right then. I had to think. I had to plan. I had to do it right if I was going to get my revenge.

And I was going to get revenge. All this time, I'd thought Rose was safe because they'd told me a lie. They'd told me he was dead. They'd betrayed me in so many ways, but this one was the worst of all. They'd pay. That was a promise I wouldn't fail to keep.

Somehow, I'd get my revenge.

I turned and met Deacon's eyes. "They can never pay enough for this. Never suffer enough. Never hurt enough. But I'm going to make them try."

"I'll help you. I promise. But first you need to tell me the rest of it."

I drew in a breath, closed my eyes, and told him everything, laying it out in painstaking detail. Rose. Lucas Johnson. The angel. The Grykon. Clarence and Zane and the training. Even the prophecy.

"A prophecy," he said, looking puzzled. "What did it say?" he asked.

"I don't know. Clarence never told me the specific wording. Just that I was the one. The one that would close the gate. Obviously that was a big fat lie."

"But it's interesting that in my vision you *were* the one who would close the gate."

"Considering I didn't close the damn thing, that's not only useless information, it's depressing." I sighed. "You saw us closing the gate, right? You and Alice. What exactly did you see? And why did you say you had her blood on your hands?"

He stood then, his expression flat and his eyes cold as he walked to the grimy window and looked out over the night. For a moment, I feared he wouldn't tell me anything, and then he spoke, still not facing me. "There are many torments for a Tri-Jal," he said, and I could hear the pain in his voice. "And I tried as best I could to hold on to my sanity. I clung to it like a life raft, and when I slipped, I searched for some piece of humanity within me. Anything that might have grown in me when I'd been in the shell of human form. I found a kernel and I clung to it." He turned and looked at me. "That kernel kept me whole, and when the pain was too great, I could lose myself in it. I could be something I wasn't. Something—*someone*—with the potential for good.

"You can't imagine the torment. It is . . . eternal. Deep and raw and unrelenting. But I found a hiding place within, and my mind would go there. One day I saw. Not in my imagination, but something outside me. A vision, laid out and clear. And in it, I was closing the Ninth Gate, and I knew that if I could do that—if I could lock the gate before the convergence—then the evil I had done would be redeemed. Not forgiven, but I would have made sufficient payment for my sins."

I watched him, the tight control that seemed to envelop his whole body. I wanted to go to him, wanted to touch and soothe him, but I feared that if I did, he would shatter into a million pieces.

"I wasn't alone. There was a girl with me. We fought. We almost died. But we did it. We closed the gate. And seeing that gave me hope." His eyes met mine. "It was that hope that kept me sane. That allowed me to survive the torment and escape the pit."

"What did you do when you were out?"

"I came to Boston. Drawn here, really. And I didn't know why until I came one day to the Bloody Tongue. I saw Alice, and I knew that she was the one. So I watched her. And I learned about her family. And I learned that she wanted out. Didn't want anything to do with the dark arts. And that fit."

"A girl like that would want the gate closed."

"So I believed. I went to her. She didn't work at the pub then. I went and I told her what I'd seen. She was terrified. Completely freaked, and she ran. Stayed away for months. I kept an eye on her, wanting to give her space, trying to figure out what to do, because the vision was so clear. I needed her. I knew it."

"But you never got her."

"No," he said. "I did. She came back one day, completely broken up. Said she'd had a vision. Told me she used to have them when she was a kid, but they'd stopped. But this one was clear. And like me, she'd seen us closing the gate." He drew in a breath. "Because of that, she went back to work at the pub. She got drawn back to that place because I told her what I saw."

"She'd seen it, too," I said. "It's not your fault."

"Maybe," he said, but there was sadness in his voice. "At any rate, I had my ally. But there was no connection between us. She was a girl that I was doing a job with, and that was fine. But it felt off. Even more so when I realized she had a thing for me."

"Imagine that," I said, with a small smile.

"She came to me one night after work. Flirted with me. Touched me." He tensed, his hands curving into fists as he fought for control.

"And she saw," I said.

"Fucking terrified her," he said. "She ran. Said she didn't know what to trust. We hadn't gotten far searching for a way to close the gate, but she was out of it now. I was on my own, and I wasn't thrilled about it."

"And then?"

"Then she came back to me. Told me she was scared. She needed to talk to me, but in secret. I was supposed to meet her after work."

"Saturday," I said, knowing where this was going.

"She didn't show. And then you were at the pub. And I knew you weren't her. I knew that right off."

"How?"

"I already told you. I wanted you," he said, and from the heat in his eyes, I knew he still did. "I wanted you the moment I saw you, and I never wanted Alice."

I swallowed, forced myself not to remember the way his body had felt against mine, the way his arms around me had made me feel both alive and whole. Had made me feel like *me*. "Why didn't you tell me? About us. About the gates?"

"Because I still believed it was *Alice* in my vision. And I knew you weren't Alice. I thought you'd killed her. Taken her place for some dark purpose of your own. I didn't know, but I intended to find out. And so I waited, and I watched."

"And you got close to me."

"Yes," he said, without remorse.

I drew in a breath, certain I would have done that very thing. Had, actually, when I'd let myself get close to him. "And Maecruth? You poisoned me in front of his house, remember?"

"I didn't know it was you. Primarily because you were covered head-to-toe in black, but also because I didn't make the connection that Alice—the new Alice—might be the rumored warrior. And I certainly didn't make the connection that the new Alice might be the woman from my vision. I saw you only as a usurper. A dabbler in magic. A body thief."

"What rumors of a warrior?"

"Whispers in the demon underground that a priest was seeking to force the gate closed, and that the demonic higher powers had delivered a warrior to make sure that didn't happen."

"You would have wanted to help the priest," I said.

"Wanted to, yes. But I was not welcome."

I frowned. "You spoke to the priest?"

"I contacted an angel."

I drew in a breath. "So there really are angels?"

"Not like what you saw the night Lily died," he said. I'd told him what I'd seen and heard. A white light. The beating of wings. And a sensation of utter beauty. "All that's a mortal affectation. But they showed you that image because they knew you needed to see it."

"In order to believe."

He nodded. "I arranged a meeting with an angel. I said I wanted to help. That I sought the light. I was spurned," he said, his voice low and dangerous. "Perhaps the creature believed a Tri-Jal could never have regrets. Perhaps it believed I was a spy. Perhaps it believed that there was no amount of light that could drown out the darkness within me. Whatever the reason, I was kicked to the curb, and soundly."

"Deacon." My voice was a whisper. "You didn't give up, though. They'll see. In the end, they'll see."

His eyes flashed with anger. "I no longer do what I do to seek entrance to the light. I do it for me, and for me alone. And, yes, I did not give up. I inquired and I searched and I killed my kind in order to find out what I need."

"You learned about Maecruth and Father Carlton."

"I did. And the rest you know."

"I do," I said. I held out my hand. "Come here." When he didn't, I stood and went to him. He kept his back to me, his eyes on the window. I put my hands on his shoulder and pressed myself against his back, wishing I could take in some of his pain. "It's better to do it for yourself, anyway. In the end, you're the only thing you can rely on. I know that now."

He met my reflection in the glass. "No faith, Lily? No blind trust?"

"Only in myself." I could see the question in his eyes and shook my head. "Not even in you. Not yet. I'm sorry." I *was* sorry, but I couldn't truly trust him. Not yet. Not after everything that had happened to me.

There was no hurt in his eyes, only a simple understanding that made my heart ache.

I stepped back and started pacing the small room, my mind whirling. "I killed real demons when I trained. They had me kill their own kind, all for the illusion."

"Not just the illusion," he said, turning to face me. "For you. You absorb their essence, right? So they were trying to mold you in their image. To make you more like them. They fucked with you, Lily," he said, and I saw the darkness stirring in his eyes. I tensed, fearful that the rage I'd seen in the church would return.

He pulled it back, though, and when he did, only warmth remained.

"Even the Grykon was real. No chance he'd gone over to the good side and they were trying to shut him down."

"I'm guessing the Grykon willingly sacrificed himself. He said as much when you were tied up, right?"

"Right," I said, remembering that first moment when I'd awakened and seen the monster. I rubbed my temples. "I was never in any danger at all. All along, I was supposed to win." I smiled a little. "But I wasn't supposed to end him, just kill him. You slammed your blade through his heart and took him out. Pissed Clarence off, too."

"That, at least, is good to know."

"And that girl in the cage. The Tri-Jal. Was she real?"

"I'm guessing yes, because she had the mark. Doubt she sacrificed herself, though. More likely she was considered a collateral loss."

I shivered. The girl had been both terrifying and pitiful, but the idea that she'd been sacrificed as part of a long con seemed obscene.

"They duped me even more with Maecruth. Got me to kill a demon who was working for the side of good." I hugged myself, remembering that vision. "Oh, God, Deacon. I saw him battling Clarence, and I went after him. Hard." I met Deacon's eye. "That son of a bitch would be dead—Maecruth would kill him. If not now, then soon. But I stopped that. Fuck. Fuck, fuck, fuck!"

"It's not your fault."

I stood and paced. "Maybe not, but it sure feels like it is. This whole thing. It's all twisted around. And the vampire. No wonder Clarence was pissed that I killed it. I'd just killed one from the home team."

I ran my fingers through my hair, on a roll. "And those demons that attacked me in the alley? Who were they?" I looked at Deacon through narrowed eyes. "Was that your doing?" I held my breath waiting for his answer.

"No," Deacon said. "I don't know who went after you."

I believed him. "Clarence," I said, as the pieces fell into place.

"Why would he kill you? He needed you."

"To make sure I fit the checklist." He cocked his head, clearly not following, so I went on. "The prophecy said that their girl would absorb demonic essence. So Clarence sent that band of demons to test me. Was I strong enough to defeat them?"

"And more important," Deacon added, "did you come back to life? Had you absorbed Zane's essence?"

"Exactly. If I did, then I'm really his girl. And if I didn't, then no great loss because I wasn't the one he needed anyway. God *damn* that son of a bitch." My breath hitched. "I've killed so many. And this one . . . tonight . . . the priest." My throat filled with tears. "Oh, God, Deacon. What have I done?"

"Shhhh," he said, pulling me into his arms.

"They used me. They tricked me. The bastards took my life and my purpose and they fucking trampled on it. And I didn't have a clue," I said, the anger shooting through me, priming me. "I didn't have a fucking clue."

"This isn't your fault."

I forced a smile. "Yes," I said. "It is. I killed him. I killed the one man who could have closed the door forever."

"Lily—"

"No." I looked at him, sure my eyes were burning. "I'm going to fix this. They gave me this power? Fine. I'm going to throw it back in their faces." I drew in a breath, rage burning through me. "I'm going to figure out how to fix what I messed up. I'm going to close that gate. And I'm going to use these powers to kill every last one of them."

THIRTY-NINE

"Lily." My name emerged from his lips whispered, a soft oath.

"I mean it," I said. "Cross my heart and hope to die. I'm taking those bastards out. Pulling the plug. They messed with me. They messed with Rose. And they are seriously toast."

He looked at me, his eyes dark. "I'll help you," he finally said.

I met his gaze. Nodded. "I know," I said, and reached for his hand, feeling the shock of connection tear through me.

"So are they done with me?" I asked, when I could no longer hold the question in. "Now that I've single-handedly destroyed the best chance of closing the Ninth Gate to Hell, are they going to try to take me out? Decide they can't run the risk of me finding out the truth?"

"I doubt it," he said darkly.

"Why?"

"Because they need you. Why stop with one gate? They're going to try to find the key to open the other eight."

I'd told him about my arm, and now I thrust it out, staring

at the currently unmarked skin. "You think Clarence has an incantation for that, too?"

"If he doesn't, I bet he's working on it."

"And the key? The legend you mentioned about a key that would seal tight all of the nine gates? Do you think he knows that incantation, too?"

Deacon looked at me, his head cocked, his expression as devious as I felt. "He just might."

"I can get it out of his head."

"No," Deacon said. "That's too dangerous. He'll see you coming. He'll *hear* you coming," he added, tapping his head for emphasis. "You said he picks up your thoughts, right?"

I nodded, realizing with a growing sense of nausea that my juvenile efforts to keep him out might not have worked as well as I'd believed. Clarence had seen my thoughts about Deacon—that was obvious to me now. But instead of attacking them directly, he'd thrown little bombs in my path. Deacon was a demon. Deacon killed Alice.

I didn't think Clarence knew about the visions, but he definitely knew more than he let on. And if I went back now, with my mind wide open, I was surely dead.

"He didn't want you dead at first," I said to Deacon. "Why?"

"I don't know. What did he tell you?"

"That you're strong."

"Well, I am."

"But later he told me that you killed Alice. What changed?"

A shadow passed over Deacon's face. "He must have figured out that I was fighting him. That I was working to close the gate, and that I'd stop you if I could."

I nodded. That made sense. "He knew," I said. "He knew how I felt about you, and he played me."

"Which is why he's going to see you coming," Deacon said. "And why you have to be prepared to kill him after you get into his head."

"Oh, I can kill him," I said. "No problem there." I frowned.

"As for keeping him out of my head, you can probably help with that. I need to find the Secret Keeper. An Alash-tijard. Do you know how I do that?"

Deacon looked at me, his expression unreadable. "You understand what you're asking?"

I nodded.

"The Alash-tijard sits and meditates. He does nothing except hold the secrets brought to him by other demons. He is passive. And he never leaves his lair."

"I know."

"He doesn't hurt. He doesn't kill. Not unless he's attacked. And then, Lily, he will defend himself."

I stood, started pacing. I didn't know that, and the knowledge made my stomach twist. "I have to," I said. "If I don't kill him—if I don't close my mind to Clarence the only way I can—then we're shut down before we even begin."

"Lily—"

"*No.* I've racked up a shitload of sins, Deacon. And when I kill this creature, then yeah, there will be one more. But I have to do this. I have to kill Johnson. I have to save Rose. I have to figure out who did this to Alice. And most of all, I have to close the gate. All of it, Deacon. I have to undo all of the bad that I did, fix everything I fucked up. And if I have to kill a demon's tool to do that, then believe me when I say I'm not even going to hesitate." I drew in a breath. "I'll find it. With or without you, I will find it. But it will be faster with you."

He was silent for a moment, and then he stood and held out a hand to help me to my feet. "All right. Let's go."

"You can just tell me where."

"I'll go with you," he said, and I understood what he did not say: He would take the stain upon his soul, too. We were partners now. For better or for worse, we were in this together.

"What about Alice?" I asked, as he led me out of the decrepit building. "Do you think she realized it wasn't her in the vision? That someone was going to take her body?"

"I don't know. Maybe that's what scared her."

I made a small noise, guilt rising. "She had a file on her computer," I said. "A photograph, and the file was passworded with your name. And it referenced Saturday. The day she didn't show up to meet you."

His brows rose. "Really?"

"You'll take a look? Maybe you'll know who's in it. What it means."

"Of course."

I mentally tried to focus on the man whose face was in the frame. The pockmarked skin. Those drooping eyes. I'd seen him somewhere, and it was right on the tip—

"Tank," I said, the memory finally bursting through. "He's the guy in that photograph. I *knew* he looked familiar. It was because I'd seen him a few days before in the picture."

"Tank," he repeated thoughtfully.

"You know him?"

"I've seen him at the pub, heard about him on the street."

"Can't say my first impression was warm and fuzzy."

"No," Deacon agreed. "He's no good. Got his hands in every scam, from spell casting to drugs. An all-around bad dude."

"I think he's got Egan involved in something bad. Drugs were my first guess, actually."

"Why? What happened?"

"I overheard them arguing. Like Egan owes him and all hell's going to break loose if Egan doesn't fork over quality goods."

"Not drugs," Deacon said, "though that's a good guess. Herbs."

"What? Like oregano and basil?"

"More specialized," Deacon said. "For ceremonial use."

I frowned. "I thought Egan didn't hold with the dark arts. I thought that's what he fought with Alice's mom about."

"I believe they did, actually. I also think that Egan is an opportunistic fellow, and the pub is often in need of cash.

He's not above catering to a demonic crowd, and he's not above importing certain herbs and selling them under the table to his clients for ritualistic use."

I glanced at him sideways. "You ever bought any?"

"No. But I keep my ear to the ground."

"Why do you think Alice wanted to talk to you about Tank?"

Deacon shook his head. "Haven't a clue, but after we take care of Clarence, we can go find Tank ourselves and ask him."

I nodded, then exhaled, feeling ripped to shreds. "That poor girl." I pressed the bridge of my nose, trying to hold back the sadness. "She was trying to do exactly what I'm doing—stop the bad guys, end this, close the freaking gate. And she died for it. She died so that they could make me, and now the gate's stuck open and it's all my goddamned fault."

The tears were back, and Deacon hooked his arm around my waist as we walked, making me feel safe, wanted. I held on, fighting through the horror of what I'd become and how. And who'd been sacrificed so that I could live.

"Those slimy, hell-bound, fucked-up *bastards*." Honestly, there weren't curses strong enough to express just how vile I thought my tormentors were. "She was only twenty-two. She'd been accepted to Harvard. Did you know that?"

He shook his head, his expression helpless.

"Her whole life ahead, and they took it from her."

"That's what they do. Even when they don't kill, that's what they do."

"I'm going to make them pay. I'm going to find out exactly who killed her, and I am *so* going to make them pay."

We wandered for an hour, finally catching the T and taking it to a section of Boston I didn't recognize. We got off, ignoring the stares of people who saw us, both filthy from battle, our clothes ripped and our faces haggard.

We crossed city streets to an urban park, then passed through, ignoring the couples out for a walk and the joggers out doing their thing.

The path led to an overpass, the walking trail going under as the cars rumbled by overhead. We stepped out of the bright day and into the shadowy darkness. I expected that we'd continue on, but Deacon stopped halfway under the bridge. "There," he said, nodding to the sloping concrete that supported the road above us.

I looked, but saw no demon.

"Where?"

"Access panel," he said, this time pointing. I followed the angle of his arm to the top, and this time saw a rectangular metal door, about one-quarter the size of a normal door. Even from this distance, I could see the warning label, prohibiting admission to all except authorized personnel.

"In there?" I asked, dubious.

"It's an equipment room for the streetlights. It opens onto the sewer system. Between the two, there's a niche. We'll find the Secret Keeper there."

I nodded, then started to climb the steep hill to the top. I reached the metal door and discovered it had no handle. A crowbar, however, had been conveniently left nearby, and I pried the door open, cringing as the metal released an angry screech.

I bent down and started to climb inside, then looked back at Deacon. "Are we doing the right thing?" I asked.

"Right or wrong," he said, "if you want revenge, it's the only thing you can do."

FORTY

We found the Secret Keeper sitting passively in the dark, and when we approached, he looked up at me with knowing eyes. He didn't speak, but somehow I knew his thoughts: *Attack, and I will defend. And beware.*

I hesitated, not wanting to do this but knowing I had no choice. Not if I wanted any chance at all of closing the gate. Did the end justify the means? I didn't know, but I thought so. I was trying to do good. By killing, I was hoping to save the world.

Ironic that that was what I'd thought I'd been doing all along.

The creature had no mouth and stringy gray hair, with skin that seemed like tissue stretched over bones and a sickly green tinge about him. "Don't help," I told Deacon. "It has to be me for this to work."

"I know," he said, then squeezed my hand and stepped back. I drew a breath, then another. And then I lunged, leading with my blade and finding that he'd pulled out a sword to match me with. He knocked my blade from my hand, his speed exceptional considering the beast rarely fought.

I grabbed a pipe in the roof and kicked, sending his sword clattering out of his hands, then dropped down and immediately went for my blade, but he turned on me, screaming, which is quite a feat for a creature with no mouth.

But I could feel it, burning inside my brain, hideous and so unexpected that I wasn't at the top of my game. He didn't hesitate, but jumped immediately on me, his hands at my throat. I felt him there, not at my neck, but poking about inside my mind, the two of us connected. I didn't want to be in his head, seeing the horrors that demons had hidden there, but I couldn't help it, and the thoughts, vile and painful, flashed like a slideshow. Glimpses and snatches. Horrid and unclear. Plans and alliances.

And blood. So much blood.

My body trembled. Pain racked through me, drawing my limbs tight, shooting fire through them until I was certain I would burn up from within. I didn't burn, though, but sank into a scorched blackness, falling deeper and deeper into the pain. Deeper and deeper into the Secret Keeper's vault.

A body. Must have the body.

The prophecy. The prophecy awaits.

Such import. The job. Heavy responsibility to bear.

Must find the vessel. Little Alice.

Important job for a little girl.

Find, find, find.

Get her from the man, the E man.

So they can kill the vessel. So that they can bring forth the One. The Champion.

She will serve the Dark. She will serve.

She will serve.

The pendulum will swing toward the Dark, and she will serve.

I saw the speaker in his mind. *Tank.* Tank had planned the kill. Had sought out Alice. *The vessel. The champion.*

And the prophecy.

I needed to know the prophecy. Needed to know if it had been fulfilled in me or if there was more.

And the only way to know was to go back in. I didn't want to—the pain, it exhausted as much as it hurt, draining me so much I wasn't certain I could break the connection. Wasn't certain that I wouldn't lose my mind inside the Secret Keeper's thoughts. And that wasn't the place I ever wanted to be.

But again, I had no choice. He wanted in my head, too, and his control over the visions was stronger than mine. Like a whirlpool, I was sucked back, my skin flayed from my flesh as I was pulled under and deeper, faster and faster, until my throat was raw from the screaming and my heart threatened to burst inside my chest.

Darkness.

A circle.

And Tank standing across from Egan. Friday. Sunrise. The girl. The little one. For the glory. For the cause.

And then Egan was leaving, and Tank was smiling.

For the glory. For the ruse. It goes on.

Tank.

And Egan.

Not herbs. Girls. One girl. A sacrifice. Tank and Egan working together.

And soon.

Someone was going to die so very soon.

My thoughts muddled. The pain. The darkness.

I tried to fight through it. I had to see. Had to see where they had her. The Little One. Had to get to her.

Had to save her.

And yet my brain was starting to melt. It was too much. He was fighting me. Fighting hard.

I wanted to protest. To find my blade. To stab him through the heart.

But my own heart had stopped. My lungs had quit drawing air. And the world was growing gray. So gray.

He'd slid inside. Inside my brain.

And he was shutting me down.

I was dying, and—

"Lily!

"Lily! Your knife! Use your knife."

The sting of a hand hard against my cheek. I gasped, and as reality returned, I thrust hard with the knife, finding the Secret Keeper's heart. It was a kill shot, and while the demonic goo eased out of him, I sank to my knees, gasping like a fish out of water as the Secret Keeper's essence flowed through and filled me.

"I thought I'd lost you. If I hadn't been here . . ." Deacon trembled with controlled rage. "If I hadn't been here, he would have burned you up from the inside out."

"I'm okay," I said, clutching his hand. "I'm okay." I sucked in a gallon of air. "Tank came to him. Gave him his secrets. I saw it all. They did need Alice's body." I shifted as Deacon helped me to my feet. "She was the shell, and I was the soul. It was planned." I met his eyes. "Egan fucking sold her to them. And all to make this prophecy come true."

"Bastards."

"And there's someone else," I said, fear and futility clogging my veins. "Unless we get to her in time, another girl will be sacrificed. Tonight."

FORTY-ONE

"Who?" he asked as we raced toward the street.

"I don't know. But it doesn't matter. We have to stop it."

Deacon stopped in front of a car, a sleek black Jaguar, and ripped off the driver's-side door. I climbed in, scrambling over to the passenger side.

"Where?" he asked, pressing his hand to the ignition slot and setting the engine firing. The sun was fast sinking, casting the street in an eerie greenish gray.

I gaped, thinking that was one damn handy trick and realizing I didn't really know a thing about this man I'd aligned myself with. "The pub. It's closed today. Plumbing." I snorted. "I'm thinking the real reason's in the basement." I remembered the metal plate I'd felt in the wall across from the stockroom. The odd symbols. *Demonic,* I assumed. Most likely a door of some sort.

Guess we'd find out soon enough.

"Was that where you woke up? As Alice?" Deacon asked, when I told him my theory.

I shook my head. "Probably moved me. Wouldn't want me going to work at the pub and recognizing the alley. The room. That would raise questions they wouldn't want to answer."

I clung tight to the door as Deacon took curves at speeds that made NASCAR drivers look like pussies. "The whole thing makes perfect sense," I said, once I caught my breath. "Those girls that went missing over the summer. That was Egan. He supplied the demons with sacrifices to get money to cover the pub's debts." I remembered what Rachel had said, and felt slightly sick. Did she realize what he'd been trafficking, or just that he'd been doing a demon's bidding?

"And then one day they come and say they need a particular girl," Deacon said. "His niece."

"And he said yes. The bastard said yes." I drew in a breath. "It makes sense now—that look in his eye when I walked in the door. He never expected to see her alive again. He knew she didn't disappear on Saturday. He sent her to the stockroom and she was taken. And when I walked in, it was like he was looking at a ghost." I snorted. "And here I thought he was being all nice and kind when he asked if there was anything I wanted to talk about. He was fishing, wondering if I remembered. Wondering if I knew what he'd done."

"He sold her," Deacon said. "He sold his own niece as a sacrificial lamb."

"And now someone else is on the chopping block."

"Not if we can help it." I looked over and saw his hands tight on the steering wheel, his face tight as he struggled to keep the rage he kept permanently at bay under control. I wanted to reach over and touch his arm, to tell him it was okay—go ahead and release the beast. Considering what Egan had done, he deserved to be consumed in fire and fury.

Fear held me back. The fear that once released, the beast within Deacon could never be harnessed again.

Instead, I sat there, hands tight on the armrest, every fiber in me willing the car to go faster.

"What I don't get is why. Why sacrifice someone tonight?"

"A ruse," Deacon said.

"That's what I heard in the Secret Keeper's mind," I said. "But I don't get it."

"A cover-up, and it's all for Egan's benefit."

I squinted at him, still not understanding. And then, as Deacon fishtailed into a parking space near the alley entrance to the pub, it all clicked into place. Egan had sacrificed Alice, but there his niece was, walking and talking. And unless the demons wanted to bring Egan in on the secret that was me, they needed Egan to think that Alice was a bust sacrifice-wise. That she was still alive and kicking with a big hole in her memory.

But Egan already had their money, and demons aren't known for their generosity. Which meant they had to hit him up for another sacrifice so that he wouldn't get curious.

This ceremony was a do-over. A sacrifice for no reason at all.

"Bastards," I whispered, as we eased quietly down the alley. There might be guards, and I didn't want us discovered before we even had a chance of saving the girl.

"She's most likely a runaway," Deacon said. "Living on the street. Easy to grab."

"Boarhurst has a lot of them." I remembered what Gracie had said about her uncle giving her pepper spray. Lot of girls around here went missing.

And then I grabbed Deacon's hand, remembering. "The vision," I said, fumbling in my pocket for my cell phone. It was still off, and I pushed the button to power it up, frantic now. "I touched Gracie and I saw a girl in a white gown in a ceremonial chamber. I thought it was because Alice had told her something. Something important hidden in her subconscious. It was so familiar—it was almost like seeing me in that room. I discounted it, because visions aren't always clear, and she was Alice's friend."

"You think she's our girl?"

"I think Egan was irritated when she gave notice." I focused on the phone. I had five new calls, but I ignored them, dialing Gracie's number instead. She answered on the third ring, and I sagged to the ground in relief. "Where are you?" I demanded.

"Alice?" Her voice was slow, groggy. "What time is it?"

"Where are you?" I repeated.

"I'm in L.A.," she said, life coming back into her voice. "Can you believe it? For work! An emergency trip, and on my very first day!"

I hung up. I'd plead broken connection when I saw her, but right then I couldn't talk. "She's okay. It's not her. We keep going."

I started to put the phone away, but scrolled through the incoming numbers first. Clarence I recognized as three of the calls, most likely calling from in front of my apartment, waiting for his report on my massacre of Father Carlton.

The other two I recognized as well. *Rose.*

With a growing sense of dread, I called voice mail, heard Rose's tentative voice.

"So, um, Alice. I . . . God, this is stupid; I don't even know you. But I still feel like someone— Never mind. I dunno. Wanted to talk to you. Give me a call."

She hung up, and I frowned, scrolling through to the final message, also from Rose.

"Things really suck right now. It's just that, you said you were Lily's friend, so I hope you're not gonna be pissed. Anyway, I figure cab fare can't be too much, right? Hopefully you're working. 'Cause I really want to see you. So I guess I will. See you, I mean. And I'm gonna take my dad's cell phone with me," she said, then rattled off the familiar number before signing off again.

I looked up at Deacon, horrified. "Here. She was coming here." Frantically, I dialed Joe's cell number. And when the damn thing went straight to voice mail, I had to stifle the urge to slam it against the wall.

"You don't think he'd—a girl walks in off the street—"

"I think if he'd planned to use Gracie, then he'd be desperate. I think he's taken girls off the street before. And I think we need to hurry."

I nodded, tears clogging my throat as I struggled to get my key into the back door lock. I couldn't—I *wouldn't*—fail my sister again.

"I'm killing the son of a bitch," I said, my voice thick. "I swear, I'm killing him for what he did to Alice. For what he's trying to do to Rose. And I'm going to make him feel every bit of the life as it drains out of him."

Deacon looked at me, and for a moment I thought he was going to argue. I didn't want to hear it, because there was nothing—*nothing*—he could say that would save Egan's life.

"I'll hold him for you."

I met his eyes. Nodded. And pulled open the door.

Whatever was in there, we'd face it together.

FORTY-TWO

We raced down the stairs toward the basement, sunrise only minutes away, and searched the wall for the metal door I'd brushed my fingers over just the other day.

Nothing.

I swallowed, panic setting in. *Rose.* I couldn't lose Rose.

I kicked the wall, willing the door to appear. Nothing.

"Dammit!"

"Egan," Deacon said. "Go. I'll stay here. Try to figure a way in."

I was halfway up the stairs before the suggestion was out of his mouth. I burst through the kitchen doors into the pub area, relief welling in me as I saw Egan pacing the length of the darkened pub. He turned, saw the knife in my hand, and paled.

"Alice!"

"How do I get in? How do I find the door, you lying, murdering bastard?"

His eyes widened and he dropped the saltshaker he'd been cleaning, the white bar rag still in his hand like a flag of surrender. "I—what—?"

After that, he was fresh out of witty conversation and raced for the front doors. He didn't make it, the knife lodging in his thigh effectively bringing him down.

I was at his side in an instant, my hand closing over the hilt of my blade. "Tell me," I said. "Tell me or I twist the knife until I reach an artery. Any idea how fast a thigh can bleed out?"

He opened his mouth, but no sound came out.

I grabbed his collar and shook.

"How do I find her? Damn you, you son of a bitch. Where do they have the girl?"

"I don't know what you're talking about. Alice, sweetheart, what's gotten into you?"

I leaned forward, getting right into his face. "Someone who's not Alice, you lying scum. That's *what's* gotten into me." I slammed my hand over his heart and looked deep into those eyes. He tried to turn away, but it was too late—I'd been sucked into the hell of his thoughts, the crimes for which I'd come to punish him right on the surface—images and thoughts mixing and swirling, pulling me into a miasma of greed and desperation that confirmed all of my worst fears.

He'd killed his own sister when she'd refused to allow the pub to be ground zero for demonic activity.

And he hadn't even hesitated when the demons had come to him and demanded a specific girl. They'd demanded Alice.

He'd sold her, thinking she was a traditional sacrifice. Thinking she was the same as the other girls he'd sold to finance the pub.

He'd sold his own niece to die at the hands of the demons, and planned the same fate for Gracie.

And when he couldn't find her, he'd snatched a helpless, damaged girl who'd come in off the street, looking for a friend.

The bastard had sacrificed my sister to cover his butt with the demons.

I trembled, rage filling me and clouding my thoughts. I wanted nothing but my hands around his neck, squeezing tight.

I wanted him dead. But I couldn't do it. Not yet. Not until I found her.

I forced myself to focus, desperate to find the control Madame Parrish had insisted I could use to navigate these visions. I couldn't break away yet, not until I learned how to open the door.

"Come on," I whispered inside my head. "Come on, you bastard."

His consciousness shrank away from me, but I followed, down the dark corridors of his mind, filled with greed and regret and fear. The liquid image shifted, clarifying, and now I was in the basement, in the hall. He was there, but not there, wanting to escape, that want so vibrant it thrummed through my head, ricocheting through my body.

"Show me . . . Show me . . ." I focused, the effort of concentrating my energy, of keeping hold of him, completely exhausting. But I had him—and as I watched, he sliced his palm, then smeared the blood on the wall. The rock seemed to melt away, revealing a metal door with odd markings on it.

Got you.

I yanked my hand back, breaking the connection, wanting free of this man. Wanting out of his head.

On the wall, the clock ticked ominously. The ceremony would be starting, and I had to hurry.

Egan struggled when I picked him up, and I was grateful for the strength of all the demons I'd killed. I twisted the knife still embedded in his leg. His shriek split my eardrums, but he froze, staying still as I hauled him down the stairs and dumped him in front of the door.

"Open it," I said to Egan.

He answered by spitting on my shoes.

"Then let me help you." The time for games was over, and my patience had run thin. I grabbed his hand, ignoring his scream as I sliced deep into his palm. I pressed the bloody hand to the stone, trying to place it where I'd seen it in the vision.

At first, nothing happened. Then, in a freaky bit of déjà vu, the rock started to dissolve, revealing the now-familiar metal door.

I ran my hand over it, searching for a latch, found it, and pushed it quietly open. Another corridor.

"Bring him?" Deacon asked, hauling Egan to his feet.

I turned to face Alice's uncle. "He's deadweight." I met Egan's eyes. "I'm ending you."

Egan swallowed. "Please," he whispered, his body shaking under my hand.

I thought of Lucas Johnson, of the revenge that stained me.

I thought of Alice.

I thought of the travesties I'd seen in Egan's memory.

I thought of my own redemption.

And then, God help me, I drew my blade across his neck and slit the bastard's throat.

He sagged, and I stepped back as Deacon let go, the body falling to the ground like so much garbage. My eyes met Deacon's, and he nodded, the slightest inclination of his head. No matter what anyone else thought, in his eyes—and in my own—I'd done the right thing.

We raced down the hall, trading silence for speed and hoping the demons couldn't hear the pounding of our feet as we raced forward. Move with stealth and the ritual might be completed before we arrived. Clatter forward at breakneck speed and the ceremony might end prematurely with a knife through Rose's neck, for no reason other than to punish her would-be rescuers.

With any luck, we'd found a middle ground: fast, but not loud. With even more luck, the ritual chanting camouflaged our approach.

I had no choice but to hope for luck, because without it, Rose was dead. Certainly, I couldn't count on the angels to step in and save her. They hadn't stepped in to save me, after all.

The corridor ended at a thick wooden door. Closed, but

not locked. We yanked the door open, and Deacon and I rushed in together, side by side.

What I saw inside was enough to make me almost stumble. Rose, clad in a long white gown, bathed in an unearthly silver glow, strapped down to a stone table, struggling and screaming against a white cloth gag as a ceremonial blade plunged downward, held by the joined hands of two black-hooded demons.

A door on the far side of the room was open, and even as I lunged for the demons' knife, I could see a figure disappear, the black cloak billowing as if in a breeze.

No time to worry about that now. I landed hard against one demon, sending the knife clattering to the ground. Deacon went on the other side of the table, tackling the companion demon, and even as I fumbled to keep the demon's hands away from the ceremonial knife, I could hear Deacon battling with his own demon on the far side of that thick stone table.

I couldn't worry about Deacon, though. The hood of the demon fell back, and I realized I was wrestling with Tank. I had my weapon out, desperate to kill the beast and get to Rose, but he was having none of it.

He thrust sideways, twisting over, then bending my hand back until he freed the blade from my grip. He straddled me, and as I used one hand to hold him back, my other hand struggled to find my blade.

I found the ceremonial knife instead, and, desperate, I thrust up, the blade sliding into his nose to embed itself in his brain.

He fell backward, and I struggled up, gasping. My knife was by the wall, and I lunged for it, then sank it deep into Tank's heart. I heard a small hiss as the black goo seeped out, and as the strength and vile essence that had been Tank surged through me, I rushed to Rose, grounding myself by looking at her face. At her eyes.

"Rose," I said as I pulled off her gag.

Whatever the silver glow had been, it was gone now. She stopped struggling, and those eyes went even wider as she stared at me. "Lily?" she whispered.

"I— My name's Alice. Remember?"

"He was here. Lily. Lily, it's him. He was here. He did something. He was here. Put something inside." The words came out in a rush, tumbling over themselves, pushed out by the fear in her eyes.

I didn't need to hear her say it to know who *he* was, but I asked anyway.

"Lucas Johnson," she said.

"I've got you now," I said firmly, as my fingers worked at the knot of her bindings. "You're safe."

But she shook her head. "Never gonna be free. Never gonna be safe." She tilted her head to the side, one eye looking up at me, and the image made me think of a cold, dead fish. I trembled, ashamed and suddenly very, very scared.

"He's in me, Lily," she whispered. "He put something in me. Him. *Part of him.* It burns. Oh, God, Lily, it burns!"

"Rose, no. You're safe. I've got you. You're safe." But she didn't hear me. How could she have over the sound of her own scream?

And then, as the scream faded, she slipped into blissful unconsciousness.

FORTY-THREE

"Could he have? Could he have put part of himself inside of her?"

We were in a pungent motel room, ripe with the stench of sex and sweat. The kind of place that took cash and didn't ask questions. Perfect, in other words.

Rose was still asleep, and I had her head in my lap as I stroked her hair. Part of me wanted to wake her up, to ask her question after question. Another part of me wanted to let her stay lost in sleep, the one place where she could escape the nightmare of reality.

"Yeah," Deacon said. "He could have."

In my lap, Rose stirred, but didn't awake. My heart, however, ripped a little. "My whole life I've tried to protect her, and look what happened. I tried to save the world, and Armageddon's closer than ever."

Everything had been turned inside out, twisted up and confused.

No more.

I knew the score now. And it was time to step up to the

plate. Time to save Rose. Time to save the whole damn world.

I stood up, feeling strong. Feeling confident.

Lily Carlyle, Demon Assassin, was pissed.

And they had all better watch out.

Coming December 2009 from Ace Books

The second book in
the Blood Lily Chronicles by Julie Kenner

TORN

Lily Carlyle continues to work for the forces of darkness—only this time, on her own terms. She's going to have to lie and kill, all in order to prove her loyalty, which she's willing to do—until she learns that her sister's life hangs in the balance . . .

Like a caged panther, Deacon paced the length of the rank motel room. He wore jeans and a white T-shirt, and the look would have been almost casual were it not for the dark glasses that he wore despite the single dim lamp and the predawn hour.

With those glasses, he looked like the consummate bad boy. Which, frankly, was exactly what he was. A demon. A Tri-Jal. One of the worst of the worst.

More than that, though, he was a demon now allied with a demon hunter—me. The irony made me smile even as a nugget of worry settled in my gut. Because this was a dangerous game I was playing. If I'd made the wrong choice in aligning myself with Deacon, I could very well end up paying the price for eternity. All I knew was that I couldn't deny him. Couldn't push him out of my life, out of my head, or even out of my heart. He'd claimed me once, gotten right inside my head and announced that I was his. *Mine,* he'd said.

And as every day passed, I feared that he was right.

Feared it and fought it, but at the same time, I welcomed it.

I didn't know where he'd found the dark glasses, and I didn't ask. What I did know was that he wore them because of me. Because if I couldn't see his eyes, I couldn't get into his head. And in his head was where the real bad boy lay. The images of past deeds. Of memories too horrible to share.

I wanted to see them. *Needed* to see them. Needed to know the heart of this man who compelled me. But he wasn't letting me in, and the glasses were just one more way of telling me not to even try.

Honestly, it pissed me off. Then again, these days, it didn't take much to irritate me. I was walking a knife-edge. Tilt one way, and I fell into rage. The other, and I slipped into despair.

"It's almost dawn," he said.

"You have somewhere else to be?" I asked. I was on the bed, my sister Rose's head cradled in my lap. And, yeah, I was tired and cranky. Too much had happened too quickly, and my head was spinning. My body might not need sleep anymore, but right then I craved a nap.

As for Deacon, I honestly didn't know what he craved. Until now I'd never been with him for any extended period, and I found myself wondering what he did with himself during the day, or during the night for that matter. I thought about asking, but since I wasn't certain I'd like the answer, I kept my mouth shut.

The truth was, I didn't want him to leave. Didn't want him to tell me he had to disappear and that he'd come back when he could. I needed help. And, selfishly, I wanted Deacon with me. Wanted the comfort that his presence provided, even a supercharged presence that looked like it was on the verge of exploding.

We'd been in our cracker-box motel for almost six hours now, having holed up there in the aftermath of a nasty little battle during which Lucas Johnson had shoved part of his demonic essence into Rose before we'd gotten her the hell out of there.

She'd screamed in pain and terror, then passed out cold.

Even now, she still slept, and to be honest, I was beginning to worry that she'd never wake up. Deacon, however, had assured me that she would regain consciousness soon, albeit with one hell of a headache. I didn't ask him how he could be so certain about the particulars of demonic possession. That was just one more thing I didn't want to know.

Add on top of all that the fact that I had, only hours prior, managed to single-handedly facilitate the imminent arrival of Armageddon, and you can probably see why I was a little stressed.

"They'll start looking for you soon," Deacon said. "We need a plan."

The "they" he was referring to was actually a "he": Clarence, in particular. My amphibious handler. A frog-faced little demon who'd run the con on me and whom I despised all the more because I'd actually been starting to like him.

"I have a plan," I said, stroking Rose's hair. "I already told you." For that matter, we'd talked of nothing other than my plan for hours. With me alternating between berating myself for failing both Rose and the world, and fantasizing in glorious detail how I would kill not only Clarence but every other demon I came in contact with.

The fantasy alone was cathartic, but not nearly enough, and I couldn't wait for the real deal. I wanted the satisfaction of the kill. The strength I gained. And, yeah, I wanted the hit of power. I drew it in when I killed them. The demon's essence. Its darkness. Its fury.

And, yeah, I was happy to embrace the homicidal happiness. Ironic, I suppose, since without all this demon-assassin, prophecy bullshit, I wouldn't be having warm, fuzzy, murderous thoughts. I wouldn't be spending every day of my life trying to suppress the demonic essence that got sucked into me with each and every kill.

And here's an interesting tidbit: You'd think that since I'd been unknowingly working for the bad guys, I would have been out there killing *good* guys that I'd been duped to whack.

If that had been the case, then I'd be filled with goodness and light, about as sweet and charming as they come, because I would have sucked in the essence of a boatload of near-angelic souls.

A nice theory, but not even close to my reality. Because Clarence and crew didn't want me sweet; they didn't want me nice. And they'd had me training on real, true, badass demons. Sacrificing their own kind so that I'd become more like them. More badass. More evil.

Apparently, it had worked. Because the darkness writhed within me.

I wanted to be over the top, and I wanted to end them all.

"We can't simply waltz in and kill Clarence," Deacon said.

"We?" I replied. "No, no, no. This one's personal. This is all me."

"Fuck that."

"Fuck *you*," I countered, demonstrating my keen skill at argument. "He's my handler. I can get close to him. Close enough to shove my blade through his heart." My plan was to go back to Alice's apartment, call Clarence, and pretend like I was the good little soldier. It didn't matter much if he believed me; it only mattered that he came over. But if Deacon was standing there beside me when he walked into the apartment, we lost the element of surprise, and what could have been a nice, clean kill would become a bloodbath.

And as much as the thought of seeing Clarence waste away in a pool of his own blood left a nice warm feeling in my gut, for this job, I preferred the subtle approach. Grab him by the short hairs, and drag my blade across his fat little throat.

"Besides," I said, "I have to get close to him, and you know it. Unless I get inside his head, this thing's over before it's even begun."

The problem with swearing on all that is holy that you are going to go forth and lock the door to hell is pretty fundamental: doors require keys. And without knowing where this particular key was, we were pretty much screwed.

Deacon and I both knew damn good and well that there was no way Clarence was going to reveal the incantation for finding the legendary key that would permanently lock tight all of the nine gates to hell.

To be honest, we didn't even know if Clarence knew the incantation, but I had to poke around and find out. And if he did know it, then we could use the spell to raise a map to the key's location on my skin. A rather handy but bizarre side effect of being Prophecy Girl.

"The moment he knows you're poking around in his head, he's going to gut you like a fish," Deacon said. "And he may be shaped like a frog, but I'm betting he can move fast. He gets you down and injured, and you might find yourself in pieces or trapped in a tiny pine box forever."

"I think I can handle Clarence," I said, even though I knew he was right. Yet another of the perks of my über-chick persona was immortality. And the idea of spending eternity awake but six feet under was definitely the stuff of my nightmares.

For that matter, if I came up against a demon with telepathic powers, I could also end up the victim of permanent brain-fry. And since Clarence had just such a skill set, I had to consider the possibility that he'd be able to whup my ass without lifting a finger.

"You're important, Lily. Don't risk yourself."

The irony was inescapable, and I bit back a laugh. "Important," I repeated. "I think Clarence once told me that very thing."

"I'm not him," he said. "And I'm not using you."

I was about to argue but kept my mouth closed. The truth was, despite the inexplicable bond I felt with Deacon, I still didn't trust him. For that matter, I didn't trust anyone. I'd learned my lesson with Clarence, and until I had a peek into someone's mind, I had to assume their agenda was their own, and I was only a pawn.

Needless to say, that wasn't a role I much liked.

"You have to trust me sometime," Deacon said. He was

looking straight at me, and I could see my reflection in the black lenses of his glasses.

"No," I said. "I really don't." I'd work with him. Truth be told, I'd do a hell of a lot more with him. But that didn't mean I had to trust him.

"Dammit, Lily," he said, grinding my name out like a curse.

That frustration in his voice irritated me, snapping the final taut string that had been holding my patience in place.

"No," I snarled as I slid out from under Rose and moved across the small room to stand in front of him. I hadn't taken off my knife, and the pressure of the thigh holster against my leg gave me a sense of confidence. Of power. "You told me you had a vision of the two of us closing the Ninth Gate. Well, good for you. But in case you've forgotten, I've already played the we-need-you-to-save-the-world game once, and I lost big-time."

I'd been told my mission was to stop a demon priest from opening a portal to hell. Instead, I'd been duped into stopping a real priest from sealing that very thing. And in only two short weeks, that portal was going to be filled with incoming demon traffic, busier than a freeway during morning rush hour.

"I screwed up," I said. "I'm not going to make the same mistake twice."

"Trusting me isn't a mistake," he said.

"Since you won't let me look in your head, I have absolutely no way of knowing if you're bullshitting me or not." I wanted to trust him—so help me, I did—but I was done being naïve.

He stopped pacing and turned slowly toward me. Too slowly, actually, and I longed to see his eyes, to have a hint as to what he was thinking. Beneath the thin shirt, his muscles tensed. An animal readying for the kill.

I took an involuntary step back, my hand going automatically to my blade even before I realized what I was doing.

"You are not going inside my head again," he said, his voice slow and deadly.

"If I want to, you can't stop me."

"Believe me, Lily," he said. "I could stop you."

"Wanna prove it?" I said, feeling pissed off and grumpy, and yeah, I wanted to hurt him. Wanted to pick a fight. The demons inside me were stirred up, gunning for some action. Violence. Pain. Sex. One at a time, or all at once in a singularly wild, erotic moment. I didn't care. I just needed the release. The catharsis.

"Back off, Lily," he said, his jaw firm and his muscles tense. He turned and deliberately looked toward Rose. "Back off and get a grip."

I exhaled, loud and long, frustrated and ashamed. "At the end of the day, I don't know a damn thing about you except that you're a demon. A Tri-Jal." I knew that, and yet I also knew that I wanted him. Knew that I'd seen the two of us together, wild and naked, in his mind. But I'd seen blood there, too. And pain. And the promise of a redemption that he hadn't yet achieved. "You're asking me to take a lot on faith."

"Yeah," he said, "I am."

"I don't have a lot of faith left in me."

"Lily . . ."

"Dammit, Deacon. Let me in. Let me see. Let me have one true thing in this completely whacked world I live in now. One thing that I can feel and touch and say, yes, I know this is real."

He moved so fast I never saw the hand that reached out and jerked me toward him. He slammed me back against the wall, his arms caging me even as my palm closed around the hilt of my knife. He was hot and hard and right there, and I could hear the blood rushing through me, could feel my body tighten in reaction to his proximity. I heard myself gasp and hated myself for it. At the same time, I wanted nothing more than for him to close his mouth over mine and make me forget everything else that was going on in this freaked-out world we were living in.

"You want true?" he whispered, leaning in close to my ear, his breath making me shiver. "Then hear this. I'm going with you. I'll wait in the back. I'll hide in a fucking closet if that's what it takes. But if it looks like Clarence is going to get the best of you, then I'm coming in and I'm taking him out. And that, Lily, is the truth."

His hand dropped down to cover mine, which was over my still-sheathed knife. "You didn't draw your weapon, Lily," he said. "I'd say you have some faith left in you."

I drew in a breath, long and deep, determined to regain a sense of control. "You can come," I said, knowing that I was conceding this round. "But we take Rose, too."

"Risky," he said. "She's your Achilles' heel, and Clarence knows that better than anyone."

I looked toward the bed, toward my little sister, curled up, broken and battered. Her once-dewy skin was sallow, and dark bags hung beneath her closed eyes. Her blond hair was dark with oil and stringy from not having been combed or washed. She looked like a street urchin instead of a princess, and I wanted the princess back. She deserved it, and I was determined to make it happen.

"She comes," I repeated, "but we make sure he doesn't realize she's there. I'm not leaving her alone."

He cut a glance across the room to the bed, then moved toward her and slid an arm under her back and another under her knees.

"What are you doing?"

"Carrying her."

"Now? We're going now?"

"You have a better idea?"

I shook my head. He was right, of course. The time for hiding in dark rooms was over.

From his arms, I heard a small mewling sound.

"Rose?" My throat was thick, my voice barely functioning.

Deacon turned, shifting her body toward me. Even despite those damned glasses, I could feel his eyes on me, watching me, gauging my reaction.

I moved closer, unable to speak from the hope that was filling my chest and my throat.

"Lily?" Her voice was weak. "Lily, what happened?" Her eyes fluttered open, her features slack but aware, and I drew in a breath, realizing the tightness in my chest was because I'd stopped breathing.

"Rose. Thank God." She was okay. She was Rose. Whatever he'd done to her, she'd fought it off. It hadn't stuck. This was my baby sister, and she was going to be just fine.

Two seconds later, she proved me a liar.

"Lily," she said, her voice sharp and panicked. "Lily, what's happening?"

"Deacon!" I cried, because I didn't know. Rose's body was convulsing in his arms, her eyes rolling back in her head until only the whites remained. I screamed her name, screamed at Deacon to do something. And then I slammed my mouth shut in horror when I heard her speak again.

"Sweet Lily," my sister said, in a voice not her own. "I'm fucking your sister. Again."